The MAGNOLIA MURDERS

SAWYER AND ROYCE: MATRIMONY AND MAYHEM

BOOK 1

AIMEE NICOLE WALKER

Everything old is new again in love and murder.

Work together, live together, and play together is the name of the game for Royce Locke and Sawyer Key. But one of those things changes when Chief Mendoza taps Sawyer to lead the newly formed cold case unit. His first task: solve the Magnolia Murders that spanned three decades and suddenly stopped in 2000.

Chaos ensues when a fourth Magnolia Queen contender is murdered during a preliminary round. With the pageant's one hundredth anniversary looming, the pressure is on to produce results. Royce and Sawyer, along with their new partners, have to team up to solve the Magnolia Murders—old and new.

As the investigation continues, a surprise visitor and an unexpected phone call force the men to face painful things from their pasts. The future Royce and Sawyer dream of is within their grasp, but first, they'll need to uproot the seeds of discontent they've buried deep.

The Magnolia Murders is the first book in the Matrimony and Mayhem trilogy, the second story arc for Royce Locke and Sawyer Key. ** New readers should start with the Zero Hour trilogy before reading Matrimony and Mayhem. ** The Magnolia Murders is a continuation of Royce and Sawyer's happily ever after as they move into the next phase of their lives—professionally and personally. Though some storylines span the trilogy, this book does not end in a cliffhanger. Heat, humor, heart, and homicide abound. You have been warned. 18+

The Magnolia Murders
Sawyer and Royce: Matrimony and Mayhem Book 1

"The two most powerful warriors are patience and time."
~Leo Tolstoy, *War and Peace*

Chapter
ONE

SAWYER PULLED INTO A PARKING SPACE BEHIND THE PRECINCT and shifted the SUV into park, then turned to look at his partner, best friend, and the love of his life. The late-January sunlight glinted off the gold watch he'd given Royce for Christmas as he tilted his travel mug to take another long drink. The high-octane java smelled strong enough to kickstart a flatlined heart. Sawyer wasn't sure if he owed his galloping pulse to a secondhand buzz off the noxious brew or from noticing how the play of light turned Royce into a gorgeous, gilded god. If he didn't know better, he'd think Royce paid someone good money to put those blond highlights in his hair.

Royce lowered his mug and met Sawyer's gaze. His mouth quirked up on one side. "Why do you look so annoyed? I wasn't the one who committed a double murder on Saturday and ruined our dinner date at Giancarlo's." He made it sound like Sawyer had been the one to pull the trigger instead of answering the call from dispatch.

"It does feel like we just left here," Sawyer said.

"This was not the exciting weekend I'd planned for us." Royce rubbed the heel of his free hand over his eyes. The ensuing sigh was as heavy as the punching bag hanging in their home gym, and Sawyer felt just as battered.

Royce had vocally promised wine and fine dining at Sawyer's favorite restaurant on Saturday, but his expression had vowed carnal delights more decadent than any dessert on the menu. Sawyer had been convinced Royce would finally present the platinum ring he'd stashed in his dresser and ask the all-important question. Sawyer hadn't meant to stumble upon the box while stress cleaning a few months ago when Royce had been loaned out to the US Marshals' fugitive apprehension task force. He'd had too much time on his hands, and Sawyer's favorite solution was cleaning and organizing everything. He'd already worked through his own dresser and had just started on Royce's when he found the box beneath Sawyer's old, faded Emory University shirt that Royce kept stealing from him. Sawyer had quickly restored the dresser contents to the order Royce had left them in. Then he tried not to obsess over when Royce might present the platinum band with two rows of sparkling diamonds and ask Sawyer to marry him. He failed miserably. He'd been breathless when he found the ring and had remained that way, even months later, waiting for Royce to propose.

Sawyer had thought for sure he'd ask on Thanksgiving, but the holiday passed by without the band making an appearance. A similar size box in his Christmas stocking turned out to be a pocket watch Royce had found in an antique store. New Year's came and went but still no proposal. Sawyer had started to believe he'd dreamed the whole thing and checked to make sure the ring was still there. He'd held his breath until he found the box in the same spot. The ring nestled in navy blue velvet was as beautiful as he remembered. Sawyer had longed to try the band on, but it would've been a step too far. Besides, he wanted Royce to be the one to slide it on his ring finger.

What the hell was Royce waiting for? Surely not Valentine's Day. Royce loathed it with the intensity of a thousand suns. When Sawyer had joked their special night out was perilously close to the "fake holiday," Royce had scoffed and said their special night was "just because." Royce

2

was waiting for a moment that felt right to him, and Sawyer wouldn't do anything to ruin it, even if he did sometimes want to shout, "Ask me already."

"It's only been six hours since we booked Davis Dingbat for the double homicide, so I'd say we just left," Royce said, cutting into Sawyer's thoughts. "And now one of us has to write up the report."

Sawyer snorted. "David *Dingby*. One of these days, you're going to screw up and use one of your nicknames in front of the press." Then the rest of what Royce said penetrated Sawyer's sluggish brain, and he narrowed his eyes. Maybe he should take a few sips of Royce's potent brew.

Royce carried on, either ignoring or not noticing Sawyer's ire. "The idiot practically left a trail of breadcrumbs from the crime scene to his front door. It's clear this guy hasn't watched a single episode of *Dateline*. I think the press would agree with my nickname."

"Well," Sawyer said, "since the case was an easy one to solve, it shouldn't take you long to write up the report. It is what we agreed to this morning before I straddled your face and took your dick in my mouth. First to come had to write the report. You shot first, so you have to do the honors. Remember?"

Royce shook his head. "I only recall your mouth on my cock. I've blocked out everything before the blow job, and I blacked out afterward." Royce cupped Sawyer's face, stroking a thumb over his lips. "Your mouth is really something, GB."

Only Royce could take a moniker he hated, Golden Boy, and turn it into an endearing nickname. His voice was really something. Sawyer nipped Royce's thumb, and he sucked in a sharp breath and pulled it free.

"And I'm sorry our weekend plans got wrecked," Royce said.

Sawyer nestled into the warmth of Royce's touch. "Delayed, not wrecked." Though he was reluctant to break the tender moment between them, their fellow officers in the Major Crimes Unit were starting to arrive for work. Monday mornings meant all hands on deck for weekly debriefings unless you were working under deep cover or pursuing a lead in an active investigation. "We better get in there before all the good pastries are gone."

Royce caressed Sawyer's lips once more, making it clear what he wanted to devour. "There are no such things as bad pastries."

Sawyer would've sucked Royce's thumb into his mouth if not for Holly making a beeline for their vehicle. Her long dark hair was pulled back from her face in a ponytail that bounced as she walked, and fire burned in her gaze.

"Uh-oh," Sawyer said. "Holls is heading our way, and she looks pissed."

"Wasn't me," Royce replied, sounding like his godsons Marc and Daniel. He unbuckled his seat belt and turned to look out his window. "Nah, that's just determination."

Royce opened the door and stepped outside just as Holly reached them. The pair had been thick as thieves since elementary school, and their bond had never wavered. Royce might've known her longer, but Sawyer didn't need a degree in Holly-ology to recognize the difference between anger and determination. Sawyer quickly followed Royce out of the vehicle so he didn't miss a second of the battle. The chilly morning air had Sawyer reaching for the zipper on the form-fitting motorcycle jacket he'd borrowed from Royce. His partner in crime zipped the bomber jacket he'd snagged from Sawyer's closet. He couldn't wait to get it back because the sandalwood, amber, and vanilla from Royce's soap would linger in the flannel lining for a long time.

"And how's my favorite bridezilla?" Royce asked. Damn, the man was always poking one bear or another.

"Fuck you, Ro. Your brother is groomzilla while I'm a paragon of patience and perfection."

Royce snorted and looked at Sawyer. "My bad," he said. "Holly is good and pissed."

"Yes, Holly is," she agreed. "Do you know what Jace did?"

Royce's bemused expression vanished in an instant. "He hasn't started drinking again, has he?"

"No," Holly said, "but I might hit the bottle soon if he doesn't stop firing our wedding planners."

"Planners, plural?" Sawyer asked.

"Uh, yeah. We're on the fourth one."

"Wow," Sawyer replied. "What did they do?"

Royce held up a finger. "The first one had a snotty attitude about their budget and made them feel bad." A second finger went up. "The next one didn't return calls or emails promptly."

"That sounds legitimate to me," Sawyer said. "And the third?"

"She screwed up the tuxedo fittings," Holly replied. "I need to give you the new appointment time."

"Breathe, Holls," Royce said as he retrieved his phone and opened the calendar. "When's the new appointment?"

Holly puffed out her cheeks and exhaled her frustration. "Tomorrow at six."

It only took seconds for Royce to move his tuxedo fitting appointment, then he hugged her tight. "Everything will work out just fine. I'll talk to Jace and try to calm him down."

"Thanks, Ro," Holly said, her voice heavy with gratitude.

The three of them headed into the precinct, and Sawyer smiled as Royce made a beeline for the box of pastries. He had nearly reached his destination when Chief Mendoza peeked his head out of his office.

"Locke, Key, I need to see you."

"Don't worry," Detective Shawn Ashcroft said as he stacked two pastries on his napkin. "We'll save you a few crumbs."

"Asshole," Royce grumbled.

"Pastry slut," Ashcroft replied.

"That's Sergeant Pastry Slut," Ashcroft's partner, Detective Kyomo Chen said.

Royce flipped them off as soon as their chief disappeared back inside his office. "I wonder what this is about?" he asked Sawyer.

"I think we both know. He's going to break us up."

Royce bumped his shoulder into Sawyer's. "He might reassign us to different partners, but there's no way he could ever break us up."

"True," Sawyer replied. They'd been dreading the moment Mendoza would assign them new partners for nearly three years. Sawyer and Royce had assumed their chief would deliver the bad news every time he pulled them into his office for a chat.

Royce opened the door and gestured for Sawyer to go first. Mendoza stood at the bookshelf to the right of his desk, watering the plants he'd tucked between the model airplanes he built with his preteen son.

"You wanted to see us, Chief," Sawyer said.

Mendoza turned and smiled. "I did." He gestured to his desk where a selection of pastries rested on a paper towel. "Help yourself. I snagged a variety since I wasn't sure what you were in the mood for."

Royce looked longingly at the single bear claw before offering it to Sawyer. As if he'd deny his man a single bite of his favorite pastry.

"No thank you," he said, picking up a glazed cruller.

Mendoza stowed his watering can in his coat closet before joining them and helping himself to a chocolate sprinkle donut. He took a big bite, and an expression of pure joy washed over his face. "The best decision Commissioner Rigby made was marrying her wife, and the second smartest was encouraging Sherry to open a bakery. Lord, the woman bakes like it's no one's business."

"Right?" Royce asked, then dabbed at his mouth with a napkin. "I was going to include hiring me in the mix, but I can't argue with your logic."

Mendoza chuckled. "Especially when your mouth is full of pastry."

Since Royce had just taken a bite, he could only bob his head in agreement.

Mendoza cleared his throat, set his donut down, and leaned back in his seat. "I've been dreading this day for quite some time now."

Anxiety felt like a lead brick in Sawyer's stomach as he waited for their chief to continue.

Royce swallowed and said, "At least you've softened the blow with pastries."

"Softened the blow? I'm not firing you, Locke."

"Will you at least let us choose our new partners?" Royce asked.

Mendoza steepled his hands at chest height and studied them with dark, intelligent eyes. The man had been their chief for nearly three years, but they still knew little about him. Mendoza was private and mysterious, which only added to his allure. "Within reason," he replied.

Royce dropped his bear claw on the desk. "What's that mean?"

"I'll tell you if you stop trying to preempt me."

"We're listening, sir," Sawyer said.

Royce nodded and resumed eating his pastry.

"The Savannah Police Department has received large donations from some very generous benefactors who have enabled Commissioner Rigby to create a Cold Case Unit and an Explorer program for teens thinking about a career in law enforcement."

Sawyer straightened in his chair. "Cold cases?"

"Yes, Detective." Mendoza's grin was sly as he opened his desk drawer, removed a shiny new shield, and slid it to Sawyer. "Make that congratulations, Sergeant Key. I can't think of anyone better suited to lead the new unit. We'll have an official pinning ceremony tomorrow."

A myriad of emotions—pride, honor, and gratitude—washed over him. "Thank you, sir. I won't let you down."

"I know you won't, Sergeant. You'll get to pick two detectives to complete the unit, but neither can be Sergeant Locke."

"Yes, sir."

Mendoza turned his shrewd gaze on Locke. "And I'd like you to set up and run our Explorer program."

"Me?"

"Yes, you," Mendoza said.

"No one wants to put me in charge of teenagers."

"I do, Locke. Are you questioning my judgment?"

"A little, sir," Royce replied sheepishly. "Surely you've heard what a wildcard I am. I'm more of a liability than a role model."

"I don't agree," Sawyer said. "I think you'll relate to the kids in ways no one else will."

Royce turned his head and narrowed his eyes. "Because I'm a kid too?"

"Nope," Sawyer said. "Because you're smart, funny, and charming. Everyone likes you."

"Well, that part is true," Royce replied.

Mendoza laughed heartily. "And so humble. I've chosen you because my gut said you're the person for the job, but Key has stated your attributes more eloquently. Locke, I won't force you to accept a position you don't want, but I will ask you to give it some serious consideration."

"Of course I will, Chief."

"Are you familiar with the Explorer program?"

"A little," Royce said, sounding overwhelmed. "I'm aware of the program's mission but not the curriculum. Do these kids come with a manual?"

Mendoza laughed again. "Of course. We're months away from implementing the program here. Prior to that, you'd go through a few weeks of training before we turn you loose with the teens. You won't be taking them on by yourself either. You'll get to choose one other detective or officer in the department to assist you, but it can't be Sergeant Key."

Royce cocked his head slightly to the side. "Is this payback for the men's hair dye prank?"

Sawyer leaned forward, pulling the chief's attention to him. "I just want to repeat that I had nothing to do with that."

Sawyer had been home recovering from his burns when Mendoza was promoted to chief. Royce had bought hair dye for Mendoza to welcome him to the MCU. Not that Mendoza needed it. The slight graying at his temples made him look distinguished and handsome, not old.

"I'm sorry you feel this is a punishment, Locke," their chief said. "I'd hoped this was a positive suggestion."

Sawyer studied Royce's pensive expression and recognized it for what it was: concern he wasn't good enough. Royce was so charming and confident it was easy to overlook the vulnerability beneath the surface.

"It is a positive announcement, sir, and I'm beyond proud you thought of me."

"After our debriefing," Mendoza said, "I want you to head over to Bryan County. I'm sure you remember my friend Abe."

No one in the room would forget the way Sheriff Beecham had rallied his team to rescue Royce, who had been kidnapped by a young woman looking to impress the serial killer she was obsessed with. Sawyer found it interesting Mendoza referred to his friend by his first name and not his official title. Royce had sworn up and down he'd detected "a vibe" between Mendoza and Beecham, but Sawyer had blamed it on the adrenaline racing through Royce's blood, making him see things that weren't there. But maybe his guy was on to something.

"Of course," Royce said.

"Abe oversees the program for Bryan County and the entire state, so I'm sending you straight to him to get the 411. He knows to expect you."

"You've already called Sheriff Beecham this morning?" Royce asked.

Mendoza arched a raven brow. "Are you fishing for something, Locke?"

8

"No, sir. Just hoping you didn't wake him up at an ungodly hour. I saw tanks smaller than Abe Beecham during my stint in the military. I'd hate for him to take his frustration out on me."

Mendoza chuckled. "I brought him up to speed over burgers and beer this weekend. It's all good." The chief glanced at his watch before aiming his piercing gaze at Sawyer. "Ideally, you'd choose your team, then sift through the case files to see which ones you think hold a better chance of getting solved."

"Something tells me you have a specific investigation in mind, sir," Sawyer said.

Mendoza nodded. "Are you familiar with the Magnolia Murders?"

"Somewhat, sir. I haven't reviewed the official file, but I'm aware three Magnolia Queens were murdered by what appears to be the same perpetrator."

"Yes. The murders took place in 1984, 1996, and 2000. Your *Sinister in Savannah* podcast buddies have been covering the deaths in-depth, which has renewed public interest. It also happens to be the hundredth anniversary of the first Magnolia Queen Pageant this year."

"Sounds like a good time to look at the case with fresh eyes," Sawyer said.

"The murders were sporadic and suddenly stopped over two decades ago. I'm not sure what kind of resolution we can get, but I'm hoping new DNA testing might help us crack it wide open."

"I agree, Chief."

Mendoza glanced at his watch again. "We'd better get started on the debriefing. I'll announce the new department and the future Explorer program, then turn you loose to set up your new office and make personnel decisions."

"New office?" Sawyer asked.

"There were a couple of rooms not being utilized downstairs, so the commissioner decided to convert them to the new CCU. It's similar to the MCU but smaller since there won't be as many officers." Mendoza looked at Royce. "Two of the community rooms down there are being converted for Explorer use as we speak and should be ready in a few months. You'll have plenty of time to consider my offer."

"Sounds good, sir. Thank you," Royce said. "Is it okay if I have a private word with Sawyer before the debriefing?"

Mendoza rose to his feet and strode toward the door. "Of course. I'll need you to make it quick because we all have a lot to do. Key, we'll meet again before your first press conference this afternoon. We'll all go to Joe's for a celebratory drink tonight after work."

"What?" Sawyer spun around in his chair to make sure he'd heard the chief correctly, but Mendoza was already gone. "Did he say I was giving a press conference?"

Chapter
TWO

ROYCE BIT HIS BOTTOM LIP TO KEEP FROM CHUCKLING AT SAWYER'S stricken expression. "Hey," he gently said, pulling Sawyer's attention to him. "You're going to be fucking amazing, and I'll be right there cheering you on."

"A press conference, though?" Sawyer was usually the epitome of calm, cool, and collected. Seeing his posture rigid and tense made Royce shove his worries aside. "Maybe he could've given me more warning. I'm not dressed for—"

Royce silenced Sawyer with a kiss. It was quick and chaste but still triggered butterflies in the pit of his stomach. It felt so good. Royce did it again, lingering a little longer. Such a simple thing was forbidden when they were partners, and they'd tried hard not to cross lines on the job. But now…Royce pressed his mouth to Sawyer's for the third time and congratulated himself when he felt the tension fade from Sawyer's lips.

Eventually, his mouth trembled and spread into a smile. Royce broke the kiss but didn't step back.

"What are you doing?" Sawyer asked.

"Pretty sure that's obvious. I'm kissing you."

"Why?"

Royce quirked a brow. "Because I can. It's the only good thing about losing you as a partner."

Not the only thing that could come of it, though. Sawyer would be able to openly wear his ring once Royce proposed. They could exchange vows and bind their lives together forever. Royce could keep his promise to marry Sawyer and create a family. That had been his intention on Saturday night before dispatch had thwarted his plans. He'd been furious when the call had first come in, but then he'd wondered if it was a sign. Saturday was just one of many interrupted attempts since he'd purchased the ring six months ago, but it was the closest he'd come to popping the question.

Sawyer's beautiful brown eyes darkened with tenderness. "Why did you kiss me now is what I should've asked. You know the chief is waiting for us."

"I did it because you were letting the idea of a press conference ruin what should be a proud moment for you." Royce kissed Sawyer again and ended it with a playful nip to his full bottom lip and a quick tongue swipe to soothe the sting. "You are going to be amazing. I am so damn proud of you."

Sawyer cupped his neck and leaned his forehead against Royce's. "I'm proud of you too. The Explorers will be lucky to have an instructor like you."

"*If* I accept the position," Royce added.

Sawyer opened his mouth to say more, but someone rapped sharply on the door. Blue said, "The chief is waiting, fellas."

Royce and Sawyer chuckled but rose to their feet. Sawyer crossed the room to open the door while Royce stockpiled a week's worth of pastries onto a paper towel.

Blue looked down at Royce's hoard and shook his head. "Your teeth are going to fall out of your head."

"Nope. I just had a checkup last week. Still no cavities," Royce boasted. He smiled broadly to show off his pearly whites before shoving a pastry into his mouth.

"Did the dentist take a picture and hang it up with the kiddies in the no-cavity club?" Blue asked.

Royce nodded and flipped his friend off before exiting the office with his hoard.

"Your jeans look a little tighter, though," Blue called out.

Royce swallowed his bite and turned to walk backward. "I volunteer this jackass as tribute, GB."

"I couldn't get so lucky," Sawyer replied. They all knew Blue loved working arsons and not just because his fiancé was a handsome firefighter.

"Tribute?" Blue asked.

Royce just laughed and faced forward once more. He received various looks from the unit when they saw his stack of pastries. Some looked amused, some looked disgusted, but a few looked annoyed Mendoza had spoiled their attempts to deny Royce. The meeting started as soon as the trio stepped into the room, so he didn't get a chance to talk smack.

One of the many things Royce admired about Mendoza was his no-nonsense handling of roll calls and debriefings. He moved through business succinctly, saving the big announcements for the end. The reaction to Sawyer's promotion was precisely what he expected. Everyone was genuinely happy for him, and Royce noticed some eager expressions when Mendoza mentioned Sawyer got to pick two detectives to move over with him. He, on the other hand, took a lot of razzing from the other detectives, who pretended being his partner was a fate worse than death.

Mendoza allowed a little teasing before he moved on to discussing the Explorer program. Since they were still in the planning stages, the chief didn't get bogged down in specifics.

After Mendoza adjourned the meeting, several detectives expressed interest in working in the new Cold Case Unit, including Holly.

"Wow," he said. "I'm truly honored and surprised so many of you are interested in moving over with me. I thought I'd have to beg people to apply and bribe them to accept. Let me get my office set up this morning, then I'll chat with each of you to determine who will be the best fit for the unit."

Their fellow detectives congratulated him again before disbanding to get their days started. Alone once more, Royce turned to face Sawyer but resisted the urge to embrace him.

"Would you like some help moving stuff to your new office before I head over to Bryan County to meet with Sheriff Beecham?"

Sawyer narrowed his eyes and cocked his head to the side. "Look who's eager to get rid of me."

Royce placed his hands on Sawyer's hips and stepped closer. "You know damn well that's not true."

"I do."

Those two words sent an arc of want and longing through Royce's body, but he tried not to visibly react. Royce was seconds away from saying "fuck it" and planting a kiss on Sawyer's mouth when someone cleared their throat.

Detective Tara South grinned at them. "Sorry to interrupt," she said, "but I thought I'd throw my ring in the hat to be your partner, Locke."

He'd expected her to say she wanted to join the Cold Case Unit, so it took him a minute to catch up.

"You've got the position," Royce said.

"Don't you want to interview me to see if we'd be a good fit?"

Royce chuckled. There wasn't exactly a line out the door volunteering for the position like there was with Sawyer's unit. Maybe he'd feel pissy about it later, but he understood the allure of working with Sawyer Key. "You're a damn fine detective, South, and you have great hair. It's good enough for me."

She'd recently cut her blonde hair from a shoulder-length bob into a quiff. The shaved sides with a swoop at the top was a drastic transformation, but the style accentuated her angular face. Royce was thinking about trying out a similar look the next time he went to the barber and had asked her what the cut was called.

South laughed. "Good enough reason as any, I suppose."

"Full disclosure. Mendoza wants me to run the Explorer program. If I accept, my partner will need to be cool with instructing teens. Mendoza is sending me to Bryan County to meet with Sheriff Beecham who's in charge of the Explorer program for the entire state of Georgia. He's going to give me a lay of the land. Are you free to tag along to see if it's something that interests you?"

Tara glanced at her watch. "I have a few interviews to conduct in ninety minutes, so there's no way we'd be back in time. I am interested and would like to hear more about it."

"Lunch?"

"Sure," South said. "Give the sheriff my best."

"You know Beecham?"

Tara's cheeks turned pink. "Um, yeah. I ran into him and the chief once. Mendoza introduced us."

Royce narrowed his eyes. "Ran into them where?"

South grimaced, and her face flushed a delicate pink. She shook her head and said, "I've already said too much. Can we pretend I didn't mention it?"

"Uh, no," Royce said. "Tell me everything."

Sawyer gripped his bicep and walked him toward the door like an unruly toddler past his bedtime. "We all have things to do. Let's move along." Royce would've liked the show of dominance if Sawyer hadn't cockblocked his gossip.

"I still outrank you," Royce grumbled.

"Only for a few more hours," Sawyer countered.

South laughed. "Let me know about lunch."

He looked at her over his shoulder. "Sure, but you should know I'm going to do everything in my power to get the rest of the story." His declaration was met with a groan. "Want to change your mind about partnering with me?"

South just shook her head. "Call me a glutton for punishment."

Sawyer dropped his arm from Royce's bicep. "You'll make an excellent team."

When they reached the bullpen, Sawyer stopped at their desks. "I guess I should try to rustle up a box or two."

The reality of the situation hit Royce between the eyes like a blow to the head with a cast-iron skillet. Sawyer's desk would be empty when he returned from the meeting with Beecham. For a moment, he recalled the intense loss he'd felt after Marcus's death, but this wasn't anything like that. Sawyer wasn't dead; he'd received a much-deserved promotion. Royce was so proud of him, and he knew Sawyer's family would be too. But that meant...

"Are you okay, Ro?"

"Yeah, why?"

Sawyer narrowed his eyes. "You're grimacing and absently rubbing the scar on your shoulder."

Royce glanced down, and sure enough, his hand was massaging the spot where a bullet had torn through his flesh when a bereaved father with a sniper rifle had taken out the man who'd killed his daughter and her fiancé. Unfortunately for Royce, he'd been escorting Wayne Miller at the time when his head exploded like a melon. The high-power round struck Royce in the shoulder, barely missing vital arteries. He'd seen his life flash before his eyes as he lay there bleeding on the pavement. Then Sawyer had loomed over him, his face gorgeous and panic-stricken. Sawyer's lips had moved, but Royce couldn't hear anything he said.

Everything after that was a blur until he woke up alone in a recovery room after surgery. He expected Sawyer to visit him at some point, but he didn't. Royce had lain awake after refusing pain meds, alternating between anger over his partner bailing on him and empathy for the fear he'd witnessed in Sawyer's eyes. Sawyer, who'd lost his husband to cancer, was allowing himself to feel again. In the blink of an eye, Royce was nearly taken from him too. So he ran. Royce had two options: allow Sawyer to pull back and protect his heart or knock down those walls. The next morning, he checked himself out of the hospital against doctor's orders and hired a car to take him to Sawyer's house. Royce hadn't left since.

He met Sawyer's gaze with a sheepish grin. "You'll need to call Evangeline and tell her about your promotion. She'll kick your ass if she hears it from someone else."

Sawyer's worried expression turned into a scowl. "True. And she'll want to make a big deal out of it."

"And every time she plans a celebration, one of us gets shot or set on fire."

Sawyer shook his head and laughed. "We broke that vicious cycle years ago."

"And I'm not looking forward to tempting fate," Royce replied. "But it's a chance we'll have to take because there's no way I want to be on Evangeline's bad side."

"You got that right," Sawyer replied. "I'll check with the chief to get firm times on the press conference and promotion ceremony and give her a call." He glanced down the front of his body. "I'll need to run home and change clothes."

There was nothing wrong with the SPD polo shirt and khaki pants he wore, but Royce knew Sawyer would feel better if he was wearing his fancier duds. "Wear your lucky tie." Royce had a particular fondness for it since Sawyer had been wearing the tie when they'd first met.

"Good idea. It will give me a chance to grab a few things for my new office."

"Such as?"

Sawyer smiled and shook his head. "You'll see."

Royce knew he should head out, but leaving was tougher than he'd imagined. He'd never been a fan of change because it rarely made his life better, but his luck had improved tremendously since meeting Sawyer.

"Christ," Ashcroft grumbled. "Just kiss him goodbye and be on your way, Sarge."

Royce shrugged and kissed Sawyer's smiling lips. "See you in a few hours."

Abe Beecham was the opposite of Emilio Mendoza in nearly every way. Beecham was big, brawny, and blond compared to Mendoza's lean frame and dark looks. The differences didn't stop with their physical appearances either. Beecham's laughter matched his physique, and there was an openness about him that directly contrasted the mysteriousness Mendoza radiated. The chief had probably worked in their precinct for six months before moving a single personal item into his office and a full year before adding his beloved plants and model airplanes. Nearly three years later, Mendoza still hadn't brought any photos of family or friends into the office. But the sheriff had filled his office with personal mementos, including a framed photograph of himself with Mendoza during an overseas deployment when they served in the military.

"Detective South sends her best," Royce said.

Beecham's big body tensed, and he narrowed his eyes. Royce knew Tara had witnessed something she wasn't supposed to see.

Knowing he was flirting with danger, Royce decided to back off. "Tell me about the Explorer program."

The tension in Beecham's broad shoulders eased as he gestured for Royce to have a seat. He spent the next thirty minutes giving Royce an overview of the program, which both intrigued and terrified him. Why would Mendoza trust him with such a big undertaking?

"Come on," Beecham said. "I'll introduce you to Deputy Mackenzie White. She's one of the instructors you'll have if you decide to proceed. The next round of training starts next week."

"Next week?"

Beecham placed both hands on his lean hips. "Lio didn't tell you?"

"No, Lio didn't," Royce replied.

Beecham chuckled and shook his head. "Sounds like his communication skills are getting rusty."

That wasn't a complaint Royce would've made about their chief in the past. "We all have off days, I guess."

"Some of us have more than others," Beecham replied before letting the subject drop. "I can tell you feel overwhelmed about running the Explorer program."

"Am I that transparent?"

Beecham laughed. "It's a big responsibility. I'd be more concerned if you didn't have reservations. Can I make a suggestion?"

"Please do, sir."

"Come to class on Monday with an open mind and see how you feel at the end of the day," Beecham said. "If you discover the course and program aren't for you, then you can tell Mendoza. He won't hold it against you."

"That's good advice. Thank you."

"And, Sergeant?" Beecham said.

"Yeah?"

"Mendoza is rarely wrong."

Royce laughed. "That's been my experience also." And the biggest reason Mendoza's decision had unsettled him.

"I'm happy to answer any questions," Beecham said after introducing Royce to Kenzie White. "Just give me a call."

"Appreciate it, sir."

Deputy White was a bundle of energy who oozed enthusiasm for the program and the kids who committed to it. She took Royce on a facility tour, which included a classroom, a gym with an obstacle course, a cyber room, and a mini crime lab.

"This is very impressive," Royce said when they finished.

"Thank you. I love working with future law enforcement officers," Deputy White said as she escorted him back to the visitor's parking lot where he'd left his ride. Royce left his SUV for Sawyer to use and had signed out a Charger from the motor pool. "You'll learn a lot in your sessions next week, and you can always consider me a resource if you need help down the road."

"I appreciate it, Deputy White."

"Please call me McKenzie or Kenzie. Everyone does."

"See you next Monday, Kenzie," Royce said when he reached his car. He'd at least attend training for a day before making a decision.

She waved and told him to be safe before heading back into the building. Royce pulled up the latest episode of *Sinister in Savannah*, then backed out of his parking spot. He'd never admit to those shitheads that he loved their podcast. They had millions of followers and didn't need to know he was one of them.

Royce's phone rang when he was just outside Savannah city limits. He didn't recognize the number, but it was local given the area code.

"Sergeant Locke," he said into the phone.

"Sorry to bother you, Sergeant, but this is Abel from the Kwik Stop."

The rage he'd long thought was gone began to simmer. It had been a long time since he'd received one of these calls about his father or younger brother. What had they done this time? Drove off without paying for gas again? Got belligerent when Abel ran out of their preferred cigarettes? "I told you they're no longer my problem, Abel." Royce replied tersely, not bothering to clarify if he was calling about Eddie or Benton.

"Don't hang up," the clerk said as Royce's thumb hovered over the disconnect button. "I wouldn't bother you over Eddie or Benton," the older man said. "I caught a teenage boy shoplifting, and he says he knows you."

Royce's blood turned to ice. "What's his name?"

"Jason Girard," Abel replied.

His sister's firstborn child who she'd named after their brother Jace. "I'm on my way."

Chapter
THREE

THE OLD NEIGHBORHOOD HADN'T CHANGED MUCH SINCE THE last Locke family dinner he'd attended more than three years ago. The streets were lined with the same derelict homes and the same broken-down cars parked in front of them. Royce's airway constricted as if an invisible fist had grabbed him by the throat. His pulse pounded, and panic surged until Royce worried he might suffocate and die in the one place he thought he'd escaped for good.

No fucking way. He had too much to live for.

Royce pulled to a stop in front of the convenience store and worked to regulate his breathing. He saw Abel talking to a tall, lanky blond through the large glass windows. Was that Jason? He hadn't seen the kid since he was twelve, and he'd been pretty scrawny then. His nephew hadn't put on much weight in three years, but he'd shot up several inches. Nothing about the teenager's profile was familiar. Had Abel gotten it wrong?

Royce braced himself for an ugly confrontation as he exited the car and strode into the store. He greeted Abel with a nod before looking at the sullen boy leaning against the counter with his arms crossed over his chest. The teen's lettermen jacket wasn't the right school colors and was too large and too battered to be Jason's. Was it something he'd inherited from Danny Girard, his loser father? Royce searched his memory for details about Danny but couldn't come up with any. The asshole had ceased to matter when he'd turned Royce's sister into a punching bag.

"Morning, Royce," Abel said. "Sorry if I pulled you away from something, but I wasn't sure what to do."

So it had been the store owner's idea to call him, not Jason's. Interesting.

"You caught me at a good time," Royce replied without taking his gaze off his nephew, who stiffened at his voice. "Jason."

The boy slowly turned his head and met Royce's gaze head-on. It was like looking at a surly, teen version of himself. Jason had inherited his blond hair and stormy gray eyes from the Locke DNA. Based on Abel's call, Jason also had the same penchant for getting into trouble. And considering his father was in prison for grand larceny, Jason and his younger brother Jared carried a double whammy in the genetics department.

"Is there something you'd like to say to Abel?" Royce asked. Jason continued glowering at him instead of responding to the question. Royce didn't want to break the stare off and give the kid a victory, but they couldn't engage in a battle of wills at the Kwik Stop all day long. Royce shifted his attention to the items on the counter and did a double take. He'd expected to see cigarette lighters, beer, or even candy bars. Pointing to the canister of baby formula and tube of diaper rash cream, he said, "This is what Jason was stealing?"

"Yes," Abel said. "It's the only reason I called you directly instead of calling it into the station."

Royce shifted his attention to his nephew. Jason's face had turned a bright shade of pink, making his gray eyes look like frosted steel. "Who's this for?"

"None of your damn business," Jason snarled.

Royce silently counted to five and reminded himself this kid had once been the little boy who'd followed him everywhere. "I'm making it my business."

"A little late, don't you think?" Jason asked.

Royce cocked his head to the side. "Late for a safe sex talk?"

Jason rolled his eyes. "They're not for me."

"Well, no," Royce said. "I didn't think you planned to drink the formula or use the cream on your ass."

"This is stupid," Jason grumbled. He turned his head to look at the store owner. "I'm sorry I tried to steal those items, Abel. I was just trying to help out a friend, but this wasn't the way."

"No, it wasn't, Jason," Abel replied.

"I'll understand if you want to press charges, but please call the station. I don't want to get lectures from this hypocrite."

Jason would've hurt Royce less if he'd punched him in the stomach, but the truth hurt like a son of a bitch. Royce had been as wild as a stallion back in the day. He wanted to think he'd made up for all his troublemaking ways, but only time would tell.

"How much for the formula and the rash cream?" Royce asked as he reached for his wallet.

Jason's expression morphed from annoyance to fury when Royce had expected a little gratitude. "Don't bother."

Abel ignored Jason and scanned the items. "Thirty-seven dollars and twenty-nine cents."

"Shit! The price of this stuff has gone way up," Royce said.

"How the hell would you know?" Jason snarled.

"I made plenty of diaper, formula, and butt cream runs when you guys were little and more recently for Candy," Royce said as he slid his credit card into the reader.

"Too bad you bailed on your family a long time ago."

Royce snapped his head in Jason's direction. "Is that what you think? That I just walked away from you boys without a backward glance?"

The color seeped from Jason's face even though he clung to his fury. "I know so."

The card reader chimed when the transaction finished, and Royce retracted his Visa and returned it to his wallet. "I'd like to discuss this with you further. How about I give you a ride to wherever you were going to deliver these items?"

Jason snagged the plastic shopping bag off the counter and skirted around Royce like he was a puddle of puke he didn't want to step in. "Hard pass," he said on his way to the door.

Royce said a quick goodbye to Abel, then followed his nephew. He had to give it to the kid. He could cover a lot of ground with his long legs.

"I don't even get a thank you?"

"Try fuck you," Jason said.

It was Royce's turn to be furious. Who the hell did this little prick think he was? Royce strode to his car, fired up the engine, and reversed out of his parking spot. Jason might walk fast, but he was no match for Royce's car unless he cut between houses and jumped fences. Royce caught up to him half a block down the street and slowed to a crawl beside his surly nephew.

He rolled down the passenger side window and said, "Come on, Jaybird. Let's talk."

Jason flipped him off. "Just go away."

"Not going to happen, buddy. It's obvious we need to get a few things straight."

Jason snorted. "Nothing about you is straight."

Royce's heart sank as hurt replaced his anger. "Is that what your attitude is about?"

Jason shot him an incredulous look but kept walking. "You better take off before someone thinks you're trying to pick me up like the pervert Grandpa accuses you of being."

"I don't care what your grandpa says about me, Jason. What do you think?"

"Since when do you care?" Jason countered.

Royce resisted the urge to drive up on the sidewalk and block his nephew's path. Later, he'd demand the universe—or maybe just Sawyer—reward him for his restraint. And Mendoza wanted to put him in charge of youths? The man had lost his mind. Royce kept a tight grip on the steering wheel and his temper as he continued cruising alongside Jason, who'd started walking a little faster.

"Get in the car, and I'll drive you over to see your kid."

Jason suddenly stopped, so Royce did too. The petulant teen stomped over to the Charger and leaned down to glare at him through the open window. Jason's face was a mottled shade of red, and a vein throbbed in his forehead.

"I told you these things weren't for me. I'm not a liar."

"Just a thief?" Royce asked. "Those things usually go hand in hand."

"I've never stolen anything before today, and I only did it because my friend is in a really bad place." Something about Jason's slumped shoulders and hangdog face made Royce think he was telling the truth.

"Get in and let me help you."

Jason held his stare for a few more minutes before relenting. He flopped into the passenger seat with all the grace of an elephant. Jason snapped his seat belt into place and continued staring straight ahead. "Don't think this makes you abandoning us okay."

Instead of pulling away from the curb, Royce looked at Jason until he turned and met his gaze. The wary expression in his nephew's gray eyes was so familiar. How many times had he worn the same look in his lifetime? Too many to count, but those days were behind him now. Jason could escape too if he put his mind to it. Royce had tried to help Benton, but his baby brother had been too stubborn, and the pills and the booze had dug their claws in bone deep. This serendipitous phone call from Abel felt like fate.

"Do you honestly think I just got sick of being your uncle out of the blue and abandoned you and Jared? Or do you think it's possible something else was at play?" He didn't want to say too much because there was a small, foolish part of him holding out hope that he could reconnect with his sister. Drusilla had asked him to make a sacrifice he wasn't willing to make, and they hadn't spoken in three years.

Jason took a deep breath and released it slowly. "I guess not. Maybe it's just easier to blame you."

"I think about you and your brother every single day. And, god, I miss your mom."

Swallowing hard, Jason dropped his gaze but only for a few seconds. "Really?"

"Absolutely, Jaybird."

Jason's cheeks turned pink, but he looked more pleased than

embarrassed. Royce wasn't foolish enough to think he'd seen the last of his nephew's sullenness, but he'd take the reprieve wherever he could get it.

"No one calls me that anymore, Uncle Ro."

Royce's heart swelled at the nickname. Another victory he'd happily accept. His joy quickly faded when he realized they needed to clear the air on one thing. Royce brought his arm up to rub the back of his neck and exhaled a long breath.

"Look, I know some things are awkward to talk about, but—"

"No, I don't think you're a pervert because you're bi," Jason said. "It was a shitty thing for me to say, and I'm sorry."

Royce reached over and ruffled his hair. "You're forgiven."

Jason chuckled as he swatted Royce away and tidied his hair. "For what it's worth, I know Mom misses you too. She told me she said some pretty horrible things to you. She wishes she could take them back."

"And Jared?" Royce managed to ask with a lump of emotion wedged in his throat.

"Jared is bi too, but Mom hasn't told Grandpa."

"That's probably for the best. I'm glad Jared has you and your mom to talk to about stuff."

Jason averted his gaze to his lap. "I know she wants to call you, but she's afraid you won't forgive her."

Royce cleared his throat, but his voice still sounded thick when he said, "Do you think it would help if I called her first? Break the ice." It was scary as hell, but he'd put himself out there if it opened the channel of communication again.

Jason snapped his gaze up, and his eyes shimmered with tears. "Please. She's having a really hard time, and Grandpa only makes her life harder."

He'd heard from Holly that Dru had started working two or three jobs after Danny went to prison. The boys spent a few nights each week with Jace and Holly at the house they'd rented from Royce. If he and Dru reconciled, the boys could hang with him and Sawyer a few nights a week. The less time they were around Eddie Locke, the better. "I'll reach out to her today."

"You'll probably have to leave a message, but she'll call you back or text when she gets a quiet moment."

"Okay," Royce said, then shifted the Charger into drive. "Where to?"

Jason directed him to a tiny bungalow house with peeling white paint. There was a faded red car with a black driver's side door. Royce could tell by the dents all around it that the vehicle had been involved in an accident. Someone had banged out the damage as best they could and replaced the door. The street was the dividing line between poverty and the middle class. The homes had once reflected the influences from both neighborhoods, but it was clear poverty was gaining the upper hand. One of the shutters was missing and another dangled crookedly, looking as if the slightest puff of air would cause the metal to lose its fight with gravity. A few of the windows were boarded up, probably from the last tropical depression that had moved through. The front door looked like someone had decided to scrape the paint off to prep for a new color before changing their mind, possibly because of the numerous layers they'd need to scrape off. He saw remnants of yellow, green, and black paint beneath what was left of the red.

"Who lives here?" Royce asked.

Jason released his seat belt and reached for the door handle. "A friend. Thanks for your help today." He pushed open the door and stepped out of the vehicle before ducking down to look at Royce. "I'll pay you back."

"You can start by telling me about your friend."

"Because you don't believe me?" Jason asked.

"No, because you said your friend was desperate. I'm a cop, and helping is what I do."

Jason started to roll his eyes but must've thought better of it. The multihued door swung open before he could say anything else, and a petite blonde stepped onto the porch. She held a tiny, blanket-wrapped bundle against her chest that she bounced gently. Even from a distance, Royce could see her eyes were red from crying or lack of sleep.

Royce started to unbuckle his seat belt to speak to her, but Jason stopped him.

"Abby and Noah are safe here, Uncle Ro. Her family is having a difficult time with their finances, and the dirtbag who knocked her up won't give her any money for the baby, even though his family is rich."

Royce retrieved his wallet, pulled out all the cash he had, and passed it to Jason. It was only sixty dollars, but it would get her another can of formula and some diapers. "Here, this will help a little. There are county resources Abby can turn to for help."

Jason shook his head vehemently. "Her parents are too proud." He tightened his fingers around the cash. "Are you sure about this?"

"Positive." Royce glanced at the porch and saw Jason's friend worrying her bottom lip. "I'll wait while you give the supplies and cash to Abby, but then I'm taking you to school."

Jason grimaced. "But the school day is half over."

"I reckon you'll need to apply yourself extra hard during the second half."

"Fine," Jason grumbled.

Royce chuckled when Jason lumbered toward Abby's porch, looking like a whipped dog. His entire demeanor changed when he reached his friend and her baby. Jason reached down and pulled the blanket aside, and Royce watched as a mixture of love and awe washed over his nephew's face. Judging by Abby's easy smile, she didn't miss Jason's adoration either.

Jason put the cash inside the plastic bag holding the formula and rash cream and held it out to Abby. She flicked her gaze between Jace and Royce, then mouthed, "Thank you," to Royce.

He waved and waited while the teens wrapped up their conversation. He half expected Jason to drag it out for as long as possible, but his nephew surprised him by jogging back to the car a few moments later. During the ride to the high school, Jason talked a lot about the baby's father, though he never stated his name. Royce learned the guy's parents were loaded, he was some super stud athlete, and he'd been too stupid to wear a condom.

"Abby is entitled to child support whether they like it or not," Royce said. "They'll do a paternity test through the county and—"

"Stay out of it, Uncle Ro."

"On one condition."

"What?" Jason asked suspiciously.

"I will give you my phone number and address when we get to the school. You tell Abby to reach out to me if she ever finds herself in a bind. No more stealing from Abel."

"Yes, sir. You have yourself a deal."

Royce stopped in front of the high school a few minutes later and parked his SUV. He exchanged contact info with Jason before his nephew opened the door and exited the car.

"Do you need anything, Jaybird? Condoms or—"

"Nope," Jason said, his face turning a flaming red. "I've been humiliated enough for one day."

He slammed the door and strode toward the high school like the hounds of hell were chasing him. Royce shook his head as he pulled away from the curb. He called Drusilla before he lost his courage and left a voicemail message when she didn't answer. He said three simple words.

I miss you.

Chapter
FOUR

ETECTIVE TOPHER CARNEGIE LUGGED THE LAST BOX OF FILES into Sawyer's office and set it against the far-left wall with all the others. Topher swept a lock of light brown hair off his forehead and smiled at Sawyer. "Does helping you move the boxes give me an advantage over the other candidates?" Good humor sparkled in the younger man's amber eyes.

Topher had been the first to apply for a position with Sawyer's new unit and was the one detective Sawyer was certain to choose. He just wasn't ready to divulge that little tidbit yet.

"It's a lot of boxes," Sawyer said. The original detectives investigated the hell out of the Magnolia Murders, which meant he had a ton of information to familiarize himself with before speaking to the press. Sawyer blew out a breath to dispel the rising panic.

"You okay, Sarge?"

It would take a minute to get used to his title. So much change all at once. New rank, new promotion, new team, and a new investigation into an old and ice-cold case. "Yeah, it's just a lot to process."

Topher nodded as he looked at the stacks of boxes. "But you don't have to process every bit of it right now and definitely not by yourself."

"True."

Topher offered him an encouraging smile. "Well, I'll let you get to it. Let me know if there's something I can do to help."

"Hey, Toph," Sawyer said when the younger detective reached his open door. "Report to me first thing in the morning."

"Yesss!" Topher said, punching the air. "You won't regret this, Key."

"No, but you might have second thoughts once we break these cases down."

Topher laughed. "It's a chance I'm willing to take. I'll see you at Joe's tonight."

"I'd appreciate it if you'd keep the news of your transfer between us until I make everything official."

"Of course."

After he was alone, Sawyer rolled up his sleeves and dug into the case files. He couldn't learn every minute detail about the murders before the press conference. Still, he wanted to know enough to speak intelligently and avoid making himself and the department look bad. It didn't take him long to become fully engrossed, so the sharp knock on his door sometime later caught him off guard. He snapped his head up to find Royce leaning against the doorjamb.

"Hi," Sawyer said.

Royce straightened and stepped fully into his office, shutting the door behind him. Something devilish and dirty glinted in his eyes, and he crossed the room and planted his fine ass on the corner of Sawyer's desk. "Hi. Did you miss me?"

"Terribly." And it was true. He was excited about the prospect of leading the CCU, but he would miss having Royce as his partner.

Royce raked his eyes over Sawyer's attire before scanning the room. "You've been home to change, and you set up your new office? And here I thought you might want my help."

Sawyer scoffed. "You want to help christen my office, which is hardly the same as unpacking the boxes and organizing my desk."

"Busted."

"You're in luck, though," Sawyer said. "I haven't had time to write up the case report for Dingbat."

Royce wagged his finger and tsked. "Look who's using childish nicknames now."

"Oh shit," Sawyer replied. "You're rubbing off on me."

Royce's grin was dark and delicious. "Every chance I get, baby." He raked his hot gaze over Sawyer. "You're wearing the pretentious cashmere thingy for your press conference. Nice."

Sawyer looked down at the storm-gray sweater vest he wore over a pale gray shirt and his lucky lavender tie. He lifted his head and met Royce's smiling eyes. "Thanks. My boyfriend bought it for me for Valentine's Day last year."

"Nope," Royce said, shaking his head to emphasize how adamant he was. "I bought it just because."

Sawyer bit his bottom lip to keep from laughing, but his restraint lasted only a few seconds. Royce rolled his eyes when Sawyer's mirth bubbled out of him. Sawyer cleared his throat and wiped his eyes, but Royce's deep scowl nearly sent him into a second fit.

"Asshole."

"Dickhead." Sawyer replied. "Can I just point out that your 'just because' gift was given to me after a candlelit dinner on February thirteenth?"

"Why do I suddenly feel like I'm on the witness stand?" Royce asked.

"Answer the question, Sergeant Locke. Do you honestly expect the jury to believe the timing of your gift was a coincidence?"

Royce crossed his arms over his chest. "Objection."

Sawyer desperately wanted to kiss his pouty lips. "The witness can't object."

"I'm also representing myself at the trial."

"So that makes you the defendant. Interesting. What crimes were you charged with? Eating cheese from a squirty can?"

Royce dropped his arms and leaned forward. "I am accused of killing off any chance another man has with you. No one will ever worship your body and heart the way I do. Now and forever." His voice was thick and husky, lighting the fuse of lust in Sawyer's core. "And, yes, counselor, I am guilty. I bought my boyfriend the super soft sweater thingy 'just because' it's the same color as my eyes, and I like to mark him in every way possible. Until today, our relationship had to be a secret at work."

A poorly kept one, but Sawyer was too mesmerized by the hunger and longing in Royce's eyes to voice his meager objection.

"What's the matter?" Royce asked. "You look lost for words."

Sawyer rose to his full height, cupped Royce's face, and kissed him hard and long. He didn't care who might walk through the door because the only person in the entire world who mattered was right there, tangling his tongue with Sawyer's and emitting soft little growls of need. By some miracle, Sawyer found the sense to pull back before they ended up christening his office. He'd been joking when he'd brought it up, but it was starting to sound like a damn fine idea.

Sawyer dropped back into his chair, which put his head way closer to Royce's crotch than was safe for work. He yanked his head back up and was relieved to see the battle raging in Royce's gaze. It was nice to know he wasn't alone in the storm.

"You should look like Mr. Rogers in your sweater."

Sawyer shook his head. "He wore cardigans."

"I don't even know what that is, but I do know I'm looking forward to stripping you bare when we get home tonight."

Sawyer inhaled a deep, shaky breath. His instincts were to bait Royce into confessing in vivid detail just what he planned to do once they were alone in their home, but he knew that would be a big mistake. He needed to focus on the press conference. Sawyer had familiarized himself with the basics of each crime scene, but he still wasn't confident enough to take questions from reporters. Then again, Sawyer wasn't sure he'd ever be ready for that.

Royce picked up the framed photo Sawyer set on his desk. It was the picture Felix had taken of them during a private moment in the parking lot of the newspaper office. Their relationship had been new, and they'd been working through insecurities and fears. Royce had gently caressed Sawyer's face while staring lovingly into his eyes. Felix had snapped the photo and sent it to Rigby to get them in trouble, a move Sawyer and Royce had given him hell for before they'd all made peace.

Royce had framed the picture for Sawyer, who'd used it to get him through the darkest days of recovering from burns at the hospital. When they removed his dead skin, the nurses hadn't permitted anyone to be in the room with Sawyer, so he'd stared at the image through blurry eyes until the pain lessened.

"This is an amazing photo." Royce's mouth hooked into a crooked smile.

"It is, and I'm so happy I can display it now."

Royce returned the frame to Sawyer's desk. "You've been so busy this morning you probably didn't even know I was gone."

"Bullshit. I feel like a part of my soul is missing when you're not around, but it will make our evenings together even more special."

"Absence makes the heart grow fonder?"

"I don't think I can be any more enamored with you than I already am, Ro."

Royce leaned forward and stopped just shy of Sawyer's mouth. "Challenge received and accepted," he said before capturing Sawyer's lips in a quick kiss.

Sawyer sighed when he pulled back. "So, how was your visit with Beecham and lunch with Tara?"

Royce's countenance darkened, his brow formed a deep vee, and the spark Sawyer loved so much dimmed the way it did every time Royce ran into one of his estranged family members. "Who was it this time? Eddie or Benton?"

"Neither." Royce launched into a recap of the phone call he received from the store owner and the subsequent conversation with Jason. "I hope I did the right thing."

"You absolutely did, and this is why Mendoza chose you to lead the Explorer program. We're about to become the proud parents of thirty teenagers."

"Thirty?" Royce asked, his voice soaring into a higher octave. "You think there will be that many kids right out of the gate?"

Sawyer chuckled. "There will be dozens of kids interested, but I'm not sure how many they'll start with. I imagine the screening process is stringent. Are you leaning toward accepting Mendoza's offer?"

Royce shrugged. "I think Mendoza sees something in me, and I don't want to let him down."

"This is your career, not his."

"I promised the sheriff I'd show up at training on Monday with an open mind, and I plan to keep my word. If I like what I see, I'll finish the rest of the training. If I don't, I'll tell Mendoza that running the program isn't for me."

"Next week?" Sawyer asked. "Mendoza made it sound like you had a few months to decide."

"I don't think he deliberately misled me. He probably isn't familiar with Beecham's minicollege." Royce explained the various classrooms and how cool it would've been to have an opportunity like the Explorer program when he was younger. "I wonder if Dr. Fawkes or someone from her office would be interested in assisting with the forensics part?"

Sawyer chuckled. "You're sounding mighty intrigued about this opportunity."

"I'm keeping an open mind. Tara seemed excited about the prospect at lunch, and she's going to join me on Monday to check out the training."

"You didn't pump her for information about Beecham and Mendoza, did you?"

"Who, me?" Royce asked though the mischievous gleam in his eyes gave him away.

"Ro."

"I didn't press her for more information, but I did notice a photo of the sheriff and our chief in Beecham's office." Royce waggled his brows.

"It's none of our business," Sawyer said.

"Fine." The little pout in Royce's voice made him smile. "Are you ready for the press conference?"

"Ha! After only a few hours of preparation? No way."

"How can I help?" Royce asked.

Sawyer quickly told him what he'd accomplished and what he still wanted to find before taking questions. Royce didn't waste his breath telling him he was over prepping; he jumped into action, digging out the detectives' summaries for the third murder.

Sawyer scanned the documents and made notes in the portfolio he planned to take to the podium. He looked up a few minutes later and caught Royce staring into space with a pensive expression on his face. "Do you think Jason was telling the truth?" he asked.

Royce turned and looked at him. "About which part? That the baby isn't his? Or that this was the first time he stole something?"

"The part about Drusilla missing you as much as you miss her," Sawyer said, knowing it was the part that rattled him the most. Royce could walk away from Eddie and Benton without a backward glance, but the chasm between Dru and Royce ate at him.

Royce ran a hand through his hair. "I want to believe Jason wasn't just telling me what I wanted to hear to get out of trouble, but I can't get my hopes up too high. I miss Dru and the boys, but she's stuck between a rock and a hard place. I hate that she has to depend on my dad for a roof over their heads, but I'd hate even more for them to get kicked out for associating with me. It's not worth the risk."

And there was the crux of the problem. Royce meant *he* wasn't worth the risk. This remarkable man still hadn't figured out his value and tied his identity to the family he'd been born into. Sawyer found it wholly unacceptable and crooked his finger for Royce to come closer. Once he complied, Sawyer cupped his face and held him in place.

"You're worth everything, baby. There's no one I'd rather have by my side—on the job and in my life. I love you enough to make up for the people who've chosen not to be a part of your life."

Royce's expression softened. "I love you too." He pressed another quick kiss to Sawyer's lips. "I'm sorry our date night got ruined this weekend."

"I still spent it with you, didn't I?"

Royce laughed. "But I had much bigger plans for us. There was something I wanted to ask you."

Sawyer's pulse leaped. "Oh yeah? You could ask me now."

Royce took a shaky breath. He parted his mouth to speak, but whatever he was going to say was interrupted by a knock at the door.

"You've got to be kidding me," Royce growled.

"Sawyer," his mother said from the hallway. He adored the woman, but she occasionally had the absolute worst timing.

Royce blew out a frustrated breath on his way to the door. "We can finish this conversation tonight. Maybe during some hot tub hijinks."

Sawyer couldn't recall the last time he'd thrown an actual fit over being denied something he wanted, but he was ready to end the dry spell until he saw his mother's luminescent face. Her sable hair framed her face in soft, romantic curls. She wore a winter white suit with a teal shirt and paired it with a teal-and-purple scarf. Her teal stilettos made her almost as tall as Sawyer. She would always be the most beautiful woman in the world to him, even if she'd arrived in sweatpants, a flannel shirt, and her hair in a messy bun. He'd seen the latter look plenty of times over the years. Evangeline knew how to dress for success but preferred to dress for comfort.

"Someone's had a blowout today," Sawyer said.

Evangeline smiled. "Someone had a very productive meeting with her agent this morning. You'll soon be seeing this face"—she paused to frame her head with her hands—"in international ads again."

"Wrinkle cream?" Sawyer asked.

She narrowed her dark brown eyes to thin slits. "Antiwrinkle cream, smartass."

Evangeline embraced Royce first. Sawyer wanted to think it was because he was closest, but he knew damn well Royce was her new favorite. The two of them conspired over nearly everything. A thought struck him. Did she know about the engagement ring tucked away in Royce's drawer?

"Mom, what are you doing here?" Sawyer asked when it was his turn for a hug. "The pinning ceremony isn't until tomorrow morning."

"Yes," Evangeline said, "but you're holding your first press conference this afternoon. I wouldn't miss it."

Sawyer nearly regretted telling her that part but realized having another friendly face in the crowd would be a blessing and not a curse. He looked at his dad standing tall and proud behind his mom. Two friendly faces were even better. His dad's once light hair was completely gray, and it made his blue eyes appear brighter. He was dressed in a suit and looked like he'd just come from his office or court. "What's your excuse?" Sawyer asked.

"Can't a father be proud of his son?"

"Thank you for being here," Sawyer said.

His dad pulled him in for a tight hug before releasing him and opening his arms for Royce.

"Barron," Royce said, returning the embrace. "Good to see you, sir."

Evangeline glanced around the small office. "Did we come at a bad time?"

"Not at all," Sawyer lied. "I was just prepping notes for the press conference."

"So we did come at a bad time," she replied. "We'll just head back upstairs and wait for you. It will give me time to plan a celebration dinner."

Sawyer and Royce both groaned.

"Mom, it's not necessary," Sawyer said.

"We don't want to get shot or set on fire," Royce added.

"Or kidnapped," Evangeline reminded them. "And I say nonsense. Every day is a cause for celebration, but some are bigger than others." She hooked her arm through Royce's. "I'm just going to borrow this guy. We have things to discuss."

Oh yeah. Evangeline knew all about Royce's intentions and wanted to know why Sawyer wasn't sporting a platinum band on his ring finger. Royce looked at him in mock horror and mouthed "Save me" as Evangeline dragged him away.

His father shook his head and laughed at Royce's theatrics. "See you in a little while, son."

Alone again, Sawyer tilted his head to one side then the other, stretching his neck to get his blood flowing. "I've got this," he said as he glanced through his notes once more.

"Ready?" Mendoza asked outside the press room.

"No," Sawyer admitted.

Mendoza laughed and said, "You'll be just fine. Keep your answers as honest and direct as possible. When they ask a question you can't or shouldn't answer, you simply reply with the standard, 'I can't comment on an ongoing investigation.'"

"Sounds simple enough, sir."

The two of them entered the press room together. The chief joined the commissioner at the front of the room while Sawyer took a seat off to the side next to Royce.

"Breathe, baby," Royce whispered.

Sawyer forced himself to sit still and not fidget when Rigby got up and approached the podium. The commissioner announced that SPD had received several large, private donations, then explained how the department planned to utilize the funds. She only fielded a few questions before turning the microphone over to Mendoza, who adopted a jaw-dropping charisma behind the podium.

Royce leaned toward him and whispered, "This never fails to shock me."

"Same," Sawyer whispered. "I can't follow that."

Royce placed his hand between Sawyer's shoulder blades. The pressure and warmth of his touch eased his nerves. "You're not a follower. You're a leader."

"I'd like to introduce Sergeant Sawyer Key, who will lead the Cold Case Unit. His first task will be to solve the Magnolia Murders." Mendoza said. "There's no one better suited to investigate the biggest unsolved crime in Savannah's history. He will relentlessly pursue justice for Barbara Jean Wright, Jessica Lynn Campbell, and Amy Lou Morgan."

A light smattering of applause broke out around the room as he rose to his feet. He strode to the podium, hoping his posture didn't reflect the abject terror gripping his body. Mendoza held out his hand, and Sawyer shook it.

"Thank you, Chief, both for this opportunity and your high praise," Sawyer said before facing the press.

He spoke briefly about the goals of the unit and what he hoped to accomplish with the Magnolia Murders before taking questions. He knew there was a lot of attention on the case due to the *Sinister in Savannah* podcast, but he didn't expect every hand in the room to go up. Sawyer started with Felix because he was a familiar face, but he should've known his friend wouldn't lob a softball question.

"How do you specifically plan to solve the Magnolia Murders after all this time?" Felix asked.

"First, I think it's important to note the original detectives conducted extensive investigations into these murders," Sawyer replied. "I plan to retrace their steps while using newer technology and processes that give us a bigger advantage today."

The next reporter asked questions about the evidence and whether DNA was likely preserved.

"I won't get into the specific pieces of evidence we have or the tests we hope to run, but of course, positive hits on DNA could be a game-changer."

Another reporter asked if they planned to run familial DNA tests, even though Sawyer had just said he wouldn't answer specific questions about testing. He politely repeated his previous answer before calling on a lady in the back row.

"Are the police feeling pressure from the attention the *Sinister in Savannah* podcast is garnering?" she asked.

Sawyer glanced at Felix, who quickly wiped the smirk off his face.

"I'm suspicious of the timing for both the newly formed unit and your investigation," she added.

"No," Sawyer said flatly.

"Just no?" she countered. "You don't care to elaborate?"

"No," he repeated. From the corner of his eye, Sawyer saw Royce laughing.

He fielded a few more questions before the reporters grew tired of his evasive tactics and fired questions at Mendoza. Sawyer happily turned over the podium to the chief and reclaimed his chair next to Royce.

"You were amazing," Royce whispered. Then he leaned closer until his mouth nearly touched Sawyer's ear. "And so fucking sexy. I can't wait to get you home."

Chapter
FIVE

BLUE HANDED SAWYER AN ICE-COLD BEER. "RAISE A TOAST TO Sergeant Key," he said, his baritone voice booming across the bar.

The detectives in the MCU, along with Chief Mendoza and Commissioner Rigby, all lifted their glasses in salute. Sawyer returned the gesture, and they all took a drink.

"And let's not forget Sergeant Locke," Chen added. "Congratulations to our new kindergarten cop."

Royce coughed and sputtered. "You nearly made me spit out my beer," he rasped after recovering. Luckily, Sawyer hadn't taken a second drink, or he would've been in the same boat. "And nothing has been decided yet. I'm just exploring my options."

Congratulatory toasts turned into jeers and good-natured roasts with Royce taking the brunt of the jabs.

"I'm not feeling the love tonight," Royce called out when their friends left them to play pool and darts or to grab another round of drinks.

Grateful it was just the two of them, Sawyer hooked an arm around his neck and pressed his lips to Royce's ear. "Let's get out of here, and I can change that."

Royce turned his head and kissed Sawyer. "One more drink, then we'll head home."

One more drink for Sawyer turned in to three because the detectives hoping to fill the slots in his unit were doing their best to get a leg up. Holly treated him to pretzel bites and beer cheese to help soak up the alcohol. Their brief night at Joe's stretched on for a couple of hours, and they ended up ordering burgers, shooting pool, and throwing darts.

Since he was driving, Royce had switched to water after two beers, making it possible for Sawyer to drink more if he wanted. Sawyer decided against it since he didn't want to contend with a hangover.

"Are you sure you want to move to the CCU?" Sawyer asked Holly when he was able to get a private moment with her.

"I'm positive."

"Do you mind if I ask why?" Sawyer inquired. "You seem to love vice."

"I do, and I'm damn good at it. My mother wouldn't recognize me when I'm in deep cover."

"So, again, I ask why?"

Holly took a deep breath. "I honestly need the change."

"You need it, or Jace wants it?" Sawyer asked.

"Both, to be honest. Vice work isn't meant for cops who want to be happily married, and I was starting to feel burned out before Jace and I reconnected. My future with him is the deciding factor but not the only one. I'm doing this for myself and for the family I hope to have one day."

"You guys thinking about having kids?" Sawyer asked.

Holly nodded. "And I'm not getting any younger."

"I'd love to have you join my unit if it's what you truly want. I've already decided to pull Topher over too."

"He's a great guy. Smart, resourceful, and diligent," Holly said. "He reminds me of you."

"Flattery will get you everywhere," Sawyer teased. "I'll see you bright and early in the morning. We'll have our work cut out for us."

"I'm up for it," Holly replied.

Royce rejoined them a few moments later. "Well, did the pretzel bites and beer cheese buy your entrance into the coolest unit?" He nudged Sawyer. "Get it? Cold cases make it the coolest unit?"

"That's hilarious, Ro," Sawyer said dryly.

"In charge of the kiddos for one day and he already has dad jokes," Holly added.

It was Royce's turn to look unenthused. "I haven't decided yet, and besides, tonight is about Sawyer's promotion."

"Promotion?" came a familiar voice behind Sawyer. "SPD must pass them out like Oprah freaking Winfrey. You get a promotion! You get a promotion! Everyone gets a promotion!"

Sawyer slowly swiveled around and gaped at Charlie Price, his former partner from the Chatham County Sheriff's Department. "What are you doing here?" Sawyer asked as Charlie wrapped him up in a bear hug.

Charlie dropped his arms and stepped back. "Saw the press conference on the news and figured you'd be here celebrating." He looked around the bar with a contemptuous expression. "You city boys couldn't find a nicer place than this dive?"

"Hey," Sawyer said, nudging Charlie. "This is a high-class joint compared to that shack the county boys hang out in."

"I've heard people throw their peanut shells on the floor like animals," Royce said.

"Yep," Charlie agreed. "It's perfect." He offered his hand to Royce, who only hesitated a few seconds before shaking it. "I see you're still bitter over losing the league softball championship to us last year."

"That was a bullshit call by the umpire in the bottom of the seventh inning, and you know it," Royce replied, not bothering to deny the loss still bothered him. "The pitch was high and outside. It was ball four, and I should've been rewarded first base to load them up for Blue."

"Strike!" Charlie shouted, mimicking the umpire who'd called Royce out on strikes.

Everyone in the bar looked in their direction. The officers who'd played on the police department's team knew what Charlie was referring to and laughed or jeered in his direction.

"Thank you. Thank you," Charlie said to his audience and bowed for dramatic effect. "You can find me here on no days ending in *y*."

Royce's scowl grew darker, and he crossed his arms over his chest.

Sawyer had seen this mixture of obstinance and pouting before, and it didn't bode well. "We'll get you back next year," Royce vowed.

"That's so far away," Charlie replied. "Why wait? Signups for spring basketball are next week. Or maybe bowling is more your speed."

Royce dropped his arms and leaned in. "I excel at both."

As much as Sawyer loved seeing Royce in all his sweaty, competitive glory, he wanted to call dibs on his man's free time, starting right then. He tried to make bedroom eyes at Royce, but he'd either lost his touch or his guy's attention was elsewhere.

"I see no need to wait. Let's settle this tonight," Royce said.

Sawyer bit back a groan and swallowed his disappointment with a drink of water.

"You're on. Best out of three," Charlie said. "Name your poison. Darts or pool?"

"Or trivia," Sawyer suggested. Both men aimed disdainful looks at him, so he held up his hands and surrendered. "My bad."

"That would give me an unfair advantage over Locke," Charlie said.

"I'm plenty smart," Royce countered.

Charlie's expression was sheer innocence, and neither Royce nor Sawyer was buying it. "Of course."

Royce's gray eyes looked glacial as he stared at Sawyer's former partner.

"Seriously," Charlie said, hooking an arm around Sawyer's neck and pulling him closer. "This guy wouldn't be in a relationship with some run-of-the-mill dumbass." Royce rolled his eyes but relaxed. "Not our Sawyer. He has extremely high standards."

Royce tilted his head back and laughed. "So you're saying I am an extraordinary dumbass."

A good-natured grin clung to Charlie's lips as he shrugged. "Hey, you said it, not me."

Royce pushed back from the table and stood up. "Trivia it is. Best of three rounds." Without waiting for Charlie's response, Royce headed to the bar to get the trivia game cards and golf pencils.

Charlie dropped his arm and straightened in his chair. When his former partner started laughing, Sawyer pulled his gaze away from Royce's sweet ass to look at his friend.

"What?" Sawyer asked.

Charlie's lips hooked into a wry grin. "Remember when he used to snarl at me if I even thought about touching you in the most innocent way?"

Sawyer narrowed his eyes. "Yeah. So?"

"I just put my arm around you and tugged you close and still managed to come away with my limbs intact. What's up with that?"

Sawyer was suddenly at a loss for words. Was Charlie implying Royce didn't feel as intensely about him? He slammed on the mental brakes before his mind could twist his friend's words and make a mountain out of a molehill. The likelier answer was that Royce had finally accepted Sawyer wanted him and only him. "He knows where my heart is."

Charlie smiled and nodded. "Yeah, he does, but it is so fun to rile him up."

Sawyer laughed because it was funny to watch sometimes, and Royce's commitment to staking a claim afterward was delicious and addictive. It had been a while since Royce's inner caveman had come out to play, and though Sawyer missed his infrequent visits, he was grateful Royce felt the need less often. Then Sawyer recalled the conversation they'd had about the cashmere sweater vest and realized Royce had still found ways to claim him. Sawyer thought about other gifts Royce had given him or gestures he'd made, looking for signs of possession.

"Oh boy," Charlie said, jolting Sawyer out of his thoughts.

"What?"

"You're wearing a very telling expression on your face."

Sawyer forced himself to relax and focus on his friend. "What do you mean?"

"Your eyes got this mushy, distant expression, and your cheeks are pink."

Sawyer laughed and clapped Charlie on the shoulder. "Yeah, they probably did. Sorry if it made you uncomfortable."

"What? Hell no. I'm stoked you've found happiness again, Sawyer. I just hate that I had to lose you as a partner for it to happen. Fucking Wheeler."

The alcohol Sawyer consumed had rounded and softened his edges, but hearing the Chatham County sheriff's name was like having a bucket of ice water dumped over him.

"Oh shit," Charlie said. "You look like a wet cat. I should've kept my mouth shut."

Sawyer shook his head. "You should be able to talk to your friend about work stuff."

"Not when the work stuff eviscerates said friend and ruins his night of celebration," Charlie countered.

Sawyer took a deep breath and exhaled it slowly. "On the contrary, you've reminded me how lucky I am to work with a wonderful, diverse group of people." A thought occurred to him. "Hey, have you ever considered moving over to the SPD?"

Royce rejoined them before Charlie could respond. "Ugh. Do I get to voice my opinion on the subject?"

Charlie ruffled Royce's hair, then snagged a pencil and trivia card from Royce's hands. "Nope," he replied.

"To which question?" Sawyer asked.

Laughing, Charlie set his trivia items on the table. "Both. I've never thought about jumping ship, and if I had, Royce's opinion wouldn't matter."

"You should consider it," Royce said, surprising them both. "What? I can be mature and shit."

Sawyer and Charlie laughed, but he could tell his friend was seriously giving it some thought.

"Did something specific happen at CCSD, or is it the overall mood dragging you down?" Royce asked.

Charlie ran his hand through his hair. "Both. Morale is at an all-time low, but Wheeler has resumed his bullying tactics. This time he has a pregnant deputy in his crosshairs."

Charlie's words landed like a physical punch to Sawyer's stomach. His gut started cramping, and a wave of heat flashed through him from head to toe, reminding Sawyer of being trapped in a raging inferno. His throat constricted, cutting off the air he needed to survive.

"Oh fuck," Charlie said. "I'm sorry. I should've kept my damn mouth shut."

"He's okay," Royce said gently. "Aren't you, GB?" Royce squeezed

Sawyer's thigh under the table, pulling him out of the fire and grounding him in the present.

Sawyer took a shaky breath and threaded his fingers through Royce's. "Yeah, I just can't stand the thought of Wheeler treating someone else the way he did me."

"Guess that sensitivity training he took didn't stick, huh?" Royce asked.

Charlie scoffed. "You didn't think for a second he actually attended classes on sensitivity and creating an inclusive workplace, did you?"

"Yes," Royce and Sawyer said at the same time.

"It was part of the settlement agreement," Sawyer pointed out. "It was the only damn thing he was required to do. Are you saying he didn't do it?"

Charlie averted his gaze but not before Sawyer saw the distress in his eyes. "I shouldn't have said anything."

"Because you're only speculating, or because you didn't mean to trigger bad memories for your friend?" Royce asked.

Charlie took a deep breath and lifted his head, meeting their gazes one at a time. "For stirring up shit that upsets my friend."

"So you know for a fact Wheeler didn't attend sensitivity training?" Royce pushed because Sawyer couldn't. The shocking revelation had made it impossible for him to voice his thoughts.

Charlie shook his head. "I shouldn't—"

"Fuck that, and fuck you," Royce snarled. "You don't get to come in here under the guise of congratulating your former partner on a promotion, drop a fucking grenade, and then dance away from the mess you've made."

"I'm not a mess," Sawyer said, finding his voice at last. "Royce has a point, Charlie. I've known you for a long time, and you're not the kind of person who goes around stirring up drama. I've also never known you to say anything you didn't mean. You said what you did about Wheeler because it's eating at your conscience. The questions on my mind are, why now, and why me?"

"Your buddy thinks *you* were the whistleblower," Royce said.

Charlie shook his head and pointed at Royce. "No, and don't you dare put those words in my mouth. I didn't just see what Wheeler put Sawyer through. I fucking lived it with him."

Someone from CCSD fed information to Felix, and he'd published a series of articles outlining the issues going on, including the reason for Sawyer's sudden departure and the subsequent lawsuit he filed. The settlement terms were simple: Sawyer was to keep his mouth shut, and Wheeler had to undergo sensitivity training. Sawyer had kept up his end of the bargain, despite Wheeler insisting he was Felix's source.

"It was you," Sawyer said softly to Charlie. He'd always known the whistleblower was someone close to him, but he couldn't allow himself to believe the obvious choice. "You fed the information to Felix."

"Fuck," Royce growled. "I never suspected you." And he wouldn't because Royce would never think about betraying a partner.

Charlie's tension drained from his body as remorse replaced his anger. He hung his head for a few seconds before meeting Sawyer's gaze. "I thought I was helping."

"By framing me?" Sawyer asked.

Charlie shook his head furiously. "No. No. Felix is responsible for the way the articles were worded."

Royce leaned forward and said, "Felix wouldn't have had an article to write if not for you, so don't think I'm letting you off the hook either." He relaxed back in his seat and blew out a harsh breath.

"I am sorry, Sawyer," Charlie said, his gaze filled with sincerity and regret. "I was so outraged on your behalf, and I wanted to make Wheeler pay. I never meant to taint your reputation."

"If I could accept that Felix's heart was in the right place and forgive him, then I can do the same for you…in time."

"You can start your atonement by telling us how you know Wheeler didn't take any of the required training," Royce said.

Charlie silently peeled the label off his beer bottle for a few seconds. Sawyer recognized one of the signs his friend was feeling anxious. He started to tell him not to worry about it, but Charlie lifted his head and locked eyes with Sawyer.

"He had a little too much to drink at the Christmas charity event at the country club and bragged to some cronies about the forged certificate he submitted."

"Did you overhear this firsthand?" Sawyer asked.

"Yeah," Charlie replied. "That's not the only thing I witnessed at the event."

Sawyer's spidey sense started to tingle. "I bet it has something to do with the pregnant deputy he's harassing."

Charlie nodded. "I saw them coming out of a room marked as staff only. She was straightening her dress, and he was tidying up his hair. They were laughing as they walked, and Wheeler patted her ass."

Sawyer recoiled. "Gross."

"Did they see you?" Royce asked.

"No. I was farther up the hallway, and they never looked behind them. I'd heard the unmistakable sound of people having sex as I walked by the room, but I never would've guessed Wheeler was that stupid."

"Even after he confessed publicly to faking his sensitivity training?" Sawyer asked.

Charlie grimaced. "Maybe I didn't think the old fucker could still get it up."

"He not only got it up, but it sounds like he's shooting live rounds," Royce replied.

"Shut up," Sawyer and Charlie said at the same time.

"Seriously," Royce said. "Do you think he's the father of her child?"

Charlie nodded. "I can't prove it, but I suspect it's the reason behind his bullying."

"That doesn't make sense," Royce replied. "Why torment her if he's the father? Wouldn't he be afraid she'd tell somebody?"

"She's married too," Charlie explained.

"And Wheeler's gotten away with bullying before," Sawyer said somberly. Guilt crushed him like a boulder. "I gave in too easily, and he thinks this deputy will do the same. I shouldn't have sold out. I should've hung in there until the bad publicity forced him to resign as Chatham County's sheriff."

"That was never going to happen," Royce said vehemently. "Even if he had resigned, you would've become a professional pariah. No department would've hired you. Rigby would've wanted to bring you on board, but the former commissioner would've vetoed it."

"He's right," Charlie said. "None of this is your fault. You're the only person who has ever stood up to him. I shouldn't have even brought it up."

"Why did you?" Royce wanted to know.

"I guess I'm looking for guidance on what to do."

"Call your pal Felix," Royce suggested. "He'll take your identity to the grave with him."

Charlie looked at Sawyer, who shrugged. "Royce has a point. You didn't have a problem airing my dirty laundry. Why the hesitation now?"

"I think the solution is bigger than me running to Felix every time Wheeler behaves unethically," Charlie said. "I think someone should run for sheriff and beat him." His friend's direct gaze created a sinking feeling in the pit of Sawyer's stomach.

He shook his head. "Cast your eyes elsewhere." Sawyer turned to Royce, expecting his man to back him up, but instead, he encountered a huge grin.

"You'd make such a good sheriff," Royce said.

"But I just got a promotion." One he was really excited about.

Royce nodded. "Yeah, but you're destined for greater things."

"You know how much I hate politics," Sawyer countered.

"No, you hate the state of our political climate today. That doesn't mean you have to deploy the same gutter tactics."

"Oh, you think Wheeler would engage in a clean campaign?" Sawyer asked.

"It's hard to say because no one runs against him," Charlie countered. He leaned forward and studied Sawyer intently. "Your unfinished business with the bastard burns in your gut. I know you, Sawyer. You don't walk away."

"Relentless," Royce added.

"I made my peace with how I left CCSD. I've moved on," Sawyer said emphatically, doing his damnedest to ignore the seed of discontent he'd buried in his soul. "I love working for SPD, and I feel like I have a real future there."

"Fair enough," Charlie relented. "It was worth a shot."

Sawyer picked up his glass to take another sip of water, but it had lost its appeal. "I want another beer."

Royce slapped Charlie on the back. "You heard the man, jackass. Buy up. It's the least you can do."

Charlie pushed his chair back and stood up. "Three?" he asked.

"I'll stick with water," Royce said, sliding his hand up Sawyer's thigh as Charlie walked away. "I need a clear head for the things I plan to do to you tonight."

"Hot tub hijinks?" Sawyer asked hopefully.

Royce nodded and pushed Sawyer's glass of water to him. "Better hydrate, baby."

Chapter
SIX

SAWYER'S HANDS GREW BOLDER AS THE NIGHT WORE ON, MAKING it harder for Royce to concentrate. He'd started with flirty touches under the table but had quickly advanced to full-on groping once they got into the SUV.

"You're the reason I lost trivia," Royce said when he turned onto their street.

"Because I'm wicked smart," Sawyer replied, sounding smug as hell.

"No one disputes that, but I think you know the real reason why I couldn't answer the most basic questions. I even missed the clue about two female police officers who combatted criminals in the streets and sexism in the precinct. You know how much I love *Cagney & Lacey*."

"I do." Sawyer slid his hand farther up Royce's thigh and traced the outline of his erection with a nimble finger. "I want this bad boy inside me."

"Trust me. I want to bury it inside you," Royce said as he shifted

Sawyer's hand to midthigh. "But that will get delayed if we jump the curb and run over pedestrians who are out walking their dogs."

Sighing, Sawyer removed his hand. "So much paperwork."

They reached their home without incident a few moments later, and Royce pushed Sawyer up against the wall as soon as they entered the house through the garage. He kissed him hungrily, raking his teeth over Sawyer's tongue and sucking it into his mouth as he removed their jackets. Royce broke their kiss and stepped back so he could eye fuck Sawyer while peeling the layers of clothes off him. Royce grazed his fingertips over Sawyer's soft skin, lightly scraped his nails over his hard nipples, and stroked his thick erection.

Sawyer tilted his head back against the wall. "Don't stop."

Royce licked his arched neck. "Not even if the world ends."

Meow.

Royce groaned, stepped back from Sawyer's tempting body, and stared down at their cat. Bones swished his bushy tail and peered at them through narrowed green eyes. His expression said, "You're late and so is my dinner."

Sawyer chuckled. "Well, maybe I'll take a back seat to Bones."

Royce kissed him soundly on the mouth. "You grab two water bottles and head out to the hot tub while I take care of this guy."

Sawyer pushed off the wall and bent over to pet Bones, but the cat darted away angrily. "Damn, we're in trouble." He pulled two bottles from the refrigerator and strolled across the house like he didn't have a care in the world. Sawyer stopped at the sliding patio door and glanced over his shoulder. "Stop staring at my ass and feed the cat. The quicker you do, the sooner you get to play with said ass." Sawyer disappeared out the door with a playful wink.

Royce retrieved Bones's pricey wet food from the cabinet and gave the pull tab a big yank.

Meow.

"I know, big guy. I wanted to come straight home to my beautiful boy after work, but Daddy made me go out for drinks."

Meow. Even the cat knew he was a bullshitter.

Royce looked out the glass doors to see Sawyer sink into the water. A look of rapture washed over his face as he tilted his head back against the headrest. Okay, Royce exaggerated everything except his love for Sawyer.

Meow.

And Bones.

"Looks like surfer's delight tonight, Bonesy Bones. We've got salmon, tuna, and shrimp." The cat had at least twenty nicknames and hated every one of them. Royce spooned half the can into Bones's dish and stowed the rest in the refrigerator for breakfast. Their beautiful boy ate with gusto, alternating between purrs of pleasure and growls of possessiveness.

Royce looked back at the patio. Sawyer's mouth had parted, and his eyes remained closed. At first, Royce worried Sawyer had fallen asleep, but then he saw his arm moving subtly in the water. His man wasn't sleeping; he was pleasuring himself. Royce stared in disbelief for a few heartbeats, a possessive growl rumbling from his chest.

"That asshole started without me."

He scooped up Sawyer's discarded clothes and headed to the bedroom. A devious plan formed along the way. He quickly stripped down, donned his robe, and slung Sawyer's over his arm. The distance from the hot tub to the house was short, but it was a nippy walk in the winter. He quickly stopped at his bedside table and slid a surprise in his robe pocket. It wasn't the ring his heart longed to give to Sawyer, but it fit the occasion better.

Royce made a beeline for the patio but paused after pulling the slider shut behind him. The steam from the hot tub mingled with the cooler air, forming a hazy fog and giving the scene a dreamlike feel. It was only fitting because Sawyer was every fantasy Royce had ever had, and a small part of him worried he'd wake up to find their love had just been a delicious dream.

A slight breeze rustled through the barren trees, lifting and dispersing the fog in swirling wisps until it was gone entirely. Sawyer slowly turned to look at him without raising his head. His dark, heavy-lidded eyes blazed with arousal and need. Parted lips curved into a seductive invitation, challenging Royce to come and get him. He thought he might combust right there on the spot if he didn't take control of the situation.

"Get those hands where I can see them," Royce commanded as he strode to the hot tub.

Sawyer lifted his hands out of the water and raised them in surrender. "I didn't do anything, officer."

Royce snorted and nodded toward Sawyer's obvious arousal. "That's not what the evidence is pointing to." He laid Sawyer's robe across the lounge chair, stripped out of his, and dropped it on top. He'd taken two steps closer to paradise when he recalled the surprise he'd planned. Royce retrieved the silicone item from the pocket, then stepped into the hot water. He lowered himself onto the curved seat and expelled a long breath as the powerful jets went to work on his body. "This feels so damn good after a long day."

Sawyer straddled him in a gracious sweep of long, toned limbs, just as Royce knew he would, which put Sawyer's cock and balls right where Royce wanted them. He didn't make his move right away, though.

Royce leaned his head against the rest and smiled at the man who'd stolen his heart so effortlessly. "Hi."

Sawyer returned his greeting with a long, scorching kiss that nearly made Royce forget his mission, especially when Sawyer pulled back and said, "Fuck me already."

Royce grinned at him. "Mighty impatient when we're tipsy, eh?"

Sawyer fisted his cock and pumped it slowly. "My eagerness has nothing to do with the beer and everything to do with you."

Royce lifted his empty hand and cupped the back of Sawyer's neck, pulling him down until their mouths hovered inches apart. "Inebriated on love, are you?"

"Yes," Sawyer whispered before reclaiming Royce's mouth.

Royce got swept away in their kiss for several long moments before moving his hand from Sawyer's neck to his cock. Sawyer bucked his hips, pushing his erection deeper into Royce's fist.

Breaking the kiss, Royce stared up at him. "Control freak."

Sawyer shrugged. "But you love me."

"More than life itself," Royce agreed. "Still doesn't mean you don't need an occasional lesson."

"Oh, teach me, baby."

Royce captured his lips once more, dialing up the intensity until Sawyer melted into him. That's when Royce made his move, pushing one silicone ring down Sawyer's shaft and securing the second around his balls.

Sawyer groaned and broke the kiss. "I might die if you don't let me come."

Royce chuckled at the petulant look on his face. "Aren't you the one who told me not to stop?" He stroked Sawyer's erection, smiling when his lover's head fell back and his lips parted on a sexy little sigh. "Have you changed your mind?"

"God no. Don't stop."

Sawyer rocked his hips, grinding his erection against Royce's, and he realized the folly of his choice. The cock ring would delay Sawyer's orgasm, but it wouldn't keep him from climaxing. His only option was to take a tighter grip on the reins and turn Sawyer into complete putty in his arms.

Royce gripped Sawyer's hips, holding him in place so he could feast on his lips. Then Royce licked a path down Sawyer's neck, sank his teeth into his pectoral muscle, sucked a hard nipple in his mouth, and kissed the scars on Sawyer's chest from the fire. Sawyer bucked and squirmed, trying to create friction where he needed it most, but Royce tightened his hold. He returned to Sawyer's mouth, sweeping his tongue in deep and circling it around Sawyer's before sucking his tongue into his mouth. Sawyer carded his fingers through Royce's hair, raking his nails over Royce's scalp.

"Fuck me now," Sawyer demanded.

Royce didn't relent. He repeated his earlier pattern of kissing, licking, and biting his way to the nipple on the other side.

"Baby, I need you," Sawyer whined.

"You have me. You always will."

Royce slid his hands down to cup Sawyer's ass, massaging the firm globes while pushing them together and pulling them apart.

"Let's go inside. I don't want the neighbors to hear," Sawyer said huskily.

"Since when?"

Sawyer looked at him with pleading eyes. "Since I'm feeling needier than usual."

Royce nearly caved but changed his mind when he caught an impish glimmer in Sawyer's gaze. "I'm not done playing with you yet."

Royce trailed a single finger up and down Sawyer's ass crack, stopping just shy of his pucker before heading back to the top. On the next downward trek, Sawyer pushed against the caress and raised his ass the scant half inch to get Royce's fingertip where he wanted it.

"Fucking control freak," Royce said as he circled his finger around the puckered rim.

Sawyer's head fell back, and he moaned needily. "Deeper."

Royce growled in response and sank his teeth into Sawyer's corded neck tendon. He pressed the pad of his fingertip against Sawyer's entrance but stopped shy of penetrating him. Water might stimulate their hormones, but it was no friend to intercourse, especially when submerged.

Sawyer yanked Royce's hair and stared determinedly into his eyes. "I need you."

"Let's go."

Sawyer stood up and held out his hand to help Royce up. The cool air hitting Royce's overheated skin was exhilarating, and it was the pause he needed to regain control of the situation. Once inside the house, Royce bypassed their bed and headed straight to the bathroom.

"Here's good," Sawyer said, bracing his hands on the vanity and presenting his ass.

"Not yet." Royce swatted a firm cheek, then cranked the faucet handle to turn the shower on.

"Fine," Sawyer grumbled as he reached down to remove the cock ring.

Royce snagged Sawyer's wrist before he completed his task. "Oh, I don't think so. I'm not done with you yet."

The shower to wash away the day and chlorine was flirty and dirty, just how Royce preferred them. His filthy words and Sawyer's moans echoed off the tile. Royce took his time toweling off Sawyer's golden skin before skimming the terry cloth over his own body.

"Look who's in a hurry now," Sawyer said.

"To get to the next phase."

Sawyer narrowed his eyes. "It better include a powerful orgasm."

"That's the phase after." Royce snagged his hand and pulled him into the bedroom. "Get on your hands and knees," he commanded once they reached the bed. "I want your sexy ass in the air."

Sawyer immediately complied, and the gorgeous sight was enough to stop Royce in his tracks.

"How are you mine?" he asked.

Sawyer turned his head and met his gaze. "I wonder the same thing about you. We could ponder the why and how we came to be, or you could get on this bed and come inside me."

"Oh, that's a good line. Borrow it from one of your audiobooks, did you?" Royce asked as he opened the drawer and removed the lube.

"Nope. Just a little something I thought I'd submit to a greeting card company."

Royce's lips twitched, then he climbed onto the bed behind Sawyer. Then the only thing he could think about was coming inside Sawyer's perfect ass. Royce dropped the lube onto the bed because they didn't need it yet. He gripped Sawyer's ass, spread his cheeks, and buried his face between the globes. Royce tongued and teased Sawyer's pucker until the only words escaping his mouth were incoherent gibberish interlaced with provocative swear words. When Royce pulled back, he wiped his mouth with the back of his hand and grabbed the lube.

"Is this the phase where I come?"

"Nope." Royce slicked his fingers and eased one inside Sawyer's tight clench, gliding it back and forth to stimulate his nerve endings. He pushed deeper, pressing against Sawyer's prostate until he arched his back and groaned.

"I can't take it anymore," Sawyer whined and tapped the bed as if they were in the middle of a hotly contested wrestling match.

"You told me not to stop," Royce reminded him.

"I meant for you to never stop loving me."

Royce lowered his head and kissed Sawyer's right ass cheek. "That's a promise I can easily make."

He continued stretching and teasing Sawyer until his entrance was pliant and needy. Royce eased his fingers free amid great protest, but Sawyer relaxed when Royce released the silicone band around his balls. He took his time working the ring down Sawyer's shaft, and his hand came away wet from Sawyer's drooling cock.

"You want me bad," Royce said. Instead of lining up behind Sawyer and pushing his dick inside him, Royce flopped onto his back. "So come and get it."

Sawyer released a hungry snarl and straddled Royce's hips, wasting no time lining up Royce's cock to his hole and sinking onto it. Sawyer's mouth fell open, and he sat still while his body adjusted to the penetration. Royce used the time to stroke his chest and taut belly before wrapping his fist around Sawyer's cock. Sawyer bucked, fucking himself on Royce's cock while driving his dick deeper into Royce's fist.

Sawyer's reserve broke, and he worked himself up and down Royce's shaft, setting an aggressive pace to hurtle them both over the cliff.

Royce tensed his body, trying to hold off a little longer. "That's it. Use my cock, baby."

Sawyer grunted and picked up the pace. "You fill me up. Make me whole."

Royce knew he wasn't talking about sex either. "Always."

Sawyer slammed down on Royce's cock once more, gasped sharply, and spurted all over Royce's chest. Sawyer's tight, spasming channel sent Royce careening over the cliff after him. The fall was the most beautiful thing he'd ever experienced. When he landed, it was in a soft bed with the man he loved draped over his chest and panting softly in his ear.

"God, we're so good at this," Sawyer muttered.

Royce slapped his ass, then rolled him to his back. He gently withdrew his softening cock before stumbling into the bathroom to clean up. Royce dampened a washcloth for Sawyer, who was barely clinging to consciousness when Royce returned a few moments later. Royce chuckled as he cleaned him up and tucked him into bed.

"Go to sleep, GB. I'm going to cover the hot tub and lock the house down."

"'K," Sawyer mumbled.

Royce tossed the cloth into the bathroom and put his robe back on before exiting their bedroom.

He made quick work of covering the hot tub and grabbed the two bottles of water they'd forgotten all about. After locking the slider, Royce grabbed the bottle of ibuprofen from the cabinet next to the sink. He had a suspicious feeling Sawyer would be feeling the beer in the morning.

He wasn't intoxicated, but Sawyer wasn't a big drinker. He preferred to stay in control of his faculties, but Charlie's remarks about Wheeler had gotten to him.

Royce had suspected the situation with the sheriff felt like unresolved business to Sawyer, though Sawyer had never said as much. The fury he'd witnessed in his boyfriend's gaze betrayed his true thoughts on the matter. Sawyer had been shocked when Charlie suggested he should run for sheriff, and both his words and actions spoke vehemently against the idea. But the glint in Sawyer's eyes led Royce to believe the situation was far from settled for Sawyer.

Royce had meant what he'd said too. The citizens of Chatham County would be lucky to have Sawyer as their sheriff. The man was a natural at fielding questions from the press. He'd been fair, friendly, and firm when he needed to be and funny when the situation allowed. His relentless streak would do well to turn the tide of corruption, and Sawyer drew people to him like a magnet. Royce still couldn't believe the number of people from their unit who'd expressed interest in investigating cold cases.

It was hard, honest work but about as exciting as watching paint dry. Cases were cold for a reason, so you needed a bulldog like Sawyer to keep grinding and churning the waters. Mendoza had chosen the perfect guy to lead the unit. So why couldn't Royce accept that Mendoza had chosen the right guy to lead the Explorers? He was much too tired to analyze how his mind worked or didn't work in some cases.

He retrieved their cell phones from their jackets so he could charge them overnight. Royce held his breath while checking to see if Dru had returned his call. Disappointment slashed at his heart when there were zero notifications on the screen. He dropped the phones into one pocket, slid the pill bottle into the other, and tucked the water bottles into the crook of his left elbow.

Bones had stretched out on the ginormous fake tree tucked in the corner of the living room. The vantage point allowed him to look out over the yard. They'd bought it for him for Christmas because he'd worn out his multi-layered carpeted contraption. Much to Sawyer's regret, he'd allowed Royce to pick out the replacement, which was how they ended up with the mammoth replica of a real tree.

Bones lifted his head and stared at Royce as he double-checked the front door, even though no one had entered through it since the last time he'd confirmed it was locked.

Meow.

Royce wasn't sure if Bones was mocking him for his routine or if he was inquiring about the bedroom activities being over so they could all go to sleep. The big guy loved his tree but knew his place was beside his humans. Royce scratched beneath the beast's chin and Bones rewarded him with a magnificent purr.

"Come on, big guy. Let's go to bed."

Bones leaped to the floor without further prompting and dashed down the hallway. He was already in bed before Royce stepped into the bedroom. Sawyer was curled up on his side and entirely lost to the world. His soft snores made Royce smile as he set a water bottle and the ibuprofen on Sawyer's bedside table. He plugged Sawyer's phone in and kissed his temple. Royce meant it to be a quick peck, but he lingered for a moment before walking around to his side of the bed. He dropped his robe to the floor, plugged in his phone, then slid between the sheets.

After turning off his lamp, Royce scooted over to Sawyer's side of the bed and spooned up behind him. He expected to fall right to sleep, but the day's events replayed in his mind like a broken record, skipping from one scene to the next before starting all over again. It had been a lot of stimuli for one day—new career opportunities, separation from Sawyer, finding out about the Explorers training, reconnecting with his nephew after he got caught shoplifting, and getting his hopes up the same could happen with Drusilla.

He was disappointed he hadn't heard from her yet but not sad or surprised. Jason had warned him it could take a while, and Royce knew he needed to be patient. He also needed to accept she might never reach out to him. And if that were the case, he'd learn to deal with it. Royce had chosen Sawyer. He'd *always* choose Sawyer. And he'd never regret it.

Chapter
SEVEN

A RINGING PHONE YANKED SAWYER FROM A DEEP SLEEP, AND HE automatically reached for his cell without opening his eyes. A predawn call at their house meant a homicide or an equally major case needed their attention.

Royce swatted him on his bare ass and said, "It's mine," before he rolled over and answered the phone.

Based on his boyfriend's short, terse responses, Sawyer could tell his first assumption was correct, so he threw back the covers and sat up. He might as well turn on the shower and get the coffee going. Royce reached over and snagged his wrist before he got very far, and Sawyer remembered they were no longer partners.

Sawyer would've burrowed under the blankets a little deeper, but consciousness made him aware of an evil elf trying to jackhammer its way out of his brain. Christ, why had he had so much to drink on a work night? Sawyer knew the answer was right there, but it hurt too much to think about, so he took a deep breath and willed his pain away. A glance at the clock revealed he had three more hours to sleep off his headache, so he tugged the blanket up around his ears.

"I'll be there in twenty," Royce said before disconnecting the call. Instead of getting out of bed, Royce curled his body around Sawyer's. "Just need another minute."

Sawyer chuckled at Royce's familiar plea, and just that minuscule motion intensified the jackhammering in his brain. "I feel terrible," he moaned.

"Yeah, I'm sure you're torn up about staying in bed for another three hours."

"Talking about my head," Sawyer whispered. "I might die."

"That's why I put the ibuprofen and water on your bedside table."

The gesture eased Sawyer's suffering slightly, allowing him to muster the courage to wash three tablets down. "You're the best," he said as he nestled back down into the warm spoon his boyfriend made.

Royce kissed the back of his neck. "Just one more minute."

Sawyer awoke to an empty bed when his alarm went off. His head felt marginally better but nowhere close to where he wanted—needed—it to be. Dragging himself into the precinct with a hangover on his first day in charge was not the precedent Sawyer wished to set for his unit. He stumbled through his routine and had already put on a dress shirt and a pair of slacks before remembering the badge pinning ceremony Mendoza had planned. Sawyer returned the items to their hangers, planning to take them with him to change into after receiving his promotion.

The more he moved, the better he felt. Then again, he could probably chalk that up to drinking Royce's high-octane coffee. He forced himself to eat a light breakfast, even though food was the last thing he wanted. Skipping the meal would lead to a severe case of jitters when the caffeine kicked in. Royce's choice of brew would pack a wallop around midmorning if he wasn't careful.

Meow.

Sawyer turned his attention from stirring the oatmeal on the stove to staring down at his beautiful boy. "Morning, Bonesington."

Meow.

"Nice try," Sawyer said and returned his focus to the stove. "I know for a fact you already ate your breakfast. It's my turn."

Meow.

Sawyer turned off the stove and slid the pan over to a cool burner. Then he walked over to the refrigerator and pointed to a magnetized task tracker attached to it. Unlike his childhood chore list, this one only had one task that read: Did you feed the cat? Beneath it, there were two options: "No, He's Starving" and "Yes, He's a Liar" available for breakfast and dinner. Between the two options was a button they could slide left or right. At the top was an adorable picture of Bones with his two dads. Candy and the kids had given it to them for Christmas, and it would come in handy now that Sawyer and Royce were on different schedules.

Sawyer pointed to the tracker and said, "It clearly states you ate breakfast already."

Meow.

"That makes you a liar, Bones." *And talking to the cat as if he understands makes you a whack job.* They continued to glare at one another for a few seconds before Sawyer sort of caved and gave the cat a few treats. Bones pranced to his ridiculous tree to resume bird watching, and Sawyer sat down to eat his breakfast.

It felt odd driving to work without Royce, but he turned on an audiobook to fill the silence. Sawyer was pleasantly surprised to find Holly and Topher had arrived before him.

"Eager to get started, or are you planning to let me down gently?" he asked.

"The former, sir," Topher said.

"Wonderful news, but knock the 'sir' crap off, Toph." Sawyer looked at Holly. "And you, Holls?"

She winked and sipped her coffee. "Let's do this."

"I'd like to go over my game plan for the Magnolia Murders before we get started." Topher and Holly nodded and followed Sawyer into their conference room where he'd moved all the case boxes. "The first step is to lay out the three cases on the conference table. The next logical step is to review the crime scene photos to form our own opinions about what we see and make a list of similarities and differences between the three scenes."

"The differences could be especially telling," Holly said.

"That's the logic," Sawyer replied. "Afterward, I want to evaluate the pictures of the evidence to see if any items are good candidates for DNA testing. Then we'll start combing through the detectives' reports and witness statements, making a list of everyone interviewed and the persons of interest."

Topher stroked his chin. "Looking for those common denominators."

"My gut tells me it's someone deeply involved in the pageant," Sawyer replied.

Holly nodded. "Seems most logical, though I can't imagine why anyone would have wanted to stab these young ladies to death."

"We'll look for similarities and connections between their families too," Sawyer said. "I'm sure the original detectives followed the same logic, but lips can loosen over time. That means I want to forge new paths and retrace their steps."

"Who were the detectives?" Holly asked.

"Gerald Donovan and John Wayne Burke," Sawyer replied. "Familiar with either of them?"

Holly shook her head.

"I am," Topher said. "Burke just goes by Wayne. He and my grandfather were partners on patrol. Wayne got promoted to detective pretty quickly, but they've stayed in touch all these years."

"Good to know," Sawyer said. The connection might come in handy. "What about Donovan?"

"He passed away a long time ago," Topher said. "He was probably retirement age when Burke became his partner."

Sawyer mentally crossed Donovan's name off the list of prospective interviewees. "During my phone conversations with the families yesterday, I promised them as much transparency as possible without jeopardizing the investigation or a future trial that might come from it." He gestured to the boxes stacked along the wall. "Based on the sheer volume of documents we need to comb through, I've asked them for a week to familiarize myself with every facet of the case before I sit down with them, which they gracefully accepted."

"Sounds like we better get to it, then," Holly said.

Topher hoisted a heavy box from the 1984 murder off the floor. "I assume you want to review the cases in order."

"Absolutely."

They worked together in companionable silence until Sawyer's phone chimed with an incoming text. He removed his phone and saw it was from Royce.

I'm so sorry, but I don't think I'll make it back to the precinct in time for your pinning ceremony. I'm proud of you, asshole.

It's the nature of the job. Love you, dickhead, Sawyer wrote back. He emersed himself back in the task and lost track of time until Holly tapped him on the shoulder.

"It's time to pin the badge on the new sergeant," she said.

Sawyer laughed. "I thought you were going to call me a donkey."

"I save my insults for Jace and Royce." She took a deep breath, steepled her hands together, and looked heavenward. "Please let the fitting go off without a hitch tonight. Those two men drive me nuts, but I desperately want to marry one and officially claim the other as my brother."

"It'll be great, Holls."

"Hello," his mother called from the main squad room.

"We'll see you at the ceremony," Holly told him.

Sawyer quickly stepped out of the conference room before she could enter. The last thing he wanted was for his mom to catch a glimpse of the crime scene photos. Evangeline halted midstride and cocked her head to the side.

"Well, it looks like someone celebrated hard last night," she said with a sly grin.

"Not really," Sawyer replied. The night started as a celebration but became something more somber once Charlie arrived. He still hadn't unpacked everything he'd learned the previous evening and had no plans to delve into it right then.

His mother hooked her arm through Sawyer's as they exited the squad room. "You can't fool me, dear. You always get a dull look in your eyes the morning after you have too much to drink."

"I'm not disputing that part."

"Oh? What happened?"

"I can't delve into it right now." He needed his head to be in the right space to find justice for Barbara, Jessica, and Amy.

"Well, I'm here whenever you're ready to talk."

"And I appreciate it."

His father waited for them upstairs and greeted Sawyer with a robust hug. When he stepped back, the smile slid off his face. "Celebrate too hard last night?"

Rather than tiptoe through the same minefield, he smiled and said, "Something like that." Before they could ask, he told them Royce had gotten called out to a scene early this morning and hadn't returned.

Evangeline shuddered. "So much violence in the world. I worry about you boys."

"Just don't plan a celebration dinner, and they should be fine," his father said.

Evangeline rolled her eyes. "Save the dad jokes for someone who appreciates them." Then she whirled around and strode into the media room where the pinning would take place.

"I thought it was hilarious, Dad."

His father laughed heartily. "It'll be our secret."

The ceremony was brief and followed by a photo opportunity with Sawyer, his family, and the chief. His parents exchanged a few words with Mendoza but didn't linger since they knew Sawyer had his hands full with his new unit and their first investigation.

He saw Felix loitering around the back of the room and suspected he wanted a word. "I'll be down in just a minute," he told Holly and Topher. "I need to have a conversation with Felix."

He broke off from them and headed toward his friend, who met him in the middle. Sawyer just hoped like hell neither Charlie's nor Wheeler's names came up during their conversation. Felix extended his hand, and Sawyer accepted.

"Congratulations on the promotion," Felix said. "I think you handled yourself brilliantly at the press conference yesterday. I see big potential for your future."

Sawyer narrowed his eyes. Had Charlie called Felix? "I have all the excitement I can manage right now."

Felix laughed. "I hear you. Listen, I just want you to know the *Sinister in Savannah* podcast team will send any leads we uncover."

"I know you will, and I appreciate it. I'm a little overwhelmed by the amount of information I need to process. What's your experience been like working with the families?"

"They've been extremely open and helpful," Felix replied. "They just want what any family would in their situation."

"I want justice for them too." Sawyer didn't press for more information because he didn't want Felix's opinions to influence the lens through which he viewed the case. "What about cooperation from the original detective?"

Felix pursed his lips and furrowed his brow. "Nonexistent," he finally said after a pause.

"Burke declined to speak to you at all?"

"Emphatically. I'd probably have more success communicating with Donovan through a séance."

Again, Sawyer didn't probe deeper because his experience with Burke might not be the same. Most cops didn't trust reporters and viewed them as the enemy. Sawyer planned to appeal to Burke with professional courtesy and see how far it got him. "I hope I have better luck."

"I hope you do too."

The two men chatted about mundane things before Sawyer excused himself to return to his team. Neither man brought up Charlie or the Chatham County Sheriff's Department. Nothing about Felix's demeanor screamed that he was on the verge of revealing another salacious scoop about Wheeler, but then again, Felix was a cool customer who kept his stories close to the vest until it was time to divulge them. And Royce had been right. Felix would take the identity of his sources to the grave with him.

Shortly after he returned to his office, a delivery man stopped in with a bakery box for him. Sawyer smiled when he saw the logo and knew who the sender was. He carried the box to his office and opened the lid. Yep. Cupcakes from his best friend.

Sawyer fished out his phone and tapped out a quick text to Kelsey. *Thank you for the cupcakes. You know these are my kryptonite, right?*

He wasn't sure the new mama on maternity leave would get his message right away, but the three dots appeared on his screen immediately.

Yay! They made it. Congratulations on your promotion! I'm so proud of you. Before Sawyer could respond, another message appeared. *Do you think I'll be congratulating you on something else soon? I figured Saturday night was "the night." What happened?*

Kelsey was the only person he'd told about his discovery. *We got called out to a double homicide in the middle of our romantic dinner.*

Her reply came quickly and made him laugh. *Proposal watch is worse than waiting for April the giraffe to give birth.*

Right? Sawyer shot back.

Whatever the reason for his delay, it has nothing to do with his feelings for you. Please tell me you know that, Kelsey wrote.

I do. Sawyer didn't doubt Royce's love and devotion for a second, and he didn't mind waiting. What bothered him was the internal battle Royce might be waging over when and how to propose or *if* he even should.

Kelsey sent a picture of baby Ella sleeping in her bassinette. The little angel had a head full of dark hair and the sweetest rosy cheeks he'd ever seen. Sawyer was surprised she still had any left after he tried to kiss them off her face when they'd last visited. Sawyer could almost smell her sweet baby-powder scent through the phone, and a pang of longing gripped his core.

Cheeks! he wrote. *Kiss her for me!*

Will do!

Sawyer continued to smile at Ella's sweet picture for a few moments before setting his phone down and rolling up his sleeves. Sawyer dialed the phone numbers he'd found in the file for Wayne Burke. A few detectives had investigated the Magnolia Murders in their free time over the years, and one of them had attached updated contact information for the retired detective. Did that mean he had been helpful at one time? Sawyer tried him at home and on his cellphone, but he didn't reach Burke. He left messages in both places, hoping he came across as eager and not pushy, then dove headfirst back into the investigation.

The team closely inspected each photo, noting significant details as they went. Sawyer laid his notebook down once they completed the task and stretched to work the kinks out of his stiff muscles. His neck and shoulders were taut, but it was expected with such a big responsibility weighing on his conscience. Sawyer's decision to drink too much hadn't helped. He heard and felt an audible pop when he leaned his head to the right, but it relieved the tension and sent a shot of endorphins through his body.

"Let's start with the similarities," Sawyer said. "The killer used the same knife, or at least the same type, in each of the three slayings. All three women were killed the night of their celebration ball after winning the crown, though the venues differed each time. There are no signs of a struggle, so it appears they trusted the assailant right up until the end. Our killer scattered magnolia blossoms all around the bodies and used the victims' blood to write 'whore' on their foreheads. The department had kept that detail out of the press, so it came as a huge shock when I saw it yesterday."

"Yeah, me too," Holly said somberly.

"It's a disgusting thing to say to a woman of any age, but these ladies were so young," Topher said. "The label seems especially harsh. We're dealing with a real sick fucker here."

Sawyer nodded. "One who killed sporadically and stopped suddenly in 2000. Why?"

"I've researched the history of the Magnolia Queen Pageant and think I know the answer," Holly said. "Up until 2001, the pageant committee required the contestants to sign a purity vow."

Topher screwed up his face. "Gross. And how did they verify it? Why had these three ladies been labeled as whores? And why had they advanced so far in the pageant if they had questionable reputations?"

"My research didn't reveal if the contestants were subjected to a physical examination during the competition process," Holly replied. Sawyer shuddered at the thought. "But I agree they would've been vetted stringently earlier on. Probably in the preliminary rounds. There are hundreds of girls vying for limited spots on the stage. Much has been written about the pageant over the years, and the purity vow became a hot-button issue. The committees in charge haven't exactly been transparent about the vetting process and always referred reporters to their official rules. Those simply claim the women are required to sign a purity vow. It sounds like the committee took their word for it."

"I have a source I can tap regarding the inner workings of the pageant and committee," Sawyer told them. "My mother won the crown in 1976, then went on to become Miss Georgia and finished second in the Miss America Pageant."

Holly cocked her head to the side. "Really? I knew she had a phenomenal modeling career, but pageants seem so tame for someone as feisty as Evangeline."

Topher snorted. "My sisters used to compete in pageants. The rivalry is fierce, and there's no room for timidity."

"Yeah, I can see that," Holly said. "Tame probably wasn't the right word. Archaic, maybe?"

"Absolutely," Sawyer said, "especially considering the contestants were still making purity pacts at the dawn of the twenty-first century." He shook his head. "There's no way my mother would've submitted to an examination to ensure she was still a virgin before competing, so the vow had to be nothing more than a token gesture for people hung up on antiquated ideas." He studied the photos of Barbara Jean, Jessica Lynn, and Amy Lou. "Someone decided these ladies weren't pure, but who?"

"And how?" Holly asked.

"I think if we can figure out the how, we might figure out who," Sawyer said. "Let's talk about the differences in the crime scenes."

"You already mentioned the different venues," Holly said. "They also didn't die at the same location within the venue. Barbara Jean was stabbed while lounging in the bathtub in her suite at the Marshall House, Jessica Lynn was found murdered in the room designated for hair and makeup at the Kehoe House, and Amy Lou was killed on the grounds of the Olde Harbour Inn. Amy could've run into her assailant, but the other two were sought out."

"The assailant seems to have gotten angrier with each kill," Topher said. "Barbara was stabbed once in the heart, Jessica was stabbed three times in the chest, and Amy was stabbed ten times. And as Holly stated, the killer posed a great risk of getting caught with Amy. Were they angrier and bolder?"

"And why stop so suddenly?" Holly asked. "I hate to say it, but we have to consider the killer might be dead."

"Or they were no longer involved in the pageant after 2000," Sawyer suggested. "That's a potential lead right there. Let's make a list of people who fit that category."

Holly sighed. "It will be a long list. After Amy's death, the pageant board made some sweeping changes that angered the longtime contributors."

"Such as?" Sawyer asked.

"They modernized the pageant, which meant they did away with the purity vow and changed the venue. The board stopped bouncing from one historic site to the other and started hosting the event at the convention center. As you can imagine, those moves went over like a lead balloon with the traditionalists, and they cut ties with the board and the pageant. They even lost a lot of sponsors because of the changes to the venue and the rules."

"We'll have to look closely at those people," Sawyer said. "It's too much of a coincidence that the murders stopped after 2000. Let's find the common denominators between the three cases. We'll start with people connected to the pageant."

They each picked a case. Sawyer read off the names in Barbara's records while Holly and Topher checked to see if they appeared in the other victims' documents. The trio worked companionably for a few hours before a knock on the doorframe interrupted them. Sawyer looked up and found Royce standing there with a few bags of food.

"Anyone ready for lunch?" he asked.

Sawyer noticed the carryout bags were from Bytes and Brew. "Chicken salad croissant?"

"Yes, but I picked a variety of others since I wasn't sure what everyone wanted," Royce said.

Topher tilted his head and sniffed the air. "Do I smell pastrami on rye?"

Royce laughed. "Yep." He handed two bags to Topher, who made a beeline for the main squad room.

"Wait for me," Holly called as she followed.

"Time to refuel," Royce said.

They went into Sawyer's office and shut the door. Royce laid the boxed lunches on the desk before dropping into the visitor's chair.

"I think we should try our dinner at Giancarlo's tonight," Royce said when they'd mowed halfway through their food. "I bet we could get a reservation for a Tuesday evening. We could pick up where we left off."

Sawyer's pulse accelerated with anticipation and excitement until he remembered Royce had prior commitments. "Tuxedo fitting," he said.

"Shit! That's tonight? Okay, we'll have to revive the magic another night."

"Or we could recreate our favorite pasta dishes at home after your fitting. I don't need expensive restaurants, linen tablecloths, or wine. I just want you."

Royce's eyes darkened, and he ignored his sandwich to kiss Sawyer's mouth. "But you already have me."

"And you're all the magic I need."

Chapter
EIGHT

ROYCE SAT IN HIS CAR AND TRIED A FEW OF SAWYER'S MEDITATION breathing exercises, hoping it would help him transition from a detective investigating a double murder-suicide to his brother's best man. After a couple of rounds of inhales, holds, and exhales, Royce couldn't deny his chest felt lighter. If only he could find a technique to erase the early morning crime scene images from his mind.

An abrupt knock on his passenger side window yanked him from the first peace he'd found since his short lunch break with Sawyer. Maybe if he ignored the intruder, they'd go away. Royce kept his eyes closed and pictured the sincerity and adoration he'd seen in Sawyer's eyes.

You're all the magic I need.

Sawyer had a valid point. Royce had been biding his time, looking for the perfect moment to pop the question. What if the perfect moment had passed them by? Or worse, what if it never came at all? Royce wondered what plans the slain parents had put off, not thinking their son would shoot them while they ate breakfast before taking his own life.

The knock on the window came again, even more persistent than the first.

"You'll get out of that vehicle, or I'll drag you out," Jace yelled through the glass.

Royce chuckled and hit the toggle to roll it down. "Freaking groomzilla. What's your problem now? This tailor isn't good enough for you?"

Jace snorted and rolled his eyes. Then he reached inside the open window, unlocked the passenger door, and let himself in. "I was worried about you," he said once he was sitting in the passenger seat. As if Royce didn't recognize the scowl or deep vee carved into Jace's forehead.

"Me? Why? I didn't bail on you." Royce gestured to the clock on the dashboard. "Hell, I'm fifteen minutes early. I was just catching my breath and trying to get myself in a healthier headspace."

Jace's gray eyes darkened, and his scowl became more pronounced. "You caught that awful murder this morning, didn't you?"

"Yeah." Royce pushed the air from his lungs in a long exhale, then scrubbed both hands over his face. "Fuck, I'm so tired." He didn't just mean from interrupted sleep either. The undercurrent of violence and fury permeating the air around them seemed to expand each day, pushing out the glimmers of light and goodness. It's no wonder cops burned out. If he didn't have Sawyer and Bones to go home to each night...Royce shuddered to think where he'd be.

Jace placed his hand on Royce's shoulder and squeezed. "I'm sorry. I saw awful things in Afghanistan and Iraq, and it fucked me up. I don't want that for you. So keep practicing meditation if it helps get you through these awful investigations."

"Or I walk away from the department and get a job working for Sal."

Jace chuckled. "I know the hardware store is your favorite place to shop, but you were born to be a cop. Walking away isn't the answer. Finding healthier ways to cope is."

Royce thought about the Explorer gig Mendoza had sprung on him. Was working with teens the break he needed for his sanity? Royce was pretty sure any parent would argue heavily against his logic, but they didn't spend their workdays solving gruesome crimes. Royce was starting to see the potential in the program rather than viewing it as punishment.

"I think maybe Mendoza was right," Royce said.

"Damn right he is. Dru told me how you stepped in to help Jason out yesterday."

Royce's heart sank. He was glad Jason had told his mother about the incident but devastated Dru had reached out to Jace instead of him. His expression must've given him away because his older brother playfully chucked him on the chin.

"Quit pouting, asshat. Dru loves you. She just doesn't know how to take back the stupid things she's said to you."

Royce huffed out a short breath. "And she's living under Dad's roof."

"And his thumb," Jace added. "She's trapped. I'm not making excuses for what she said. I'm just trying to explain why she's hesitant to respond to your message."

"She told you I called her?"

Jace nodded. "I heard the longing in her voice. Give her time."

"I'm trying. I wish I could find a way to get Dru and the boys away from Eddie and Benton. Did you know Jared is bisexual? Jason said he's come out to his mom."

"No, I didn't," Jace replied. "That's a brave kid right there. I'm proud of him."

"I am too. I'm just really worried for Jared."

Jace's lips curved into a wry smile. "You know, there's a straightforward solution."

"I'm not kicking you and Holly out of Aunt Tipsy's house."

Jace rolled his eyes. "It's *your* house. We just rent it from you."

He'd tried to give the property to them, but Jace had refused. Royce then offered to sell it to them for what Aunt Tipsy had paid for it, but Jace shot him down. They'd insisted on renting it at market value—a fact that still grated on Royce's nerves.

He narrowed his eyes suspiciously. "Is this why you refused my generous offers?"

"Yeah. I thought there was a good possibility Dru would come around and need someplace to stay. Why else would I have refused?"

"Because you didn't think my relationship with Sawyer would work out and suspected I'd need a place to live when he got sick of me."

Jace just blinked for a few seconds before slowly shaking his head. "The thought never occurred to me. I knew Sawyer was your future the first time I saw the two of you together." Jace tilted his head, and his eyes briefly took on a faraway look until he straightened his head and met Royce's gaze once more. "I take that back."

"No takebacks. Sawyer is the one for me."

"Duh," Jace said with an exaggerated eye roll. "I knew he was the one for you when I saw him in the emergency room after you got shot. All the reasons you hadn't settled down yet had become crystal clear. I'd chalked up your bachelorhood to the Locke genes until then, but you're Mom's son. Domesticity looks damn good on you, brother."

Royce grimaced. "I'm not sure if a thank-you or a fuck-you is in order."

Jace threw his head back and laughed. "I probably deserve both."

Feeling much lighter than when he'd arrived, Royce rolled up Jace's window and turned off the engine. "Time to get fitted for your wedding tux, groomzilla."

Jace flipped him off and shoved open the passenger door. "You're the least supportive best man on the planet."

Royce stepped out of the SUV and shut the door behind him. He stepped onto the sidewalk and hit the button on his fob to lock the door. "You'll thank me for it when you stop nitpicking and enjoy your wedding day."

"I don't nitpick." Yet Jace's reserved attitude shrank with each step they took toward the tuxedo shop. His expression and body language grew tense, and new energy crackled in the air around him. "There are only eight weeks until the wedding. I read most tailors need—"

"Shut up," Royce growled. "Did you tell the shop when you're getting married?"

"Yes."

"Did they tell you they'd be able to accommodate your needs?" Royce pressed.

"Yes."

Royce reached for the door to the shop but paused before opening it. "Then calm the fuck down."

Jace puffed out a short breath and nodded.

Bells jingled overhead when Royce pushed the door open. He gestured for the groom to go first and smirked when Jace's mixed bag of emotions settled on awe once he stepped inside.

"Be right there," a man called out from the rear of the store.

Jace slowly spun around in a circle as he took everything in. There were racks and displays of everything a groom could need neatly arranged by style and color. Mannequins decked out in full wedding attire were strategically placed throughout the space, showcasing the shop's different wedding fashion styles.

"I'm kind of partial to the one with the tails, vest, and top hat," Royce teased.

That seemed to snap Jace out of his stupor. He turned and looked at Royce with a horrified expression on his face. "You can't be serious?"

"No?" Royce asked. "What are you thinking? The modern look?" He glanced over at the mannequin wearing a slim-fitting, sleek tuxedo. Sawyer would look damn fine in the style.

"I'm not sure," Jace admitted. "I'm a little overwhelmed."

"That's where I come in."

Royce and Jace jolted and spun around to find a slender, brunet man smiling at them. His green eyes were a few shades lighter than the emerald vest he wore over a crisp white shirt. Was vest even the proper term? The velvety fabric had gold embroidery woven throughout and looked more structured than a typical vest. It was very tight, molding to the man's lean torso. Was that the reason for his impeccable posture? And all those tiny green velvet buttons lined up in a meticulous row. Damn, there had to be at least two dozen of the pearl-sized things.

"Sorry," the man said. "I didn't mean to startle you. My name is Julian, and I'm excited to help you pick out the perfect tuxedos for your wedding. Which one of you is Jace?"

"I am," Jace said. "And this is my brother, Royce."

Julian shook their hands. "It's nice to meet you both. I know this place feels a little overwhelming, but I promise you're in excellent hands."

Jace exhaled and nodded. "Yeah. I definitely need to calm the hell down."

"The best place to start is with color," Julian said, holding up his hand like a game show host and doing a half turn to encompass the right side of the room. "Over here, we have the traditional blacks and grays. As you can see, there is no such thing as one shade of black or gray." Julian continued his pivot and gestured to the left side of the room. "And here, we have the lighter color tuxedos and even some bolder hues which tend to be more popular with prom attendees."

Royce's gaze snagged on the back of Julian's emerald vest and didn't budge. There was a one-inch gap in the fabric with golden laces pulling the two pieces of velvet together. The vest was both formal wear and lingerie for men. Royce had never seen anything like it.

Julian pivoted once more and caught Royce staring at him. "It's a corset vest."

Royce snapped his fingers. "Corset. That's the word I was searching for."

He looked over at the display of vests on the far side of the room. He saw a variety of textures in every shade and color, but none looked like the one Julian wore. Jace nudged him with his elbow, so Royce refocused his attention on his brother and the tailor.

"Let's talk style," Julian said. "Are you thinking tuxedo or suit?"

"I don't want anything fussy or with tails."

Julian walked over to a mannequin dressed in a black suit, crisp white shirt, and a gray and pink striped tie with a matching pocket square.

"I do like the way that looks," Jace said.

"Keep in mind there are hundreds of combinations to choose from when it comes to the tie and pocket square. You can mix and match patterns and solids."

Jace puffed out his cheeks and released a slow breath.

Julian chuckled and patted him on the shoulder. "No stressing. We've got this."

Jace still looked thunderstruck but nodded.

"About the color," Julian said. "Do you want to do classic black, or are you thinking navy blue or gray?"

Jace turned helpless eyes on Royce, who held up his hands. "I'm not the person you should ask. My idea of fashion is sweats and a T-shirt."

Julian swept an appraising gaze over Royce's black button-up shirt, dark jeans, and black motorcycle boots. "You do okay."

Jace snorted. "His boyfriend picks out his outfits."

Julian's mouth twitched on one side. "Is that so?"

"Does not," Royce retorted.

Jace dismissed him with an annoying wave, pulling the tailor's attention back to groomzilla. "I haven't seen my wife's dress, but I've heard her say it's ivory."

"And it has a lot of lace," Royce added.

Jace aimed a dark scowl his way. "You've seen Holly's dress?"

Royce smiled smugly. "She showed me a picture. You're going to bawl your eyes out when you see her. I can't wait."

"You're such a dick."

Shrugging, Royce said, "Sawyer doesn't call me dickhead for nothing."

"What about her attendants? Do you know what colors they're wearing?" Julian asked.

Jace grimaced. "Um, pink. The exact color has fled my mind, even though our wedding planners managed to work it in a dozen times during every conversation."

Julian smiled patiently and said, "There are a billion shades of pink. Let's start with light or dark?"

"*Blush* pink," Royce said, managing to sound bored and smug at the same time. He turned to his brother and threw up his hands. "What kind of groomzilla are you?"

Jace laughed and playfully punched his arm. "I think my brain blocked the word to preserve my sanity."

Julian removed a book of fabric samples and opened it to reveal a hundred different shades of pink. "Which one is closest?" Royce and Jace both pointed to the same square, making Julian laugh. "You can't go wrong with black, gray, or navy blue."

"Not blue," Jace said, walking along the black and gray suits. "I'm thinking more classic, but I'm not sure I like the starkness of black against the softness of the pink." He stopped and trailed his finger over the sleeve of a dove gray tuxedo. "Too light? Too soft?"

Julian stepped over with his fabrics book and laid the sleeve next to the blush pink swatch. "I think they complement each other beautifully." Julian assessed Jace's face and nodded. "And with your complexion and coloring too."

"Well, that was fast."

Julian laughed and snapped the book shut. "We've only just begun."

Royce and Jace tried on several different styles until they found the one they liked, which Julian called a hybrid of modern and traditional.

"Are we ready to say yes to the tux?" Julian asked.

Royce and Jace looked at one another, then nodded.

The tailor stepped back and eyed them critically. "A few adjustments here and there, and they'll be perfect." He reached into his pocket and pulled out a measuring tape before dropping to one knee in front of Jace. Julian placed the edge of the tape up by his crotch and unrolled down the length of his leg.

Jace jolted and said, "Whoa there."

Royce covered his mouth but couldn't stifle the snicker.

Jace turned an incredulous expression on him. "Grow up. I've never been fitted for a tuxedo, and the only dudes who've gotten this close to the goods were doctors who checked me for hernias to clear me for sports or military service." He looked back down at Julian. "Sorry if I came off like a homophobic asshole."

Julian laughed. "Not at all. I should've given you a warning."

"Or bought him dinner first," Royce added.

"If it makes you feel any better," Julian said, "you're not my type." Then he pointed to Royce and said, "He is, though."

Jace crossed his arms over his chest. "We're nearly identical."

"It's not the looks," Julian replied. "It's his aura."

"His aura is taken," Jace reminded the tailor.

Julian grinned. "I don't see a ring." He held up the measuring tape for Jace to see. "Coming in hot. I still need to measure the other leg."

Jace chuckled. "Go for it." Once Julian resumed his measurements, Jace turned a curious look Royce's way. "What happened to your plans to pop the question this weekend, a full three weeks before Valentine's Day, so no one could accuse you of proposing on a cheesy greeting card holiday? Why aren't you engaged, Ro? And do not try to feed me a bull-shit story that Sawyer turned you down."

Royce blew out a frustrated breath, earning a curious glance from Julian. "I'd planned to ask Sawyer this weekend," he admitted. "I made reservations at his favorite restaurant. There was candlelight and wine and a stellar breadbasket. It was perfect."

Jace laughed. "And?"

Julian rose to his feet and instructed Jace to hold his arms out like a scarecrow. He looked over at Royce and said, "Go ahead. We want to hear the rest."

"There's not much to tell," Royce replied. "Dispatch called, and we had to leave our dinner to head to a double homicide."

"That was four days ago," Jace pointed out.

"And we spent all of Sunday and into the early morning hours of Monday investigating the crime. Sawyer deserves better than some random proposal over a quick bowl of ramen noodles at three in the morning. Then there were sweeping changes at work yesterday and another grisly crime scene for me to investigate this morning."

Jace scowled. "I can't believe Sawyer eats ramen."

Royce laughed because everyone knew his guy was a food snob. "We were desperate."

Julian circled his finger in the air for Jace to turn around, and his brother complied. "If you wait for the perfect time, you'll be waiting forever."

"He's right, Ro," Jace said softly. "Look how many years I wasted without Holly before I found the courage to pull my head out of my ass."

Royce stiffened. "I'm not afraid."

"Bullshit," Jace replied. "Maybe you're not admitting it to yourself right now, but you're finding any reason not to go after your heart's one true desire because a part of you doesn't think you deserve him."

Royce groaned and scrubbed his face. "You sound like a Hallmark movie."

Jace ignored his barb and kept talking over him. "And I know exactly how that feels. I kept my distance from Holly, thinking the perfect man for her would come along someday. The jackass never showed up, and it took me years to realize *I* was the jackass."

"I've been calling you that since we were kids," Royce protested.

Julian laughed and said, "This is the most fun I've had in ages." He dismissed Jace, who, instead of changing back into his clothes, continued to stand there haranguing Royce while the tailor measured him for alterations.

"I realized one day that no one would ever love her the way I did," Jace added. "Instead of allowing someone else to steal my girl, I became the man she deserved."

"Sawyer and I have built an incredible life together," Royce said. "I make sure he knows he's the love of my life."

Julian sighed. "I'm getting misty."

"Your sweaty balls are making his eyes water," Jace said, lightening the mood. "So maybe take a shower before asking Sawyer to marry you."

Julian popped up in front of Royce. "He's right, you know."

"My balls do not stink," Royce grumbled as Jace howled with laughter.

Julian's face turned pink. "Not that part. I'm sure they're fine. I agree that waiting for the right time is an exercise in futility. Take something imperfect and make it perfect." He gestured to his torso. "I found this vest at a secondhand shop. Someone had gotten rid of it because it no longer fit or wasn't in style. It was a few sizes too large for me, but I saw the potential and turned it into a corset."

"You made the vest?" Royce asked. "I'm impressed."

"Side hustle. Don't tell," Julian whispered. "Okay, scarecrow arms."

Royce did as instructed, then turned so Julian could complete his task. He thought back to what Sawyer had said to him. Royce was all the magic Sawyer needed, so why did his knees quake at the thought of retrieving the ring box as soon as he got home?

Because Jace had been right about that too. Maybe Royce had inherited more of his mother's goodness, but the Locke genes were strong. No one could self-destruct like them, and innocent people always got caught up in the explosions. The morose thought put a damper on Royce's mood for the rest of the appointment, and though he smiled and joined in the conversation, Jace aimed worried glances at him every few minutes.

Once they left the shop, Jace threw his arm around Royce's shoulders.

"I'm sorry I overstepped and ruined the night. Blame it on big brother birthright."

Royce slung an arm around Jace's waist. "You didn't ruin anything. My day went sideways before the sun even came up. You're just looking out for me, and I appreciate it."

Jace released his shoulder, got Royce in a headlock, and furiously rubbed his knuckles over his head.

"No noogies! You'll mess up my hair!" Royce yelled as he managed to spring free and juke to the right when Jace reached for him again.

They continued the brotherly games to Royce's SUV. Once there, Jace pulled Royce into a tight hug.

"Just ask him already."

A horn sounded, pulling the brothers apart.

"Look at the queers," a familiar voice called out.

"Get a room," said another.

Royce looked at the rusted Oldsmobile that had stopped beside his SUV. Eddie was behind the steering wheel, and Benton leered at them from the passenger seat. Jace started for the street, but Royce put his arm out to stop him.

Benton mimed jacking off before Eddie sped off.

"They're not worth it," Royce said.

Marrying Sawyer would subject him to their brand of abuse for the rest of his life. How long before Sawyer thought Royce wasn't worth it either?

Chapter
NINE

SAWYER'S HEART WAS IN HIS THROAT AS HE JOGGED UP THE PORCH steps of the lovely Victorian manor belonging to Jennifer Wright-Stevens, Barbara Jean's oldest sister. The property was nestled among a row of similarly constructed homes with matching live oaks and magnolia trees. The houses were all gorgeous and worth a small fortune.

Sawyer had discovered Lizette, Barbara's mother, had moved in with Jennifer's family after her husband died. And since Lizette was in her eighties, he felt it was appropriate to schedule their interview through Jennifer, who'd been gracious and inviting since their first phone conversation. Then why the hell was he so nervous? Simple. After a week of reviewing documents, making lists, and triple-checking them, Sawyer was no closer to solving the case than he'd been on day one.

It wasn't like he'd expected the team to unearth the smoking gun, or the bloody knife in this case, just by scouring photos and case documents and listening to the interviews. They weren't the first team to take a crack at it; they were just the latest. But they were the first group of detectives who could devote their entire energy to the investigation. Not even the original detectives, Burke and Donovan, had had that luxury when the crimes first occurred. Still, they had worked the homicide investigations mercilessly and had the documentation to prove it.

Christ. Sawyer, Topher, and Holly had spent Thursday, Friday, and Saturday listening to recordings of the interviews. On Sunday, they'd cross-referenced the tapes to the written accounts and witness lists, thinking they'd find a discrepancy pointing to why such a thoroughly investigated case remained unsolved. Sawyer refused to believe the killer had committed three perfect crimes, which had allowed them to go undetected for nearly thirty-eight years. It was either extraordinary luck or they'd had help. But from whom? If the murders were poorly examined, he could at least say police ineptitude was the killer's accomplice, but that wasn't the case here.

So why was Wayne Burke avoiding Sawyer? He'd tried to reach him twice more but had had to leave messages. He'd hoped appealing to his professional courtesy and praising the man's work would grease the wheel, but Sawyer had come up empty all three times. He asked Topher to take a swing at him since he had a personal connection to Burke. The retired detective had been kind enough to return Toph's call but had firmly declined to get sucked back into the cases that had consumed him during his time in the SPD. Topher had pressed for more, but Burke had quickly disconnected the call.

Sawyer tried to remain objective but failed to understand why Burke didn't want to do everything in his power to solve cases he'd been obsessed with. It flew in the face of logic. Did Burke expect Sawyer to believe his subconscious also retired when the man had left the department? Sawyer had read the man's words and could almost place himself in Burke's shoes. No fucking way would his psyche let him sleep at night, knowing these women never found justice. Unless Burke had a more sinister reason for his silence. Sawyer couldn't ignore the possibility.

The dark red door on the pale blue Victorian swung open before Sawyer had a chance to knock. A petite woman with a mop of riotous salt-and-pepper curls greeted him with a smile. Sawyer noted the expression in her brown eyes was equally as warm.

"Sergeant Key," she said, extending her hand to Sawyer.

His big paw dwarfed her dainty hand, but her grip was firm and assertive. He got the unspoken message loud and clear. Though she may be petite and friendly, this woman was a force of nature. "Yes. Mrs. Stevens, I presume?"

She sighed and shook her head. "Oh, yes. Please forgive my poor manners. I have the advantage of recognizing you from the interview last week." She stepped aside and waved him in. "Please come in. My sister and mother are waiting for us in the dining room. Can I get you a cup of coffee?"

He'd already consumed two cups before leaving the house. More caffeine was the last thing his nerves needed, but he was expected to accept his host's offer. Besides, she'd just ask at least two more times, so it was easier and more efficient to say yes and sip the brew.

"I'd love a cup," Sawyer said, then followed her down a long hallway of family photos with beautifully adorned rooms opening to the left and right.

Jennifer stopped at the second to last room and gestured for him to enter a formal dining room decked out with priceless antiques. It felt like he'd stepped back in time when he crossed the threshold.

Lizette sat at a long, polished table that gleamed beneath a chandelier. She wore a pale lavender cardigan over an ivory blouse buttoned primly to the top. The long strand of pearls at her neck matched the earrings in her lobes. Her makeup was artfully applied with a light hand to accentuate her natural beauty. Lizette's snowy white hair was pulled back from her face and secured in a bun. A few wispy curls had managed to escape and framed her pretty face, and she looked at least twenty years younger than her actual age. Time and genetics had been very kind to Lizette, even if life had treated her cruelly.

A nearly identical version of Jennifer, whom he presumed to be Sara Beth, the youngest sister, rose to her feet and extended her hand when Barbara made introductions. Like her sister, Sara Beth came across as a petite powerhouse, and he found himself liking them, even though he needed to maintain neutrality.

Lizette remained seated and assessed Sawyer coolly. He saw no censure or anger in her sharp gaze, just curiosity. Sawyer held her regard until she gave him a subtle nod, and he pulled back the dining chair across from her and sat down. Sara Beth reclaimed her seat, and Jennifer excused herself before walking to the buffet and pouring Sawyer a cup of coffee from a silver pot.

"Do you take cream in your coffee, Sergeant Key?" she asked.

"Yes, ma'am."

Jennifer set the cup of coffee on a silver tray, then added a spoon and a silver caddy containing several types of creamer and sweetener. She placed the tray in front of him and sat on the other side of her mother.

He felt their eyes on him as he swiftly and neatly doctored his coffee. Though he'd initially accepted the offer out of politeness, the scent stirred his taste buds, and he took a quick sip to steady his nerves. The java was strong with a hint of something extra he didn't expect to find in Savannah.

"Chicory?" he asked.

Lizette's eyes brightened, and she smiled, revealing teeth as pearly white as her jewelry. "It reminds me of my Owen. You can take the man out of New Orleans, but you can't take the chicory from his coffee."

Jennifer and Sara Beth simultaneously reached over and covered their mother's hands. The gesture might've appeared staged to some, but Sawyer thought it was a subconscious act rather than a director's cue.

"It's a daily thing we do to keep Daddy's memory alive," Sara Beth said.

Jennifer sighed. "I miss the smell of his pipe tobacco."

Lizette released the tiniest sniffle, but it was enough to pull her daughters from their musings. They both gave her a gentle pat before retracting their hands. Sawyer observed it all while taking another sip of coffee.

Barbara Jean's mother squared her shoulders and managed to look taller. "How can we help you solve my daughter's murder, Sergeant Key?"

"Tell me about Barbara Jean." He'd spent a week combing over every detail about her death and the journey two men had taken to find justice. He knew nothing of how she lived, and therein lay the key to solving his case.

Sawyer forgot all about his nerves as he listened to the women talk, first freely about their beloved daughter and sister, and then later when he walked them through a series of questions about what had been happening in her life at the time of her murder. He laughed along with them when the women recalled Barbara Jean's antics growing up. It turned out she was a tomboy right up until she turned thirteen.

"One day she was climbing trees with the boys, and the next, she was wearing makeup and ribbons in her hair that perfectly complemented her outfits," Lizette said.

"If someone predicted Babs would enter a beauty pageant someday, I would've laughed in their face," Jennifer said.

Sara Beth nodded. "Such a tomboy."

"My wild child," Lizette said in a watery voice.

"Was there a particular boy or group of boys Barbara Jean still hung out with?" Sawyer asked. "The original detectives mostly interviewed female friends from school or the pageant."

Jennifer's gaze sharpened, but Lizette stared off into space, seeming lost in the memories only she could see or hear.

"Why do you ask?" Sara Beth inquired.

"If I'm to solve this case, I need to find the one person who knows or saw something," Sawyer replied.

Jennifer and Sara Beth exchanged a glance before meeting Sawyer's gaze. "Tommy Hasselback," they said at once.

Sawyer asked for the spelling of Tommy's last name, and after a quick debate about one *s* or two, the girls agreed on the latter. He wrote the name down in his portfolio, then dug deeper into their relationship.

"Tommy was the boy next door and Barbara Jean's best friend," Lizette said softly. "They were inseparable."

"Our parents were dear friends for decades," Jennifer added.

"We didn't have a single celebration growing up that didn't include the Hasselbacks," Sara Beth said. "Which is why it's so silly I couldn't spell their name right."

Jennifer smiled at her younger sister. "Gene and Clarice have been gone for ten years or longer, and Tommy hasn't been back to Savannah since he sold their place." She turned her attention back to Sawyer. "I don't want to be rude, but can I ask a blunt question?"

"Of course."

"Why are you asking about Barbara Jean's friends? I mean, I'd understand if it were just her death you're solving, but my sister's killer went on to butcher two more women. It surely has to be someone connected with that insidious pageant."

"Unless you think Jessica and Amy were victims of a copycat killer," Sara Beth said.

Christ, everyone was a damn expert now thanks to true-crime documentaries and podcasts.

"I cannot afford to rule anything out until I've followed every possible thread to the very end. Detectives Burke and Donovan turned over every stone in their investigation. I not only need to revisit those stones, but I need to find some new ones. I plan to kick up the dirt everywhere I can until I figure out who killed Barbara, Jessica, and Amy."

Lizette tilted her head. "I think you mean it."

"Yes, ma'am, I do. I won't make you any promises I can't keep, but I won't stop until I've exhausted all resources."

She closed her eyes, and a single tear trickled from the corner of her eye. She lifted a wrinkled hand and dabbed it away with a tissue before meeting his gaze. "I believe you."

Sawyer steered the conversation back to Tommy, gently probing to see if there'd ever been romantic feelings between them. "Even one-sided," he said.

"Babs had a crush on Tommy, but he viewed her as one of the guys," Sara Beth replied.

Sawyer made a note, then continued. "Do you think that's the reason for her abrupt change from tomboy to beauty queen at thirteen?"

Jennifer worried her bottom lip for a second. "I'm concerned you'll get the wrong impression and…"

"I'm not looking to railroad innocent people, Mrs. Stevens."

"Call me Jennifer, please."

"Okay," Sawyer said. "I simply want to get to the truth, which is someone effortlessly and without drawing any suspicion managed to kill three young ladies. It was someone they trusted up until the last moment."

The three women flinched, and he regretted his bluntness. "I apologize. I didn't come here to hurt you."

"No," Lizzette said, dabbing at her eyes. "You're right."

"And I guess it's possible one of Barbara's friends worked for the catering staff at all three venues, but it seems unlikely," Jennifer remarked.

"But unlikely doesn't mean impossible," Sara Beth added. "But all three of them? Why?"

"And that is the crux of the mystery," Sawyer said.

Their killer had marked these three ladies as whores. How had they decided? Why had their judgment resulted in deaths? Sawyer couldn't tell from the detectives' notes if the families were informed of the bloody word scrawled on their loved ones' foreheads. He was confident the medical examiner's office would've washed it off before turning their bodies over to the funeral directors. That left only the detectives or the persons who'd discovered the victims.

The woman who'd found Barbara Jean in the bathtub was Cicely Turner, her pageant coach. Sadly, the woman had passed away ten years later from cancer. If Cicely and the investigators hadn't mentioned the ugly epithet, Lizette, Jennifer, and Sara Beth probably didn't know. Sawyer might reach a point where he felt it necessary to tell them, but he wasn't there yet.

He cycled through several more questions as he finished his coffee. Barbara had offered to refill his cup, but he declined and wrapped up the interview.

"I appreciate your time," he told the three ladies as he rose to his feet. "Feel free to call me anytime if you think of something. No lead is too small."

Jennifer quickly stood up and clapped her hands. "I just thought of something that might come in handy. Will you excuse me a moment?"

"Of course."

She returned a few minutes later with a pink journal in her hands. Jennifer took a deep breath and extended it to Sawyer. "It's Barbara's journal. I've held on to it all these years, reading every word and looking for clues I somehow missed. She wrote about her feelings for Tommy and the petty fights she had with girls her age. The last entry was dated the night before her death."

Sawyer gently took it from her hands. "Thank you." He met Lizette's gaze once more. Tears streamed down her face, reminding him grief like hers had no expiration date. "I promise I'll take excellent care of this and return it to you as soon as possible."

She sniffled and nodded.

"I'll walk you out," Jennifer said. Once they reached the foyer, Jennifer placed her hand on his forearm to stop him. "My sister was naïve to the ways of the world. She wasn't a whore."

Sawyer's heart broke over the agony he saw in her eyes. "Of course not." He nodded his head toward the dining room. "Do they know too?"

"God no. That would've killed my parents. I could tell something was weighing heavily on Cicely's conscience and confronted her about it. She told me in strictest confidence, even though the detectives forbid her to speak about it."

"I hope she found peace after unburdening herself to you, though I hate that you've shouldered it alone for almost thirty-eight years."

"I have so many questions," she said sadly.

"And I hope I can answer them all someday." He held up the journal. "I'll get this back to you ASAP. Take care, Jennifer."

Sawyer hadn't expected to learn much, so coming away with a new name to track and Barbara's journal felt like a big victory. Sawyer had more than an hour to kill before meeting with Jessica Lynn's family, so he swung by the precinct to secure Barbara's journal in his desk. Holly and Topher were in the field reinterviewing the victims' friends, so Sawyer didn't loiter in the quiet squad room. If he sat down and looked through Barbara's journal, it was highly likely he'd lose track of time and be late to the Campbell's home. Instead, he updated the evidence log and locked the leather book in his desk.

Feeling jittery after too much coffee, Sawyer swung by Bytes and Brew to grab a turkey sausage breakfast sandwich. He looked for Levi like he always did, then recalled he and Diego were on their honeymoon in Hawaii.

"Would you like a salted caramel coffee?" Micah asked once Sawyer placed his order. He should be embarrassed they knew him so well.

"Not today, but thank you."

Sawyer stood off to the side and played around with his phone while waiting for his sandwich. He was halfway through a level of *Best Fiends* when an incoming message notification interrupted him. If it had been from anyone other than Royce, he would've dismissed it and kept playing.

"Here you go, Sawyer," Micah said.

Turning, he accepted the paper bag. "You're a lifesaver."

Afterward, he walked to his car so he could read Royce's message in private. It was likely to make him laugh, cuss, or spontaneously combust. Royce had still been on the fence about the Explorer program and had needed extra encouragement before leaving the house.

Sawyer swiped his thumb up and read Royce's message. *You were right.*

He could've toyed with Royce and reminded him he usually was or he could've played dumb and acted like he didn't know what his boyfriend was talking about. Before he could type a response, he saw the three bubbles pop up on his screen.

You're debating between a sincere and smartass reply, aren't you?

Sawyer laughed and typed, *Maybe.*

Ha! I knew it. I'll go with sexy. You were right that your lips around my cock would take the edge off and help me relax. Love you, asshole.

I live to be helpful. Love you too, dickhead.

Sawyer set his phone aside and carefully ate his sandwich to avoid getting anything on his shirt and tie since he was cutting it close and wouldn't have time to change. He wanted to make a good impression on the families. Once finished, Sawyer shoved the trash into the paper bag and checked his reflection in the visor mirror. He didn't see any grease smears on his face, so he folded the visor, checked his side mirror, then eased into traffic.

Bruce and Janet Campbell lived in a small trailer park outside the city limits. The homes were small but tidy. Some had flower beds or flower baskets hanging from the awnings, while others were free of decoration. An older man with a gray buzz cut and rigid posture answered his knock.

"Are you Key?" he asked in a surly voice.

Sawyer fought off the urge to salute. "Yes, sir. Are you Mr. Campbell?"

The man didn't suggest Sawyer call him by his first name; he just stared at him unblinkingly. "Who the hell else would answer my door?"

Mr. Campbell heaved a weighted sigh and stepped aside. "Might as well get this over with."

Sawyer paused before crossing the threshold. "Would another time work better?"

"For you to blow smoke up my ass and then do absolutely nothing to solve my daughter's case? I'd prefer to tell you to go fu—"

"Bruce!" a lady yelled over him. Seconds later, a tall woman with long wavy hair muscled the angry man out of the way and smiled worriedly at Sawyer. "I'm so sorry about my husband's attitude. Please come in."

"Ma'am, I'm Sergeant Key."

"Please call me Janet."

Sawyer agreed before turning to Mr. Campbell. "Sir, I understand how frustrated you are with—"

"How? Was your daughter killed by a madman who should've been caught before he could strike again?"

"Bruce," his wife hissed. "Stop it right now. This man isn't our enemy. He could be the last hope our Jessie has of getting justice. Stop being belligerent and help us."

The man peeled his eyes away from Sawyer to look at his wife. That's when Sawyer witnessed a slight softening in his dark eyes. Mr. Campbell looked at Sawyer once more and gave him a jerky nod.

Janet gestured to the small table tucked into the corner of their kitchen. Sawyer was beyond grateful she didn't offer him coffee because he'd had enough for two people.

When Sawyer asked the Campbells to tell him about Jessica Lynn, the husband and wife just stared at one another for several moments before returning their gaze to him. Mr. Campbell's brown eyes filled with tears.

"Call me Bruce," he said and proceeded to talk for two hours about his precious little girl. Sawyer learned that Jessica had been an accomplished equestrian. "I don't remember what horse movie she saw as a little girl, but she became obsessed with them. We obviously couldn't keep a horse here, so I took on extra jobs to board her mare and pay for lessons."

"Her name was Snow White," Janet whispered, then smiled. "Jessie loved her so much."

Sawyer only interrupted long enough to find out where they'd boarded her horse and who'd given Jessica lessons since those details hadn't been included in the investigators' notes.

"Our girl was fierce and had a great head on her shoulders," Bruce said, then lowered his gaze to the table. "She met a lot of wealthy families once she started running with the equestrian crowd. Sometimes she was ashamed of her humble life."

"But never us," Janet quickly added. "She was never spiteful or harsh. Our Jessica just wanted more from life."

"She started competing in those beauty contests for the scholarship money," Bruce said. His voice broke, and he cried softly for a few minutes before pulling himself together. "She didn't want us to work so much to help offset the cost of her education." Bruce put his arm around his wife and smiled at her. "Her mama created the most beautiful gowns for Jessie. My heart swelled with pride when the people around us murmured in awe as our girl walked onto the stage. She was pure magic."

Janet nodded. "My baby burned too bright for this world, and that's why God called her home. Not a day goes by that I don't miss her. I'd give anything to hear Jessie's sweet laughter just one more time." Her chin wobbled, and she covered her mouth with her hand. Janet shut her eyes, and a tremor quaked through her before she steeled her resolve and met his gaze. "Sorry."

"I'm the one who should apologize for making you relive the most difficult time in your lives."

"Do you have children?" she asked.

"Not yet, but I will someday." Royce had promised him, and he always kept his word.

"Cherish every minute, Sergeant Key. Never let minor things steal a single moment of your joy. They grow up so fast, and this world can be so cruel." She laughed dryly. "Good lord. I'm talking to a man who investigates homicides for a living. I don't need to tell you."

Sawyer smiled gently. "A reminder to embrace joy never hurts anyone."

The Campbells didn't know of any young men Jessica might've been dating, and they also didn't bring up the insult written on her forehead. The stylist hired to do her hair and makeup for the celebration ball had discovered Jessica's body. Like Cecily, she'd probably been sworn to secrecy.

Bruce shook Sawyer's hand at the door and apologized for his surly behavior. The interview hadn't uncovered any new potential leads, but Sawyer hoped Mr. Campbell slept better knowing he cared about getting justice for their Jessie.

Sawyer grabbed a salad and caught up with Topher and Holly by phone on his way back to the precinct. The duo sounded a little dejected since they hadn't learned anything new, so he gave them a pep talk before disconnecting. Then he reminded himself to take his own advice.

Amy Lou Parker's family lived in a comfortable middle-class neighborhood. Sawyer met with Dean and Dinah, Amy's parents, Andrea, her younger sister, and Alex and Adam, her older brothers. They all had brown hair and brown eyes, though the shades ranged from very light to nearly black.

The Parkers' reaction to Sawyer's presence was somewhere between the first two interviews. They weren't as hostile as Bruce initially had been, but they weren't as open as the Wrights either. Their interview neither revealed new facts nor boosted their faith, but they seemed to find pleasure in talking about Amy, so he listened.

Dinah kept absently stroking her hand over an ivory cross hanging from a leather cord around her neck. Sawyer remarked that it was pretty, and she told him Amy had made it.

"My father made the most beautiful things from leather," Dinah said. "Belts, handbags, bracelets, wallets, and so many things. He was teaching Amy the trade, and they'd worked for hours in his workshop. My daddy died from a broken heart not long after we lost our Amy."

"I'm so sorry to hear that," Sawyer said.

"Please find who killed our daughter and bring them to justice," Dean said.

"I will do my best, sir."

Though his time with the Parkers was the shortest, their interaction weighed heaviest on his heart as he headed home after an emotionally draining day. Amy's family was afraid to hope, which resonated deeply with him.

He would never compare losing Vic to the Parkers' tragedy. His husband had lived a full life, even if it had been cut short. Barbara, Jessica, and Amy had been killed before their lives could even take off. Sawyer knew what it felt like to fear hope, and he wouldn't wish that on anyone. Without hope, there was nothing.

Instead of going straight home, Sawyer took a detour. He needed to understand Wayne Burke's decision not to speak to him. On its face, his actions looked suspicious, but maybe the retired detective had given up hope too.

Wayne Burke lived a few streets over from the Parkers. Flowerbeds surrounded the red brick ranch, and Sawyer imagined they would burst with color and vitality in the spring and summer. A Winnebago camper was parked on the far-left side of the driveway. Sawyer pulled up behind a black Ford Ranger and killed the engine. He could feel someone watching him approach the house and figured Burke had seen him pull into the drive.

The door swung open before Sawyer could ring the bell. Burke wore faded jeans and a red-and-black flannel shirt over a black T-shirt. He ran a hand over his bald head, which seemed more like a habit than a show of vanity. The weariness in his eyes made him look older than midsixties. "I told Topher I wasn't interested." Burke's voice was gruff, bordering on mean.

"You know who I am?" Sawyer asked.

The older man pinned him with a belligerent stare. "I saw the news conference."

"Detective Burke, I could use your help. If you—"

Burke slammed the door in Sawyer's face before he could finish. He stood there on the porch for several seconds, unable to decide whether he was furious or humiliated. What the fuck was Burke's problem?

Sawyer turned around and headed back to his car. His phone vibrated and he pulled it from his pocket. Sawyer smiled when he saw it was a text from Royce.

On my way home. Don't work too late. I have a surprise for you tonight.

Sawyer's heartbeat stuttered and galloped. Was this the night?

Chapter
TEN

ROYCE SMILED WHEN HIS GARAGE DOOR ROLLED UP TO REVEAL Sawyer's Audi already parked inside.

"He must really want his surprise."

Or he'd had a rough day meeting with the families. The thought put a damper on Royce's excitement. He'd spent the day getting to know officers from other departments at the Explorer instructor course, but Sawyer had relived three families' worst nightmares.

Royce shut his vehicle off, hit the button to close the garage door, and snagged Sawyer's surprise off the passenger seat. Bones was waiting for him inside because he associated the rumbling garage door with the snick of the lid on his cat food. Royce was confident Sawyer had already fed the beast, but he let Bones do his best to manipulate him until he could verify his assumption.

"Are you my starving boy?"

Meow.

"Daddy didn't feed you?"

Meow. Bones added a dramatic tail swish as he darted into the kitchen. Royce pulled up short because Sawyer was staring into the open refrigerator with a blank look on his face. Royce glanced over and saw the ingredients for their favorite pasta dish scattered on the kitchen island. He ticked off the items to figure out what Sawyer had forgotten, but everything was accounted for, so why was he staring off into space? The noise-canceling headphones he was wearing meant he was listening to an audiobook or podcast. The distraction would make it easy for Royce to sneak up on him undetected, so he set Sawyer's surprise on the counter and stealthily stalked across the room.

"Oh yeah," Sawyer muttered. "That's really good." He was definitely listening to an audiobook.

That's when Royce noticed the can of squirty cheese in Sawyer's right hand and the open bag of sliced pepperoni and sleeve of crackers on the shelf in front of him. *Son of a bitch!* Sawyer had helped himself to Royce's secret stash of fake cheese in a can. His shock was replaced by outrage when Sawyer made himself another cracker, piling on two slices of pepperoni and adding a very generous amount of cheese. Sawyer popped the entire thing in his mouth, closing his eyes as he chewed like it was the best thing he'd ever had.

"So good," Sawyer mumbled around a mouthful of cracker.

Royce crept up beside him and said, "Isn't it?"

Sawyer let out an inhuman squeak, whirled, and shot Royce in the face with the squirty cheese.

"My eye!" Royce shouted, covering the right side of his face and staggering over to the counter.

Sawyer shoved his headphones down around his neck and rushed to his side. "Baby, I'm so sorry. You scared the hell out of me." Sawyer wrapped his long fingers around Royce's wrist and tried to tug his hand away. "Let me see. We need to wash the cheese out of your eye. I can't begin to imagine the chemicals in that orange shit."

Royce's charade crumbled when he burst into laughter. He lowered his hand and showed Sawyer the cheese had landed under his eye, not in it.

The love of his life fell back against the cabinets in relief. "You're such a dickhead."

"And you're a sanctimonious asshole for"—Royce held up one finger—"invading my secret stash." Two fingers. "Eating my guilty pleasure behind my back." Three fingers. "Talking with your mouth full." Four fingers. "And having the gall to lecture *me* about how unhealthy the cheese was after *you* got caught eating it." Royce shook his head sadly. "Who are you?"

Sawyer grimaced as he snagged a paper towel from the roll and gently wiped the cheese off. "I can't take your lecture seriously with this shit on your face."

"The shit you were moaning and groaning about just now?" He settled his hands on Sawyer's hips, pulled him closer, and nuzzled his lips against Sawyer's neck until he relaxed. "Stress eating?" he asked.

"Guilty as charged."

Royce pulled back and looked at him. "I'm sorry you had a bad day."

"But are you sorry for scaring me?"

Royce pressed several kisses along Sawyer's jaw until he reached his earlobe. He nibbled the tender flesh before pulling back to stare into Sawyer's dark eyes. "That too."

"And for shaming me?"

"Hell no," Royce replied. "You've given me so much shit for loving my stupid canned cheese. There's no way I'm letting you off the hook for enjoying it behind my back."

"Fair enough." Sawyer pressed a quick kiss to Royce's lips before taking a step back. "How was your day?"

Royce snagged Sawyer's hips before he could get too far. "Huh-uh. You first. It's my policy." He could tell Sawyer was going to remind him about the bet he'd lost the previous Monday morning when he came first, but Royce wasn't having it. "Don't deflect. Talk."

During dinner prep, Sawyer recapped his interviews with the three families. Royce remained silent while he talked, passing the vegetables so Sawyer could finely slice them for sautéing. Sawyer's tension seemed to ebb as the mountain of zucchini, yellow squash, peppers, onions, and mushrooms grew. Royce realized he'd cut enough vegetables for three dinners, so he retrieved the freezer bags and a head of garlic from the pantry.

He set them on the counter, then pressed his chest to Sawyer's back and looped his hands around Sawyer's waist. Royce kissed the back of his neck before resting his chin on Sawyer's shoulder. "I love you."

Sawyer sighed and leaned his temple against Royce's. "I love you most."

"You're going to figure this out. I know it."

"God, I hope so."

Leaving their work outside their home had been easier when they were partners. Sawyer hadn't needed to dredge up the worst parts of his day for Royce because he'd experienced them alongside him. This was another change they needed to adapt to because bottling up their feelings was a breeding ground for resentment. They'd need to make space for heavy conversations, and Royce thought cooking dinner together was the perfect solution.

He reluctantly loosened his arms from Sawyer's waist and resumed assisting him with dinner. But first, he snagged a few mushrooms and green peppers. Sawyer eyed him with an adorable smirk.

"Snacking on fresh vegetables before dinner? Who are you?"

"Hardy har har," Royce said as he retrieved the pot for the pasta. He added water and sprinkled some salt before turning the burner on. "So what if I've developed a more sophisticated pallet while yours has diminished."

"It was a moment of weakness," Sawyer pleaded.

Royce snorted. "Said the cheating douchebag husband on *Dateline* last week."

Sawyer spun around and narrowed his eyes. "Are you comparing me to the guy with multiple identities, wives, and girlfriends?"

"Nooo," Royce said slowly, "but I am concerned it's a slippery slope."

Sawyer backed him up against the cabinet on the opposite wall. He rested his hand against Royce's throat and pressed his thumb against Royce's pulse. Excitement raced through his body, and there was no way Sawyer missed it. His nostrils flared as he inched his face closer, stopping only a few scant centimeters from Royce's lips. "Do you know what you can do to my slippery slope? You can ride it, suck it, or fuck it. But don't you *ever* doubt it belongs to anyone besides you."

Sawyer kissed him then, hard and hungry, pushing his tongue inside

Royce's mouth and dominating him with a single swipe. Royce groaned, gripped Sawyer's hips, and met his passion with equal fervor.

Meow.

Sawyer broke the kiss, and they both looked down at their favorite little cockblocker.

"You've already eaten," Sawyer said.

Meow.

"Maybe that's his 'take it to the bedroom' plea," Royce suggested.

Sawyer laughed and stepped free from his embrace. "And I plan on it. You promised me a surprise."

Royce chuckled. "It wasn't sexual."

"Since when?"

"Since Sheriff Beecham had our lunch catered, and it included this salted caramel pretzel bar as one of the dessert offerings."

"Where?" Sawyer asked.

Royce chuckled and retrieved the napkin-wrapped dessert from where he'd left it. He uncovered the caramel cookie bar and waved it under Sawyer's nose.

"Feed it to me while I cook," Sawyer said. "You can tell me about the rest of your day."

"Dessert before dinner?"

Sawyer added olive oil to the skillet, then looked at Royce over his shoulder. "You're my dessert."

Royce sauntered over to his side, broke off a chunk of caramel cookie bar, and placed it in Sawyer's eager mouth. Sawyer's slutty moans made Royce want to postpone their dinner and conversation plans. "The things you do to me with the slightest sound."

"More," Sawyer said greedily as he added vegetables to the hot skillet.

Royce had heard a similar tone when he'd had his head between Sawyer's thighs that morning. He'd had his hands in Royce's hair tugging at the strands as he'd struggled to regain control after Royce had pinned his hips to the bed and edged him for a good five minutes. He saw the answering desire in Sawyer's soulful, dark eyes and knew it would take very little convincing to get his man into their bedroom. An emotion more profound than lust urged him not to stoke those fires just yet, so he broke off another chunk of cookie and held it up.

Sawyer snatched it from his fingers and did a silly shimmy, allowing Royce to admire his taut ass and lean hips. He suddenly couldn't stop himself from imagining what Sawyer might look like in one of those corset vests. It would hug his torso so beautifully and frame his sweet, sweet—

"Eyes up here, or I'll burn dinner," Sawyer said.

Royce darted his glance up and wanted to kiss the smug smile on Sawyer's lips. Instead, Royce settled his free hand at Sawyer's nape and fed him another bite. He slid his hand down Sawyer's spine, imagining how those corset laces would feel against his hand. What if Sawyer wore the vest and nothing else? Would it end at the top of his ass crack? Royce bit his lip to keep from groaning as he imagined parting Sawyer's taut cheeks and shoving his face between them.

"Talk," Sawyer groused. "I want to hear about your day."

Royce cleared his throat and helped himself to a bite of Sawyer's cookie bar, earning a wounded look in return. "Sorry," he said sheepishly. "Today was a little boring because the instructors spent most of the day talking about rules and regulations." Royce sighed. "Did you know I would be in charge of raising funds to continue the program beyond the first year?"

"I do now."

Royce stretched his head to the left and right, fighting off the urge to tense up.

"Do they at least make suggestions on how to raise money? Please don't tell me the kids will have to peddle cookie dough, fruit, or popcorn."

Royce chuckled and shook his head. "It's usually community events like working concession stands and assisting with venue parking. Most organizations will share a percentage of the profits or pay a certain amount per hour."

"Well, that's better."

Royce sighed and drew lazy circles over Sawyer's lower back. "I'd also be in charge of the budget for the program. There will be oversight, of course, but there will be bookkeeping and auditing."

"But surely they give you guidelines to follow? They don't just toss the checkbook at you and say good luck, right?"

"Don't call me Shirley," Royce teased, nipping Sawyer's ear. He picked up the salt and pepper shakers and seasoned the vegetables. "But yeah. I have a thick binder full of dos and don'ts."

"So you're going back tomorrow."

The thought still terrified him, but Royce nodded. "Tara is too."

Sawyer poked a zucchini slice with a fork to test its tenderness, then squeezed three garlic cloves through the press. He gave the skillet a good stir to thoroughly mix the contents. Royce sniffed the air, loving the aroma of sautéing garlic and vegetables. He never would've guessed he'd like a meatless pasta dish. Cooked zucchini and yellow squash? Sawyer had opened his eyes to a bevy of possibilities, and his food preferences were just the tip of the iceberg.

"Do you think you'll like the program once you get past the boring stuff?" Sawyer asked.

Royce walked around him and dumped the whole grain penne pasta into the boiling water. "Yeah, I honestly do. I admit I'm starting to feel burned out, and I don't want to end up like Burke."

"Is that what you think his problem is?" Sawyer asked. "Or do you think it's more sinister?"

"I thought you said the guy thoroughly investigated the murders."

"He did," Sawyer replied, "but what if the plethora of paperwork is to hide his duplicity? Think about it. What supervisor would've looked at the volume of reports he composed, considered the hours he worked, and concluded anything less than total dedication on Burke's part?"

Royce tipped his head to the side. "Bury the truth like a needle in a haystack?"

Sawyer shrugged. "It's a theory."

Stirring the pasta, Royce looked up and studied his face. "It's also just as probable those murders consumed Burke's life, and he's afraid they'll do it again. His obsession could've wrecked his marriage or chased away his children. I mean, that happens a lot to guys like us."

Sawyer stared pensively at the vegetables until Royce scooted the jar of pasta sauce made with fire-roasted tomatoes and herbs his way. Sawyer twisted the lid off and poured the sauce over the vegetables. "You make a valid point. I guess the respectful thing to do is to honor his wishes."

"It's the only thing to do," Royce said. "There are two types of retired cops. Some walk away and don't look back, and the others can't seem to let go. The McDonald's is filled every morning with former jocks and cops who relive the glory days over senior coffees, breakfast sandwiches, and hash browns."

Sawyer laughed. "That's what we have to look forward to, huh?"

"Not us," Royce said as he carried the pot of cooked noodles to the sink and strained them through a colander. "You've never been a status quo kind of guy, and you'd never let me become an old curmudgeon like Burke." Royce gave the colander a good shake before crossing back to Sawyer and adding the noodles to the skillet with the vegetables and sauce.

Sawyer gave it a stir while Royce retrieved a wedge of Parmesan and the handheld cheese grater for garnishing the completed dish. He set those on the counter and sliced four pieces of crusty French bread. Royce arranged them on a small cookie sheet, then generously smeared a layer of cheesy garlic spread on top.

Meow.

Royce popped the cookie sheet under the broiler and smiled down at Bones. "No. The vet said it isn't good for you." But as soon as Sawyer turned away, Royce pinched off a tiny chunk of bread and fed it to Bones.

"I saw that," Sawyer said.

Their children would get away with nothing. The thought was both sobering and exhilarating, an odd combination that felt like fizzy soda bubbles were trapped in his chest. He so badly wanted to marry Sawyer and start a family, but he also feared it. Strands of his conversation with Jace replayed in his mind. He wanted to be as brave as his brother, and he tried every day to be the man Sawyer deserved, but he wasn't sure he'd reached the high bar.

Unaware of Royce's inner turmoil, Sawyer continued stirring the pasta dish on the stove. "I sock money away for retirement like everyone else, but I haven't thought much about what I'd like to do with the money once I get there. Have you?"

"Recently, yes," Royce replied.

Sawyer turned off the burner and faced him. "You have?"

Royce narrowed his eyes, then hip-checked Sawyer out of the way to check on the bread. It was golden brown and bubbly, so he pulled the sheet from the oven with a mitt and set it on the stove. He looked at Sawyer, who continued to study him closely. "Why do you sound so surprised?"

"Did I? I'm sorry. It's just something we haven't talked about, so I figured you were like me. I didn't know you'd concocted a big plan already."

Royce slid his arms around Sawyer's waist and rested his hands at the small of his back. He pressed a quick kiss to the lips pursed in suspicion. "There's no need to look brooding. Everything I picture involves you."

Sawyer swooped in and nipped Royce's bottom lip. "And what do you envision us doing in our golden years?"

"Besides straining something every time we have sex?" Royce asked.

Sawyer snorted. "Pretty sure our bodies will turn on us long before then, but yes. What besides sex do you see us doing as old fogies?"

Royce took a deep breath. "The idea came to me recently when I was at Sal's."

"Like most of them do," Sawyer quipped. "The hardware store is your favorite place to shop."

"I've loved Sal's since I was a kid," Royce said. "I'd like to own a hardware store like it someday."

Sawyer's penetrative stare made Royce want to squirm. He was trying to figure out if Royce was telling the truth or pulling his leg. After a moment, he gave a brief nod. "I like it."

Royce brightened. "Really? It doesn't sound lame?"

Sawyer grinned broadly. "I think it sounds peaceful. You're very handy and knowledgeable. Besides, you'd get to drink coffee and bullshit with your customers all day." He narrowed his eyes, and Royce could almost hear his gears grinding.

"Spit it out, GB."

"Have you talked to Sal about buying into his store now to make the transition easier down the road?"

"No," Royce admitted, "but I will now."

"Can I swing by for coffee sometime?"

Royce nuzzled Sawyer's neck. "Don't expect a fancy machine like yours."

"Ours."

Royce nodded. "Ours."

After dinner, Royce and Sawyer stretched out on the long leather sofa to watch television and wrapped up with one of the afghans Royce's mom had made years ago.

Sawyer pushed back into Royce's body and sighed happily. "We haven't shared enough of this lately." They'd both been working insanely long hours, which barely left enough time for eating, sleeping, and sex. They needed other types of intimacy to sustain a healthy relationship.

Royce tightened his arms around Sawyer and pressed a kiss to the back of his head. Valentine's Day was still two weeks away, so he had time to plan a romantic night out and pop the question without getting caught up in clichéd tripe. Royce appreciated Sawyer's insistence that he didn't need fancy dinners and candlelight, but Royce wanted Sawyer to have them.

He closed his eyes and made a mental note to make a dinner reservation for Saturday. The next thing he knew, Royce's vibrating phone woke him from a deep sleep. His man wasn't in the last place he'd seen him, but Royce knew where he'd find Sawyer.

He rubbed his eyes and remembered the reason he'd woken up. Royce pulled his phone from his pocket and sucked in a sharp breath when he saw a text message from Dru. His thumb shook when he swiped up to read the message.

I miss you too. Thanks for helping Jason.

Royce inhaled deeply as hope surged in his heart. It wasn't the apology he wanted—*needed*—but her text was a good start. Royce stood up, tucked his phone away, and sought out Sawyer, who was exactly where he'd suspected.

Bones was stretched out on Sawyer's desk, and Bones's daddy was leaning back in his chair, reading a pink leather book.

"Is that Barbara's journal?"

Sawyer squealed again for the second time that night and slammed the book on the desk. The noise sounded loud in the small space. Bones jumped up like someone had shot at him and bolted from Sawyer's office. "Must you sneak up on me?"

"Must you sneak out on me?"

Sawyer smiled softly and rubbed his eyes. "Sorry. I hadn't planned to abandon you, but you fell asleep, and I..."

"Have three homicides to solve. I get it. The best thing you can do right now for Barbara, Jessica, and Amy is to get a good night's sleep. Look at things with a rested brain and fresh eyes."

Sawyer pushed back from his desk and stood up. "Fine. But don't expect me to be happy about it."

"I'll take that challenge."

Chapter
ELEVEN

SAWYER CURLED THE WEIGHTS UP TOWARD HIS SHOULDERS AND his biceps begged for mercy. Instead, he focused on watching his form in the mirror. *Just a few more. Five, four, thr—*

Royce appeared in the doorway, naked as the day he was born and sporting a semi-erection. Their eyes briefly met in the mirror before Royce dropped his gaze to Sawyer's ass. Instead of stopping, Sawyer kept curling the weights, flexing his biceps and the glutes that held Royce's rapt attention, and was equally fascinated watching Royce get hard just from the visual stimulation he afforded him.

Sawyer nearly dropped the weights on his feet when Royce reached down and lazily stroked his cock. He set the weights down before he hurt himself and crossed the room without pausing to towel off his sweat. Royce remained in the same spot as if rooted to the floor but continued to pump his hand up and down his shaft.

"Aren't you cold?" Sawyer asked.

Royce's mouth quirked up on one side. "Do I look cold?"

Sawyer lunged the last few feet and knocked Royce's hand away from his prize. He ghosted his fingers down the center of Royce's chest from his clavicle to his neatly shorn pubic hair. Sawyer curled his fingers around Royce's erection, provoking a strangled moan for his efforts. Sawyer gave him a firm, slow pump. "You're smoking hot."

Royce's eyelids drooped, but he kept them open. A pretty pout formed on his mouth. "Then why do I keep waking up alone?"

Sawyer kissed Royce's lips until they parted on a minty-fresh sigh. "I figured you needed your sleep more." Fears he'd kept hidden managed to escape Pandora's box like little wisps of smoke through a keyhole. If he wasn't careful, the tendrils would form an ominous fog that would take Sawyer to the darkest recesses of his mind where the memories of Vic's illness and death waited. Unexplainable exhaustion was the first sign that something hadn't been right with his husband. Sawyer managed to rein in his thoughts but not before he voiced them. "Are you feeling okay?"

Royce's gaze and pout softened because he knew all too well Sawyer's biggest fear was losing him. "I'm fine, baby. My dick hurts, but I'm sure you have the cure for that ailment."

Sawyer snorted and tightened his grip. "I've got your number."

Royce placed his hands on Sawyer's hips, brushed his nose against Sawyer's, and pressed soft kisses to his mouth. "Stay in this moment with me. You won't want to miss this." Royce kissed a path down Sawyer's neck, and he began walking him backward. "Or this." Royce sank his teeth into the tender flesh where Sawyer's neck curved into his shoulder. Sawyer gasped and shivered. "And you definitely don't want to miss this." The back of Sawyer's legs bumped into the chest press bench.

"I'm sweaty and gross," Sawyer warned.

Royce shook his head. "Sweaty and delicious." He yanked Sawyer's shorts and underwear down his legs and pushed him onto the bench. Sawyer hissed when his bare flesh touched the cold vinyl. "Lie back," Royce urged.

Sawyer immediately complied, turning his head to watch Royce in the mirror. He walked over to the storage cabinet in the corner of the home gym and removed a bottle of lube they kept tucked away there. This room had been the first where they'd shared intimacy, and it continued to see a lot of action. Working out made Sawyer horny, and watching Sawyer sweat and strain always revved his boyfriend up.

Royce looked like pure sin as he strode back to the workout bench. He straddled Sawyer's hips, then lowered his upper body so they could kiss. Sawyer curled his tongue around Royce's and sucked it into his mouth while Royce ground his ass against Sawyer's erection. Royce pulled back suddenly, and they stared into each other's eyes while breathing heavily.

"This connection is insane," Royce said, his words laced with awe. "It keeps getting stronger."

"I wouldn't want it any other way."

Royce gripped the bar over Sawyer's head and lifted his hips. Sawyer retrieved the lube, slicked up two fingers, and massaged Royce's opening to stimulate the sensitive pucker and arouse him. Royce closed his eyes and let his head fall forward.

"Fuck, that feels good."

Sawyer pushed the tip of one finger inside the tight ring, slowly working it in and out.

Royce's breathing got heavy, and he used his strong legs to ride Sawyer's finger. "Quit being a stingy bastard and give me more." Sawyer added a second finger, making Royce snarl and buck against him. "I need you."

Sawyer withdrew his fingers, smeared more lube on his erection, then gripped the base and held it steady as Royce sank onto it.

"Fuck. Burns so good," Royce said, his voice raw, gruff, and needy.

He set a slow pace, taking his time working up and down Sawyer's shaft. The tight friction made Sawyer's eyes roll back. Royce quickened the tempo, dropping both hands to Sawyer's chest to brace himself on his pectoral muscles. Sawyer hissed when Royce's palms grazed his sensitive nipples. Royce smiled wickedly as he slowly lowered his hands until the tips of his middle fingers brushed over the hard disks.

"Fucking tease," Sawyer growled.

Royce pinched his nipples and twisted hard enough to detonate fireworks in his core. Sawyer gripped Royce's thighs, bouncing him harder and faster on his shaft, spiraling them toward a hard crash. Sawyer felt Royce's body tense with a climax, and his balls drew tighter against his body in reaction. Royce painted his chest and stomach while Sawyer filled his ass. They floated back down to earth on tender kisses, touches, and even softer words.

Royce plastered his chest against Sawyer's, not caring that he was lying in his own cum. He nestled his nose against Sawyer's neck and sighed happily.

"I could stay here all day."

Sawyer tightened his arms around Royce's back. "I wish we could."

Royce braced his hands on Sawyer's chest and pushed up. "I have a later start with training, so how about we take a quick shower, and I can make you a nice breakfast." He tipped his head to the side. "Or would you prefer to finish your workout?"

Sawyer snorted. "On these limp legs?"

Royce winked and slowly eased off Sawyer's cock. He stood up and offered his hand to help Sawyer up. They headed into the master suite and went through their usual morning routine.

Royce finished his shower first and stepped out so he could get breakfast started. Sawyer was still drying off when Royce disappeared into the bedroom to get dressed. At this pace, he expected Royce to already be in the kitchen by the time he made it to the bedroom, but he was standing buck naked at his dresser. A drawer—no, *the* drawer—was open, and Royce was staring into it.

Sawyer's muscles seized and his lungs froze. Waiting for Royce to propose was pure torture. Sawyer reached over and twisted the phantom ring on his left hand, a move he'd made countless times when married to Vic. It was something he'd absently done whenever he worked through a problem, a tell Vic had never missed, and it had taken him months after removing Vic's ring to break the pattern. Sawyer stared down at his bare hand, realizing old habits indeed died hard. He ached to feel the cool metal of Royce's ring on his finger and wondered again how he could help Royce find the confidence to remove the band from the drawer. He shook himself free of his stupor and placed his twitching hands on his hips. "I think your lucky underwear are in the hamper."

Royce flinched, snagged a pair of red briefs, and slammed the drawer shut. He turned and faced Sawyer with a cocky grin on his face as he stepped into his underwear. Royce pulled them up his legs but paused when he reached midthigh. "When you're this good…"

Sawyer crossed the room and stopped in front of Royce. He reached down and gripped his briefs. "You don't need luck," Sawyer said, finishing his words as he tugged the underwear into place.

"Besides, I already have you," Royce said.

The sincerity in Royce's expression eased the frustration licking at Sawyer's psyche. He knew damn well Royce was madly in love with him and wanted the same future. Sawyer just needed Royce to believe he deserved it.

Royce's smug smile melted into a frown. "Isn't this the part where you return the sentiment?"

Sawyer lowered his hands and gripped Royce's ass with both hands. "I could…but you won't believe me."

Royce narrowed his eyes. "Try me anyway."

Sawyer lifted his hands to cup Royce's face. "I'm the lucky one."

He saw the responding spark in the gray eyes he loved so much. Royce *wanted* to believe, which had been enough for Sawyer for three years, and it would be enough for today.

Sawyer left the house earlier than he'd planned and swung by the bakery, not that he had room for pastries after Royce had fed him turkey bacon and crepes.

Sherry Rigby glanced up from filling an order when he walked in. Her red hair was pulled back from her face in a braid, and her eyes twinkled with happiness. She smiled at him briefly before refocusing on the person in front of her. Sawyer recognized more than half the customers from the precinct, and though Commissioner Rigby was popular among the men and women in blue, her wife had earned a reputation on her own merit.

Three bakery employees were serving the customers, so the line moved quickly. Sherry was helping the woman who'd been in front of Sawyer, so he called out a quick greeting before placing his order with the young guy whose name tag identified him as Zak. Unsure what to get, Sawyer asked Zak to box six of his favorite pastries and added a large coffee to the order.

"Be safe, Sergeant Key," Sherry said between customers.

"Thanks, ma'am."

Once back in his car, Sawyer started having second thoughts about his plan. He didn't even know when the idea had come to him, but he suspected his conversation with Royce the previous night was the culprit. He parked behind Burke's Ranger again, and just like the first time, Sawyer felt Burke's attention on him as he made his way to the front porch. This time, Burke didn't answer before Sawyer could ring the bell, and he didn't answer afterward.

"Detective Burke, I just stopped by to apologize. I'll just leave my peace offering and disappear. I won't bother you again, sir."

Sawyer set the box of pastries and cup of coffee on the porch, then took two steps backward. The door swung open just as he turned to leave.

"Did anyone ever tell you you're an asshole?" Burke asked.

Sawyer met the older man's scowl with a grin. "Every single day of my life."

Burke grunted, and Sawyer saw a slight thaw in his grim expression. He ran a hand over his bald head but made no move to pick up the pastries and coffee from the porch. He shook his head before bending over and accepting Sawyer's peace offering.

"Might as well come in."

Sawyer was surprised and stood there for a few seconds, wondering if he'd heard the man correctly.

"Or not," Burke said as he started to shut the door in Sawyer's face again.

Sawyer shook himself from his stupor and followed the man inside. The interior of the home matched the era of construction. The tiny house was dominated by a dark brown, avocado-green, and burnt-orange color scheme, which they'd tried to temper with beige and ivory here and there. He'd only seen the bold patterns and colors in photos of his parents' childhoods.

Sawyer knew better than to react or comment, so he followed Burke into a living room where the only modern furniture was a worn-out leather recliner, but even it was brown.

"Have a seat," Burke gruffly said as he carried his donuts and coffee to his throne. Once settled, he set the pastry box on the end table and pulled the lid off the coffee. "Oh, good. No creamer. It's smart you didn't assume." Burke looked at him. "Did you put any sweetener in it?"

Sawyer shook his head. "No arsenic either, sir."

Burke paused with the cup halfway to his mouth. "You think you're funny?"

"Sometimes," Sawyer replied.

Burke continued to study him for a moment before he took a sip of coffee. Surprise registered on his face, and he looked at the bakery logo on the cup. "Is this the place the police commissioner's wife owns?" Burke's expression was blank, and Sawyer didn't hear any derision in his voice.

"Yes, sir."

He took another sip and nodded. "She makes a damn fine cup of coffee."

"The pastries are even better."

Burke set his cup down without putting the lid back on and retrieved the box. He flipped it open with a flourish and stared at the contents. Burke pulled out a bear claw and took a big bite. He made an appreciative hum and nodded as he chewed. "These are delicious." Burke glanced in Sawyer's direction before taking another bite. After he swallowed it, the retired detective took another drink of coffee before setting the pastry and coffee down and returning his full attention to Sawyer. "My Alma would be furious at me for not offering to share."

Sawyer held up his hand. "I wouldn't accept. I brought those for you."

"To butter me up?"

"To apologize," Sawyer said. "I need to respect the toll those murders would've taken on you and not pile on more pressure." Sawyer took a deep breath. "I can be pretty relentless sometimes."

"I'm sure it serves you well on the job." Burke offered a sly grin. "I was a lot like you. Those three homicides consumed my life, though. I spent every minute of every day thinking about what those young ladies went through. It nearly destroyed my marriage." Burke sighed. "I was lucky my Alma was cut from sturdier cloth than most of my friends' wives. She had a health scare toward the end of my career, and it was my wake-up call. I put my thirty in and got out. We bought a Winnebago and traveled all around the country. It felt like I was getting to know my wife for the first time, and you know what?" Burke didn't wait for an answer. "I was one lucky son of a bitch."

Sadness washed over his features as he stared into space. "But my Alma got sick for real a few years back, and cancer took her fast." Something else they had in common. "I promised her before she passed that I would make peace with my inability to solve the Magnolia Murders." Burke quirked a wiry gray brow. "Pretty sure a dogged fellow such as yourself knows how it's going."

"Sir, I can honestly say your investigations were some of the best I've ever seen. I'm not just telling you that because I think you want to hear it. I'm telling you because it's true. I'm working with two additional detectives, and we've combed through every file at least twice. You did good work."

Burke took a deep breath and relaxed his shoulders. "I wanted nothing more than to find justice for those young ladies. I dreamed of my Alma last night, and she admonished me for being rude to you and reminded me of my promise. I wish you luck, Sergeant Key, I really do. It's not that I *won't* help. I just don't think I *can*."

Sawyer nodded. "I understand, sir. Can I ask you one question?" Burke hesitated for a moment before nodding. "If there was something you could've done differently, what would it have been?"

The older man rubbed his chin, the friction against bristles there sounding like sandpaper. "I've asked myself that question every day for nearly thirty-eight years. I feel like I ran down every lead. Maybe new DNA technologies will come through for you. The testing wasn't around in 1984 and courts were still uncertain of it in 1996. The technology was better in 2000, but you still needed a pretty big sample for testing. Things have changed so much in the last two decades. If you catch a break, I think that's where it will come from."

"I agree. My team has an appointment with the crime lab in a few hours." Sawyer rose to his feet. "Thank you for your time, Detective Burke."

"Call me Wayne," he said as he stood up from his recliner to walk

Sawyer to the door. "I'm really sorry you became a widower at such a young age. Have you remarried?"

Sawyer shouldn't have been surprised by the question. Of course the man had done his homework, or maybe he'd remembered Sawyer's story from the articles five years ago. "No, sir," he said after a pause.

"I didn't mean to make you feel uncomfortable, Sergeant," Burke said. "My apologies."

"None needed, sir. You just managed to catch me by surprise."

Burke chuckled and paused at the front door. He placed his hand on the knob but didn't turn it. "Bet that doesn't happen very often, does it?"

Sawyer returned his grin. "No, sir."

"Back in my day, we didn't talk about things like you kids do today." Sawyer hadn't been a kid in a very long time, but he didn't see a need to interrupt the man when he was on the verge of imparting his wisdom. "Not saying we were right and you're wrong, mind you. It's just different." Burke tilted his head to the side and nodded as if he'd replayed his words back in his head and approved of his wisdom. "Do you have someone special in your life?"

Sawyer quirked a brow. "Please tell me you're not hoping to fix me up with a relative."

Burke laughed heartily. "No, I'm just trying to make sure you don't make the same mistakes I did. Keep your feet firmly planted on the ground, young man."

"Yes, sir. And I do have someone special in my life. I hope to someday call him my husband."

Burke narrowed his eyes. "You don't strike me as the type to wait around for someone else to make a move."

Sawyer laughed. "Not normally." But this was something Royce needed, and Sawyer wouldn't deny him.

Burke released the doorknob and extended his hand to Sawyer. "Hopefully your young man will take that leap soon."

"Thank you. I appreciate it."

"And I'm sorry I couldn't be more helpful, but I can't think of anything I could've done differently." He narrowed his eyes and stared off before refocusing on Sawyer. "But I wish I could've shut down the Magnolia Queen Pageant after Barbara Jean was murdered." He held up his hands like Sawyer might defend the pageant's existence. "I'm not morally opposed to the beauty contests themselves, but there was something sinister about that particular pageant. I could never put a finger on what bothered me or point it at the person responsible for the feeling. I just couldn't shake it."

Burke was the second person in twenty-four hours to imply the pageant was insidious, making Sawyer even more confident their killer was involved in the inner workings.

The retired detective opened the door, and Sawyer thanked him again for the chat. Then he got into his car and headed toward the station. Sawyer was more determined than ever to find the common denominator tying all three murders together.

Chapter
TWELVE

GETTING A LAST-MINUTE RESERVATION FOR SATURDAY AT A FANCY restaurant had been impossible, even though Valentine's Day was more than a week away. Royce had planned to improvise and cook Sawyer a romantic dinner until Candy called. She'd sounded a little down, so Royce had invited her and the kids over for pizza, snacks, and games.

He glanced up from slicing carrots into sticks and got mesmerized by the sight of Sawyer painting Bailey's tiny toenails while her brothers romped in the living room. His little buttercup had run right past Royce with her arms up and her tiny fist clutching a bottle of hot pink nail polish.

"Unc Saw do it!" she'd yelled.

Sawyer had gathered the three-year-old in his arms, and the rest of them were all but forgotten. Royce couldn't be mad about it when he was so relieved to see Sawyer relaxing after a long week.

Beside him, Candy snickered and gently removed the knife from his hand. "Snap out of it, buddy. You'll either slice off a finger or set the living room on fire with your smoldering stare."

Royce chuckled and snagged a carrot. "Will not," he grumbled before biting into it with a *crunch*.

Candy rolled her eyes and shook her head before nudging him entirely out of the way to resume the task. "And stop pouting. You know damn well that little girl loves you like crazy. She's just extremely picky about who gets to paint her nails." Royce eyed her speculatively and she crossed her heart. "Not even I'm good enough."

Royce resumed watching two of his favorite people bond over the pink polish. Sawyer returned the brush to the bottle, then lifted Bailey's Flintstone foot and blew on it. Their little angel giggled and wiggled to get free. Early in their relationship, Sawyer had vowed to become Bailey's favorite uncle, and he'd followed up the promise with a decisive victory.

Candy cleared her throat to get his attention. "So…"

He recognized the tone and said, "Don't start."

"What did I say?"

"It's how you said it. That one word was as heavy as the anvil you'd like to drop on my head."

"So, I'm Wile E. Coyote and you're Roadrunner in this scenario?" she asked. "Hmmm. Kinda poetic, don't you think?"

"I'm not sure I follow," he lied.

"Elusive and hard to catch. Ring a bell?"

Royce snorted. "Don't be ridiculous. I'm well and truly caught. Jace has lectured me enough about my cowardice, and I don't need it from you too." His words came out surlier than he'd intended, so Royce apologized for his tone and slipped an arm around her shoulders.

Candy leaned into him, resting her head against his chest. "We just want you to be happy, Ro. You've come so far. Look around at the amazing home and life you've built with Sawyer." But Candy knew Sawyer wanted—needed—more. Royce did too, which was why he'd become more and more frustrated. Why couldn't Royce vocalize what he wanted most in the world? Why was he fearless everywhere but the place it counted most?

"I can't take credit for the house," Royce said. "He owned it before we met."

"Idiot," Candy hissed as she lightly whacked him on the back of the head. "Your presence is everywhere I look because the two of you have blended your lives so beautifully. You give me hope, Ro." He started to respond, but she cut him off with a wave. "Do you know what your problem is?"

"I have a feeling you're about to tell me," Royce replied. Candy tried to cuff him again, but Royce deftly darted out of the way. "You projected your move, Candy Crush."

Nonplussed, Candy said, "You're too complacent and comfortable. It's never good to take your relationship for granted."

All humor and cheer drained from him, leaving Royce feeling as hollow as a husk. "I am not complacent, and I don't take Sawyer for granted." His voice sounded as dry and brittle as brown autumn leaves crumbling beneath his boots, which was only fitting since Candy's accusation trampled his heart into dust. He was going to say more, but the doorbell rang.

"Probably the pizza," he mumbled before leaving the kitchen.

"This conversation isn't over," Candy yelled.

That's what she thought.

"Unc Ro," Bailey yelled. She lifted her foot so he could fuss over Sawyer's handiwork.

"So pretty, buttercup." He kissed her cheek before dropping one on Sawyer's head. "You do good work, GB."

"I still have openings available," Sawyer suggested. "Shall I pencil you in?"

Royce chuckled and continued through the living room. He glanced over just as Marc pinned his younger brother to the rug.

"Surrender now, and I'll go easy on you," Marc told Daniel.

"Eat dirt," Daniel replied, then did an impressive maneuver to wiggle free from his brother's grasp. His face was red and mutinous, and Royce knew his clenched fist spelled trouble.

"Do not hit your brother in the balls," Royce said firmly. Daniel, who'd just committed to the swing, jerked and the blow landed on Marc's thighs.

"You're going to pay for that," the oldest Wilkes said.

Royce stopped and pinned them with a fierce look. "You're both going to settle down and wash your hands for dinner."

"Boring," Daniel griped.

"Lame," Marc added.

"Yeah, that's a good one," Daniel said, high-fiving his brother. At least they'd found something to bond over.

The doorbell rang again, and Royce resumed his trek to the front door, pulling it open with an apology. It wasn't the delivery person standing on the porch, though. It was Tara. She'd left her sunglasses in his SUV on Friday night after their final day of Explorer training. He'd texted her when he saw them on his Saturday morning run to the hardware store, and she said she'd stop by sometime to grab them. "Hey, South," he said. "I thought you were the pizza."

Daniel and Marc started whooping about something, and Tara looked around him.

"Did I catch you at a bad time?"

"No, come in," he said, stepping aside. "Candy and the boys are here for pizza. Have you eaten?"

"Nah, but that's okay. I don't want to intrude."

"You're not intruding," he said, ushering her through the house. With South there, Candy wouldn't start in on him again. Royce regretted he'd told so many people about the ring he'd bought for Sawyer. It was just added pressure he didn't need. Evangeline, the one person he'd expected to be impatient, had been sympathetic and encouraging. And, damn it, if he'd been smart enough, he'd have asked Evangeline to call Giancarlo's for a table. They'd likely clear half the restaurant if she requested it.

Bones jumped down from the tree and greeted the new visitor.

"Damn, that's a big cat," Tara said.

"He's our beautiful boy," Royce cooed.

"Is it okay if I pet him? I don't want to lose a finger."

Bones sniffed Tara's leg and immediately started rubbing against her jeans. The big cat purred, and Royce gave her the all clear. The furry attention whore soaked up all the petting and praise Tara heaped upon him. Afterward, Royce introduced her to Bailey.

Tara studied Sawyer's progress as he slowly painted the toenails on Bailey's other foot. "You're a man of many talents, Key."

Sawyer looked over his shoulder and smiled at Tara before locking eyes with him. "That's what I keep telling Royce."

"I appreciate every one of your talents," Royce said, hoping he didn't sound defensive in the wake of Candy's comments.

In the kitchen, Royce said, "Candy, you remember Tara South, right?"

Candy glanced up midslice and froze. Her lips formed a silent *oh*, and she blinked at their visitor.

"Hey," Tara said. The word managed to sound thicker than its casual purpose.

Candy responded with a blush and stuttered, "H-hi."

Well, well, well. What did we have here? Royce figured a severed finger if he didn't act fast. He moved in beside Candy and eased the knife from her just as Tara took a few steps away to answer her ringing phone.

"Pull yourself together," he whispered. "You look like a blow-up doll."

Candy snapped her mouth shut and turned a menacing glare on him. "Don't think you can distract me from my purpose."

Royce tipped his head in Tara's direction. "Perhaps you need to start giving your own romantic relationships more thought."

Candy's eyes narrowed to mere slits. "I *think* about it quite often, thank you very much."

"When was the last time?" Royce pressed.

"This morning when I added batteries to my grocery list."

Did Candy really think she could embarrass him with a vague reference to sex toys? Ha! Royce leaned closer and whispered, "They make rechargeable vibrators."

Candy's lips trembled at the corner, but she fought off her smile like a heavyweight champ. "I am aware, and it's all well and good until the harried single mom forgets she left it charging in her bathroom and her sons decide to play pirate with the cool new sword they found."

Royce fought off his glee long enough to say, "Sword? Wow. She likes 'em big." Then he set the knife down on the kitchen island and doubled over laughing.

"Dagger," Candy amended as she tried to kick him.

Royce darted out of the way, and her foot connected with the cabinet instead. She cursed a blue streak, which only made him laugh harder. The commotion grabbed Tara's attention, and she spun around with a quirked brow and stern expression. Royce felt properly chastised for his childish behavior and fought off the urge to stand at attention and salute her.

Candy sighed and whispered, "Fuck, that's hot."

Royce leaned his head closer and said, "Play your cards right, and maybe the two of you can have a sword fight later."

Tara kept her gaze on Candy and told the person on the other end of the phone she wouldn't make dinner after all. "I've had a change of plans." Tara disconnected the call and crossed the room to stand on the other side of the kitchen island. She stared at Candy until his friend blushed and looked away. Candy's hand shook when she tucked her hair behind her ear. She mumbled something about checking on the boys and left the kitchen.

Tara watched her flee with unabashed interest before returning her focus to Royce. "Are you sure it's okay if I stay?"

"Of course. I ordered plenty of pizza."

Tara chuckled and shook her head. "I wasn't concerned about the quantity of food. I meant—" She jerked her head toward the living room.

Royce looked out and saw Candy flicking her attention between her sons and Tara. He had no idea what she was saying to them, but Royce would bet a week's worth of Sawyer's blow jobs that she was reminding them of the behavior she expected them to exhibit. Royce figured it was best if Tara witnessed her darling monsters in their full glory right out of the gate. If they were too much for her now, she need not pursue the attraction pulsing between them. Tara cleared her throat, reminding Royce he owed her an answer. Or maybe she was seeking his blessing.

"Yeah, I think you should definitely stay."

Tara smiled and relaxed. "Please tell me there's at least one pizza without pineapple."

Royce laughed and pushed the plate of veggies toward her. "I like you, South."

Tara *crunched* into a stick of celery and chewed thoughtfully. "You're okay, Locke."

An hour later, Royce had Sawyer all to himself while they cleaned the kitchen together. He thought back to what Candy had said about complacency and relationships getting stagnant.

Sawyer stood up from loading the dishwasher and said, "This is bullshit."

"We could've left it for the morning. Or I could've taken over so you could paint more toenails."

Sawyer snorted. "I'm not grumbling about this. I'm pissed about that," he said, pointing to the living room.

Bailey had commandeered Tara's lap while the boys tried to impress her with their wrestling prowess. Candy split her attention between the woman sitting beside her and the little jokers she'd brought into this world.

"You're pissed because Tara is trying to steal our girls?"

Sawyer turned his entire body to face Royce. "Girls? I meant Bailey. What are you talking about?"

Royce gestured to the couch where the women sat. "Haven't you been paying attention?"

Sawyer looked at Candy and Tara, then back at Royce. "I noticed they chatted about people they knew in common." It turned out Tara's younger sister worked at the hospital with Candy. That's who Tara was supposed to meet for dinner before she'd taken a detour to their place to pick up her sunglasses. "What do you see happening?"

Royce was stunned Sawyer hadn't picked up on the little signs that Candy was swooning over Tara. He repeated the interaction between the women upon reintroduction and watched as awareness dawned on Sawyer's handsome face.

"Stay out of it, Ro."

"Why? I have a proven track record. Diego and Levi are married and currently enjoying their honeymoon, aren't they?" Royce wished he could take the words back. He'd just claimed marriage was the pinnacle of a healthy relationship, knowing it was what Sawyer wanted most in the world.

Sawyer scowled and shook his head. "Fine, but that's one couple."

Royce narrowed his eyes. "Didn't I tell you years ago something was going on between Mendoza and Sheriff Beecham?"

"You did," Sawyer admitted, "but I've yet to see the proof. And now Tara and Candy?" He gestured to the living room, and they both looked in time to catch Tara handing her phone to Candy, who quickly entered something before returning it. Tara did a little typing of her own, and Candy retrieved her phone a second later. She glanced at the screen then blushed profusely. Tara reached over and tucked a wayward strand of hair behind Candy's ear, and her finger lingered to trace the outer shell. "Oh," Sawyer said.

"Pretty sure Candy just said the same thing," Royce did a victory shimmy, which included some impressive hip thrusts if he said so himself. Sawyer must've agreed because his gaze dropped down to Royce's groin and lingered for longer than was polite.

Royce's gloating turned to gluttony, and he suddenly wanted everyone out of their house so he could spend the rest of the weekend worshipping Sawyer's body. He truly hoped Sawyer knew Royce was precisely where he wanted to be. Two questions consumed his thoughts, but he only dared to ask one.

He closed the gap between them and cupped the left side of Sawyer's face. "Do you have any idea how much I love you?"

Sawyer turned his head and kissed Royce's palm. Their gazes met once more, and it felt like Royce was falling into a vat of melted chocolate. "I have a pretty good idea, but I'm always happy for a demonstration."

Royce leaned his forehead against Sawyer's. "There's no one I love more. I cannot imagine a single day without you in my life." He took a shaky breath. Hell, he was halfway to the proposal he'd imagined, even if the setting was vastly different. Sawyer had stated he didn't need fancy dinners and romance. Would he settle for pizza and—

"Whatcha doing?" Candy asked loudly from the other side of the island.

Royce groaned and turned to look at her. Hadn't she just told him to pull his head out of his ass? He'd freed himself to his ears and was working on the rest before she'd shoved his head back in. He bit back a groan and looked into the living room, noting a certain detective's absence.

"Where's Tara?"

"Kids scared her off," Candy said breezily. A moment later, her cell phone pinged, and Candy checked it. Giggling, she glanced up at Royce. "I don't suppose…"

He'd do anything to keep hearing that sound of happiness. "Get out of here and leave the munchkins with us." Then a thought sobered him. "Be careful, okay? South's reputation with the ladies is legendary."

Candy smiled softly and came around the island to kiss his cheek.

"Thank you for loving me. I'm not looking for happily ever after right now. Just a little *hell yeah.*" She smooched Sawyer's cheek next. "I'll be back by ten."

"No way," Royce said, shaking his head in disappointment.

"Nine?" she asked nervously.

Royce rolled his eyes. "I was thinking more like eleven. Give those swords a chance to charge back up for another fight."

"I don't even want to know," Sawyer said.

Candy laughed on her way to the living room. She hugged and kissed each of her kids before heading out to meet Tara. Royce hoped he hadn't made a mistake when he'd greenlit the pairing. He hadn't been joking about South's lady-killer reputation.

"No," Sawyer said firmly. "Stay out of it."

"What?"

"Wipe the innocent expression off your face. I know damn well you're planning to have a conversation with Tara. Do not ask what her intentions are toward Candy."

"I wasn't going to." But he had planned to remind Tara that Candy hadn't been in a relationship since Marcus died. He rubbed the back of his neck and heaved a sigh. "You're right."

Sawyer grinned and tugged him closer. "Every dog has their day. Look how we turned out."

"Dog, huh?" Royce pictured Sawyer on his hands and knees in the center of the bed. Yeah, he definitely brought out Royce's baser instincts.

"There are children present," Sawyer said, dumping ice water on his libido.

"For now."

Sawyer chuckled. "Think you can manage to stay awake until eleven?"

"Yeah, but you better hope Candy is on time because eleven thirty is my limit."

Sawyer laughed and tugged him into the living room where they played games and watched movies with the kids until Candy returned at ten fifty, looking like she'd just smoked ten joints. Her mussed hair, loose posture, and dopey smile betrayed the good time she'd had. Royce snorted when he greeted her at the door but didn't comment further. By ten fifty-five, Royce had the sleepy kids bundled up and loaded into the van.

Candy turned in her seat and watched him secure their little miss in her booster seat. "It would be so easy to overlook your vulnerabilities with all the preening you do."

Royce dropped a kiss on Bailey's nose as he stood back. "Preening?"

"You put the cock in peacock. Everything you do is effortless and loose-limbed, but now and then, cracks form in your façade. I don't know Sawyer as well, so it took me longer to see his fissures. The man is holding his breath and waiting for you to make the next move, Ro. Don't keep him waiting and guessing."

Royce's first instinct was to dispute her claim, but he couldn't because she was right. "Be careful, Candy Cane. Text me when you get home."

By the time he reentered the house, Sawyer had double-checked the other doors. Royce slid the deadbolt home on the front door and smiled devilishly at him.

"Naked. Now," Royce demanded as he crossed the room.

Sawyer met him in the center, and they kissed and touched their way through the house. They'd nearly made it to the bedroom when Sawyer's phone rang.

Sawyer growled and removed his phone. "This can't be good."

"Dispatch?" Royce asked.

"Mendoza."

Royce immediately stilled. It was never a good sign when the chief of police called them at home at eleven o'clock on a Saturday night, especially when Sawyer wasn't working new cases.

"Chief," Sawyer said into the phone. A slide show of emotion played on his face as he listened to whatever Mendoza had to say. Royce saw disbelief, horror, and shame flash through the expressive eyes he loved so much before Sawyer closed them. Royce cupped the back of his neck and Sawyer met his gaze once more. "Yes, sir. Right away." The conversation was brief and one-sided, but the haunted look in Sawyer's brown eyes exposed its potency. "He needs us at Mansion on Forsyth," Sawyer said.

"Us?"

Sawyer nodded. "There's been another Magnolia Queen murder."

Chapter
THIRTEEN

"**D**ID MENDOZA SAY WHY HE WANTED ME TO TAG ALONG ON your case?" Royce asked when he turned onto Drayton Street. Sawyer still hadn't adjusted to them working separate investigations. "He just said it would be obvious when I saw the crime scene."

"That's not at all ominous."

"Christ," Sawyer muttered when he saw the pandemonium surrounding the hotel. First responders had already cordoned off the hotel's perimeter, and several officers stood guard to keep the gawkers and large media presence at bay. Cop cars and news vans lined around the block. The medical examiner's office had driven their van onto the manicured lawn beyond the barricade and backed up to the hotel's grand entrance. "This reminds me of the circus surrounding the first homicide we worked together."

They'd been called to the home of a disgraced shock-jock who had been clubbed to death in his sound booth while spewing hate on his podcast. The grisly murder had been captured on the recording and uploaded for millions of people to hear before the cops were even aware Roland Putzinski was dead.

"But that case had been easy to solve," Sawyer said. Whoever killed the first three Magnolia Queens had gotten away with murder for decades. Sawyer worried they'd get away with a fourth unless they'd gotten sloppier with age.

"I thought the Magnolia Queen Pageant wasn't until April," Royce said as he parked the SUV as close as he could get to the police barricade surrounding the massive historical hotel.

Mansion on Forsyth had been built in the late eighteen hundreds as the personal residence of someone who must've seen themselves as royalty. The enormous brick structure looked like a castle decided to have a love child with a Victorian home. *The stories this grand lady could tell.*

"Several preliminary rounds lead up to the big event," Sawyer explained. He took a deep breath, hoping it would settle his nerves. Breaking news: it did not. "Fuck, Ro. Did I poke the hornet's nest? Is that why this young woman is dead?"

"Oh no," Royce said, shaking his head. "You aren't responsible for her death. No one gets to pin this on you." He reached over and squeezed Sawyer's hand before removing his seat belt. "Do your magic breathing, square your shoulders, and plaster a neutral expression on your face. Don't give the press the satisfaction of making a story off morose posture or grim countenance. Make them work for it."

Sawyer nodded because he knew Royce was right. He followed Royce's advice before reaching for the door. The throng of people surged in his direction when they stepped out of the SUV. This wasn't his first time walking through a gauntlet of reporters, and it wouldn't be the last. He politely responded to their inquiries about the victim and the circumstances of her death, but his "No comments at this time" didn't go over well.

"Do you feel responsible?" a male reporter asked when they ducked under the tape.

"Just keep moving forward," Royce said softly.

They signed into the crime scene in the hotel's grand foyer and donned their protective gear away from the press's prying eyes. Commissioner Rigby headed their way as soon as she saw them. She wore her police uniform and had pulled her hair into a severe bun. The severity of the situation was etched on her face.

"Commissioner," Sawyer said solemnly.

She nodded at them both. "I don't have to tell you what kind of nightmare we're experiencing."

"Yeah, we just walked through it," Royce said.

"Mendoza is waiting for you upstairs," she said and provided the room number.

The lobby was old-world opulence meets modern art. Their footsteps echoing off the polished floor sounded like an ominous soundtrack to the misery squeezing Sawyer's heart. He mentally gave himself a good shake because moping didn't solve cases. Sawyer caught Royce's worried expression in the elevator's gilded reflection and briefly met his gaze.

"The bastard screwed up," Sawyer said.

Royce nodded. "And we'll make them pay."

Mendoza was waiting in the corridor outside the hotel room. Sawyer saw camera flashes every few seconds and picked up bits and pieces of communication between the medical examiner and the crime scene unit.

"The latest victim is Rachel Ann Morgan, a twenty-year-old college sophomore competing for the Magnolia Queen crown. Mrs. Morgan discovered Rachel after returning from the lounge."

"Do you think this is the original killer or a copycat?" Sawyer asked.

Mendoza pinched the bridge of his nose and exhaled sharply. "We'll chat after you've had a chance to assess the scene."

When Sawyer first entered the hotel room, he noticed the similarities to the three original murders. A young woman was killed, marked as a whore, and surrounded by magnolia blossoms. But the similarities ended there.

"This isn't the same killer," Sawyer said as he swept his gaze over the room again. "Everything is off."

He eased closer to the bed where Rachel lay naked on the carpet beside it. The nightstand had been overturned, so the hotel lamp and alarm clock had tumbled to the floor along with a laptop and a purse. The latter's contents had spilled out onto the carpet and had been stepped on and scattered during the struggle. An open tube of blood-red lipstick immediately stuck out. Sawyer diverted his gaze back to Rachel's forehead and realized *whore* had been written in lipstick, not blood. Rachel hadn't been stabbed; she'd been strangled with what appeared to be a black lace bra.

There were vicious scratches above and below the fabric from where she had tried to claw the ligature away from her neck. Sawyer noticed blood beneath her fingernails and wondered if she'd possibly scratched her assailant as she fought. Barbara, Jessica, and Amy had not struggled with their killer either because they were incapacitated somehow or caught entirely unaware. The number of magnolia petals surrounding Rachel was significantly higher than the first three victims. The handwritten "whore" wasn't as neat, didn't have a capital *w*, and was written in lipstick.

"This isn't the same killer," Sawyer stated again.

Royce, who'd been remarkably quiet, said, "Tell me why you're so confident."

Sawyer tipped his head to the corridor where Mendoza waited so he could tell them both at the same time. Royce followed him out of the hotel room and listened as Sawyer recounted his observations.

"So even the similarities are different," Royce said.

Sawyer nodded. "Very."

"Allow me to play devil's advocate," Mendoza said. "Perhaps their element of surprise failed, allowing Rachel to fight back. Maybe she knocked the knife out of the assailant's hand, and they improvised by strangling her. Or the murder seems hastier because the killer was restricted by time or fear of discovery, especially since the overturned nightstand would've been loud enough to get someone's attention. It's been more than two decades since the last murder, so maybe our perp couldn't remember if they capitalized the *w*, and handwriting worsens over time."

While Mendoza made valid points, Sawyer's gut said they were dealing with a copycat with intimate knowledge of the original murders.

"But I agree with you, Key," Mendoza said after allowing his words to sink in. "That's why I wanted Locke here. He and South will take the lead on Rachel Morgan's homicide while your team continues to work the cold cases. I want the five of you working together behind the scenes, pooling resources to find the connection between the copycat and the original killer. There has to be one."

"Yes, sir," Sawyer and Royce both said.

"The media is going to go wild with speculation and theories. I'll meet with the press to give you time to investigate, but I can't stall them forever. Be prepared to speak with them in the next forty-eight hours."

"Yes, Chief," they said.

"I want you to call Stein, Carnegie, and South to help you run interviews. Talk to every person involved in the pageant and every member of the hotel staff who worked during Rachel Ann's stay. I've already requested footage from all the security cameras, but I've been told there aren't many inside the Mansion."

"What? Why?" Royce asked.

"It would ruin the historical aesthetic," Mendoza replied dryly. "I'll let you know when I get my hands on whatever is available."

"Where's Mrs. Morgan?" Royce asked.

He rattled off a hotel room number a few floors down. "She's with some friends. Key, I'd like you to sit in during the interview on the off chance this is the same killer and they just changed their MO to throw us off."

"Yes, sir," Sawyer said.

He dismissed them with a curt nod, and they immediately reached for their phones to call in the others on the way to the elevator. They heard the grieving mother's mournful wails as soon as they stepped onto the floor. A brunette woman with bloodshot eyes and a messy bun about to lose its battle with gravity answered their knock. Since the sobbing came from somewhere deeper in the room, Sawyer knew they weren't looking at Rachel's mother.

"I'm sorry to intrude at such a terrible time," Royce said and introduced them. "May we please speak to Mrs. Morgan?"

The brunette's bottom lip trembled, and she briefly pressed slender fingers against her mouth. She lowered her hand and stepped back. "Come in."

"Can I ask your name, miss?" Royce asked.

"Charlotte Evans, but my friends call me Lettie."

"Thank you, Ms. Evans."

"Missus," she clarified.

Royce nodded and added that to his notes.

She gestured to a sitting area where a petite blonde sat between two raven-haired women. Mrs. Morgan had her head resting on one woman's shoulder and held the hand of the other. As they approached, the bereaved mother shot to her feet. Black mascara streaked her tear-soaked face, and she stared daggers at Sawyer as she advanced on him.

"You have some nerve showing your face around me. This is all your fault. None of this would've happened if you'd just left things alone. You taunted the psycho, and they killed my baby."

Sawyer felt the blow in his gut. It would've hurt him less if she'd kicked him in the balls.

"Samantha," the raven-haired women said as they rushed forward.

"She doesn't mean it," the one on the right said softly. "I'm Marissa, and this is my sister, Miranda."

Royce wrote their names down while Sawyer made introductions. Lettie joined the trio, and the four women squeezed onto the small couch. The friends all found ways to comfort Samantha Morgan through physical touch. They stroked her hair, held her hand, rubbed her back, or attempted to wipe her tears.

"We are truly sorry for your loss," Sawyer said. "The last thing we want to do is make you relive your trauma, but it's important we get as much information upfront as possible."

Samantha narrowed her eyes and pointed at him. "I won't sit idly by for twenty years while you dillydally around. I will be in your face at least once a week until you find out who killed my baby."

"I understand, ma'am. I promise you there's nothing we want more than to get justice for your family."

Miranda brushed a stray lock of hair off Samantha's face. "Honey, you can't expect him to solve cases in a week that others couldn't solve in decades."

"She's right," Lettie said, reaching over to tuck a strand of hair behind her ear. "Give them a chance, okay?"

She closed her eyes and took a shaky breath. When she met Sawyer's gaze again, some of the fire had faded. Royce took over, guiding the four ladies through their evening. Mrs. Morgan stuttered in some parts and sobbed in others, but she helped them create a rough timeline.

The four women had dinner with their daughters in the hotel restaurant, finishing just after eight. Miranda showed them the text from her credit card company to confirm the charge. The mothers had decided to unwind over drinks and commiserate over what they called "judgment day," when they'd learn if their daughters advanced to the Magnolia Queen Pageant. None of their daughters were of legal age to drink and had decided to let off steam another way. Tabitha, Marissa's daughter, and Taryn, Miranda's daughter, went to see a movie while Jasmine, Lettie's daughter, joined another group to go shopping. Rachel Ann had decided to head back to her room to study for an upcoming college exam.

"Is that typical behavior for Rachel?" Sawyer asked gently. Her laptop had been out, but Rachel might've been using it for other purposes.

Mrs. Morgan closed her eyes. "Not really, and I should've asked more questions. Do you think she planned to meet this person?"

Neither detective wanted to speculate, so Sawyer pivoted to asking about the door. "Were there any signs of forced entry? Had the door been locked or left ajar?"

"Locked," she whispered. "I had no clue something was wrong until I w-walked into the r-room and saw her on the f-floor." Another wave of grief crashed into the woman, and she swayed on the sofa.

At that point, they had to put Samantha Morgan's health before the case. Miranda promised they'd call her family doctor and stay with her, but Royce called for an EMT instead. In a matter of moments, the woman had gone from sobbing loudly to looking nearly catatonic. The paramedics suggested they take her to the ER, and Royce agreed. Lettie went with her while Miranda and Marissa gave Royce their contact information. Sawyer noticed the ladies had become increasingly curious about Royce once Samantha had left.

"I know this is terrible timing and wholly inappropriate," Miranda said, stepping closer to Royce. "But are you…" She let her words trail off while batting her eyelashes at him.

Sawyer's mind started to fill in the blank. Single? Available? Horny?

"No," Royce said firmly and met Sawyer's gaze. "Not even close."

"That's unfortunate," Miranda said.

"We'll need to speak to your daughters as soon as possible. We'd like to know what Rachel might've said privately to them about her plans. Where are they now?"

"In my room," Marissa said, then gave the number to Royce. "I'll call my daughter and let them know you're coming. I'd like to hope they wouldn't answer the door otherwise."

"Do you need us to come with you?" Miranda asked.

"Unless they're minors, we'd prefer to speak with them alone," Sawyer replied.

"They'll be less likely to speak freely with their mothers around," Royce added.

The women looked disappointed but nodded.

Marissa's phone rang, and she looked at the caller ID. "It's Bryan." She stepped into the bathroom and closed the door. Sawyer heard her voice through the wood but couldn't decipher what she was saying.

"Who's Bryan?" Royce asked.

"Rachel's father," Miranda answered. "Poor guy is in Houston on business. Samantha broke the news to him over the phone. He's probably calling back with his travel itinerary."

Royce entered another note. "Do you have his number? I'll need to speak with him."

Miranda had started thumbing through her contacts when Marissa returned from the bathroom with her cell phone extended. "Bryan would like to speak to the detective in charge."

"That's you," Sawyer said, then waited while Royce had a brief conversation with Mr. Morgan and exchanged contact information.

Afterward, they said goodbye to Marissa and Miranda and stepped into the hallway. Sawyer's phone buzzed, and he read the text from Topher.

"The gang's all here," he told Royce.

"Tell them we're on our way down."

Sawyer tapped out a quick message and put his phone away. He wished the hotel's concern for their historical aesthetic extended to the elevator because he'd love nothing more than to lean into Royce.

Their conversation with Topher, Holly, and Tara was brief. Royce brought them up to speed and asked them to start interviewing hotel employees. Royce and Sawyer were going to speak to Rachel's three friends before joining them. After the staff, they'd start working their way through the beauty pageant contestants and organization members still at the hotel. They'd span out to interview anyone who'd already left before Mrs. Morgan found Rachel.

When Jasmine answered their knock, she looked so much like Charlotte that Sawyer experienced a moment of déjà vu. Tabitha and Taryn were their mothers' doppelgangers right down to Taryn's immediate fascination with Sawyer's man, but he couldn't blame them.

He and Royce had discussed a strategy on the way up and decided to interview the ladies together to make them more comfortable. The women's accounts matched what their mothers had said. Tabitha and Taryn produced movie ticket stubs. Jasmine explained she'd only been window shopping, which is why she'd gotten bored and came back to the hotel before them.

"Uber?" Royce asked.

She shook her head. "City bus."

"Someone's daddy took her credit card away for blowing her budget last month," Taryn said, then smiled at her friend. "But those Jimmy Choo stilettos were worth it."

"Are we suspects?" Tabitha asked tearfully.

"No, ma'am. We're just creating a timeline, and receipts are constructive."

Tabitha sighed. "Oh, good."

"Did you find it odd Rachel went back to her room to study?" Sawyer asked.

The three girls looked at each other before emphatically affirming Rachel's behavior was atypical.

"Rachel was in school to get a good husband," Taryn said.

"Tare!" Tabitha said.

"It's true, Tabby, and you know it."

Jasmine nodded. "It is true."

"Was she dating anyone?" Royce asked.

"Not since she and Benji broke up about seven months ago," Tabitha replied.

"Benji?" Royce asked.

Jasmine stiffened and whirled on her friend. "Don't drag him into this, Tabby," she said. "He's a total sweetie and would never harm a hair on her head. Besides, he's over their breakup."

"Then he shouldn't mind talking to the police," Tabby fired back. She returned her attention to Royce. "His name is Benjamin McKay."

He looked at Taryn who hadn't answered his question. She was looking at her lap instead of following the conversation. "Taryn, do you know something that could help me?"

"Maybe," she said softly.

"Really?" Tabitha asked.

"You've been holding out on us?" Jasmine accused.

"Tell us anything you know," Royce told Taryn, who worried her bottom lip through her teeth.

Sawyer could almost hear her gears grinding as she wrestled with her conscience. "I know it might feel like a betrayal to talk about your friend's personal life, but you might help us catch her killer. Isn't that more important right now?"

Taryn straightened her posture and nodded. "What do you want to know?"

"Everything," Royce replied. "No detail is too small right now."

"She's been chatting with some guy online. He's older and his name is Jake."

"How much older?" Royce and Sawyer both asked.

"He's thirty or thirty-five, I think," Taryn replied.

"Whoa," Tabitha whispered. "That old?"

"Ouch," Royce teased.

Tabitha blushed. "Sorry."

"No worries," he replied. "I would've thought thirty or thirty-five was old at your age too."

"How old are you?" Taryn asked Royce.

"Old enough to know better," he quipped.

"That's unfortunate," Taryn said, sounding like her mother.

Royce steered her back to the guy Rachel was chatting with online, but they learned very little. Rachel hadn't shared any other details about him.

"I caught her sneaking off with her phone between prelim rounds and called her out on it," Taryn said. "I reminded Rach the crown was hers for the taking if she didn't get distracted and blow it."

Sawyer quirked a brow. "What do you mean the crown was hers for the taking? The pageant isn't for two more months."

Tabitha aimed a pitying glance at him. "The winner is rarely a surprise, Sergeant. We've known since we started pageants as little girls the crown was Rachel's destiny."

"She was Miss America material," Taryn added.

"Maybe even Miss Universe," Jasmine said. Her face crumpled, and she began to cry. "I can't believe she's gone."

The other two girls started crying too, then they took a few minutes to comfort each other. The interview resumed when everyone had settled down. Sawyer and Royce directed Taryn's focus to Rachel's reaction when she approached her.

"She got bitchy about it and told me to mind my own business," Taryn said. "It hurt my feelings, and she apologized. Rachel told me winning the crown wasn't as important as it used to be. She admitted she'd met a wonderful man and dreamed of building a future with him. She specifically said if everything went according to plan, she'd be dropping out of school and picking out a wedding dress soon. She told me her parents wouldn't approve because Jake was in his thirties."

"Whoa," Tabitha said. "You should've gone straight to Samantha with this information."

Taryn's eyes widened. "Is this my fault?"

"No," Royce said quickly. "There's no way you could've known. We don't even know if the guy she's been chatting with is the person who killed her. Did you get a glimpse of a profile picture or anything?"

Taryn sniffled and dabbed at her eyes with a tissue Jasmine handed her. "No. Rachel moved her phone away before I could see much." She stiffened suddenly and gasped. "Oh god. I did see a message."

"Go ahead," Royce prompted.

"It said 'tonight' followed by a question mark. But that could mean anything, right?"

"This is great information, Taryn," Royce told her. "Can you remember who sent it?"

"It was in a blue bubble, so Rachel sent it."

Rachel had either invited her boyfriend to the room or confirmed a suggestion he'd made.

"Thank you," Royce told her.

They continued the interview but called it off when the girls ran out of important things to say and started rolling out phrases like "She had a smile that could light up a room" and "She loved life."

Once outside in the hall, Royce said, "They sound like they're rehearsing for their interviews with Keith Morrison."

"This is the kind of case that draws *Dateline* to a city," Sawyer replied.

They rode the elevator down to the first floor and caught up with Topher, Holly, and Tara.

"We've interviewed the front desk staff, housekeeping, and management," Tara told them. "We're down to kitchen staff, butler service, and maintenance."

"Nice work," Royce said.

Sawyer and Royce jumped into the fray. Sawyer started with the kitchen staff while Royce spoke with the maintenance crew. Jubilee, the kitchen supervisor, told Sawyer someone in Rachel's room had placed an order for strawberries and an assortment of desserts.

"What time?" Sawyer asked.

Jubilee checked the computer. "The order came in at eight twelve."

Long enough for Rachel to return to her room and confirm plans with her online friend? "What time was the order delivered?"

Again, Jubilee referred to the screen. "The butler arrived at the room at eight fifty-one. The guest didn't answer the knock. The front desk called the room, but no answer."

"What's the protocol?"

"It's assumed the guest fell asleep or left the room, so the order comes back to the kitchen. We can't serve it to another guest, so the staff eats the food, or it gets tossed."

"I'd like to speak to the butler who delivered the food."

"Ian," Jubilee called out. "The sergeant would like a word with you."

A twentysomething kid with curly brown hair and piercing green eyes stood up and crossed the room. His hotel's butler uniform was a three-piece black suit, white gloves, and shoes so shiny Sawyer could check his reflection in them. Sawyer introduced himself and shook Ian's hand when the kid presented it. He caught Royce's eye and gestured for him to join the conversation.

"Do you still need me?" Jubilee asked.

"Hang out here for just a minute," Sawyer replied, then repeated what he'd just learned from Jubilee.

Royce introduced himself to Ian and the two men shook hands.

"How can I help?" Ian asked.

They went through the timeline with him, and he verified what the computer said. He hadn't heard any noises coming from the room, and he hadn't seen or heard anything out of the ordinary before or after when he'd made other deliveries.

"It's been a zoo around here," Ian said. "I've made more room service deliveries today than all of last week combined."

"It's true," Jubilee confirmed.

Sawyer asked for a printout of all the orders between seven thirty and nine, and she gladly obliged.

"Thanks," he said to Jubilee and Ian. He gathered their information and moved on.

Royce gripped his bicep and pulled him off to the side. He stepped in close to have a private conversation. Notes of sandalwood, amber, and vanilla tickled Sawyer's senses, and he resisted the urge to bury his nose in Royce's neck.

"Don't look at me like that," Royce whispered.

"How am I looking at you?"

"Like I'm all you could ever want."

Sawyer winked. "Where's the lie?"

Royce chuckled and said, "So it's likely Rachel was killed sometime between eight twelve and eight fifty-one."

"Unless she was in the shower and didn't hear Ian at the door or the phone ringing."

Sawyer nodded. "It's possible, especially if she performs solo concerts every time she steps beneath the spray like some people I know."

"You're welcome for the free entertainment," Royce replied. "The front desk didn't receive any loud noise complaints, but I noticed the carpet is thicker than you typically find in hotels. The dense fibers might've muffled the sound."

"Plus, this place is hopping with young ladies and their families," Sawyer said. "I'm thinking slamming doors and excess chatter in the corridors make people less observant over time because they tend to tune it out. A gunshot would've stood out, but the overturned nightstand might've sounded like a distant door slamming."

"I want to speak to anyone staying above, below, or beside her room. Just because they didn't complain doesn't mean they didn't hear anything."

Sawyer and Royce split up again to work the interviews more efficiently but didn't uncover any new facts to confirm or contradict the timeline they'd built.

The five detectives briefly met once they released the kitchen and maintenance staff back to their duties.

"The front desk manager gave me a list of guests registered as part of the pageant," Tara said. She pulled the printout from her portfolio and handed it to Royce, who let out a whistle.

"That's more people than I was expecting," he said.

"There are seventy-five ladies registered for this preliminary round. The rest are hairstylists, makeup artists, judges, organization members, and pageant coaches."

"Pageant coaches?" Tara asked.

"It's a huge business," Topher said.

Sawyer blew out a breath. "This is going to be a very long night."

Royce rested his hand on Sawyer's shoulder. "Let's divide and conquer, people."

The five of them wrapped up the last interviews at eight the following morning. The press was still in full force outside the hotel, and they came to life when the detectives stepped outside. Whatever Mendoza had said to the media hadn't satisfied them.

Sawyer remembered Royce's advice and ignored the questions they shouted at him. They'd almost reached their SUV when Sawyer saw a familiar face on the periphery of the barricade.

"Hey," he said to Royce. "I see someone I need to talk to. Give me a minute."

The crowd of reporters started heading in Sawyer's direction the moment he veered away from Royce.

"Fuck," he growled.

Catching Burke's eyes, he gave a subtle nod to the SUV Royce climbed into. Burke nodded and they both headed in that direction.

Burke and Sawyer made it to the SUV about the same time and quickly got inside before the voracious reporters blocked them in. Sawyer made hasty introductions as Royce put the SUV in gear and got them the hell out of there.

"Good to meet you," Burke told Royce.

"Likewise, though I wish it were under different circumstances," Royce said.

"Is it the same guy?" Burke asked. His voice was strained, and he looked like he'd been up all night.

"We're pretty sure it's a copycat," Sawyer replied.

"One with details never shared with the press," Royce added.

Sawyer turned in his seat to face the older man. "I hate to ask—"

"Tell me how I can help," Burke said.

"Would you be willing to review the new crime scene photos and give us your opinion?"

The retired detective swallowed hard. "If you think it will be helpful."

Sawyer told Burke he'd be in touch once he had the official photos, and Royce dropped him off at his Ranger.

They rode in silence for a few blocks before Sawyer said, "No one is going to believe Rachel is a victim of a copycat killer."

"They will when we solve both cases," Royce said.

He sounded so confident and convincing. "I nominate you to speak at the press conferences."

Royce glanced over with a wicked smile. "We could always wager on it like we did with writing incident reports."

Sawyer laughed. "You're always thinking about your dick."

"Almost as much as you do," Royce countered.

Sawyer searched his tired brain for a counterargument, but why bother lying? "Busted."

Chapter
FOURTEEN

"IT'S BEEN A MINUTE SINCE I'VE HAD TO SIT WITH A GRIEVING family immediately after losing their child," Tara said once they left the Morgans' house late Sunday morning. Royce had sent the rest of the team home to rest as they waited for Bryan Morgan to arrive back in Savannah. "That was brutal."

"It was," Royce agreed. He'd never get used to that part of the job, and he wouldn't lie to Tara and tell her it got better. It fucking didn't.

The Morgans were as different as night and day. Bryan was tall and muscular to Samantha's petite and dainty. He was swarthy and dark to her peaches and cream. He seemed to dwarf her as they sat together on a loveseat. The only similarities were the matching expressions of shock and misery evident in their facial expressions and body language. Red, swollen eyes had stared at Royce and Tara, silently pleading with them to do or say something that would wake them up from their nightmare.

Tara heaved a deep sigh, and Royce glanced over at the passenger seat. It felt strange to be working a case with someone other than Sawyer. Royce sometimes partnered with the marshals' fugitive task force without Sawyer, but it was rare to find one of them without the other. Three years wasn't a long time in the grand scheme of things, but Sawyer Key had burrowed himself so profoundly into Royce's soul that he was confident his boyfriend had permanently altered his genetic makeup. Sawyer had wrapped himself around Royce's DNA strands as easily as he had his heart. Royce had blond hair, gray eyes, and now came complete with a six-foot Adonis who loved him more than life itself. And Royce was more than okay with his altered genetics. Sawyer made him a better man.

But Tara looked anything but fine, so Royce said the first thing he could think of to distract her. "Was it as brutal as me having to watch you seduce my best friend with smoldering glances?"

Tara snorted. "*Smoldering glances.*"

"Going to put that on your dating site bio?" Royce teased. He could tell Tara was staring at him, but he didn't meet her gaze until he stopped at a red light. "What?"

Tara's right brow arched, and her mouth quirked into a smirk. "You think I'm some player, huh?"

Royce offered an easy smile before returning his attention to the traffic light. "No, I don't, but you have a lady-killer reputation. I think still waters run deep, and there's a lot I don't know about you."

Tara chuckled. "It really kept our unit on their toes, yeah? They were hiding their wives from both of us."

Royce laughed too. "Have you met Ashcroft's wife yet?"

"Nope," Tara replied. "You?"

"Yeah. He introduced us once I came out," Royce said.

The memory of kissing Sawyer in front of their unit at Joe's still heated his blood and made him smile. They'd been there to celebrate Royce's promotion to sergeant, and he hadn't liked the way Diego Fuentes, who'd been a patrolman at the time, kept flirting with his man. The kiss had started out as a chest-thumping gesture but had become so much more.

Sawyer hadn't pressured Royce to come out, but he'd existed in the shadows long enough, always living vicariously through others. Sawyer made Royce want more out of life than just existing, so that press of lips in a crowded bar had been his phoenix rising. And for three years, what they'd had together was enough. Royce had known Sawyer was ready for matrimony and babies, but he hadn't pushed. Not even when invitations to weddings and baby showers for their friends arrived in the mail. Sawyer just patiently waited until Royce was ready.

And like the ginormous turkeys Evangeline roasted for Thanksgiving, Royce's internal thermometer had popped, yet he continued baking in his fears of inadequacy. If he weren't careful, he'd end up like the husk of a turkey on *National Lampoon's Christmas Vacation*, the only Christmas movie worth watching besides *Die Hard* and *Lethal Weapon*.

A horn honked behind them, yanking him out of his reverie. He hit the gas and drove through the intersection, wondering how long he'd sat through the green light. The bigger question was why Tara hadn't spoken up. He glanced over and saw she was gazing out the window. Maybe she was caught up in a quagmire of her own making.

His new partner took a deep breath and seemed to shake herself loose from her thoughts. "So, what's Ashcroft's wife like?"

"She's sweet as pie and really cute." Much like Candy, but Royce kept that remark to himself.

Tara laughed. "You're so damn transparent sometimes, Ro."

"I am?" he asked. *Was he?*

"Yeah," Tara replied. "Did I screw up on Saturday night? I don't want things to be awkward between us. No dancing around subjects and being weird. I don't dance, and if I did, you wouldn't be the partner I'd choose. No offense."

Royce hadn't thought of himself as a dancer either until he'd turned lazy circles with Sawyer in the kitchen while cooking dinner, their bodies and mouths fused. Just once was all it had taken before Royce had found a new addiction. Maybe Tara hadn't met the right person yet, or perhaps she had and was fighting her instincts as he'd done with Sawyer. Either way, it wasn't his business.

"None taken," Royce said. "And, no, things aren't going to be awkward between us. I'm not going to demand to know your intentions toward Candy." He glanced over and saw a lecherous smile tugging at the corner of Tara's lips. Royce stifled a chuckle and continued. "You're both consenting adults, and I know you wouldn't do anything to hurt her or the kids."

"I wouldn't."

"I'm a good listener," he said. "And objective if you don't mind me bragging a little on myself." Tara chuckled, so he pressed on. "I think the two of us are a lot alike in many ways."

"Besides the bogus lady-killer reputations?" she asked, confirming what Royce had already suspected.

He glanced over and saw the panic in her light eyes. He recognized the expression well. It was moments like these that Royce believed there was no coincidence, and people really did come into his life at precisely the right moment. "Yeah."

"I'll keep your offer in mind. Thanks."

They spent the rest of the drive to Benji McKay's home in companionable silence.

Tara let out a whistle when Royce pulled into the driveway and stopped at an ornate wrought iron gate. They could see only a glimpse of the massive white brick manor at the end of a long, tree-lined drive. "I hope they string lights around these trees for Christmas," Tara said.

Royce glanced over at her before pushing the intercom button. He'd never have pegged Tara as a Christmas lover.

She shrugged her shoulders and said, "The lights cheer me up. Our job sucks, man. Let me find joy where I can."

Royce held up his hands in surrender. "Not judging you." Then he pushed the button and identified himself to the person answering the page. Moments later, the gates opened, and he drove through. "This would be magic with lights," he admitted.

The winding driveway circled in front of the house. Royce parked under the portico, and the two of them made their way toward the front door, which opened before they could ring the doorbell.

A woman with dark red hair, porcelain skin, and sad blue eyes greeted them. She wore a burgundy suit with a cream silk blouse beneath the jacket. Her hair was pulled back at the nape, showing a triple strand of pearls around her neck that matched her dangling earrings.

"Please come in," she said, stepping aside and gesturing for them to enter. The entryway was a grand, opulent space with white-and-gray marble floors leading deeper into the home. On both sides of the corridor, ornate staircases led to the second floor.

"I'm Benjamin's mother, Maggie McKay."

Royce made introductions, and Maggie firmly shook their hands before leading them to a sitting room just beyond the double staircase. An older man wearing a dark suit and a grim expression stood up. Royce thought he might be the family attorney until he introduced himself as Harris McKay. Royce knew he couldn't go by looks to determine someone's age, but he appeared at least twenty-five years older than Maggie, not that it mattered.

Harris gestured to a young man with a lighter shade of red hair than his mother. He wore a pale green dress shirt, black pants, and a pair of black Chucks. "This is our son, Benjamin."

The young man lifted his head and met Royce's gaze. His dark green eyes were red and swollen, and he wore an expression Royce could only describe as numb.

"Stand up and shake the detectives' hands," Harris said tersely.

His son flinched and shot to his feet. "Sorry," he said to Royce.

"It's okay," Royce said. "You've had quite a shock. I'm very sorry for your loss."

His eyes widened like maybe it was the first time anyone had acknowledged his pain. "Thank you."

"Won't you sit down, detectives," Maggie said. "Would you like some coffee or tea?"

Royce and Tara sat across from Benji and declined a beverage.

"We won't keep you long," Royce said. "I can't tell if you just arrived home or were preparing to leave." They might have dressed up every day, but he doubted it.

"We just got back from church," Maggie said as she crossed her legs and rested her hands on her kneecap. "They dedicated the service to sweet Rachel. I hope Bryan and Samantha could feel the outpouring of love we sent them."

Recalling their grieving expressions, Royce doubted it but said, "I'm sure it's appreciated." He homed in on Benjamin, who plucked at the folds of fabric at his knees.

"Stop fidgeting," Harris said. "And make eye contact before they think you're trying to hide something."

"Honey," Maggie said softly. "Go easy. He's had a terrible shock."

"I'm just looking out for our son," Harris replied. "Everyone knows the boyfriend or ex-boyfriend is the first place the police look when a woman gets killed." Royce wanted to point out that not all women date men, but he let the remark go.

"We're talking to all of Rachel's friends today," Royce said, hoping to ease the sudden tension in the room. "You are someone who knew Rachel better than most, so I will have a different set of questions to ask you. I apologize if you feel they're too personal."

Benji raised his head to meet Royce's gaze, then nodded. "I understand."

Royce started with easy questions, taking him through how long he'd known Rachel and how long they had dated. Was their breakup amicable?

"Should we have a lawyer present?" Harris asked before Benji could answer.

"That's entirely up to you, sir," Royce said. "We can reschedule this interview for another time at the station if you would prefer to wait. I just thought your son would be more comfortable in his own home."

"Here is fine," Benji said. "I don't have anything to hide, Dad. Just let me do this."

Harris studied his son for a few moments before gesturing for them to continue.

"Amicable means on friendly terms, right?" Benji asked him. When Royce nodded, Benji continued. "I wouldn't say we ended on a high note, but it wasn't as dramatic as some of our high school breakups."

"Define dramatic," Tara said.

"So you can blame my son for Rachel's murder?" Harris asked.

"No, sir," Tara replied firmly, "because learning everything we can about Rachel will help us solve her case. We need people to be honest with us about the kind of person she was."

Maggie sighed. "People do tend to overlook peccadillos after someone passes."

"Um," Benji said, running his hand through his hair. "Rachel slashed my tires the first time we broke up. She thought I was cheating on her with her enemy, Rebecca Howard."

Royce jotted the name down. No one had mentioned her name to them yet.

"Talk about someone with a motive for murder," Maggie said. "Rachel was awful to the poor girl." Benji's mom shook her head. "She can't be the killer, though, because she's at Harvard."

Royce jotted the information down, then prompted Benji to keep talking about his history with Rachel. He stumbled and teared up a few times, and Royce had to admit his sorrow appeared genuine. The interview moved along smoothly until they got to the part where Royce needed Benji to account for his time on Saturday night.

"Here we go," Harris said.

"Hush," Maggie told him.

Benji ran him through his entire day. He'd had physical therapy for his knee early in the morning. He'd blown it out during a college basketball game, and the injury had required surgery and months of physical therapy.

"I'd graduated to a smaller knee brace and was finally cleared to drive again," Benji said. His somber expression eased, but the reprieve didn't last. He closed his eyes and took a deep breath.

"The doctor also said he might never play basketball competitively again," Maggie said softly.

Benji stiffened and forced his eyes open. "I call bullshit."

"Son," Harris said. "Save your crude language for your townie friends."

Benji pursed his lips and nodded. "I was in a bad place after I got home. I went upstairs and took a nap. I woke up and ate dinner with my parents. I couldn't shake the funk and decided to go out for my first solo drive in months. I headed to the mall for some retail therapy. I bought these Chucks and ate some mall pretzels."

"About what time?" Royce asked.

Benji fished receipts from his wallet and handed them to Royce. The timestamp for the shoes was seven fifty, and he purchased the pretzels at eight.

"You can have those," Harris said. "We have copies."

"Okay, thanks." Royce tucked them inside his portfolio and continued. "What did you do after you ate pretzels?"

"I jetted when kids from high school showed up at the food court. I wasn't in the mood to talk about my knee or receive pitying glances. I sure as hell hadn't been in the mood to run into Rachel."

"So you came straight home?" Tara asked.

"No, ma'am. I just drove around. I rolled the windows down and tried to clear my head. I got home sometime after ten."

He'd just driven around aimlessly for two hours? Not impossible but highly unlikely. Benji claimed not to have stopped anywhere and didn't have any other receipts to help corroborate his story, which meant he didn't have a solid alibi for when Rachel died.

Royce and Tara wrapped up the interview, expressed their condolences again, and thanked them for their time. Once back in the car, Tara yawned big enough to crack her jaw, triggering Royce to do the same.

"Stop that," Royce said after trading another round of yawns. "We've been at it for twelve hours, so why don't we both try to catch a power nap and meet back at the station tonight. Mendoza said we should have security footage soon."

"Sounds good to me. Six?" Tara asked.

Royce checked his watch and figured it would give them four or five hours of sleep and a chance to eat. "Works for me."

Royce dropped her off at the precinct, then dialed Sawyer, who answered on the second ring.

"Hey, baby."

Just hearing his voice breathed new life into Royce. Bustling conversation in the background reminded Royce he should be at Evangeline and Barron's for Sunday brunch.

"Hi," Royce said.

A chair scraped against the floor, and the background noise got quieter as Sawyer stepped out of the room. Royce pictured Sawyer leaving the gathering to have a private conversation with him. His brow would be furrowed, and his warm brown eyes would shimmer with worry and love. Royce ached for that. He could eat Evangeline's yummy food, soak up Sawyer's love like a greedy sponge, and still have time to nap. "I'm heading over for a little bit."

"As much as I want to see you, I'd prefer you go home and sleep. I'll bring food home for you."

"Tired of me already, huh?"

"You know damn well that's not true," Sawyer replied. "More like I can't be trusted to keep my hands to myself when sleep is what you need most."

"You know what helps me sleep really well?"

Sawyer's warm chuckle washed over him, making Royce shiver. Sleep suddenly seemed like the last thing he needed.

"I'm hanging up now. Go home and get some rest," Sawyer chided.

"I love you, asshole."

"Love you most, dickhead."

Bones gave him hell the moment he stepped through the door, really laying his abandonment woes on thick in hopes the guilt would make Royce reach for the treats. It nearly worked, but instead of going for the snacks, Royce picked up the mammoth cat and cradled him in his arms.

"I missed you too, Bonesy."

His feisty feline continued his vocal displeasure until Royce set him down on the bed.

"Shower. Nap. Then some extra treats."

Bones's growl reminded Royce of a grumpy old man, and he spent his time in the shower wondering if cats aged like dogs. He'd heard people refer to age in dog years but never cat years.

"That's because cats have multiple lives. And now I've reached the level of exhaustion where I not only think the most random things, I speak them out loud to myself."

Meow.

Royce shut off the faucet and slid the frosted shower door open to see Bones watching him from the vanity. Steam rolled out of the enclosed shower, and cool air stirred goose bumps all over his body. Sawyer always snatched a towel right away and began drying off, but Royce found the chill exhilarating like the tingle from a peppermint patty.

Meow.

Royce snagged the towel and began rubbing it over his chest. "Fine, I speak my random thoughts out loud to you too, but I don't think that's an improvement."

Bones jumped down off the vanity and ran into the bedroom where Royce found him stretched out once he'd finished drying off. He pulled on his favorite pair of sweats, then climbed between the sheets. Bones settled on his chest and gave him a no-nonsense stare. Royce scratched behind the cat's ears and rubbed his chin, earning rumbling purrs in reward. The weight and heat of the cat combined with the vibrations lulled Royce to sleep right away.

Unfortunately, his wired brain wouldn't allow him to slumber long. He woke up alone in an eerily quiet house. Royce didn't need to search their home to know Sawyer hadn't returned yet. He'd hoped to spend some quality time together before returning to the precinct, but he wouldn't ask Sawyer to come home just to be left alone again. Royce had no idea how long he'd be at the station reviewing security camera footage.

Royce threw back the covers, got dressed, and made a quick bite to eat. As promised, he slipped Bones a few treats before leaving. He should've been surprised to find Tara already at the precinct, but he wasn't. She was sitting at her computer scrolling through Facebook. A glance at the screen confirmed she was looking through Rachel Morgan's social media accounts.

"Did you get any sleep?" Royce asked.

"Probably as much as you," she replied. "The security footage hasn't arrived yet, so I put another call into the manager. She promised it will be here soon." Tara sighed heavily, and Royce glanced over in time to catch her shaking her head. "Do these kids not know these social media sites have settings to make their profiles a little more private? Any random stranger can read their every thought and track their movements."

Royce chuckled and dragged his chair over to Tara's desk. "I think, to them, that's the point. Learn anything useful?"

Tara paused her scrolling and consulted her notes. "Let's see. Of her four thousand, six hundred, and twenty-nine friends, she"—Tara made air quotes—"*knows* twenty-five guys named Jake. I've scrolled back a year and can't find a public interaction with any of them." She looked at Royce. "I hope you don't think I overstepped, but I reached out to the Law Enforcement Reaction Teams for all the major sites and requested access to Rachel's private messages, likes, comments, and even group activity. They might balk and insist on a warrant, or they might help us out without one."

"You didn't overstep. Thanks for acting on your hunch."

Tara huffed a sigh. "It will be an arduous task because this girl was on social media dozens of times a day."

"What have you learned from Rachel's posts?" he asked.

"The tone has changed a lot since her breakup with Benji. There were a lot of memes about betrayal and backstabbers, but those shifted to girl-power anthems about forging your own path and fighting for what you deserve. A few months ago, the tone shifted again to something softer. She started talking about fate and people coming to you when you need them most." A sentiment Royce had grown fond of since falling in love with Sawyer. "Her last post expressed gratitude to her creator for life's unplanned miracles."

"Unplanned miracles?" Royce asked. "Was she pregnant?"

"That wasn't the impression I got from the post, but you weren't the only one who wondered about a hidden message. Several people asked if she was pregnant. She emphatically denied it in the comment section, but we'll know for sure when we get the ME's report." Tara found the post and turned her monitor so Royce could read the comments for himself.

Royce leaned back in his chair once he finished. "What do you think she means by an unplanned miracle?"

"I think her posts depict a young woman who had her heart broken, someone who was determined to be resilient and not get hurt again, and someone who was completely smitten with a person she never saw coming." Tara turned and met his gaze. "And I think they killed her."

"We need to learn everything we can about this Jake," Royce said.

They shifted to Benji's social media accounts next. If you trusted his posts, the guy wasn't harboring any ill will toward Rachel. He liked and commented on many of her posts. When Rachel posted about her nervousness over the preliminary rounds, he remarked she was born to wear the crown, encouraging her to smile and be herself. Then there were the photos and location updates of Benji hanging out with two dozen girls since their breakup. He'd shared updates about his injury and pictures of his biggest supporters keeping him company while he recuperated.

Royce's eyes zeroed in on a recent collage Benji had posted. Up at the top right corner was a photo of Benji with his arm around Rachel's friend, Jasmine. Benji was smiling at the photographer while Jasmine was looking at Rachel's ex the same way Royce gazed at Sawyer. The reason for her robust defense of Benji became crystal clear.

"This is one of Rachel's best friends," Royce said, pointing to the photo.

Tara snorted. "I recognize her from Rachel's timeline. I'm not sure I'd consider them best friends. Their relationship is the textbook definition of passive-aggressive and toxic as hell."

"Interesting," Royce said. "I'll have to deep dive into Jasmine's social media after finishing with Benji's. How likely do you think the LERTs would be to give us copies of Benji's and Jasmine's social media activity?"

"Probably not without a warrant," Tara replied. "Rachel was the victim of a violent crime, so I expect them to step up and offer support. They've been known to flag accounts and notify authorities if someone logs in to a victim's profile after they died. There's a lot they can do behind the scenes to help us but not without probable cause."

"Like retrieving deleted messages?" Royce said.

"Yeah, but with Benji and Jasmine, I think they'd require more than just our hunches."

Royce nodded. "Fair enough."

They searched social media accounts for a few hours, printing off anything they felt might be crucial to their investigation. They even cross-referenced Benji's location updates with Jasmine's to see if they could find any patterns. Royce found at least a dozen instances in the past month where the two of them were in the same place simultaneously, even though they didn't appear in one another's photos. It didn't take a super sleuth to figure out the two of them were spending a lot of time together.

Royce hit the print command once more, then stood to stretch his spine. He spotted Sawyer walking toward the bullpen with a large paper bag. Damn, he was a sight for Royce's sore eyes, even wearing his stupid Duke University sweatshirt. Sawyer smiled when their gazes collided, making Royce forget all about the printout and his aching back.

"You want me to head out for a bit?" Tara asked.

"Hell no," Royce said. "Judging by the size of that bag, he's brought enough food for both of us. If we're fortunate, it'll be leftovers from Evangeline's brunch."

Sawyer was still smiling when he pushed open the door and stepped inside. Royce met him in the middle of the room and kissed him hard.

"Are you sure I shouldn't leave?" Tara asked.

"Yes," they said.

Sawyer hoisted the bag higher. "I come bearing gifts from Evangeline's." He set the bounty on his old desk and began unpacking containers. "I have French toast casserole, a potato dish that's to die for, spiral sliced ham, biscuits, and red-eye gravy." Royce moaned his appreciation, and Sawyer paused his unpacking to kiss him. "There's some fruit, yogurt, and granola too."

"Oh, man," Tara said. "I could kiss you too."

Royce growled like a junkyard dog while Sawyer laughed.

"Take it back before he pees on my leg," Sawyer said.

When Royce had been insecure about his role in Sawyer's life, he'd gotten jealous whenever someone flirted with Sawyer, either real or imagined.

Tara shuddered hard. "Gross. I take it back." Instead, she held out her fist for Sawyer to bump.

Royce's phone pinged with an email alert. "The security footage has arrived," he said, suddenly forgetting all about the food.

Reading his thoughts, Sawyer snagged the phone out of his hand. "Go get plates and silverware from the kitchen. I'll cue up the footage and start on it while you and Tara take a break and eat."

"I'll go get the plates and cutlery," Tara said. "You two can make kissy faces at each other."

"I'm going to do more than make faces," Royce boasted.

Tara just waved as she exited the bullpen.

Royce snagged Sawyer close. "I miss you."

"I miss you too. Maybe between the three of us, we can work through the footage so you can get home at a decent time." Sawyer swept his thumb under Royce's eye. "Did you sleep at all?"

"A little." There was no point in lying. He figured he was starting to look like the walking dead by this point, but his man still leaned in for another kiss.

Tara returned before they could deepen the embrace, but the smell of leftover brunch eased his frustrations a little.

Royce filled his plate as if it were his last meal while Sawyer accessed Royce's email and uploaded the security footage. Royce sat with Tara, and they both dug into the food while discussing the few things they'd found.

"Uh, guys," Sawyer said. "I think I found something."

Royce and Tara stood up and walked over to him.

"Already?" Royce asked.

Sawyer pointed to the computer where he'd paused the video on a couple approaching the side entrance to the Mansion. Royce smiled when he recognized the pair.

"Isn't that Jasmine?" Sawyer asked. "She said she rode the bus back to the hotel."

"Yes, it is," Royce said. "And that's Benji." Parked near the door was the black Corvette Royce had seen in several of his social media posts.

Sawyer smirked. "The ex-boyfriend Jasmine defended."

"Yep." Royce checked the timestamp. "They arrived at eight twenty."

Tara sucked in a breath. "Guess we know where Benji McKay went after leaving the mall."

The Mansion had cameras on the public entrances and exits, the lobby, the elevators, and emergency stairs but not in the corridors, public gathering places, service areas, or private rooms. Sawyer switched over to the footage for the elevator closest to the recorded entrance. They watched in uncomfortable silence as the young couple groped each other during the ride to Jasmine's floor.

"But what time did he leave again?" Royce asked.

Sawyer went back to the elevator feed and scanned forward until the two arrived on the scene after getting the call from Mendoza. He tried the other elevators but didn't find Benji on any of them. They checked the emergency stairwell, but he didn't appear there either.

Sawyer returned to the camera feed trained on the parking lot where Benji had left his Corvette. At nine fifty, Benji casually strolled to his vehicle from the opposite direction.

"He's not acting like he recently strangled his ex-girlfriend," Royce said.

"But where'd he come from?" Tara asked.

Royce rubbed his chin while he thought it over. "Must've used the service elevator or stairs that allow the staff to move around unseen. The Mansion doesn't have security cameras there or aimed at the employee entrances in the back of the building."

"I wonder what time he left Jasmine's room?" Sawyer asked.

Royce stared at the still frame of Benji climbing into his Corvette alone. "You can bet I'll find out."

Chapter
FIFTEEN

THE FORTY-EIGHT-HOUR MEDIA REPRIEVE MENDOZA HAD GIVEN them was up. Fortunately, the chief showed Royce and Sawyer mercy and volunteered to face the firing squad from the podium. They had a debriefing scheduled in a few hours, allowing Royce to speak privately with Bryan and Samantha Morgan about what he'd learned so far. He glanced down at his watch and realized he only had thirty minutes before the Morgans were due to arrive at the station. Royce checked his appearance in the locker room mirror and almost didn't recognize the haggard man staring back at him.

His stubbled jaw, wild hair, and puffy eyes wouldn't instill confidence in the Morgans—or the public—that Royce could solve this case. He needed to mask the effects of no sleep and too much caffeine. And not nearly enough intimacy with Sawyer. These cases had consumed them, and what little time they had carved out together was spent sleeping. Royce hadn't been home since his catnap the previous day. He'd intended to leave after they finished combing through the hotel security footage. Royce had sent Sawyer home, promising to follow after updating his notes, but Rachel's social media records arrived in Tara's inbox. A quick scan had revealed a bigger problem than they had realized, and he and Tara hunkered down and dug in.

And now, Royce was in desperate need of Sawyer, food, a nap, and a shower. The latter was the only thing he could muster before meeting the Morgans.

Royce stripped down at his locker, grabbed his grooming kit and towel, and headed to the shower room. He chose a stall in the far corner, set his stuff on the bench, and closed the door. The water heated quickly in the new building and the pressure was divine. Royce sighed heavily when he stepped beneath the spray and shut the curtain. Now, if he could just share this blissful break from the madness with the man who owned his heart...

As if the universe heard his plea, the outer stall door rattled as someone reached over the top and slid the lock free. Royce's pulse galloped in anticipation as he listened to the same someone stripping down on the other side of the curtain. He tipped his head back into the spray like he hadn't heard any of it and patiently waited for Sawyer to whisk the curtain aside and join him. Luckily, his man was just as eager to see him and didn't draw out the anticipation too long.

The curtain rings rattled against the metal bar, and there he was. Royce raked his starved gaze over six feet of sleek, naked muscle and—

His brain short-circuited when he reached Sawyer's face.

"Baby, you look like roadkill," Royce said. Hearing the words echo in the shower made him grimace. What the fuck kind of greeting was that? One Sawyer found amusing because he laughed and circled his arms around Royce's waist, stepping under the spray with him. Royce lifted his hand and gently caressed the dark circles under Sawyer's eyes.

"Yeah?" Sawyer said. "You look like roadkill after vultures have picked over the carcass for about three days."

Royce slid his hands down to grip Sawyer's firm ass. "Oh, good one."

"Did you find anything promising in Rachel's social media activity?" Sawyer asked.

Royce's stomach pitched. "So much. None of it good. This Jake person Rachel was talking to is a predator, plain and simple."

Sawyer sighed. "That's awful."

"And I'm starting to have more doubts about running the Explorer program after spending the night reading awful messages between young adults," Royce said.

"That bad, huh?"

Nodding, Royce said, "Tara made a color-coded spreadsheet to keep up with it all."

Sawyer winced. "Well, I think the point of the Explorer program is to give teenagers direction and purpose. Instructor Royce could make all the difference in the world."

He squeezed Sawyer's ass. "We're here together, naked and wet. Do you really want to talk about the investigation right now?"

Sawyer kissed him hard, pushing his tongue between Royce's lips and sweeping inside his mouth. He pinned Royce against the shower wall and fisted their cocks together in his talented hand. Royce's eyes rolled back in his head on the first stroke, and he fought off the urge to moan like the needy slut Sawyer turned him into at the slightest touch.

Sawyer twisted his fist on the upstroke and thrust his dick against Royce's. Sparks danced like fireflies behind Royce's closed eyelids. He wrenched his mouth free and panted in the humid shower. Sawyer immediately started attacking Royce's neck.

"Fuck, I've missed you," Royce whispered. He fisted his hands in Sawyer's hair and yanked his head up so they were eye to eye. "You're going to spend the rest of your life with me."

Sawyer's stroking faltered, and his hand tightened around their shafts. "Are you ask—"

Royce cut him off with a hard, quick kiss. "No, I'm telling you how it will be." Nothing about the moment was ideal. They were up to their assholes in complicated investigations, he hadn't slept for almost twenty-four hours, and he couldn't remember his last decent meal. But speaking his deepest desire out loud lifted a weight off his shoulders and made the impossible seem possible.

Sawyer's lips slowly curved into a devastating smile, easing the tension in his face. "Yeah, okay."

Royce jutted his hips forward, thrusting his dick through Sawyer's stilled fist. "Now jerk us off, asshole."

Sawyer kissed him aggressively as he pumped his hand up and down their shafts. Royce's body tensed as pleasure built, and he curled his toes against the tile floor when the dam broke. His mouth parted on a silent scream when the head of Sawyer's dick brushed against the sweet spot beneath his crown.

"Right there with you," Sawyer said savagely.

Royce looked down to watch their joint release geyser from their cockheads and coat Sawyer's fist. They shared soft, sweet kisses as Sawyer lazily stroked until they became too sensitive for anything more.

Royce wanted to linger in the private moment Sawyer had carved out for them, but he needed to finish his shower and get dressed. He owed the Morgans his very best, and thanks to Sawyer jumpstarting his stalled engine, Royce felt better able to handle the tough interview and debriefing that followed.

Pressing his forehead to Sawyer's, Royce said, "I love you."

Sawyer gave him a quick kiss, then said, "I love you too. We better get a move on because your breakfast sandwich is getting cold." Sawyer's thoughtfulness never failed to move him.

The two of them washed quickly with Royce's shampoo and body wash. He loved knowing Sawyer would spend the rest of the day smelling like him. Once outside the shower, Royce caught a whiff of the breakfast meal Sawyer had brought for him, and it spurred him to move even quicker. With the towel wrapped around his waist, Royce took his kit to the bathroom sink and shaved his face. He studied his appearance in the mirror once more and smiled at the noticeable improvement in his reflection. Royce still looked like picked-to-the-bone roadkill, but he no longer looked like he was recovering from a month-long bender.

"Fucked and fed looks good on you," Sawyer whispered when they stopped down the hall from the conference room where the Morgans waited for him.

"Fucked and fed feels even better," Royce replied. Christ, Sawyer deserved a better proposal than the shitty demand he'd issued midcoitus. What had he been thinking? The timing and circumstances were terrible, and they hadn't improved since he'd spoken his most profound need out loud.

Sawyer gave him a reassuring smile, then tilted his head toward the closed door. "You better get in there, yeah?" Dread settled in his throat like thick phlegm, making it impossible to speak, so he nodded. "I'll see you in Mendoza's office for the debriefing." Sawyer winked before walking away.

Royce watched until he turned the corner at the end of the corridor and disappeared. He received a text just as he started toward the conference room. Tara was working on crucial steps, so Royce couldn't ignore his phone. He pulled it from his pocket and confirmed the text was from Tara.

Jasmine is coming in tomorrow for her follow-up interview. She has exams all day and is over an hour away. Sent search warrant for Benji's cell phone records to judge.

Great job, Royce replied and followed it with another text. *Can you schedule a second interview with Benji McKay? Let's talk to him after our interview with Jasmine.*

Sure thing.

You should go home and get some rest, Royce wrote.

I will when you do, Tara fired back. *Partners.*

Royce smiled and typed furiously. *You want to join me for the meeting with the Morgans?*

About as much as you want to help me update the social media spreadsheet, Tara replied.

Fair enough. I'll find you afterward.

Royce tucked his phone away, straightened his posture, and reached for the door handle. Cheerful whistling down the hall caught his attention and he turned to find Diego Fuentes striding down the corridor, looking sun kissed and blissed. It must've been one hell of a honeymoon. Diego's joy was infectious, and Royce smiled at the dopey look on the man's face. Remembering where he was and what he was about to do, Royce sobered his thoughts and expression before stepping into the conference room.

The couple launched to their feet, and Royce wouldn't have recognized them if he hadn't been the one to request the meeting. Samantha Morgan's blonde hair hung limply around her makeup-free face, and her sweater was so loose she looked like a little girl playing dress-up in her mother's clothes. The dark circles under their eyes and gaunt faces gave them a zombie-like appearance, which was only fitting since they were walking through a living hell. The shroud of misery clinging to them had only worsened since he'd left them the previous day. Royce's heart went out to them, and he dreaded the conversation they needed to have.

"You have some nerve trying to pin Rachel's murder on Benji," Bryan Morgan said before Royce could speak or even shake their hands. Royce wasn't sure where he'd gotten the false narrative, but he'd place a bet on Harris McKay. "Benji is a good kid, and he'd never hurt Rachel." That is not a hill Mr. Morgan would choose to die on if he knew Benji had repeatedly called his daughter a whore, the same slur written on her forehead. "I won't let you ruin his reputation and railroad an innocent man," the devastated father added.

It wasn't unusual for a parent to channel their grief into anger at the police, and Royce didn't take it personally. It also wasn't uncommon for the grieving family to be in total denial about a person of interest's likelihood of guilt. Instead of lashing back at Mr. Morgan, Royce gestured to the chairs and encouraged them to have a seat.

Samantha flopped back down in her chair like a ragdoll and looked at him with dull, lifeless eyes. Bryan remained standing, his hands at his hips and rage burning in his eyes. Royce figured it was the only thing preventing the man's heartbreak from swallowing him whole. He couldn't begrudge him his fury.

"Can I get you something to drink before we start?" Royce asked.

"What are you doing to find my daughter's killer?" Bryan yelled. He leaned forward and banged a fist on the table, making his wife flinch and burrow deeper into her oversized sweater. "And why the hell weren't the police at the hotel to prevent this sick fuck from killing another innocent victim? Why didn't someone have the foresight to consider all the attention from the press would trigger him to kill again? Why did my daughter have to die because of this department's ineptitude?"

The bereaved father's sharp accusations came at Royce like nails from a pneumatic gun and were twice as deadly when they struck. Even if he weren't exhausted, Royce wouldn't have ducked.

Samantha wrapped both hands around her husband's forearm and tugged. "Sit down, Bryan. You're not helping the situation. We discussed this. And all I've heard from you since your return is your worry about what the police think about Benji or plan to do with him. Even in death, Rachel is barely a blip on your radar."

The man turned his glare on his wife. "And I told you I'm not interested in what you have to say since you're the one who pushed this pageant bullshit on our only child. You didn't do it for her, Samantha. You did it to live vicariously through our daughter because you never won the crown for yourself."

The woman shrank back as if her husband had physically struck her.

"Mr. Morgan," Royce said firmly. "I understand how devastated you are right now, but blaming your wife isn't the solution."

"So now you're a fucking counselor?" the surly man asked. "You didn't save my daughter, so you'll save my marriage?" Bryan balled his hands into fists and looked ready to take a swing.

"Sit in the chair and calm down, or I'll remove you from the room and the conversation. I empathize with your grief, but it doesn't mean I'll be your punching bag." Verbal jabs were one thing, but Mr. Morgan wouldn't like the result if he upped the ante. "I invited you here to speak with you before going public with our preliminary findings."

Mr. Morgan's expression didn't change, but he dropped back into the chair and gestured for Royce to continue.

"Rachel's assailant wasn't the person who killed Barbara, Jessica, and Amy," Royce said.

Bryan snorted and threw up his hands. "I told you they'd say that," he said to his wife.

"Hush," Mrs. Morgan replied without taking her gaze away from Royce. "Please continue, Sergeant."

"The method, manner, and timing don't match the three original crimes," Royce said. "This homicide occurred during a preliminary round instead of the celebration ball after the crowning."

"She was a shoo-in," Samantha whispered. "Everyone knew it."

"That's what I gathered from interviewing the other contestants, the committee, and judges," Royce admitted, then, as sensitively as possible, expanded on significant differences between her murder and the original three. "There were a few similarities, but—"

"Such as?" Bryan asked.

"We're not sharing those details with the public right now," Royce said. Mr. Morgan opened his mouth to speak again, but Royce cut him off. "Hear me out, please."

Bryan glared at him for a few moments before giving him the slightest nod.

"Thank you." Royce explained how law enforcement withheld specific details from the public to corroborate physical evidence and witness statements or confessions once they made an arrest. "In Rachel's homicide, even the similarities differ from the first three."

Both parents flinched at hearing him use their daughter's name, but it was vital for them to realize Rachel wasn't just a case number to him.

"W-were the other women called wh-whores too?" Samantha asked before bursting into tears.

Her mournful sobs melted her husband's icy demeanor. Bryan wrapped her in his arms. "Oh, honey. Rachel was many things, but she wasn't a whore." He met Royce's gaze. "Were the other ladies called that awful name?"

"I cannot answer your question right now, but I need you to promise not to reveal anything you saw in the room," Royce said. "Not to family, friends, and especially not to the press. No one."

Samantha sniffled and pulled a few tissues from the box in the center of the table. She dabbed at her eyes and wiped her nose. "I promise," she said.

"Thank you."

"I understand there are differences, but don't the similarities prove the killer is the same?" Bryan asked.

"No, sir. It just means they had insider information about the first three murders." Before Mr. Morgan asked, Royce continued. "There's always a possibility someone leaked information they shouldn't have. And the details got to someone who used them to their advantage."

"How?" the Morgans both asked.

"To divert our attention away from the truth." Royce took a fortifying breath because this was the part he hated the most. "I believe your daughter was killed by someone who stalked her on social media and laid a trap she couldn't resist."

Samantha gasped and cried into her hands while Bryan cursed.

"And you can prove this?" he asked.

"Yes, sir," Royce said.

"How?" Bryan and Samantha both said.

"We obtained warrants for her phone activity and social media accounts," Royce explained. "It would usually take us a little longer to get them, but a witness claimed Rachel was interacting with a man she'd met online. We don't have her phone records yet, but the social media activity painted a vivid picture."

Mrs. Morgan narrowed her eyes. "Who told you about the guy?"

"I'd rather not say right now because it could discourage them from divulging additional information."

"Basically," Bryan said, "you asked us to come here so you could blame my daughter for her death because she was stupid."

"Bryan!" Mrs. Morgan exclaimed, whirling on him. "The sergeant didn't say that, but it's obvious you think it. First, Rachel's death is my fault, and now you're saying it's hers."

"I never said—"

"You did!" she cried. "I've heard nothing but insults since you came home."

"Maybe you should've been paying closer attention to what Rachel was doing or who she was talking to," he fired back.

Samantha physically bristled. "She was an adult, Bryan. I had no desire to micromanage Rachel's life and make her miserable as my mother had done with me. Despite what you think, our daughter wanted to enter that pageant. She told me it would open doors for her."

Mr. Morgan closed his eyes and shook his head. When he reopened them, Royce saw the vacant expression his anger had hidden. Royce would prefer the man's hostility to the desolation he was witnessing. Bryan Morgan crumbled into himself. "My baby girl," he said, sobbing as he leaned into his wife's embrace. "I'm so sorry, honey. Please forgive me for the awful things I've said. You lived and breathed for our daughter."

Samantha tightened her arms and kissed the top of his head as tears streaked down her face. "I know you didn't mean it."

"Would you like me to step out of the room for a minute?" Royce asked.

Samantha shook her head, and Bryan sat up. "No," he said. "I owe you an apology too."

Royce held up his hand. "You don't. Let's just work together moving forward, okay? We all want the same thing here, and I will not stop until I find Rachel's killer. You have my word."

Bryan held his gaze for a few minutes and nodded.

"About six months ago, someone created a fake profile on Facebook under the name Jake Evans and befriended Rachel. And before you ask, yes, we are certain it's a fake profile. Our cyber unit did a reverse search on the pictures used on the account and traced them to the real person who lives in California. At the time of Rachel's murder, this unsuspecting gentleman posted about his honeymoon in Italy." Tara was in the process of tracking Scott Buyers down to obtain proof of his whereabouts just to rule him out officially.

Samantha started crying harder, and Bryan pulled her into his embrace.

"You're certain this Jake profile was fake?" he asked Royce.

"Absolutely." What he didn't know was if Benji McKay was behind it or someone else who wanted to hurt Rachel.

"How old is this guy?" Bryan asked.

"His profile states he's thirty-five."

Mr. Morgan blanched. "Why would Rachel want to date someone fifteen years older than her?"

"And he told her everything she wanted to hear, right?" Samantha asked.

"Yes, ma'am."

She took a deep, shaky breath. "C-can I read the messages, please?"

"No," Bryan and Royce said at the same time.

"Why?" she asked.

Bryan deferred to Royce with a gesture.

"The messages will be evidence we use to arrest and convict her killer. After I make an arrest, I'll share them with you if you still want to read them. I won't let you get caught off guard during a trial." He wouldn't want to show Rachel's parents because of their sexually explicit nature, but as awful as that would be for them to see, the messages about Rachel's deepest feelings toward her parents would devastate them. Reading her words wouldn't heal their broken hearts or the strained marriage their daughter had discussed with a stranger.

"No," Bryan said, tightening his arms around his wife. "No good will come of it."

Samantha pulled free and turned toward him. "You can't make this decision for me."

"I'm putting my foot down on this," her husband returned.

Samantha narrowed her eyes. "And I'll just shove it up your ass so your head won't get lonely."

Royce could see the fight brewing in their body language and decided to head them off before he lost control of the meeting. "Mr. and Mrs. Morgan," he said firmly.

They ignored him for a few seconds before ending their glaring contest and looking at him.

"Jake set up a rendezvous for them on Saturday evening. Rachel had given him her schedule and stated she'd be free by eight or eight thirty. She told him her father would be out of town and her mother would spend the night in the lounge with the other moms. She figured they'd have until midnight."

Samantha blushed and averted her gaze. "It was only a few drinks. She made me sound like a lush."

"If the Jimmy Choo fits," Bryan replied. His wife gasped, and he threw up his hands in surrender. "That hit was below the belt. I'm sorry." He scrubbed his hands over his face, dragging the skin and giving him a distorted, funhouse mirror effect. After a moment, Mr. Morgan dropped his hands to his lap and took a fortifying breath. "Was our daughter just in the wrong place at the wrong time to attract this man's attention?"

"I want to point out we don't know if the killer is a man. We only know they used a masculine profile to spring a trap. And no, based on the evidence, we feel this person created the profile with the sole purpose of snagging Rachel's attention."

"What?" Samantha cried. "Why? What could our girl possibly have done to invite such viciousness?"

"And how could you even know that?" Bryan asked.

"We're working with the Law Enforcement Reaction Teams on the various sites to obtain all the information on Jake's profile." Royce had nearly slipped up and used the Fake Jake nickname he'd given the account, which could've sounded flippant and callous to Rachel's family. Sawyer's cautionary warning the previous week had been timely. "The person created the account a week before reaching out to Rachel, and she was the only person they interacted with. Jake attempted to delete all the messages and deactivate the account, but nothing is truly deleted or deactivated in cyberspace. This person created a profile they thought would catch Rachel's eye. Then they joined most of the groups she was a member of and interacted with her there to build a rapport before they started interacting privately."

"How could our daughter fall for this?" Samantha asked. "I don't understand."

"Whoever set this up knew a lot of information about your daughter and knew the right chords to strum. This Jake didn't just build a bare-bones profile either. They created a comprehensive account filled with stolen pictures and experiences." Royce paused a moment to weigh his words. "They knew intimate things about Rachel that lead me to believe this is someone she knows in real life."

The Morgans flinched as if he'd struck them.

"You think this is someone we know? A person we invited into our lives?" Samantha asked.

"Impossible," Bryan insisted.

"It's not only possible; it's highly likely," Royce said patiently. "It doesn't necessarily have to be someone you're familiar with. They might've met at school or have mutual friends."

"And they hated our daughter so much they created a fake profile to make her fall in love with them, set up a meeting, and kill her?" Bryan asked.

"I know it sounds outlandish, but I'm basing this on my experience as a homicide detective and from reading the messages Rachel exchanged with Jake."

"The messages you won't share with us," Samantha said.

"Yes, ma'am."

She shook her head. "Our daughter might not have been the best student, but she was savvy. There's no way she would've fallen for such an obvious ruse."

"Mrs. Morgan," Royce said gently, "Rachel looked for what she wanted to see."

"Which was?" she countered.

Royce hesitated because he didn't want to add insult to injury. They'd been hurt enough.

"We can take it, Sergeant," Bryan said firmly. "Give us this much."

"Rachel was looking for a way out," he replied. "She hated school and wasn't happy at home. Jake promised Rachel everything she needed to hear. Jake knew intimate things about her like the clothes, food, and music she liked. Yes, those are things you can glean from someone's posts, but this went deeper to include intimate habits and preferences she didn't post about."

"Intimate as in sexual?" Samantha asked hesitantly.

"Yes."

The person had sent expensive lingerie to Rachel without asking for her address. She'd been too flattered to dig deeper. She'd posed in the lacy garments for Fake Jake. Royce had been shocked to discover the lacy bra used to strangle her was part of the gifted set and had cost over three hundred dollars. The matching underwear was nowhere to be found in the hotel room, and Royce suspected the killer had taken it as a trophy.

Mrs. Morgan looked at her husband, who'd turned white as a ghost. "Why wouldn't that freak her out? This random guy on the internet knew these things about her?"

Bryan nodded. "Didn't she question them?"

"She did," Royce said. "But they were prepared with an answer each time, then they would reference fate, instinct, and destiny."

"If you have access to their social media account, you should have access to their IP address," Bryan said. "Why haven't you tracked them down?"

"They used a burner phone and a VPN to hide the IP address. We are working with the cellular provider and should have the complete phone records today."

Mr. Morgan blew out a frustrated breath. "What's next?"

"I'm sending a group of detectives to her university to interview students and faculty. We're also going to reinterview people associated with the pageant or who worked at the hotel. Once we have the burner phone records, we'll look at every tower it pinged from and hope to find area businesses with exterior security cameras. We need to find out who would go to such lengths to hurt your daughter."

And they couldn't afford to have tunnel vision on Benji McKay, especially not when Rachel had been embroiled in many arguments.

"I replayed every petty argument Rachel had since she started school," Samantha said. "She was a magnet for drama it seemed, but to hate her so much someone would want her dead? Over what? Getting beat out for the cheer squad? Losing homecoming queen?" She shook her head. "I don't buy it."

Bryan studied Royce for several tense moments. "I don't think he's trying to sell us anything, dear."

"Fair enough," his wife said. "This is just a bitter pill to swallow, Sergeant Locke."

"I know, ma'am, and I'm truly sorry."

"Don't be sorry," she said. "Be relentless."

Her comment reminded him of Sawyer, and it provided the jolt of adrenaline he needed. "Yes, ma'am."

The couple slowly rose to their feet. If possible, they seemed to have aged even more since the meeting had begun. He held open the door for them and promised to be in touch as they exited the room. Royce observed them walking down the hallway and felt a modicum of hope for the couple when they reached for one another at the same time.

Once they were out of sight, he shut the door and headed downstairs to Sawyer's office. Royce found him at his desk studying four pieces of paper laid out before him. Sawyer snapped his head up and smiled at Royce.

"How'd it go?"

Royce flopped down in the chair and exhaled slowly. "Brutal." He gestured to the sheets of paper. "What are you up to?"

"Cross-referencing the names of the people involved in the pageant at the times of all four murders."

Royce pursed his lips. "Why? I thought we agreed Rachel's murder wasn't connected."

"Burke stopped by when you were meeting with the Morgans. Tara showed him the crime scene photos, and he emphatically stated we're looking at a copycat."

"So why are you still comparing all four crimes?"

"I said the murders weren't committed by the same person, but I didn't say they weren't connected. Whoever killed Rachel had information only a few people knew. I think they know who killed Barbara, Jessica, and Amy."

"That's a huge leap."

"Is it?" Sawyer asked. "There hasn't been so much as a whisper about the magnolia flowers and the slur written on the victims' foreheads in thirty-eight years. We didn't even know about it until I opened the case files. The families wouldn't have released such a humiliating detail. Donovan is dead, and Burke hasn't spoken to anyone about the case since he retired."

"True," Royce said, "but what about the first responders and medical examiner's office?"

"Not a whisper in thirty-eight years," Sawyer reminded him. "We live in the South where gossip moves faster than the speed of light. I stared up at the ceiling all night, trying to figure out the connection, and I kept coming back to the pageant. It's time for me to bring in the big gun."

Royce quirked a brow.

"Evangeline. I want to get permission from Mendoza to show the list of names I compiled from the four cases to my mother to see if anything jumps out at her."

"It's probably a long shot, but at this point, we have to explore every avenue and tap every source." He checked his watch and said, "It's time to debrief the chief."

Chapter
SIXTEEN

"**O**H MY GOODNESS," EVANGELINE SAID WHEN SHE STEPPED into Sawyer's office a few hours later. "You both look awful."

His mother looked like a million dollars in her dark-wash skinny jeans, a camel-colored sweater that matched her ankle boots, and a plum cashmere coat.

Sawyer kissed her cheek. "Thanks, Mom." He felt like someone had dragged him over a cheese grater, especially after the hostile press conference. Mendoza might've done all the talking, but Sawyer and Royce had become everyone's favorite targets. The public was scared, the press was suspicious, and he couldn't blame them.

"Death warmed over?" Royce asked her.

"Worse." Evangeline hoisted an oversized picnic basket onto the desk with a *thud*. "But I can make it better." She lifted the lid, and the aroma wafting out of the basket made Sawyer's stomach rumble like thunder.

Royce tilted his head back, closed his eyes, and inhaled deeply. "Is that your famous fried chicken?"

"The very same," she said proudly. "Extra crispy for my special boys."

"What's the secret?" Royce asked. "I can make decent fried chicken, but this is better than anything I've ever eaten."

"A lady never tells," Evangeline said coquettishly.

"She uses a double dredge system," Sawyer said. "A light dusting of flour, egg wash, and buttermilk with a little hot sauce mixed in and a final dredge through seasoned flour. Each layer adds a new herb or spice to enhance the flavor."

"Hush, Sawyer," his mother said, swiping at him. He danced out of the way and circled his desk to peer inside the basket. She'd included containers of potato salad and baked beans and packed plates, napkins, and cutlery. "Have you boys been sleeping?" she asked.

"A little," Royce lied, "but don't try to distract me from my interrogation."

Evangeline chuckled, threw her hands up, and walked over to Sawyer's bookshelf to study the family photos he'd placed there.

Royce narrowed his eyes. "You know how to make this chicken but don't?"

Sawyer shrugged. "I can't show up my mother."

Evangeline snorted. "As if."

Royce heaved an exaggerated sigh. "This changes things between us."

Seeing the spark of playfulness in Royce's eyes for the first time in days made Sawyer forget they weren't alone. He reached into the basket, picked up a drumstick, and bit into it, savoring the combination of flavors and textures. "So you no longer want me to love you for the rest of my life?" he asked after swallowing the bite.

Royce had just reached into the basket to pull out a piece of chicken but froze and looked up. "Don't be ridiculous. But I'd like to insist on a new promise."

"I'm listening."

"You're going to love me *and* make this chicken for the rest of your life," Royce said.

"Yeah, okay. But I'm only making the chicken for special occasions."

Royce smiled seductively as he snagged a thigh out of the basket. "Define special."

Sawyer reached out, hooked his finger in Royce's belt loop, and tugged him closer. He knew exactly what he wanted to feast on.

"Such as when I'm not here," Evangeline suggested.

Royce flinched. "Oh shit."

Evangeline giggled. "You boys make my heart so happy, even if you look awful. Promise me you'll get some sleep."

Sawyer could promise he'd be horizontal with his man as soon as possible, but that wasn't what she wanted to hear.

"We'll do our best," Royce said, not taking his eyes off Sawyer.

"Time for me to go," Evangeline said as she headed toward the door.

Sawyer snapped out of his trance and stopped her before she could escape. "Mom, we could use your help on this investigation."

She slowly turned around and beamed at him. "Me? How?"

"Before discussing this case with you, we have to do something first," Royce said. He reached into his pocket and pulled out one of the plastic shields the department handed out in elementary schools. "Evangeline O'Neal, please raise your right hand and repeat after me." Royce swore her in and handed her the badge. "Okay, you can discuss the investigation with her now that she's officially one of us."

Evangeline's lips tilted up at the corners as she clutched the badge to her chest. "This is an honor I'll cherish forever."

Sawyer shook his head over their antics and removed the four lists he'd created. "Mom, I'm trying to find the common thread between these four murders. I think the killers are connected to the pageant, but I keep running into roadblocks."

Evangeline furrowed her brow as she scanned the first page. "I thought your official stance was that Rachel Morgan wasn't murdered by the same person as the other Magnolia Queens."

"That's correct," Sawyer said. "But I still think the murders are connected. Can you look at these lists and tell me if any of these people are related or interact outside the pageant?"

"I'll do my best." She compared the first page to the second, noting the relationships she knew about before moving on to the third page and the fourth. She knew more about the people on the first two sheets but very little about the last two. She sat back with a dejected expression on her face. "I don't think I was very helpful."

Royce crunched through his third piece of chicken. "You're a lifesaver."

She kissed both their cheeks, told them she loved them, then headed out.

"So much for my hunch," Sawyer said once they were alone.

"Hey," Royce said, lifting a forkful of potato salad to Sawyer's mouth. "Just because the answer didn't come to us right away doesn't mean your hunch is wrong."

Sawyer cleaned off the fork and chewed thoughtfully. It felt like he was on the defensive, throwing everything he had at the wall and hoping something would stick. Royce dropped the fork into the basket, placed his hands on Sawyer's hips, and tugged him closer.

"You're the best investigator I know," Royce said. "Keep working every angle, and you'll get to the truth."

Sawyer leaned in to kiss Royce, but his door flew open and banged against the wall.

"I got it!" Evangeline exclaimed. "You didn't ask me the right question."

Sawyer cocked his head. "What do you mean?"

She crossed the room and pointed to the lists still spread out on his desk. "You should've asked me if any names were missing from the list."

"Are there missing names?" Sawyer asked.

Evangeline rolled her eyes. "Would I have barged in here and said you asked the wrong question if there wasn't someone missing from your list?"

"Who?" Royce and Sawyer both said.

"Marilyn Moynihan." Evangeline's voice rang with smug superiority until she failed to get a response from either of them. "Marilyn Moynihan," she repeated. "How can she not be included on those lists?"

Sawyer and Royce looked at each other and shrugged.

"Her name appears nowhere in the case files," Sawyer told her. "She wasn't listed as a witness or even a person associated with the pageant."

Evangeline's mouth gaped uncharacteristically. "You must be joking," she said once she recovered from her surprise.

"I assure you I'm not," Sawyer replied. They'd meticulously reviewed the files and checked their lists enough times to make Santa Claus look like a slacker. Even so, a shadow of doubt crept in. Had he given Mendoza wrong information? Fuck. The chief had trusted him to lead this investigation and—

"Knock it off," Royce said firmly. "There's no way you missed her name once, let alone three times." Royce reading his mind didn't surprise Sawyer, but it did make him smile. Royce winked at him and gestured to the twin seats in front of the desk and said, "Please tell us everything you know about Marilyn Moynihan."

Evangeline removed her plum coat and draped it over her arm before gracefully lowering herself into a seat. Royce sat on the corner of Sawyer's desk instead of taking up the other chair. Having him within touching distance went a long way to settle Sawyer's stretched nerves.

"Marilyn is a past Magnolia Queen from 1964. The pageant is a steppingstone to something greater for most of us. It's meant to open doors and introduce the queens to influential people and new experiences."

"But not for Marilyn?" Sawyer asked.

Evangeline shook her head. "No. It became her crowning glory. Instead of setting her free, it boxed her in, and she couldn't let go. It was as if Marilyn was permanently stuck in 1964. The sixties were a tale of two decades rolled into one. The early years were a carryover of the fifties' attitudes and norms where women's defined purpose was to get married and raise a family. There's nothing wrong with women choosing to stay home and raise their babies. I did. The key is being able to choose your own path." Sawyer was prepared to guide his mother back on topic, but he didn't need to. "The latter part of the decade saw women protesting war, burning bras, and asserting their own will. They went to college to better themselves and train for careers, not just to find husbands. But not Marilyn. She was still stuck in a time warp when I won the crown in 1976 and hadn't budged when we last argued in 1999."

"What did you argue about?" Sawyer asked.

"The future of the pageant. Marilyn fought any changes suggested by the committee and voted on by the board."

"Can you give us an example?" Royce asked.

"The biggest clash was the purity vow," Evangeline replied with a dramatic eye roll.

Royce looked between Sawyer and Evangeline. "The what now?"

Sawyer was so used to working his cases with Royce that he forgot his boyfriend hadn't been privy to all the discussions. "Up until 2001, all the Magnolia Queen contestants signed a pledge claiming they were pure of heart and virtue."

Royce's eyes widened, and he snapped his head in Evangeline's direction. "*You* willingly signed that document?"

"I wanted the scholarship money and the open doors, Royce. The life Barron and I provided for our children was the opposite of the childhood I had." She batted her eyelashes innocently. "Besides, I had a pure heart, and I didn't think a committee mostly consisting of men had a right to decide my virtuousness."

"So the committee just took your word for it? There was no physical exam?" Royce asked. Evangeline pinned him with a dark look for even asking. He put up his hands in surrender. "I take it back."

"Marilyn got angry when someone suggested they do away with the purity vow?" Sawyer asked, steering them back on topic. "What else?"

"She was infuriated when *I* suggested we do away with the purity vow," Evangeline replied, then bumped her fist against Royce's. "And she argued against any motion that physically and figuratively moved the pageant into a new era."

"So she got upset when the committee changed the venue to the convention center after 2000?" Sawyer asked.

"Upset? I'd say she was livid, and it was the final straw. She and several others disassociated with the pageant afterward."

"Were you involved in the pageant during 1984, 1996, and 2000?" Royce asked.

"No, I was big and pregnant with Sawyer in 1984. Marilyn complained that subjecting the ladies to my condition would be vulgar and untoward."

"Christ," Sawyer said.

"I was deeply hurt at the time, so I didn't fight back when the board chairman called me at home and said my help wasn't needed. I rewashed all Sawyer's baby clothes and rearranged his nursery instead."

Royce looked over at Sawyer. "Now I know where you get it."

Sawyer exchanged an amused glance with his mom. "Yep. If you can't meditate your nervous energy away, it's best to use it for the greater good." Rearranging closets and organizing sock drawers wouldn't win Sawyer a Nobel Prize, but he felt peaceful after exerting the energy. And he'd learned the hard way to leave Royce's stuff alone after stumbling across the ring.

Royce leaned forward and kissed him. "Never change."

"Probably too late now," Sawyer admitted.

"Good."

"Should I go?" Evangeline asked.

Sawyer and Royce returned their full attention to her.

"What else besides dropping the purity vow and changing the venue angered Marilyn? You said those were the last straws."

"The first blow came when they removed her as the beauty pageant coordinator the year I competed for Magnolia Queen. The committee had decided to go with someone younger and prettier."

"Ouch," Royce and Sawyer said.

"It was a jerk move," Evangeline agreed. "Marilyn was a pageant icon, and they couldn't just blow her off, so the board created an honorary role for her. Marilyn became the Magnolia Mentor to the contestants. I think the board envisioned a surrogate mom to ease tense moments for us backstage, but Marilyn created more stress with her opinionated, critical remarks."

"About what?" Royce asked.

"Everything! She thought our hairstyles, makeup trends, and fashions were trashy." Sawyer sat up straighter. "You should've seen the meltdown she had when the contestants were permitted to wear two-piece bathing suits. She was vicious and cruel."

"And yet the pageant board kept her around?" Royce asked.

"She'd entrenched herself into every aspect of the event and made them think they couldn't run it without her," Evangeline replied.

"You said Marilyn was vicious and cruel," Sawyer said. "To whom? The contestants?"

"Yes," Evangeline said, "though I can't recall the precise slurs she used."

Alarm bells were going off in Sawyer's mind, but he urged himself to remain calm. "What else can you tell us about Marilyn Moynihan? Is she still alive?"

"I believe so, but I think she had a stroke or something a few years ago that seriously impacted her motor skills. I've heard she lives in a nursing home, but I don't know which one."

Sawyer tamped down his disappointment. Interviewing Marilyn would be off the table if Evangeline was right. "What about her family? Does she have children who are now involved in the pageant?"

"Oh, heavens no," Evangeline said. "She never married." His mother's eyes sparkled with mischief, and she leaned forward. "I'm almost positive Marilyn was in love with Neil."

Neil? Sawyer narrowed his eyes as he searched his memory. "Neil Henshaw?" The man had hosted the pageant for decades, starting in the midseventies and continuing until 2005.

"Yes," Evangeline said. "He was a local television anchor and a bit of a celebrity, at least in his own mind. I think his first year as pageant host was 1975. You should've seen Marilyn swoon whenever he walked into the room. She had it bad for him."

"He didn't return her affection?" Royce asked.

"Oh, Neil dialed up the charm and strung her along," Evangeline replied. "Marilyn was a stunningly beautiful woman in her midforties, but her mannerisms made her seem much older. Good ole Neil only had eyes for the contestants." She sniffed. "He tested his charms on me a time or two, but I quickly shot him down. I could smell a player from a mile away, even back then."

Sawyer narrowed his eyes. "How did Neil respond when you rebuffed him?"

Evangeline waved her hand. "Please. He wasn't going to waste energy on one debutante when there were forty-nine others."

"Were there ever any rumors about Neil succeeding occasionally?"

Evangeline snorted. "Some ladies viewed sleeping with Neil as a rite of passage. There were more fights over that man than anything else."

"Which must've been painful for Marilyn to witness," Royce said.

"Oddly enough, the girls banded together to keep her from finding out once it became obvious who Neil preferred."

"Gross," Sawyer said.

"I agree, but these were consenting adults."

Sawyer narrowed his eyes. "Doesn't make it right."

"But it doesn't make it illegal either," she said. "Neil held no sway with the judges or committee. He was nothing more than a smarmy stage decoration with a microphone."

Sawyer crossed his arms over his chest. "I guess. I just struggle to picture you in that world."

She smiled indulgently. "Honey, I struggled while existing in that world, so I fought hard to change the pageant from the inside. I lost more than I won, but I think I made a positive impact."

Sawyer forced himself to relax so he didn't sound like such a judgmental asshole to the woman who'd always had his back come hell or high water. "I've got no doubt, Mom."

"What's the likelihood Marilyn caught Neil sneaking around with a few ladies?" Royce asked.

Evangeline cocked her head to the side and considered the question. "Anything is possible. Marilyn had become so ingrained in the pageants that she became part of the backdrop. She could probably move around without drawing notice."

"But why wasn't her name listed as associated with the pageants?"

"As I stated, it was an honorary position. If you can get your hands on a pageant program from those years, you'll see Marilyn's photo and biography."

Sawyer looked at Royce. "We need to get our hands on those programs." He wanted to ask Burke why they'd never interviewed Marilyn Moynihan.

"Try your friend at the paper," Evangeline replied.

Royce hooked his thumb in Sawyer's direction. "His friend. I just kinda put up with Felix."

"Why would the *Savanna Morning News* keep copies of the pageant programs?" Sawyer asked.

"Because they're the ones who pay for and print the programs each year," Evangeline said. "I'd think they keep them in their archives."

Royce glanced at him. "It's worth a shot."

Evangeline rose to her feet and dusted her hands. "My work here is done."

Sawyer and Royce both stood up and hugged her.

She cupped their faces one at a time and made them promise to eat and sleep better.

Royce raised his hand. "I swear."

Evangeline narrowed her eyes. "Is this the same thing as me claiming to be a virgin so I could enter the Magnolia Queen Pageant?"

Royce snickered. "You don't see me signing my name to anything, do you?"

Evangeline swatted him before breezing out of the room.

Royce shut the door and crossed to Sawyer. "Maybe this is the break we've been looking for?"

"Marilyn Moynihan didn't kill Rachel Morgan," Sawyer said.

"No," Royce agreed. "But Rachel's killer knows things about those murders they shouldn't."

"Marilyn doesn't have any family," Sawyer said absently.

"No," Royce corrected. "She doesn't have children."

"I need to learn more about her."

Royce nodded. "Start with your friend Felix. Even if the newspaper doesn't have archived copies of the programs, I'm willing to bet the podcast has ferreted out information about Marilyn."

Sawyer rubbed the back of his neck. "It's worth a shot. Maybe if I learn more about her, I'll understand why the police never interviewed someone so involved with the pageant."

Royce glanced at his watch. "I need to hit the road."

"And go home to get some sleep," Sawyer said. "You're running on empty."

"We're canvassing Rachel's college today. I need—"

Sawyer silenced him with a kiss. "You go home and catch a few hours of sleep. I'll head out with the team. Text South and tell her she's running point."

Royce looked like he would argue until Sawyer fisted his shirt and tugged him close for another kiss.

"And we'll have dinner together, watch the latest episode of *Dateline* you recorded last week, and sleep in our bed."

Royce started backing toward the door. "Just sleeping?"

"Depends if you can stay awake."

Royce stopped and reversed his direction, not stopping until they were chest to chest. "Are you calling me old?"

Sawyer snorted. "I'm calling you exhausted. Go home, baby. Get some sleep. Trust me to step in for you, okay?"

It wasn't in Royce's nature to back down from any challenge, including ones he created in his mind. Sawyer recognized the battle brewing like a storm in Royce's mercurial eyes, but he was smart enough to know his very human limitations. Royce cupped the back of Sawyer's neck and pulled him in for a too-brief but still-devastating kiss.

"I'll take a power nap and meet the team there in a bit."

Sawyer narrowed his eyes, prepared to bargain harder for a kinder concession until Royce chuckled.

"Like you'd be home sleeping if you were the one leading Rachel's investigation," he said. "How many nights have I woken up and caught you reviewing files and strategies in your office?"

"Too many to count," Sawyer admitted.

"Power nap, and I'll be good to go." Royce added a lascivious wink. "You'll see."

One final kiss from Royce, and he was gone.

Sawyer stowed the leftover food in the refrigerator in their small breakroom, then headed out to meet Tara, Holly, Topher, Diego, and Chen at Rachel's university.

Tara divided the tasks, and the team spent several hours interviewing students and faculty. Sawyer assumed Royce had arrived at some point until the detectives rendezvoused in the parking lot after they finished. Sawyer checked his watch and saw it was after six. Royce must've been more exhausted than he realized. Pandora's box shook a little, but the lock held and his fear remained confined inside it. Sawyer talked himself down off the ledge, reminding himself there were many explanations for exhaustion besides a terminal illness.

"Did anyone else have an entirely different experience with this round of interviews?" Tara asked.

Grateful for the distraction, Sawyer spoke up first. "Oh yeah. Instead of hearing her smile lit up the room, I was told her presence sucked the air out of it."

"Same," Topher said.

"I had a few people with kind things to say," Holly replied. "But not many."

"I wasn't involved in the first round of interviews," Chen said, "but I didn't get favorable input. If I were basing an investigation off today's interviews alone, I'd feel overwhelmed with suspects."

"My experience is the same as Chen's," Diego said.

"Let's head back to Savannah," Tara said. "I want everyone to write up a quick summary while the interviews are fresh on our minds and email it to Locke. Just hit on the comments and interviews that stood out to you the most so he'll have our top impressions to work with until we finalize our official reports."

Everyone agreed and headed to their vehicles. Sawyer decided he would give an oral report instead.

The house was dark and silent when he arrived home an hour later. Sawyer was shocked Bones hadn't greeted him at the garage door with his usual demand for food. A glance at the refrigerator revealed the beast hadn't been fed his dinner yet. Sawyer flipped on some lights as he walked to the bedroom where Bones and Royce slept peacefully. He kept the room dark, but the light from the hallway illuminated the four-poster bed. Sawyer stood at the bottom and watched his guys sleep. Bones was curled in a tight ball on Sawyer's pillow while Royce had kicked his covers off and lay stretched across the bed in nothing but a pair of gray sweatpants.

Royce's steady, even breaths soothed him in ways no amount of meditation ever would. He was tired, not sick. Tears burned the back of his eyes and stung his nose. Sawyer closed his eyes and matched his breathing to Royce's. It was scary as hell to love someone this much.

Bones let out a little growl and stretched before tucking himself back into a tight ball.

"I think he missed me," Royce said. His gruff, sleepy voice made Sawyer's spine tingle.

"We both did." Sawyer wrapped his hands around the top of Royce's feet and pushed his thumbs into Royce's arches.

Royce groaned lustily. "Damn, I love it when you touch me."

Sawyer shifted his hands up to massage the balls of Royce's feet and his toes before working his way back down to the arches and beyond to his heels. Royce moaned and shifted restlessly on the bed but never tried to pull his feet free from Sawyer's grasp.

"Feel good?" Sawyer asked, though he didn't need to hear the words when he saw Royce's reaction tenting his sweatpants.

Royce's eyes looked dark and sparkled like sin in the half-lit room. "Would feel even better if you went higher."

Sawyer shifted his hands up to Royce's calves, massaging him through the fabric. "Here?"

Royce smirked as he trailed his fingers over his nipples, then down his chest to rest just above his waistband. "Getting warmer."

Sawyer worked his hands higher, stopping at Royce's knees. He moaned when Sawyer dug his thumbs into the back of his knees but wiggled when Sawyer found his ticklish spots just above his kneecaps.

"A little higher," Royce said once he quit fidgeting on the bed. He grew impatient when Sawyer stopped off to pay homage to his toned thighs. Royce slid his hand under the waistband of his sweatpants and started stroking himself.

Sawyer responded by gripping the fabric and tugging it down Royce's long legs. "So impatient," he said once the sweatpants cleared his feet. He dropped them onto the floor, grabbed Royce's ankles, and yanked him down until his knees were at the edge. Bones growled his displeasure before jumping off the bed and running from the room.

"He's scandalized," Sawyer said, releasing Royce's ankles so his legs could dangle over the end of the bed. He gripped Royce's wrist and pried his hand off his cock. Seeing a trail of precum on Royce's palm, Sawyer leaned over and swiped it with his tongue. "Mine," he said hungrily.

Royce's cheeks looked flushed in the dark, and his eyes crackled with need. He smirked and tucked his hands under his head. He spread his legs wider, propping his feet up on the bottom bed rail and exposing his entrance to Sawyer. "Yours."

Sawyer took a moment to appreciate his lover's surrender before he resumed massaging Royce's thighs, loving how the muscles flexed beneath his ministrations and how Royce's cock jerked in response to Sawyer's touch. "You want me so bad."

"Nice observation, Captain Obv—" Royce's words cut off when Sawyer dropped to his knees at the foot of the bed, bringing him up close and personal with Royce's cock. Sawyer swiped his tongue along his shaft and swirled it around the crown and back down again.

With a playful growl, Sawyer buried his nose in the juncture of Royce's hip and leg where his essence was most potent. Closing his eyes, Sawyer breathed Royce's scent in deep. This was home to him, not a set of brick walls and a roof. Royce grew even more impatient, but Sawyer wouldn't be denied. He turned his face and nuzzled his nose against Royce's sac before sucking one ball into his mouth, then the other.

Unable to remain passive, Royce double fisted Sawyer's hair and tried to drag his mouth to where he wanted it most. Sawyer ignored his demands and relished the stinging sensation in his scalp brought on by Royce's desperation. He licked and sucked his sac before teasing Royce's taint with his tongue.

"You sexy fucker," Royce growled as he thrust his hips up and down, rubbing his cock and balls against Sawyer's face. "I need you."

Sawyer laid his forearm over Royce's hips to hold him still, then swallowed his cock to the root. Sawyer stayed there, breathing through his nose, while Royce squirmed and cursed him.

"Fuck, baby. Please. More."

Sawyer extended his tongue to tickle Royce's balls, then kept it out while he slowly retracted his mouth, dragging his tongue along the thick vein on the underside and teasing the sensitive spot just beneath the crown. Royce rewarded him with a bead of precum, and Sawyer eagerly lapped it up.

"Christ, I love when you do that," Royce said. "Keep it up, and I'm going to come already."

Sawyer met his desperate gaze with a smug smirk before repeating the sequence he knew would be Royce's undoing. Bracing his hands on Royce's thighs, he felt the orgasm building on the second sweep, so on the third, he buried his nose in Royce's pubic hair and swallowed around his swollen head.

"Fuck!" Royce shouted as he came down Sawyer's throat, holding him in place until the last drop fell.

Sawyer's pleasure vibrated through him in a hum as he slowly released Royce's spent cock. He laid his head on a hairy thigh to catch his breath. Royce carded his fingers through Sawyer's hair while he came down from his high.

"Your turn."

Sawyer raised his head and smiled at Royce. "I just wanted to take care of you. Stay here and rest while I feed the cat and make dinner." Sawyer pushed off the bed and watched Royce stretch like a lazy cat. He expected him to crawl back up the bed, but Royce surprised Sawyer by springing to his feet.

Royce was on him before Sawyer knew it, shoving him against the dresser hard enough to rattle the stuff on top. One of the metal drawer pulls dug into his hip, but he was too mesmerized by the sight of Royce dropping to his knees to care.

Royce didn't take the time to undress him. He only loosened his belt and lowered his pants enough to free his cock and balls. Royce shoved Sawyer's dress shirt and sweater vest up and out of his way. It was rough, fast, and so fucking dirty that Sawyer came just as quickly as Royce had.

He sagged back against the dresser as his legs trembled with the strength of his orgasm. Royce took his time licking his spent cock until he became too sensitive for more, then he stripped Sawyer down and coaxed him into bed. Royce spooned up behind Sawyer, getting as close as humanly possible.

"Still not close enough," Royce whispered sleepily. "Never enough." His breaths evened out, and Sawyer thought he'd fallen back asleep until he tried to get out of bed. "Where do you think you're going?"

Sawyer chuckled. "To the kitchen. I need to feed Bones and start dinner."

"Just give me a few more minutes, then we'll feed the cat and cook together. We can catch up on *Dateline* and my man, Keith, afterward. It will be so nice to do something normal for a change."

And it was.

Chapter
SEVENTEEN

"**W**E DON'T HAVE BENJI'S PHONE RECORDS OR SOCIAL MEDIA activity reports yet," Tara told Royce on Tuesday morning as they headed toward the interview rooms. "I followed up with the phone carrier and the LERTs to confirm they received the signed warrants. We should have everything later today or tomorrow."

"Nice." Royce had hoped to have them before they met with Benji and his attorney later, but he'd make do. The exchanges between Benji and Rachel on her social media accounts were damning enough. He bumped his fist against Tara's. Royce felt like a new man after recharging his batteries and was twice as determined to solve Rachel's homicide. "What room is Jasmine in?"

"Three. She didn't bring an attorney."

Sleeping with a friend's ex-boyfriend wasn't a crime, and Jasmine hadn't drawn a correlation between Benji's presence at the hotel and Rachel's death. And maybe she did so for valid reasons that had nothing to do with her being blinded by desire or petty jealousy. Royce was willing to give Jasmine the benefit of the doubt until she proved she didn't deserve it.

"Care to join me?" Royce asked.

Tara stopped, forcing Royce to pull up too. "Because the interview requires a delicate touch, and I'm a woman?"

Royce chuckled. "Delicate touch? I saw you knock out a challenger in the boxing ring in less than five minutes. If anything, you're the heavy hitter in this duo. I asked you to join me because you're my partner."

"Well, in that case, yes." Tara gestured to interview room three.

Royce pushed the door open and stepped inside. "Good morning," he told Jasmine, extending a hand to her.

The young lady ping-ponged her gaze between them as they took seats opposite her. Jasmine's focus eventually settled on the file in Royce's hand.

"Can we get you something to drink? Coffee, perhaps?" Royce asked her.

Jasmine snapped her eyes up and smiled. She glanced in Tara's direction and said, "No, but thank you. Detective South already offered." Her brow furrowed slightly, and she pursed her lips. "What happened to the other guy? Your partner?"

"Sergeant Key isn't my partner," Royce said. "Well, he is, but not on the job." Royce figured if he opened up to her a little, she'd show him the same courtesy. A little quid pro quo.

"Oh," Jasmine said. Then her eyes widened. "Ohhh."

"Sergeant Key leads the Cold Case Unit and is investigating the original Magnolia Murders."

Jasmine's confusion returned. "Wouldn't that apply to Rachel as well? They referred to her as Magnolia Murder Number Four in a news report I heard on the way here."

Royce clamped his jaw shut until the urge to curse passed. They could give the press hourly updates, and they'd still report whatever stories they wanted to tell.

"I'm sorry the news outlets referred to your friend as a number," Tara said. "That's awful."

Jasmine smiled and nodded. "Thank you."

"As our police chief stated yesterday," Royce began, "we're investigating Rachel's homicide as a separate incident."

"My parents said you were, but I had a hard time believing it."

"Why?" Royce asked.

Jasmine took a deep breath and dropped her gaze down to her pale yellow sweater where she became fixated on a loose strand of yarn. Jasmine plucked, twisted, and pulled at it long enough for Royce to realize she'd checked out and gone someplace else.

"Jasmine," he said gently.

She lowered her hand and raised her head. "Sorry. Um, it's easier for me to blame it on a faceless killer who preyed on beauty queens than to believe someone I know wanted to kill my friend."

"You don't know anyone who would've wanted to harm Rachel?" Royce pressed as he opened the folder on the table.

Jasmine's eyelids twitched, and her body tensed, but she kept her gaze trained on him. "No." She swallowed hard. "Not really."

Royce removed the top picture, turned it around, and slid it to her. Jasmine looked down at the photo of her and Benji entering the hotel and sighed. Her shoulders slumped as the tension rolled down her body like an avalanche.

"I was so tired of keeping this secret," she whispered. "I've been seeing Benji for a few months now."

Royce flipped the next photo in the stack over. There was no need to show them making out if she admitted their relationship. "The security footage shows you arriving back at the hotel at eight twenty," he said. "Would you say that's accurate?"

Jasmine nodded. "Sounds right."

Royce made a note in his portfolio and looked at her again. "What time did Benji leave?"

Jasmine's cheeks turned pink, and she cleared her throat nervously. "Um, like eight forty-five."

"Are you sure?" Tara asked.

Jasmine's delicate blush darkened to a scorching red. "It could've been eight forty. He didn't last—um, didn't stay long."

Royce showed her the photo with the timestamp showing Benji getting into his Corvette at nine fifty.

Jasmine snorted. "No way. I already told you the original time was accurate. It might've been off by a minute or two, but this," she said, tapping the photo, "is off by more than an hour. Benji McKay left my room no later than eight forty-five."

"Did Benji mention plans to see someone else after leaving your hotel room?" Tara asked.

Jasmine's bow mouth fell open, and all the color drained from her face. "Are you saying…"

"We're not saying anything," Royce said. "We're asking you if Benji might have stopped off to see anyone else in the hotel." She shook her head, but Royce continued. "Someone employed there or another Magnolia Qu—"

"No," Jasmine snapped angrily. "Benji was done with Rachel. So done with her."

Royce recalled the private messages Rachel had exchanged with Benji. He'd called her a whore more than once and told her she'd get what was coming to her. Was death what Benji had thought she deserved? Those were questions Royce would save for his primary person of interest.

"Have you spoken with Benji since Saturday?" Royce asked.

She shook her head. "I've called him a few times and left messages. I thought he ghosted me until he texted me on Monday morning."

"May I see the text?" Royce asked.

Jasmine thought about it for a few seconds before pulling her phone from her purse. She tapped on the screen a few times before sliding the mobile device to Royce.

Hey, baby girl. Sorry I've been so quiet. I'm still in shock about Rach, you know? The cops were here. They think I killed her. Maggie and Harris want me to keep a low profile. You know I didn't kill her, right? Didn't I show you how much I want to be with you on Saturday night?

There was nothing of an evidentiary nature in the message unless he counted Benji's denial about his prowess. Royce had devoted a longer time making love to himself than Benji had spent with Jasmine. Oh, and Royce learned Benji referred to his parents by their first names.

Royce slid the phone back to Jasmine. "Thank you for coming in today. We appreciate your honesty and cooperation."

She bounced her gaze between Royce and Tara again. "That's it?"

"Is there something else you'd like to add?" Tara asked her.

Jasmine squared her shoulders and notched her chin up higher. "Rachel Morgan didn't light up a room with her smile. She drew the air out of it like a soul-sucking vacuum stuck on an all-you-can-eat setting. There were plenty of people who couldn't stand her. It wouldn't be fair to only focus on Benji."

"I assure you we are not unfairly targeting anyone. We will follow all leads until we've arrested the right person."

She nodded and rose to her feet.

"Jasmine," Royce said before she could take a step. "Now that you've adjusted your story, I'm afraid I'll need you to account for your evening after Benji left."

Her eyes widened. For a moment, Royce thought she would burst into tears or express disbelief he would even ask. Jasmine took a deep breath instead. "Fair enough. First, I finished what Benji started but couldn't complete, and then I ordered a brownie sundae from room service and took a long hot bubble bath. Is there anything else you'd like to know?"

Royce fought off a smile. Her moxie reminded him of a former Magnolia Queen who'd raised the man he loved. "That's all for now. Have a good day."

Jasmine nodded and left the room.

Tara giggled after a moment. "Jasmine is going to rule the world someday," she said.

"Yeah, she's going to do all right." Royce stretched his neck. "Let's debrief the chief and get ready for our meeting with Benji later this morning." The two of them stood up and headed to the door. "What's the likelihood we'll have his phone and social media records before they arrive?"

Tara snorted. "I hear brownie sundaes make good consolation prizes."

Benji arrived early at the precinct for his appointment, and he hadn't come alone. The tall, redhead was flanked by his parents on his right side and a man he presumed to be Benji's legal counsel on the left. The elder McKays wore matching stoic expressions and somber suits in what Royce thought of as funeral black, while the lawyer had chosen a less severe charcoal gray, three-piece ensemble with a pale blue silk tie. His expression was the kind of smug that dared someone to take a swing at him. Royce's brawling days were over, but he wouldn't mind seeing Tara lay him out.

Benji wore a pair of jeans, a light-gray hoodie with a logo Royce didn't recognize in the center, and the new Chucks on his feet. Benji either hadn't received the memo on what to wear to the precinct, or he'd set out to prove just how little Royce concerned him. They'd see how long his nonchalance lasted once Royce revealed his cards.

Royce shook their hands and asked Benji and his attorney, Langston Short, to follow him. Maggie and Harris wanted to come along, but Langston discouraged it before Royce shut them down.

"But he's our son," Maggie said as the first cracks in her façade appeared. She'd wrung her hands a few times before clasping them until her fingers turned white.

"He's an adult who's accompanied by his attorney," Royce replied. "Please have a seat."

"But," Maggie said, stepping forward and clutching Benji's sweatshirt sleeve. "I'm his mother. He needs me."

"Cut the cord, Maggie," Harris said bitterly and sat down in one of the vinyl chairs. "Remember what I said, son."

"Yes, sir."

Harris pulled his phone from his suit pocket and proceeded to forget about everyone around him.

Benji patted his mother's hand. "I'll be fine, Mom."

She reached up and stroked his hair. "Do what Langston tells you."

"I will," Benji said, sounding and looking mortified.

Maggie sat down in the chair beside her husband and crossed her legs.

Royce led Benji and his attorney to the interview room where Tara was waiting for them.

"Good to see you again, Benji," she said politely.

"I wish I could say the feeling is mutual. No offense."

"None taken," Tara said, gesturing for them to have a seat.

Royce sat across from them in the empty chair next to Tara. He stated the date, time, and people present for the video recording while Benji looked at the camera aimed at him.

"You're recording this?" he asked.

"Benji, we talked about this," Langston said. "Just do as I tell you and everything will be fine."

The young man nodded and relaxed until Royce began reading his Miranda rights.

"Wait," Benji shouted and turned on his lawyer once Royce finished. "You said they weren't arresting me."

"Benji," Royce said patiently, "you're not under arrest, but if I want to use this recording as evidence in a trial—"

"Who's trial?" Benji demanded to know.

Langston pinched the bridge of his nose and muttered, "Christ."

"Anyone's," Royce said. "This is how I ensure the evidence I collect is admissible in court. It's one thing to arrest a person, but it's an entirely different ball game to prosecute them."

"But I don't know anything," Benji protested. "There's nothing I can tell you."

"The thing is, you might not know you've stumbled onto something unless we take you through that night," Tara told him.

"But I already did," Benji argued.

Royce tilted his head and studied him. "Did you tell us everything?"

"Quit dancing around and ask the boy your questions," Langston told them.

"I just asked him a question," Royce pointed out. "Benji, can you recount your whereabouts on Saturday evening for the recording?"

Benji huffed a sigh and repeated his story verbatim, which in itself was suspicious. He'd had days to think up new details but hadn't embellished his story one iota.

"You said your breakup with Rachel wasn't contentious," Royce said. "But I've come across an exchange of social media messages between you and Rachel that says otherwise." He showed them a printout of what he'd thought of as their greatest hits. And for effect, he read his favorite part out loud. "'You're a whore, Rachel. You'll get what you've got coming to you.' And she replied with 'I'm the whore? How's your son?'" Royce looked at Benji. "Care to comment."

"No," Langston said, but his client wasn't listening.

"I don't have a son," Benji said tersely. "The bitch was lying. Fine, Rachel and I got into a few arguments after breaking up. Big deal."

Bitch. Whore. Royce recognized a pattern here. What a charmer.

"Benjamin, I've asked you not to speak without my permission," Langston said.

Royce kept pushing forward. "Benji, can you confirm what time you arrived at the Mansion on Forsyth on the evening of February sixth?"

Benji scrunched up his brow. "I didn't say anything about being there."

"You didn't," Tara said, pulling a photo from the folder and setting it in front of him. "We're saying it. The timestamp says you arrived at eight twenty. Would you say that's accurate?"

Benji opened his mouth to speak, but Langston cut him off with a wave. "Do not answer that question."

Tara showed Benji a still frame of him and Jasmine making out in the elevator.

"Oh no," the redhead whispered and slouched in his chair.

"Not another damn word," Langston said.

Tara showed the final photo of Benji getting into his car at nine fifty. The young man seemed to shrink farther into himself.

Langston looked at the photo and back up at Tara. "What am I missing here? It seems to me my client has an alibi for when Miss Morgan was killed."

"He would if Jasmine hadn't stated Benji left her room at eight forty-five," Royce said. "Miss Morgan was killed sometime between eight thirty and nine fifteen. Benji didn't exit the hotel until nearly ten o'clock."

"And Benji doesn't appear in any interior security footage," Tara said. "Which means he used the service access elevators or stairwells."

Langston sighed heavily. "I don't hear a question in there anywhere."

"Okay," Royce said, "Let me give it a try. What were you doing for over an hour after you left Jasmine's room, and how did you know about the service passages?" Royce asked. "That's two questions, counselor."

Benji straightened and started to answer, but Langston cut him off. "I'd like a private word with my client first."

"Sure," Royce said and turned the recording equipment off. "We'll just be out in the hallway."

He and Tara exited the room and walked a little way down the empty hallway.

"Well?" Royce asked.

"He looked guilty of something, but his body language didn't scream at me."

"Yeah," Royce agreed. "He looked more embarrassed than anything."

They didn't have long to speculate because Langston opened the door and popped his head out. "We're ready."

Royce and Tara returned to the room and reclaimed their seats. Benji McKay's entire demeanor changed. Instead of slouching, the redhead sat tall and looked more alert. His eyes brimmed with unshed tears, making Royce curious about what the lawyer had said to him.

"Where were you between eight forty-five and nine fifty?" Royce asked.

"I met up with Ian Boyd. He works as a butler there."

Royce recalled the guy from the long night of interviews. He was the one who'd delivered food to Rachel's door just before nine and reported there had been no answer.

"You're friends with Ian?" Tara asked.

Benji shook his head. "We went to high school together for a few years, but we weren't friends."

"Why not?" Royce asked.

"There'd been, um, a misunderstanding between us, and I avoided him."

"What kind of misunderstanding?" Tara pressed.

"Why does it matter?" Langston questioned.

"It just does," Royce replied. "Please answer the question."

Benji scrubbed his face for a few seconds before lowering his hands. "Sophomore year, Rachel and I had broken up for a few months."

"Is that the time she slashed your tires?" Royce asked.

"Detective," Langston warned.

"It's sergeant," Royce reminded him. "Please answer the question, Benji."

"Yeah," Benji said. "Ian was Rachel's tutor at the time. They started hanging out a lot, and Rachel flirted with him at school to make me jealous."

"Did it work?" Tara asked.

"Yes, ma'am. I couldn't understand why she was spending all her free time with him and not giving me another chance. Around Christmas break, Rachel found out she'd brought all her failing grades up, so she dumped Ian and took me back." Benji's eyes went vacant, and a smile tugged on his lips until Langston yanked him out of his fond memory with a sharp elbow jab. "Sorry."

"Then what happened?" Royce asked.

"Rachel got her Sweet Sixteen trip to Cancun," Benji said.

"That's not what they meant," Langston chided.

"Sorry," Benji repeated. "Well, Rachel told me I'd been jealous for no reason and that I was the one Ian wanted, not her. She claimed Ian did her homework and helped her pass her tests to get closer to me."

"But you were broken up."

"I was a horny teenager who would've believed anything to get back in her pants," Benji admitted. Another smile tugged at his lips, but he shook himself from his reverie. "Rachel didn't stop at just telling me Ian had the hots for me. She told the entire school. By the time we returned from winter break, everyone knew and made his life a living hell to the point he switched schools by February."

"Including you?" Royce asked.

Genuine remorse shone in his eyes when Benji nodded. "I'm not proud of it."

"What changed?" Tara asked.

"I ran into Ian at a friend of a friend's house a few months ago. We, um, smoked some weed and talked it out. I found out what had really happened between him and Rachel." Benji took a deep breath. "I don't want to say bad things about Rachel, especially after someone hurt her."

"We won't find her killer if all we hear are stories about rainbows and kittens," Royce said. "We need the truth, Benji."

"Rachel had been providing Ian with sexual favors and stringing him along to do her homework and get her ready for her exams." Royce wanted to point out that homework was prepping for exams but kept his mouth shut. "Once she finished with Ian, she shoved him aside and took me back. I don't know why she had to hurt Ian the way she did, but that was Rachel. She was so beautiful she stole my breath, but she could be vicious and cruel. She played me like a puppet." Benji took a shaky breath, then began to cry softly. "I'm going to miss her for the rest of my life."

"So you and Ian bonded over the experience?" Royce pressed.

"Yes, sir." Benji smiled sheepishly. "Mostly, I wanted access to weed, and Ian has a great hookup." Benji stilled, and his face went white.

"Relax, kid. I'm only interested in solving Rachel's murder." Benji's shoulders slumped again, and Royce continued. "Did you visit Ian often at the Mansion? Is that how you knew where the service passages were?"

Benji nodded. "Every Saturday night when my parents go out."

"You just got permission to drive, though," Royce said. "How were you getting there?"

"Um…"

"You drove anyway," Royce said.

"I hurt my left knee, so I could drive just fine. Stupid doctor's rules," he said, rolling his eyes. "Sometimes I took an Uber there and back. Ian always takes a break when I get there, and we smoke in his car and listen to music and stuff." Royce was curious about the "stuff" but didn't think it was relevant.

"And that's all my client is willing to say," Langston said. "You asked for his alibi during the missing time, and he gave it to you." He gripped Benji's bicep and pulled him to stand. He dropped a business card onto the table and directed them to arrange any further interviews through him.

Once alone, Royce turned to Tara. "I want to speak to Ian Boyd again."

"I'll make it happen."

Chapter
EIGHTEEN

"**N**ow we're getting somewhere," Sawyer said, gripping the steering wheel tighter. "The truth will prevail."

The audiobook paused just as the fictional detective eased the door open with the barrel of his gun. Sawyer's phone rang through the speaker, and he growled at the interruption until he saw the identity of his caller.

He pushed the button on his steering wheel to answer. "Hello, Sergeant Locke."

Royce snorted. "Why so formal?"

"Well, I wasn't sure where you were calling me from or who might be around you."

"Yeah?" Royce asked huskily. "And if I told you I was in a room all by myself?"

Sawyer smiled and played along. "I'd ask what you were doing or maybe what you're wearing."

Royce chuckled. "I'm just a man, standing in an empty office, wondering where the love of my life has gone."

"He's headed over to the newspaper to meet Felix," Sawyer replied.

"And the other yahoos in your unit?"

Sawyer laughed. "I'll be sure to share your high opinion with them. Holly is interviewing more of Jessica Lynn Campbell's equestrian friends and trainers."

"And Toph?"

"He's on his way to Jacksonville to speak with Tommy Hasselback. He grew up next to Barbara Jean Wright. They were best friends as kids, and Barbara developed quite a crush on him as a teenager. If something had been going on in Barbara's life, she probably would've told Tommy. None of her family or friends mentioned him to the police, so it doesn't appear Donovan and Burke interviewed him. Topher tracked him down, but Tommy has dodged his calls so far. It was time to visit him."

"Alone?" Royce asked. "Sounds like the guy might have something to hide."

"That's why Mendoza loaned me Diego for the day."

"I was just in the chief's office a few minutes ago giving him an update before his daily press conference. You'd have thought he would've told me about loaning out one of my detectives."

Sawyer could hear an edge of excitement in Royce's voice, and the hairs on his neck stood up. "Are you close?"

"Getting there," Royce said.

Sawyer bit his bottom lip as he turned into the newspaper lot. He found a spot near the front of the building but didn't shut off his vehicle. "Are we still talking about your case?"

Royce chuckled. "What case?"

Sawyer pictured Royce sprawled in his office chair with his zipper down and dick in his hand. An abrupt knock jerked him out of his trance. Sawyer flinched and wrenched his head toward the window to glare at Felix.

"Whatcha doing?" the reporter asked, though his crooked smile said he had a good idea.

"Ugh, that guy," Royce said, but there was no animosity in his tone.

He'd never admit it to Felix, but Royce held him in high esteem…for a reporter. "Tell him we're almost done."

Felix grinned because he could hear Royce through the speakers. He gestured for Sawyer to roll the window down, and he complied. "Royce, is that you?" Felix asked.

"Who the hell else would Sawyer be having phone sex with?"

Sawyer laughed. "We were not having phone sex."

"Okay, well, one of us was having the sex while the other was thinking about it," Royce said.

"Was not," Sawyer denied again.

Felix's lips turned down at the corners dramatically enough to make a clown instructor proud. "Are these investigations cutting into your alone time?"

"Fucking Felix," Royce said. "That would be his clown name." His remark reminded Sawyer of just how in sync they were.

"Sounds more like a talent to me," Felix countered, waggling his brows.

"Time for me to go. I'll catch up with you later, GB." Royce disconnected before Sawyer could respond. Not using a proper goodbye to end a phone call was one of Royce's biggest pet peeves, so Sawyer would need to call him out on the lackluster signoff.

He rolled up the window, killed the engine, and climbed out of his vehicle. "Did I catch you at a bad time?"

Felix's lips twitched. "Pretty sure that's my line. You looked all blissed out and happy."

"So you knocked on the window and ruined it?"

The reporter shrugged. "Just being a friend who didn't want you to get caught doing something you shouldn't."

"As if," Sawyer scoffed. But hadn't he been careening down a steep hill on a three-wheeled skateboard?

"And, actually," Felix said, "your timing is perfect. I've just come back from an interview with Sheriff Wheeler."

And another wheel popped off, pitching Sawyer face-first onto the pavement. He gritted his teeth to keep from spewing any of the vitriol resting on his tongue. Sawyer had worked through his bitterness toward his former employer in therapy, and until Charlie had shown up at Joe's, he'd convinced himself it had worked. Instead, Sawyer realized he'd only buried his rage. Each positive stride forward had been a shovelful of dirt, some occasions earning more than one. A fresh start with SPD. Three shovelfuls. Falling in love with Royce. Ten shovelfuls. Taking the love and building a life around it. Fifty shovelfuls followed by heavy tamping to really pack the dirt tight.

But Sawyer hadn't eradicated his fury; he'd unknowingly blanketed it with denial in the guise of fertile soil. Charlie's remarks had shaken his foundation, causing cracks to form and making it possible for sunlight and water to reach the feelings he'd so deeply buried. Sawyer had been so caught up with his investigation that he'd avoided feeding the seedling, and delving into the touchy subject with Felix was a surefire way to fertilize the damn thing.

"I don't see how your interview with Wheeler involves me," Sawyer said, making a last-ditch effort to block the sun.

"You wouldn't because you don't know the nature of my visit with him."

"And that would be?" Sawyer heard himself asking, even as his soul shouted, "No! No! No!"

"To find out if he was running for sheriff again," Felix replied. His lips quirked up on one side. "Well, that's the bullshit reason I gave to get an audience with him."

Sawyer snorted. "He's not royalty."

Felix sobered. "He thinks he is, and quite frankly, his untouchable attitude should concern everyone."

Irritation sparked in Sawyer's gut. Or was that the seed of discontent unfurling and taking root? "Again, I don't see how this involves me."

"Don't you?" Felix asked. He didn't buy Sawyer's faux nonchalance one bit. "I think you'll change your mind once you hear what Wheeler had to say."

"I've avoided reading every article written about the man since deciding to leave him and CCSD in the past."

"I'll let you hear the unabridged audio version of it."

"I'll pass," Sawyer said.

Felix stopped suddenly and spun to face him, making Sawyer jerk to an abrupt halt. "This isn't just about one man's history with a corrupt lawman, Sawyer. The problem is much bigger."

Sawyer narrowed his eyes. "Did Charlie call you? Is that what this is all about?"

Not even a minuscule expression of recognition or surprise registered on Felix's face. "Who?"

Sawyer snorted. "Charlie Price, my former partner. He showed up at Joe's the night of my promotion celebration and told me everything, Felix."

"And you expect me to know what *everything* entails?"

Sawyer had to hand it to him. Felix was smooth. "Charlie told me he was your source for the articles you wrote about the sheriff's department. Are you going to deny it?"

"I will neither confirm nor deny my source." Felix's rote remark fueled Sawyer's irritation until it threatened to become an inferno.

He turned and headed back to the parking lot with Felix following fast on his heels.

"Where are you going?" Felix asked.

"Back to the precinct. This was a big mistake."

"When did you become a quitter?"

Sawyer stopped and whirled on him. "I'm not quitting. I'll find out my information another way." He wasn't quite sure how. Maybe he could bypass Felix and work with Minerva, the paper's editor. "I thought we'd worked through our past issues, but I can see how wrong I was."

"Wait," Felix said.

Sawyer quickened his pace instead.

Felix released a sound that was a combination of frustrated growl and wounded animal. "I'm sorry, Sawyer." If not for the pleading tone, Sawyer would've kept going back to his car where he'd pretend a wild idea wasn't germinating in the soil.

Sawyer stopped and slowly faced Felix. "What exactly are you sorry for?"

"So many things, and I don't know where to begin."

Sawyer crossed his arms over his chest in a Royce-like move. "I have time."

Felix chuckled. "Doubtful, but I appreciate the patience." He puffed out his cheeks and released a slow breath. "I'm sorry, but I can't let this thing with Wheeler go, even if I understand why you have. It's much more personal for you, and you deserve to rise above it and be happy. I'm a petty bitch who wants to drag the fat bastard to the deepest pits of hell." Felix widened his eyes a bit and staggered backward a few steps. "Whoa. That truth bomb was explosive."

And Sawyer felt its blast to his core. He could feel the fissures in his denial growing wider. He should've accepted Felix's apology and gotten the hell out of there. "I hate him too," Sawyer admitted. "I'm not over what he did. I just stopped letting it consume me. I wouldn't give him that kind of power over me then, and I won't now."

Felix searched his gaze for a few seconds before giving a subtle nod. Had he heard something in Sawyer's voice or seen something in his eyes to make him relent? Or was he just biding his time until he could bring it up again? One key thing Sawyer learned in therapy was to celebrate all victories, no matter how big or small. Felix backing down was a huge win.

"Let's go inside and talk about the Magnolia Murders," Felix said. "You reached out to me, and I really want to help. No more talk about he who shan't be named."

Sawyer chuckled and followed Felix inside. He passed on his offer of coffee but accepted a bottle of water.

"How can I help you?" Felix asked.

Sawyer took a sip, then grinned. "First off, you need to know this is not a quid pro quo kind of thing. I'm here seeking information but will not share anything about my investigation in return." He raised his hand when Felix started to speak. "But I will grant you an exclusive interview once I make an arrest."

"Deal."

"Has the paper kept copies of all the Magnolia Queen programs?" Sawyer asked.

Felix tilted his head to the side. "Why would we?"

"Because the paper pays for and prints the programs."

Felix smiled. "Come on."

They exited his office and went downstairs to a cavernous archive room.

Sawyer swept his gaze over the space. Huge filing cabinets lined the room's perimeter, and rows of multitiered metal shelving units sat in the center. A rod went through the middle of each shelf, and stacks of old newspapers were draped over it as far as Sawyer could see. Paper, dust, and history permeated the air. This is what heaven would smell like to him. "I'd love to spend about a week in here."

"I could arrange that," Felix said.

Sawyer snorted. "Not for the price I'd have to pay."

"Not even for unsupervised time in there?" Felix asked, gesturing to a vault on the far wall Sawyer hadn't seen. "It's where we stash the good stuff."

"Tempting, but no."

Felix shrugged. "Can't blame a guy for trying."

Sawyer followed Felix to a filing cabinet where he withdrew the programs from 1984, 1996, and 2000. He wasn't surprised Felix was familiar with the layout of the archive room, but the speed with which he located the items was telling. What had they gleaned from the glossy pages?

Sawyer thumbed through the list of sponsors in the front and stopped when he got to Marilyn Moynihan's tribute. A collage of images of the woman from her various pageant roles took up one page. The first was of her crowning in 1964. She wore a ballgown, sash, and a smile more dazzling than her sparkling crown. In another, Marilyn wore a prim suit and ruffled collared shirt and held a clipboard in her hand instead of a bouquet of roses. Around her, several pageant contestants were raptly listening to whatever she had to say. Well, all but the one who appeared to be daydreaming or perhaps just tuning out Marilyn. Sawyer smiled down at the younger version of his mother.

"What's so funny?" Felix asked.

Sawyer tapped the photo. "This is my mom. She didn't have time for Marilyn's bullshit in 1976."

"Or anytime afterward," Felix said. "Their arguments are legendary, and curiously, they both ended up walking away from the pageant."

"But for very different reasons."

Felix hummed for a few seconds. "What do you hope to find in the programs?"

Sawyer shook his head and kept perusing the slick pages, pretending he hadn't already completed his objective. He stopped on the image of Neil Henshaw and studied his handsome face and toothy grin.

"What do you know about this guy?" Sawyer asked.

"I'd heard many rumors about him, but nothing I could substantiate, so we left him out of the podcast."

"What kind of rumors?" Sawyer asked. He listened as Felix delved deeper into the issues Evangeline had highlighted. He mentioned Marilyn's name a few times, but Sawyer forced himself not to react as he continued thumbing through the magazine.

He picked up the next one from 1996 and repeated scanning the pages while Felix continued talking, only glancing up when he cut off suddenly.

"What?" Sawyer asked.

"Are you listening?"

Sawyer smirked. "To every word. Did you interview a lot of people for your podcast?"

"Dozens," Felix said. "Not everyone wanted to go on record or appear in the episodes."

"Give me the CliffsNotes."

"You'd know if you listened to the podcast. I'm hurt you haven't," Felix said, adding a few sniffs.

"I'm hurt you think I'd allow it to influence my investigation."

"Yet here you are."

"Yet here I am," Sawyer agreed.

Felix caved and talked about his favorite interviews while Sawyer confirmed Marilyn was still the Magnolia Mentor in 2000. He quickly skimmed past her bio but noticed they still used the same old photos.

"And what about Marilyn and Neil?" Sawyer asked when Felix finished. "They were staples of the pageant for decades."

"He died a few years ago," Felix said.

"And Marilyn?"

Felix crossed his arms over his chest and smirked. "You may live with the king of bullshitters, but you're still transparent. What do you want to know about Marilyn and why?"

Sawyer returned to perusing the final program, allowing Felix to stew in his juices. After a few minutes, Felix sighed heavily.

"Fine, but I'm holding you to the exclusivity you promised me."

Glancing up, Sawyer said, "I keep my word."

"Marilyn lives at the same retirement community as Rocky's grand-mother, but she has advanced dementia. Only family can visit her, but Rocky's granny is a fount of information." It took Felix a second to recall which one of the retirement communities she lived in. "Ask for Beatrice Jacobs and hang on to your wallet."

Sawyer chuckled and handed the programs back to Felix. "Thief or card shark?"

"Depending on who you ask, those terms mean the same thing." Felix returned the archived documents to the filing cabinet and closed the drawer. He gave Sawyer his full attention. "Was the information on Marilyn Moynihan the reason you stopped by?"

"I will neither confirm nor deny."

Felix chuckled. "Touché."

Chapter
NINETEEN

Sawyer's call to Royce rolled over to voicemail, and he disconnected without leaving a message. He stepped out of the car and zipped up the leather jacket he had taken back from Royce. Ducking his face from the wind, he caught a whiff of his boyfriend's familiar scent. It warmed Sawyer's blood quicker than Royce's beloved hot tub.

His phone rang as he approached the retirement center's main entrance. He fished his phone from his pocket and smiled at the display.

"Hey, baby."

"Christ, Sawyer," Royce said, sounding rushed and out of breath. He went on immediate alert.

"What's wrong?"

"I'm in a room full of people, and you answered the phone with your bedroom voice," Royce replied.

Sawyer's pulse simmered from a gallop to a fast jog when he

realized he'd been played. "'Hello, sergeant' was too formal, and 'hey, baby' is too sexy. Dickhead, it is."

Royce chuckled. "How'd it go with Felix?"

"Huh-uh," Sawyer said. "You were going to tell me about your interviews before Felix interrupted us."

Royce recapped his meeting with Jasmine first.

"Ouch," Sawyer said when Royce got to the fudge brownie remark. "I mean, she's not wrong. Who doesn't love those? What did Benji have to say?"

"I didn't question him about his prowess."

Sawyer snorted. "I suppose not. What about the rest of it?"

Sawyer's feet stilled, and he forgot about the chilly air as Royce recounted Benji's odd friendship with Ian and his admission that they'd been smoking pot together.

"Sounds like both had a motive to harm her, and Ian had access to her room and would've known how to avoid detection. Do you think they acted together?"

"It's a strong possibility," Royce said. "We're trying to find Ian now. We went by his home and the hotel, and he wasn't at either location."

"You think Benji tipped him off and he's lying low?"

"Maybe. He wasn't on the schedule at work, so it wasn't like he was a no-show. How'd the chat with Felix go?"

Sawyer didn't tell him about their argument over Wheeler. The last thing he wanted to do was stir up tension between Royce and Felix again. He stuck to Felix's one-sided chat about the rumors swirling around the pageant people and the admissions Felix had sussed out from interviewees.

"Are you headed back to the station?" Royce asked.

"After I make a quick stop at Magnolia Manor."

"The retirement community?"

Sawyer chuckled. "Yeah. I figured I'd give them a down payment to secure a villa for when we're older." He looked at the large pond and manicured lawns with dormant magnolia trees dotting the landscape. It would be a beautiful place in the spring when the trees were in full bloom. "We could do worse."

"I'll live anywhere as long as it's with you," Royce said.

Movement in his periphery caught Sawyer's attention. He turned his head and locked eyes with Royce's sister, Drusilla, as she exited the retirement community, wearing pink scrubs and a black fleece jacket zipped up to her chin. He hadn't seen her since the ER waiting room after Royce had gotten shot on one of the first cases they worked together. The Locke clan had stared at him with various levels of suspicion and hostility. Sawyer had thought he'd glimpsed something else like fear sparking in Dru's eyes that day, but she'd blinked, and loathing had replaced distress.

Three years later, Dru looked like a deer caught in headlights. She froze and stared at Sawyer, and he did the same.

"I need to go, Ro. I'll call you back after I talk to Rocky's grandmother."

Royce chuckled. "Don't accept an offer to play cards, and don't take any of her bets."

Sawyer laughed. "Felix warned me about her, but how do you know about her proclivities?"

"Beatrice was dear friends with my Aunt Tipsy."

"It really is a small world."

"Hey," Royce said gruffly before Sawyer could hang up. "I love you."

"I love you most." Sawyer was close enough for Dru to overhear, and there was no mistaking who he'd been speaking to.

Sawyer and Royce exchanged their goodbyes, and he pocketed his phone. Drusilla had remained frozen in front of the double doors he needed to enter, and Sawyer hadn't budged from his spot either. A strong wind whipped through, ruffling his hair and sending a shaft of cold air down the back of his jacket.

"We'll turn into popsicles if we continue to square off like it's high noon," Sawyer said.

Dru's mouth twitched, but she didn't smile. She stepped aside and gestured to the doors. "By all means."

Sawyer had intended to walk past her without another word, but he couldn't. This woman was someone Royce loved deeply, and Sawyer would regret it forever if he didn't at least attempt to make peace with her. Her son and Jace had both told Royce that Dru missed him. She'd said as much in her text, even if she'd gone radio silent since. Valentine's

Day was right around the corner, and what better way was there to express his love for Royce than by giving him the only thing he truly wanted—a chance to reconnect with his sister and nephews. So he stopped and turned to face her.

Drusilla's eyes were a lighter shade of gray than Royce's. They were wide and wet with unshed tears, making her irises look like shimmering mercury. Sawyer wasn't sure if the moisture gathering there was from emotion or the biting wind. He preferred one option over the other but was afraid to hope.

"You mean it, don't you?" she asked softly.

He just blinked for a second while he tried to figure out what she meant. The phone call. "That I love him?" She nodded. "More than anything or anyone. There's nothing I won't do for him…except give him up."

"Simmer down, Rick Astley," Dru said. "I'm not asking you to give him up."

Sawyer smiled despite the awkwardness. "I'm never gonna let him down."

"Yeah, I get it," she said. "You won't run around and desert him." Dru took a deep breath. "Good. You make him happy in ways I never could've pictured for someone named Locke."

"What about Jace? He's getting married in a few months."

Dru nodded. "They deserve all the happiness in the world."

"So do you, Dru. We'll all be here for you when you realize it."

She shook her head, and the dam broke. Tears slid down her cheeks, and she swiped angrily at them.

"I'm sorry," Sawyer said. If she were someone he knew well, Sawyer would've pulled her into a hug. "I didn't mean to make you cry."

She sucked in a shaky breath. "I'm crying over my own stupidity. You don't get to take credit for my tears, pal."

"Men are the worst," Sawyer said, coaxing a surprised giggle from her.

"Sometimes," she said. Then Dru tilted her head to the side. "But some of them are pretty amazing. They take on the world to keep you, sticking around through thick and thin and vowing never to give you up."

Sawyer felt incredibly moved, and more than ever, he wanted to bridge the divide between brother and sister. "There's nothing Royce won't do for you either, and you get me by default."

"A bonus brother," she said dryly. "Just what I always wanted. Thank goodness I get to claim Holly as a sister soon." They shared a brief laugh, and Dru sobered. "I'll call Royce soon. I don't mean to keep him hanging, but I'm working three part-time jobs right now. A full-time position is opening here soon, and if I get it, I can quit the other two jobs. Magnolia Manor pays great, has excellent benefits, and treats its staff and residents really well. I've been saving every spare penny so the boys and I can get our own place. Things are starting to look up."

"Good," Sawyer said, and he meant it.

Dru shivered, and he felt horrible for keeping her out in the cold.

"You better get going before you freeze to death."

Dru nodded and took a few steps forward before she stopped, spun around, and launched herself into his arms. "Thank you for loving him so much."

Sawyer's eyes stung, and he knew damn well it had nothing to do with the wind. "Please text Royce and tell him how you feel. If time and space are what you need, he'll give them to you. If it's money—"

Dru pulled back and shook her head vehemently. "No. I have to do this on my own. For my boys and, more importantly, for myself. But I will text him. Thank you."

Sawyer nodded and watched her leave. She got into a small sedan that was probably as old as he was, but it fired up right away, and the engine ran smoothly as she drove out of the parking lot. He stood there for a few more seconds after she left to pull himself together, then he opened the doors and headed inside Magnolia Manor.

Feeling rattled from his unexpected run-in with Dru, Sawyer's thoughts were a little jumbled as he asked for and received directions to where he could find Beatrice Jacobs. He was charmed to know she was in the middle of a card tournament. Hopefully, she'd spare him a few minutes to talk about Marilyn Moynihan.

Sawyer's thoughts turned to Royce. Should he tell him about the conversation with Dru? Would it make Royce feel better, or would it worsen his pangs? Would it bolster his hope or make it that much harder for Royce to wait?

He recognized Beatrice Jacobs without an introduction because of the laserlike focus she had on the card game in front of her. Sawyer wouldn't play against her nor would he accept any bet she offered.

She glanced up and narrowed her eyes as he approached. Was she trying to figure out who he was, or was she annoyed at the interruption?

Sawyer smiled to soften his cop face. "Excuse me, which one of you lovely ladies is Beatrice Jacobs?"

"Who wants to know?" asked the lady to her left.

"Run, Bea," the one on her right said.

A gentleman across from Beatrice chuckled and pointed at her. "Hope your taser is charged and ready, mister."

Sawyer chuckled. "No tasing necessary." He met Beatrice's shrewd gaze and introduced himself. "I'd just like to have a private word."

"Who the hell called the cops on us?" Beatrice asked.

"No one, ma'am, but your name did come up during an investigation."

Beatrice pushed back from the table and rose to her feet. "How exciting for me." She started to walk away from the game but turned around to sweep her cards off the table and drop them in her cardigan pocket. "Better take these with me."

"She's probably got an ace up her sleeve anyway," another gentleman groused.

"Like I need to cheat to win against the likes of you. It's like taking candy from a baby." She gripped Sawyer's bicep when she reached him, then gave an extra squeeze. "So firm. You must spend a lot of time in the gym."

"I do," Sawyer replied as he guided her over to an arrangement of furniture next to a crackling fire. "It keeps me sharp."

Beatrice settled herself into a chair. "That's why I play cards." She tapped her temple then dropped her hands into her lap. "I'm still sharp as a tack, even though I'm twice as round as I used to be. What can I do for you today?"

Sawyer introduced himself, explaining their connection through Rocky and Royce.

Love and adoration softened her features, and she smiled wryly. "Bet those two keep you on your toes."

"Yes, ma'am."

"How can I help you, Sergeant Locke?"

He explained he was taking a fresh look at the Magnolia Murders and interviewing folks involved in the pageants.

"That wasn't me," Beatrice said. "I didn't exactly howl at the moon or turn men to stone, but no one would ever call me a looker."

Sawyer disagreed. Beatrice Jacobs had a natural beauty that drew a person to her. "We're also talking to friends and acquaintances of people involved."

"But I don't know any—" Her eyes widened, and she leaned forward. "Oh! You're here for gossip about Marilyn Moynihan."

Sawyer chuckled. "Not gossip, but I was hoping you could offer some insight since Marilyn can't speak to me."

"I've known Marilyn since we were little girls, so I know plenty about her, but I'm afraid I can't offer you much insight into her role in the pageant, other than that she lorded her crown over our heads."

"She didn't talk about why she left?" Sawyer asked.

Beatrice snorted. "Oh, she bitched nonstop about the progressive changes to the pageant, but it didn't stop her from tuning in each year. She complained the entire time, so the other residents stopped watching it with her. Marilyn has always been a wet blanket, but it's gotten worse with age. She always turned us into the retirement village director for one rule infraction or another. We pay good money to live here, and we should get the experience we want…within reason."

"Of course," Sawyer agreed, though he figured their definitions of "within reason" varied greatly.

"What did she have to be so uppity about anyway?" Beatrice asked. "Sure, she won the Magnolia Queen title, but it didn't get her anywhere. She never married or experienced a great love of any kind that I'm aware of. And not every woman wants a spouse and kids, which is perfectly fine, but they usually have passion for something in their lives. A career or causes near and dear to their hearts, perhaps? Marilyn only loved the pageant and has been stuck in 1964." She tipped her head to the side and sighed. "I have to wonder if it's because her *father* was so cold and indifferent to her. Winning the title might've been the first time she felt cherished and valued. So sad."

"I couldn't help but notice your emphasis on father," Sawyer said. "Can I ask why that is?"

Beatrice looked around to make sure no one was listening in. "It's just a rumor, mind you, but the story goes that Marilyn was born only seven months after her parents got married. I'd heard the Moynihans tried to pass her off as a premature infant, but no one bought it."

"So Marilyn's mother was pregnant when she got married."

"Yes, and I'd bet my last dollar Seymour Moynihan isn't her biological father."

"I'm not going to take that bet," Sawyer said. "I've been warned about you."

Beatrice cackled and slapped her knees. "Well, you can't blame a girl for trying."

"Is there a rumor about who her biological father might be if not Seymour?"

"Nope. It's one of the best-kept secrets in Savannah."

"What about siblings?"

"Marilyn had a younger sister and brother. Both have passed away."

"Nephews or nieces?"

"Yes, but they weren't close to her, so they never visit." Her eyes widened. "There is someone, though. Marilyn has a great-nephew who visits her frequently. From what I understand, he's the trustee for her estate and will inherit everything once she passes. Her great-nephew truly cares for her. Some might say he cares a little too much. He hovers and fusses quite a bit. There's a fine line between being tossed in here and forgotten and being smothered with attention to assuage guilt."

"You think her nephew feels guilty over placing Marilyn here?" Sawyer asked, gesturing to their lovely surroundings.

"I think he's too young to feel guilty about much," Beatrice replied.

Sawyer narrowed his eyes. "How young?

"Late teens or early twenties."

Marilyn's involvement with the pageant was left out of the investigation, and she has a great-nephew around Rachel Morgan's age. Things were starting to click into place.

"That's a big responsibility for someone so young," Sawyer said. "It might explain why he hovers."

"Maybe. The guy just makes me uneasy."

Sawyer tilted his head. "Why?"

"Honestly, I can't put my finger on it. Maybe it's because he insists the staff put Marilyn's crown on her every day. He gets really pissy otherwise." Beatrice rolled her eyes. "Perhaps it's just a sweet gesture, or maybe he's as obsessed with it as Marilyn. I trust my instincts, and the kid is off."

"Do you know his name?"

Beatrice inhaled slowly and pursed her lips. "Starts with an *e*. Ethan, maybe." She looked beyond Sawyer and straightened. "Don't look now, but he's wheeling Marilyn past the rec room."

Sawyer pivoted and bit back a smile as Ian Boyd, Royce's person of interest, wheeled a frail, white-haired woman wearing the same crown he'd seen in the pageant program. The sparkly adornment sat slightly crooked until Ian paused and straightened it.

Well, well, well.

As if sensing his attention, Ian turned his head and locked gazes with Sawyer. The young man stiffened and resumed pushing Marilyn past the ample gathering space.

Beatrice sucked in a sharp breath and hissed, "I told you not to look. You scared him off."

Sawyer laughed and spun around. He rose to his feet and crossed to Beatrice. "You, ma'am, are a true delight and have been most helpful." He extended his hand, which she accepted and used to pull him down. She tapped her cheek with her free hand, and Sawyer placed a kiss there.

"You just made my day," she said.

Sawyer helped her to her feet, and she tucked her arm through his and gripped his bicep as he escorted her back toward her table. He smiled when she copped an extra squeeze. "And you mine," Sawyer said. "Good luck in your card tournament."

"Bah," she said, waving her hand. "Who needs luck with this lot. Maybe you come back and give me a run for my money."

"Fine, but I'm bringing backup."

She cackled. "Please do. I haven't seen Royce in a few years. You tell him to get his ass down here so we can relive some of Darla's finest moments. God, I loved that woman so much."

At long last, he'd learned Aunt Tipsy's real name. "I'll do so, ma'am."

Sawyer helped her back into her chair at the table and gave her one of his business cards. She promised to call him if she thought of anything helpful, and Sawyer bid everyone a good day before walking away. He'd dialed Royce before he reached the rec room door.

"How much do you love me?" Sawyer asked when he answered.

Chapter
TWENTY

"**I**S THAT EVEN A REAL QUESTION?" ROYCE ASKED. "AND WHY DO you sound out of breath?"

"Not now, dickhead. Listen! I know where Ian is."

Royce bolted up from his chair, snagged his jacket off the back, and headed out of the bullpen. Under normal circumstances, he would've had a snappy comeback, but this wasn't the time. Fuck it. "Hey," he gruffly said as he walked through the precinct. "You don't say anyone else's name but mine in that voice."

"What voice?"

"Breathless and full of anticipation," he said. "It's mine."

Sawyer took a shaky breath. "Everything I have is yours, including my knowledge. Your *person of interest* is at Magnolia Manor visiting his great-aunt. Guess who she is."

Royce stared out his windshield for a minute as the puzzle pieces clicked into place. "No way."

"I'd say her name, but I might still sound excitable, and you're touchy about it."

"I got your touchy right here," he said. Royce shifted his SUV into drive and pulled out of the parking lot. "I'm on my way to you. Tell me everything."

Royce listened in disbelief as Sawyer repeated everything Beatrice Jacobs had told him. "It had to be either Burke or Donovan who kept her name out of the case files," Royce said once Sawyer finished. "Burke is too young to have been her dad, but he could've been a brother. Donovan was definitely old enough to be her dad. Holy shit. Marilyn and Ian are the fucking connection tying the original three murders to Rachel's."

"Yeah, but the connection alone doesn't prove either is a murderer."

"Patience, love," Royce said. "Keep digging. That's what we do."

They discussed the next steps in both cases until Royce pulled into the parking lot at Magnolia Manor.

"Wow, this is a nice place," he remarked. "Did you secure our villa?"

"Um, I forgot about it."

"Because you're on the hunt," Royce said as he parked next to Sawyer's car.

"Yes, but that's not what threw me. I ran into your sister on my way in."

"Drusilla?"

"Do you have another sister I don't know about?" Sawyer asked.

Royce chuckled, but it sounded dry and brittle. "Probably."

Sawyer came through the double doors and headed toward the SUV a moment later. They stayed on the phone, but neither of them spoke. Royce's mind was too busy spinning all the horrible things Dru might've said to Sawyer. He missed his sister so much, but he'd abandon his attempts to reconcile if she behaved cruelly to Sawyer.

"Breathe, baby," Sawyer said.

Royce inhaled slowly and watched as Sawyer's long strides ate up the distance between them. And then he was there, in the SUV and leaning across the console to kiss Royce.

"Did she…" Royce couldn't finish.

Sawyer cupped his face. "She hugged me and thanked me for loving you so much. Dru just needs time, Ro." Sawyer told him about her dreams of landing a full-time job at Magnolia Manor and the difference it would make for her and the kids."

"But I could help her gain her independence quicker," Royce argued.

"She doesn't feel like accepting help from one person to get away from another is flexing her independence. That's how Dru got into her current situation. It might be frustrating, but it's also admirable. I made it very clear we're willing to help her and the boys however we can."

Royce swallowed hard. "Of course you did. I love you so much."

"Love you most."

"I can be patient. You've taught me that."

Sawyer winked and leaned in. "I've taught you lots of things."

Heat unfurled in his core. "Yeah, you have." Royce had planned to say more, but Ian Boyd stepped through the double doors. "There's my guy."

"It's my turn to drag my knuckles," Sawyer said sulkily. Royce wished he could kiss those pouting lips until they turned into a smile or parted on a sigh, but it would need to wait.

"Want to question him with me?" Royce asked.

"Nah, I'm going to head over to Burke's house. See what he can tell me about Donovan. I have a hard time believing Burke covered anything up for his former partner. The man went to extraordinary lengths to solve the murders."

"Keep me posted," Royce said.

"You too."

They exited the SUV simultaneously, causing Ian to pause midstride. For a brief second, Royce thought he would run, but he didn't. Ian continued toward them like he didn't have a care in the world.

Sawyer headed to his car, and Royce waved when he drove off.

"I remember you from Saturday night," Ian said. "But I can't place your name."

"Sergeant Locke," Royce said. "Can we have a chat? It won't take long."

"Here? It's like forty degrees outside," Ian said.

Royce wasn't sure if his hard shiver was genuine or for effect, but he gestured to his SUV. "Step inside my mobile office." Ian hesitated long enough to make Royce more suspicious. "Or we could head to the precinct. Up to you."

Ian straightened and smiled awkwardly. "Here's fine."

Royce fired up the engine, blasted the heat, and gestured to the controls to heat the passenger seat. Royce didn't hesitate to turn on his ass burner in the winter or the ass chiller in the summer.

"While reviewing security footage, we caught Benji McKay entering the hotel with a lady friend a little after eight. He didn't return to his car until nine fifty. Benji claims you're his alibi. He says the two of you were smoking pot in your car." Ian's eyes widened and his entire body tensed. Royce believed his surprise was genuine. "Hey, I'm not here to bust you for recreational use. If I thought you were dealing out of the Mansion, I might feel differently. Even then, I have bigger concerns right now."

Ian swallowed hard and ran a hand through his hair. "You think Benji killed Rachel."

"I've seen plenty of evidence to indicate he had a reason to harm her, and now I know he was there when she was murdered."

Ian shook his head. "Benji was with Jasmine until I went on break, then we, um, hung out in my car."

"What time did you go on break?" Royce asked.

Ian closed his eyes and pursed his lips. He was either thinking back to Saturday or buying time. "I already told you I knocked on Rachel's door at nine. I finished a few more deliveries and took my break."

"What's your best estimate?"

"Nine fifteen," Ian said.

"Benji left Jasmine's room at eight forty or eight forty-five, which gave him a solid thirty minutes before you saw him. A lot can happen in that amount of time."

Ian narrowed his eyes. "Do you really think Benji left Jasmine's room and strangled Rachel, then casually strode down to my car and waited for me?" They'd released Rachel's manner of death to the press, so it wasn't surprising Ian knew.

"I'm not sure what to think," Royce told him. "Do you think Benji could've strangled her? From what I've seen, he was very angry with Rachel."

Ian's face flushed red. "Angry? He hated Rachel. She was threatening to tell his parents about his little bastard. Benji had no one to blame but himself there. He's the one who couldn't keep it in his pants and knocked the gold digger up. Rachel broke up with him over it, not that Benji should've been mourning the loss."

"Benji told me what Rachel did to you in high school. You must've hated her."

Ian narrowed his eyes. "I've learned the trash tends to take itself out. You just have to get out of the way and wait patiently."

Royce's stomach soured. It sounded like he'd taken a page right out of a white supremacy handbook, and there was an edge to him that made Royce very uncomfortable.

"About this baby," he said. "Why didn't Benji want his parents to find out?"

Ian laughed. "Are you kidding? His mother would've wanted to keep it, and Benji wasn't willing to lose all her affection and play second fiddle to his brat. Have you met his dad? Christ, what a cold fish. Good ole Harris would probably try to have mom and baby killed."

"And Benji?"

"He just keeps pretending none of it's real," Ian said. "The weed helps."

"What was Benji's demeanor like on Saturday?"

Ian seemed to hold his breath while he pondered the question. Was he struggling to remember or to manufacture an answer to help his buddy out? Ian expelled his breath in a rush and said, "Agitated, which is surprising since he'd just gotten laid. It took him two joints to calm the hell down."

"Why didn't you tell us Rachel's hostile ex-boyfriend was in the building when she was murdered during your initial interview on Saturday?"

Ian scowled. "I didn't know he was in the building until you told me just now. Benji was waiting for me at my car like he is every week." His eyes widened when he realized what he had said. "I'm not dealing."

"Relax," Royce said. "You just told me Benji was uptight even after having sex."

Ian put both his hands up in front of him. "Because he told me he hooked up with some random chick. I didn't know it occurred at the hotel."

"Would you have told us if you had known?" Royce asked.

"No," Ian said without hesitation. "I wouldn't have wanted to get him in trouble when there were plenty of people at the hotel who'd fantasized about murdering Rachel Morgan."

"Including you?"

"Many times, sir. I'm not proud of it, but you asked for honesty. I didn't kill Rachel." He glanced over at the clock on the dashboard. "If you don't mind, I should get going. I need to go home and shower before my shift at the Mansion. I smell like commercial grade bleach and my Aunt Marilyn's perfume. Pretty sure the shit has fermented in the bottle."

Royce had a sensitive sniffer, and all he detected was bullshit. Ian had no idea Royce had already stopped by the Mansion and found out he wasn't scheduled to work for the next few days. Royce also found it odd Ian hadn't inquired about what he and Sawyer were doing there in the first place. Royce sure as hell wasn't going to volunteer any information that would tip the kid off.

"I won't keep you, then," Royce said. "Have a nice night."

Ian nodded and exited the SUV. The kid burrowed down into his coat and made a beeline for a pale gray sedan. It might've been the weather hastening his stride, or it could've been self-preservation spurring him on. Regardless, Ian Boyd was on his radar, and he'd remain there until Royce cleared him.

Chapter
TWENTY-ONE

AFTER LEAVING MAGNOLIA MANOR, SAWYER DECIDED TO RETURN to the precinct to make three calls before he confronted Burke with what he'd learned about Marilyn. So far, he had a lot of supposition and very few facts. Yes, he'd proven Marilyn was involved with the pageants when Barbara, Jessica, and Amy were murdered, but no witness or interviewee had placed her at the celebration balls. Was it because she so seamlessly blended into the background as his mother had claimed? If so, how could Marilyn be both a nuisance and forgettable? Those things didn't tend to go together.

Sawyer ran into Holly on her way out to meet Jace for lunch. She hadn't uncovered any new leads but had discovered a newfound love for horses.

"Think Jace will buy me one as a wedding present?"

"If he's half as sentimental as Royce, you shouldn't mention it to Jace unless you're serious."

Holly laughed. "So true. Want to join us for lunch?"

Sawyer thanked her and explained why he had to decline.

"Holy shit," Holly said. "This is our first solid break. Let me call Jace and—"

"Nope," Sawyer said. "Keep your lunch plans. I'm just going to make a few calls and run by Burke's house. We'll all meet up later with Royce and Tara for a big debriefing."

After a few rounds of "Are you sure" and "Yes, I'm sure," Holly and Sawyer parted ways. Sawyer headed straight for his office and called Lizette Wright, Janet Campbell, and Dinah Parker.

The mothers were surprised to hear from Sawyer so soon after the last update and spoke candidly about their interactions with Marilyn. Sawyer struggled to keep up as he took notes and had to double back a few times to ensure he got everything down. The more they spoke, the more he wondered how Marilyn had escaped mention for nearly forty years. So Sawyer asked them point blank. He was still pondering their answers when he drove to Burke's house because he wanted to have the conversation face-to-face.

The retired detective's truck was in his driveway, but the motorhome was gone. Sawyer rang the doorbell anyway. No answer. Burke hadn't mentioned he was leaving town when they had last spoke. His parting words had been an assurance he'd help Sawyer in any way he could. Had Burke changed his mind? Had he left to avoid the press? Or was this sudden trip owed to something more sinister?

Sawyer rolled his eyes at his conjecture. More sinister? He sounded like he was rehearsing for an appearance on Felix's podcast. He returned to his car and called Burke's cell phone. The retired detective answered on the second ring, and Sawyer was relieved to hear his gruff voice. He liked the man and didn't want him to be involved.

"I stopped by to give you some updates on the case, but you're not home."

Burke chuckled. "And you thought I fled in my RV."

"No," Sawyer said too quickly. "Well, maybe for a minute."

"I'm having the old girl serviced one last time so I can sell her," Burke said. "I'm getting too old to be driving something so big, and I have no desire to travel alone." Burke rattled off the name of the RV dealership. "I was just going to hang out in the reception area, but they've got the television turned to a local news channel where they've been talking about the Magnolia Murders out both sides of their mouths for the past half hour. If that wasn't enough, the pompous windbag of a sheriff just gave a press conference. How that man keeps getting reelected is beyond me. And, boy, does he have it in for you."

Burke's remark caught him off guard. He didn't have time to prevent the seed of discontent from cracking open. Charlie and Felix had propagated the kernel, and against Sawyer's will, the little fucker had sprouted. Tiny tendrils of resentment would become destructive vines, choking out the beautifully manicured life he was building with Royce, if he didn't weed them out immediately.

"You still there, Sawyer?"

Burke's voice cut through his introspection. "Yes, sir."

"Would you mind swinging by here to pick me up?" Burke asked. "Or I guess you could hang out at my place, and I'll see if I can get someone at the dealership to drive me home."

"I'll come get you. Have you eaten lunch?"

"No." Burke chuckled again, and Sawyer couldn't imagine what was funny about his question. "I figured I'd just run through a drive-thru, but then I remembered what I was driving."

"I know a place that serves great sandwiches and coffee. The dealership should be done with the RV by the time we're through, and I can run you back there."

"Sounds perfect."

Twenty minutes later, they walked into Bytes and Brew at the perfect time of day. It was late enough to avoid the lunch crowd but too early for the rush-hour commuters or dinner swarm.

Levi smiled when he glanced up and saw who'd arrived.

"Someone looks tan and happy," Sawyer said, then introduced Levi to Burke.

"I recognize a vacation glow when I see one," Burke said.

"Honeymoon in Hawaii," Levi told him.

"Congratulations," Burke said.

Levi smiled and thanked him. "I love my job, but it was hard to come back. And I can't stop talking about my trip." Sawyer chuckled, and Levi turned his big blue eyes on him. "Is Diego driving you nuts with stories?"

"Just Topher," Sawyer replied. "I might've received a few 'help me' texts from Toph during their road trip. Diego is smitten and is highly recommending married life." Unfortunately, that was the only thing Topher had to report.

The interview with Tommy had been a bust. The guy avoided Topher's calls because he hadn't wanted to get persecuted in the press or on a true-crime podcast. Tommy hadn't been able to offer any new leads, but he'd stated he adored Barbara Jean. He'd had a major crush on her but viewed her as out of his league. It made Sawyer sad that Barbara Jean had never told Tommy about the feelings she'd written about in her pink leather journal. At least Sawyer could return it to her family as promised.

Levi blushed adorably. "Diego's going to become a matchmaker like Royce, isn't he?"

Laughing, Sawyer shrugged. "Maybe, but it's a wonderful compliment. He's deliriously happy and wants everyone else to be too."

After a sweet sigh, Levi took their orders. Sawyer asked for his usual chicken salad croissant with a salted caramel latte while Burke got a double-decker turkey club on rye and plain black coffee. Once their orders were ready, the two men settled into a corner booth.

Sawyer allowed them time to enjoy a few bites before delving in to why he'd wanted to talk to Burke. The retired detective quietly ate his food as Sawyer recounted the events from the past few days, starting with the Marilyn Moynihan lead he'd received from his mom and ending with the Magnolia Manor bombshell. Burke kept his eyes locked on Sawyer for most of their one-sided conversation, but his gaze wandered a few times, and he seemed to get lost in thought. Something Sawyer said always snapped Burke's attention back to him.

"This is the first time I've ever heard Marilyn Moynihan's name," Burke said. His voice was neutral, and if Sawyer hadn't been looking at him, he would've missed the brief lowered brow, squint, and tense posture. Burke blinked and his expression cleared, and Sawyer thought he might've found a card player who could give Beatrice Jacobs a run for her money. "But no wonder you were getting ready to put a BOLO out on me," Burke said. "I'm not sure I'd believe you if the situation were reversed."

Sawyer snorted. "I was not, and I didn't mean to put you on the defensive. I don't think Marilyn's omission from the file was because of shoddy detective work on your part, and I know you can't be her father."

Burke snorted. "I can't even be her brother or cousin. My entire family is from Mississippi, and I met my Janie there when she attended college. I didn't move to Savannah until a few years after we got married. My wife's people are from here, and she was really homesick for them."

"Do you think Marilyn could be Gerald Donovan's daughter?"

Burke considered the question for a few moments before answering. "I know he fathered children with his wife, so he was capable. But, man, I have a tough time imagining Donovan covering up this woman's alleged crimes. Daughter or not." Burke paused and briefly grew pensive again before he resumed his line of thought. "The only way she stays out of the files is if she had help."

"Maybe," Sawyer said. "I can't overlook that possibility right now."

"It'd be hard to miss the giant elephant in the room," Burke remarked. "Can anyone place her at the scene? Is it possible she was involved with the pageant but didn't get an invitation to the celebration ball?"

"I considered that too," Sawyer said, "so I called Lizette Wright, Janet Campbell, and Dinah Parker. I didn't want to hit you with unsubstantiated conjecture. All three of them confirmed Marilyn had been on the scene and dressed for the gala when their daughters were killed. According to them, all former queens in attendance were to be honored at the beginning of the dinner."

"I'm stumped," Burke said. "She's been described as this annoying, antiquated woman, but she didn't warrant a mention from someone connected with the pageant or the victims' families? That doesn't make sense."

"I agree. And I don't want to muddy the waters further—"

"Oh boy," Burke said, making Sawyer chuckle. "Sounds like I should've made this an Irish coffee."

"Those who didn't describe her as a rude meddler kind of compared her to drapes."

Burke scrunched up his brow. "I don't follow."

"When you walk into someone's home, how much attention do you pay to the drapes?"

Burke snorted. "You've seen my home. What do you think?" His eyes widened. "I get it. She was just kind of always in the background."

Sawyer thought back to the photo of his mom looking on while Marilyn spoke. Evangeline had tuned her out, and Sawyer was willing to bet others had too. "I think it's possible Marilyn's honorary title didn't earn her any respect with the ladies. I think she was like the crazy uncle who gets invited to all the holiday gatherings. You know the ones I'm talking about. They're obnoxious but basically harmless."

"Know them?" Burke asked. "I am that uncle."

Sawyer laughed. He figured the gruff man was probably the family favorite but kept his opinion to himself. "Then you would know the uncle is tolerated but pretty much ignored. Unless he does or says something extreme to grab attention, he can move around at will, and no one pays him any mind."

Burke narrowed his eyes. "And when attendees are asked to recall their evenings, he wouldn't warrant a mention."

Sawyer nodded. "But if someone asked them specifically if their Uncle Joe was there, they'd confirm he was."

"So I didn't ask the right questions." Burke's morose voice squeezed Sawyer's heart. The man had truly cared and still did.

"Or Marilyn had help keeping her attendance quiet."

Burke sighed and scrubbed a hand over his wrinkled face. "Both of those things can be true."

"Yes, and they'd be hard to prove without a confession," Sawyer said.

"But you said she has dementia. It would be unethical to interview her, and even if it weren't, nothing she says could be used against her."

Sawyer smiled. "Nothing she says now can be used against her, but how likely is it that her great-nephew just happens to work at the hotel where this Magnolia Queen candidate died? And Rachel Morgan's assailant had intimate knowledge about the original murders."

Burke nodded. "And as far as we can tell, the parts we held back from the press and public have remained a secret all this time. Did this kid have a motive for killing Rachel Morgan? The press is focusing on the ex-boyfriend, Benji McKay."

It wasn't Sawyer's place to disclose anything about Royce's case, so he simply told Burke that Ian checked several boxes. He was in the right place at the right time, he had a motive, and if Sawyer's hunch was correct, he was related to the original killer.

"So the ex-boyfriend is a red herring, a patsy, or an accomplice." Burke held up his hand. "I have so many questions, but they're not your answers to give. Guess I'll wait to see how this shakes out."

Sawyer's respect for the man grew. "I'll fill you in as soon as I can."

The two of them finished eating, then Sawyer dropped him back off at the RV dealership. He started his audiobook on the way back to the precinct, and a call came in almost immediately. He didn't recognize the number and briefly debated sending it to voicemail before answering.

"Sergeant Key," he said.

"Thank goodness you answered," a woman whispered. It took him a second to place the voice.

"Beatrice?"

"Yes. I have a scoop for you."

"Why are you whispering? What are you up to?"

Sawyer heard a door shut, and Beatrice sighed. "Back to my room safely," she said in her normal pitch, though she sounded out of breath.

"Where were you?"

"Relax, I haven't escaped the home," Beatrice replied. "Whew! I just need a second to catch my breath. This investigating is hard work. No wonder you're so fit and trim."

Sawyer felt his brow arch high on his forehead, and a huge smile stretched across his face. He glanced in the rearview mirror, and sure enough, he looked like a cartoon villain. "What investigation?"

"Into Marilyn," she said like Sawyer was as dumb as a box of rocks.

"Beatrice, I—"

"Just let me get this out before I forget," she said.

"I thought you were as sharp as a tack?"

"How sweet of you to forget the twice as round part," Beatrice quipped. "I worry the oxygen deprivation might impact my memory."

"You make it sound like someone held a pillow over your face," Sawyer said. "Or are you just looking for an excuse to breathe heavily in my ear?"

She cackled. "I really like you."

"The feeling is mutual," he said.

After another few seconds, Beatrice admitted her heart was racing with excitement.

Concern replaced his amusement. "Do you need to call for a nurse?"

"Heavens no." She took a deep breath. "I just came from the clinic, and that's how I overheard them talking about Marilyn."

"Why were you at the clinic?" Sawyer asked suspiciously, wondering if he should call Rocky and rat her out.

"That's where you go to get the juiciest gossip. The nurses either don't think we can hear or don't think we care what they're talking about, so I *occasionally* use it to my advantage. I faked a small injury—"

"How small?"

"You sound just like Rocky. He doesn't like it when I run an investigation either, but it gets boring here. I haven't had a good mystery in a long time, and fate dropped you in my lap."

Sawyer bit back a groan. He'd never forgive himself if he caused Beatrice harm. "What did you overhear?"

"Marilyn has been extremely agitated after her great-nephew's past few visits. She keeps saying he's going to kill her."

Sawyer pulled over and gave Beatrice his full attention. "Does she specifically say the nephew's name, or could it be a memory from her past?"

"I can't say for sure, but I think she's just using a pronoun in place of a proper name. The nurses remarked it was something new and started within the last few days. Regardless of the source, Marilyn was genuinely terrified to the point they had to sedate her and are considering asking the doctor to restrict her visitors."

Christ. Had Ian confessed he'd killed Rachel Morgan to his great-aunt with dementia? Or had he always been violent toward the woman and she was just now reacting?

"This is excellent information, Beatrice. I need you to make me a promise right now."

"Maybe," she replied noncommittally.

"Let me take it from here, okay? I want you to stay far away from Marilyn and her nephew."

"Okay."

"Nice try," Sawyer said. "I want to hear the words *I promise*."

Beatrice sighed. "Fine. I promise."

"Are your fingers or toes crossed?"

"No," she said, then chuckled. "You didn't ask about my saggy boobs, though."

"Goodbye, Beatrice."

"See you around, handsome."

Sawyer laughed all the way back to the precinct. He and Royce gathered their teams to catch everyone up. Then the two of them met with Mendoza, who, like usual, steepled his fingers and let them lay out everything they'd learned.

Afterward, he pursed his lips as he thought. "You've made some great advances."

Royce turned to Sawyer. "I hear a *but*."

"But," Mendoza said with a chuckle, "it's too circumstantial to get a warrant." Before they could argue, he added. "It is, however, enough for me to authorize round-the-clock surveillance on Ian Boyd and Benji McKay."

Sawyer and Royce groaned. Surveillance. It was a bittersweet victory.

Chapter
TWENTY-TWO

ROYCE'S PHONE RANG AND HE KNEW WHO WAS CALLING WITHOUT looking. Keeping his eyes trained on Benji through his binoculars, Royce answered his phone with his free hand. The kid was leaning against the hood of Ian's car in the employee parking lot at the back of the hotel.

"Hey, baby," Royce said.

"There are a billion things I'd rather be doing than staking out these two numbskulls on a Saturday night."

Royce squirmed in his seat a little. "A billion, huh? I was thinking of ten or fifteen. I feel so inadequate."

"Nothing about you is inadequate, and I'll prove it when we hand over babysitting duties in a few hours."

The two teams split shifts and had been tailing Benji and Ian since Tuesday night. It was about as exciting as watching paint dry. "Either these guys are extremely dull, or they're playing it safe because they know we're following them."

Sawyer chuckled. The rumbly sound washed over Royce, making him fidget a little more. "If that were the case, the 'two yutes' wouldn't be meeting up to smoke pot behind the Mansion."

Royce laughed at Sawyer's Joe Pesci impression from *My Cousin Vinny*. "The two what?" he asked, imitating the judge's response to Pesci's remark in the courtroom. "And you make a good point. We only have their word that weed is involved in their rendezvouses."

"What else would they be doing?" Royce asked.

"You mean in a parked car in a dark lot? I could think of—"

"A billion things," Royce finished.

"I was going to say a few things this time."

"So you think it's possible these two are hooking up?" Royce asked.

"Benji is loaded. I bet his monthly allowance is bigger than my salary. Do you honestly think he couldn't find someone at his college to supply his weed habit? There's a reason he's chosen this guy. I think Benji may be using the weed as a crutch to get what he really wants."

Royce considered it. Ian wasn't an unattractive kid, but the ladies Benji had dated were all knockouts. Royce also knew there was so much more to loving someone than their physical looks, so he couldn't discount Sawyer's theory. "If you're right, it gives Ian more reason to want Rachel out of the way. I read the text messages Benji sent to her. He had wanted to get back together until Rachel dropped the bomb that she knew about his kid. I'm not sure he really loved Rachel, though. I think she was familiar, safe, and someone his parents approved of."

"Did it sound like Rachel planned to use the knowledge against him?" Sawyer asked.

"Actually, no. She encouraged him to do the right thing and support the baby's mama."

"Do we know who the mother is?"

"Neither of them mentioned her name or even how old the baby is," Royce replied. He glanced at the clock and saw they only had a few minutes left before Ian would go on break. "Wanna place a bet?"

"What are the stakes?"

"Loser writes the report," Royce said.

"What side are you taking?"

Royce slowly inhaled as he debated. "I think they're just smoking pot together."

Sawyer chuckled. "Will you never learn? They're totally boning each other. What will it take to prove it? A kiss? We won't be able to see a hand job from this distance."

"Blow job," Royce said. "If one head disappears beneath the dash, you win."

"I'll take that bet," Sawyer said.

Royce suddenly realized how ridiculous his stance had been. "Shit. I should've wagered on how long Benji lasted."

"Knock it off," Sawyer said. "We can't all be Lotharios like you. I embarrassed myself a time or two back in the day."

Sawyer was such a methodical lover. Royce couldn't imagine him rushing anything, not even as a virgin.

"I told you I lost my virginity in college, but you didn't tell me when you lost yours," Sawyer said.

"It was in the stockroom at Sal's," Royce said. "I started working there on the weekends when I was sixteen."

"Ahhh," Sawyer said. "No wonder you have such fond memories of the place. God, you're not going to put up a commemoration plaque when we own the store, are you?"

When we own the store.

"I fucking love you," Royce said.

"Because you didn't think of the idea first?"

"No, because you take my dreams and make them your own." Royce would do the same by asking Sawyer to marry him but not during a stakeout. "And my love for that store has nothing to do with losing my virginity there." The reason was so much more complicated and harder to admit. "It was a special place for my dad and me. I'd always go there with him on the weekends when I was little. It would be just the two of us. There was no yelling. No violence. Eddie explained the different tools and their uses as we walked up and down the aisles. Later, he taught me how to use them in the garage. Eddie was a completely different person there. He forgot he was supposed to be this badass abuser and was just my dad. He's the reason I've become so good with my hands. I feel guilty for remembering any of the good times with him. He's vile and doesn't deserve my positive memories."

"But you deserve them," Sawyer said. "Sometimes the good, the bad, and the ugly become so entwined we have a hard time remembering the good even existed. There's a big difference between accepting what could've been and pining for what will never be."

"Sawyer?"

"Yeah," he said huskily.

"You make me glad I'm so good with my hands."

Sawyer's laughter rumbled through the speaker. "That makes two of us."

A moment later, the Mansion's back door opened, and Ian stepped out. He made a beeline for his car and Benji.

Royce straightened in his seat. "Showtime."

Benji pulled Ian against him and planted a hard kiss on his mouth.

"First base," Sawyer said jubilantly. "I'm just a base hit away from not having to type a report."

Royce snickered. "I should've bet on stamina."

The two young men got into Ian's car and continued kissing. Eventually they did break apart to pass a joint between them. Once it was gone, more kissing ensued before Ian's head disappeared beneath the dashboard.

"Eureka!" Sawyer said.

Royce groaned. "Damn it. You win." He looked away from the action. He was many things, but a pervert wasn't one of them.

"God, they so did this murder together, didn't they?" Sawyer said.

"It's possible. Maybe even likely. Are they done yet?"

"I'm not looking," Sawyer said. "I have my eyes trained on the back door so I'll know when Ian goes back in, and I'll resume following Benji."

"While I sit here bored out of my mind playing *Best Fiends*." Just thinking of the game made Royce swipe up on his phone. "Let me know when the coast is clear."

"Are you playing the game now?" Sawyer asked.

"Yep."

"You think Benji's detail is more exciting?" Sawyer asked. "We went to physical therapy, the bank, and the mall today. The kid dropped enough money to pay off your hot tub."

"My hot tub?" Royce asked. "I don't hear you complaining when you ride me like I'm your personal stallion."

"Fine. Our hot tub." Sawyer laughed, and before Royce could ask why, Sawyer said, "They're done already."

"What?" Royce looked through the binoculars and saw Benji standing alone in the parking lot. Not only had they finished, but Ian was already back inside. Benji was tucking in his shirt and straightening his jacket and didn't notice the shadowy figure approaching him from the other side of the car.

"Shit!" Royce and Sawyer said at the same time.

"Should we move in closer?" Sawyer asked. "I don't like how that person is moving toward Benji."

"Yeah, let's go. I'm not writing up a report that ends with this idiot kid getting killed like in some slasher film."

Royce switched the speakerphone off and held the phone to his ear as they headed toward Benji. The dark shadow was gaining on him fast. Just as Royce was about to warn Benji, the clouds parted, and a ray of moonlight illuminated the parking lot.

"Wait a minute," Sawyer said. "I'd recognize that stride anywhere. It's equal parts swagger and pissed at the world." Royce recognized it too. He'd just seen it recently after taking a call from the Kwik Stop owner. "It's built into the Locke DNA, it seems," Sawyer added.

"What the hell is Jason doing here?"

"Pull back now that we know who it is," Sawyer replied. "Let's see how this unfolds."

Benji whirled around and clutched his chest when Jason drew near. Royce was close enough to hear Benji's nervous chuckle.

"Dude, you scared the fuck out of me," Benji said.

"Did you bring it?" Jason asked.

"Yeah," Benji said, then reached inside his jacket.

"Wait," Jason said when Benji started to withdraw his hand. "Nice and slow."

"Oh, fuck you, Girard. I'm not armed."

"You've been questioned by the police a few times since your ex-girlfriend's murder, so forgive me if I'm being cautious."

"Give me a break. You of all people know I didn't kill her." That caught Royce's attention. Benji withdrew a white envelope and held it aloft. Royce's mind went straight to drugs, and he felt sick to his stomach.

"Don't assume the worst," Sawyer whispered. His voice was a balm to Royce's soul.

"Want this or not?" Benji asked.

Jason held out his hand, and Benji smacked the envelope into his palm.

"I don't ever want to see you or talk to you again, loser," Benji said.

Jason tucked the envelope away and headed back to the shadows. "Makes two of us. Have a miserable life, asshole."

"You first," Benji retorted before continuing to his Corvette.

"I'm heading back to my car to follow Benji," Sawyer whispered. "You intercept Jason and find out what the hell is going on."

Royce felt numb, frozen to his hidden spot.

"Ro," Sawyer whispered urgently. "Stop assuming the worst."

He flinched and rubbed a hand over his face. "Hard not to," he whispered back. "As you said, the Locke DNA is strong with this one."

"You're the finest man I know. If the kid is half as good as you are, he's set for life, even if he doesn't know it yet."

"Your faith in me is…"

"Unshakable," Sawyer said. "Relentless."

Royce's breath caught in his throat at the reference. Damn, he loved his man. Royce stayed hidden even after Benji drove away, then kept to the shadowy tree line as he pursued Jason. "I was going to say touching, but those work too."

"Touching comes later."

Royce tucked his phone into his pocket after they said goodbye and quickened his pace to catch his nephew. The kid wasn't old enough to drive yet, but he could've hopped on a bus or caught a ride from someone else. Then again, by Jason's age, Royce had already hotwired Dru's car and taken it on a joyride. Royce's mind wouldn't rest until he knew what was in the envelope.

When Royce eased from the shadows onto the street, he was half a block behind Jason, traveling away from the closest bus stop and heading in the opposite direction of home. Royce thought about calling out, but chances were good Jason would beat him in a foot chase if the kid decided to run. So Royce shifted his pace into a higher gear and broke into a jog, catching Jason at a street corner while waiting for a light to change.

"Hey, buddy," Royce said, clamping his hand tightly on Jason's shoulder. "Whatcha doing?"

Jason heaved a fifty-pound sigh. "You again?"

"Like a bad case of herpes. Let this be a lesson to you."

Jason looked at him with the trademark Locke smirk. This kid. "Got it. I'll double bag it."

Royce laughed despite the situation but sobered quickly. "What's in the envelope, Jaybird?"

A red flush swept over his nephew's cheeks, and he tried to pull free. Royce tightened his grip and gestured to the crosswalk sign with his free hand. They stepped off the curb and headed across the street.

Halfway there, Jason said, "I can't believe you were following me."

"Don't flatter yourself, punk. You weren't my target."

Jason stiffened beneath Royce's hand but didn't try to pull away. "I should've been smarter."

"Yes," Royce agreed.

"You don't even know why I was there," Jason countered.

"You were slinking around in the shadows. How good could your intentions have been?"

"Asks the guy lurking in the shadows," Jason said.

"Pretty sure you know why I was following Benji McKay."

Jason veered to the left once they stepped onto the other curb, but he didn't go far before he stopped and whirled on his uncle. "Here," he said, pulling the envelope out of his pocket and extending it to Royce. "Go ahead and look." He kept his face averted so Royce couldn't read his expression, but his tense body language could signify several responses.

Royce took a deep breath, forcing himself to calm down. "I'd rather you tell me."

Jason lowered his hand and raised his head, meeting Royce's gaze. The stubbornness, determination, and swagger in Jason's eyes made Royce feel like he was looking at a younger version of himself. Luckily, Royce didn't read shame or guilt, and he realized Sawyer was right. This kid was going to be okay. They'd make sure of it.

"Do you remember my friend Abby?" Jason asked.

"The one with baby Noah, right?"

Jason took a shaky breath. "Yeah."

He recalled the heated text exchange between Rachel and Benji, and the comments Jason had made about Noah's dad. All the pieces clicked into place. Benji was the rich daddy that didn't want anything to do with the baby.

"Did Benji give you money for Noah?"

"Better," Jason said. "He signed away his parental rights."

"May I see the document, please?" Royce asked. "If the signature wasn't notarized, it won't be legal."

"You can't keep it as evidence, Uncle Ro. Abby needs that form."

Even if Benji killed Rachel to keep her quiet about the baby, he saw no need to involve Abby and her family. "I need you to trust me, Jaybird."

Jason handed the envelope to Royce, and he scanned the document. Benji's signature had been notarized earlier that day, which might have explained his trip to the bank.

"Looks legit," he said, returning the document to the envelope and handing it back to Jason. "Why does she need it?"

Jason swallowed hard. "So she can give Noah up for adoption. Her family can't afford to keep him, and Abby can't afford to do it on her own. And yeah, she could go after Benji for support, but then his parents would find out. They'd want visitation rights or suc for full custody. That's the last thing anyone wants for Noah, especially Benji. He's a douche bag, but he's not a complete monster. Signing this document is probably the first selfless thing he's ever done."

"Jason, I'm not an expert, but Benji's parents would probably find out through official proceedings and would have the right to apply for full custody. I don't think Abby or Benji should consider this a done deal."

"Abby found a private adoption attorney who said all she needed to do was get Benji to sign the document. They'll handle the rest."

Royce narrowed his eyes, not liking the sound of that at all. "His signature isn't legal if obtained under duress." Royce had read through Benji's recent text messages and social media activity. There was no indication

Abby or Jason were trying to blackmail him, and Royce hadn't found any evidence to indicate Benji was Rachel's Fake Jake either.

"We didn't pressure Benji. I just met up with him last Saturday night, and we talked man-to-man."

Royce didn't point out that Jason was only fifteen, and Benji, though legally an adult, didn't act like one. Which brought up another question. How the fuck old was Abby? Before he could ask, Jason's response sank in. "Last Saturday? What time?"

"Same time as tonight. Benji isn't as discreet as he thinks."

"So, nine-ish?" Royce pressed.

"Well, a little earlier. I got to him before Ian took his break. I didn't want to arrive mid-blow job." Jason's eyes widened. "Not that there's anything wrong with it."

"Relax, kid," Royce said. "Tell me what happened."

"I got to the employee parking lot early. Like eight thirty, maybe. I waited for Benji's Corvette to pull up, but I didn't see it. Around eight forty-five, I saw him come out of the employee door."

"Are you sure about the time?"

Jason fished his phone from his pocket and checked his text messages. "I texted Abby at eight forty-six and told her I had eyes on Benji. Then I approached him with the papers."

"How long did this man-to-man chat last?"

Jason narrowed his eyes, not liking the question, but he didn't call Royce out on it. He rechecked his phone. "I texted Abby at nine eleven to tell her the meeting went well and was on my way back to her car."

And that meant Benji McKay had a solid alibi. "Screenshot those messages and text them to me."

"Uncle Ro, I told you I don't want Abby involved."

"I understand, and I will do everything in my power to prevent it, but your conversation with Benji means he couldn't have killed Rachel Morgan."

"I told you he's not a complete monster," Jason mumbled as he took a screenshot of the texts and sent them to Royce.

He made sure they came through before returning his attention to his nephew. "Jaybird, I need to ask something, and I need you to be honest with me."

"Yeah, okay."

"Is Abby your age?"

He shook his head. "She's eighteen and would've graduated in the spring if she hadn't had Noah."

Royce wanted to believe Jason, but he needed to make sure Abby wasn't a victim of statutory rape, so he pressed a little further to see if Jason contradicted himself. "How'd you meet?"

"Band camp. I play in the drumline, and Abby is—was—our field commander. She gave me rides home from practice a lot." His answer came quick and seemed sincere.

"I didn't know you played in the marching band," Royce said.

"Lame, huh?"

"What? No. I think it's awesome, and I want to see you in action."

Jason blushed and averted his gaze. "I'll give you a schedule next year." He looked down the street and shuffled his feet. "I should get going."

"Wait," Royce said. "Is Abby sure she wants to give up her baby? Is there any other alternative?"

"I honestly don't know. Abby loves Noah a lot, but he cries so much. She said she's too young and doesn't know what she's doing. She keeps saying she wants a better life for him." Jason sighed. "I thought about asking Mom if we could take him in, but we're broke, and Mom has her hands full."

"And babies aren't puppies," Royce said.

"Really? Why didn't I think of that?"

Jason's phone pinged and he looked down. "I gotta go. Abby is getting anxious."

"No," Royce said. "I want to talk to Abby. She could be making a huge mistake here, and someone needs to look out for her." He softened his voice. "For both of you."

Jason looked down the street and back at Royce. He could see the struggle in the kid's eyes as he wrestled with his loyalty. Finally, the tension faded from his shoulders, and he said, "Come on."

Royce followed him down the street. They made a turn at the next corner, and the same faded red sedan with the black driver's side door came into view. It was idling in a parking spot halfway down the block.

"Please don't scare her with cop talk, okay?" Jason said as they approached.

Royce nodded and concentrated on slowing his galloping heart. Royce stopped Jason near the car, and he knew Abby could see them in the rearview mirror. "You go first to settle her nerves. Assure her I only want to help. Then I'll come over when you give me the go-ahead."

Jason nodded and continued to the car. He opened the front passenger door and leaned down to speak to Abby. His posture remained loose and calm, and he spoke so quietly Royce couldn't hear him. Royce could feel her appraisal and knew she kept her eyes on him in the rearview mirror. After a few moments, Jason stood up straight and waved Royce over.

He approached slowly like he would with any wounded thing. He couldn't begin to imagine all the emotions warring inside Abby, and he didn't want to make things worse. He just didn't want her making such a big decision under duress.

Royce eased the rear passenger door open and climbed in, careful not to wake the sleeping infant. Noah had a shock of dark red hair and skin so pale it looked like porcelain. He wanted to stroke his finger over Noah's velvety cheeks and cradle the little cherub close. Royce's brain chose that exact moment to spit out a scenario where he presented a swaddled baby to Sawyer. He hadn't picked out a Val—er, "just because" gift…Royce gave himself a good mental shake until the picture cleared, reiterating to himself that babies weren't puppies.

And for fuck's sake, he still hadn't worked up the courage to propose yet. His midmasturbation demand didn't count.

Abby kept her wary gaze trained on Royce in the rearview mirror. He clasped his hands in his lap instead of fussing over the baby like he wanted to.

"I think you're courageous, Abby," he said.

"You don't know me." Her voice was small and so very tired.

"I know you love Noah, and you're scared about your future. I can see you're exhausted and feel like the two of you have no place to turn to for help. And I'm worried about both of you."

Abby's chin wobbled, and she began to cry. "Why do you care?"

Royce leaned forward and ruffled Jason's hair. "Because I've loved this guy since his first breath. You're very important to him, so you matter to me. I need you to hear me. It's okay if you don't believe it right now, but please listen to me. Jason has my contact information and address. If you ever need anything—money, shelter, food…I want you to reach out to me because I can and will help you."

Abby cried harder and nodded.

"This is not the time for you to make life-altering decisions. I'm not trying to sway you one way or the other about giving Noah up for adoption, honey. I just know you need to wait until you're in better physical and mental health. Would you agree?"

Abby nodded.

"How can I help you right now? Do you need money? Formula for the baby? Food for yourself?"

She covered her face with her hands and sobbed quietly.

"A hug?" Royce asked.

Abby laughed through the next sob but nodded.

Royce pushed open the door and stepped outside. "Come on, honey."

Abby unbuckled her seat belt, exited the car, and approached him slowly at first but quicker when he opened his arms. She barreled into him, sobbing against his jacket.

Jason got out too, looking utterly helpless and maybe a little defeated. Royce loosened an arm from Abby and waved him in.

"Come on, big guy. Group hug."

Jason rolled his eyes, but he joined them.

"I'm so proud of you, Jaybird."

Abby pulled back and looked up at Jason. "Jaybird?"

Jason rolled his eyes and flushed pink. "No one calls me that anymore."

"They should," Abby said, then repeated, "Jaybird. We're keeping it."

Jason gazed at her upturned face and nodded.

Royce would worry about his nephew getting his heart crushed another day. The priority was making sure Abby and Noah were safe and cared for. He gave her cash for food, formula, and diapers.

"Are you still good on the diaper rash cream?"

Abby stared down at the cash in her hands, then looked back at Royce. "Yes. Thank you so much."

"My pleasure. Do you feel safe at home?"

"My parents aren't abusive. They're just indifferent and broke."

Royce disagreed with her assessment but didn't want to risk alienating her.

"I'm just so tired," Abby said. "If I could get a few hours of sleep…"

"Jay, call Holly and ask if she'll watch Noah for a little bit so Abby can crash. Let me know if she's busy. I can check with Candy or someone else."

"I'll call Holly right now." Jason took a few steps away and dialed her number. "Hey, Aunt Holls," he said when she answered, "I have a big favor to ask."

Abby watched Jason for a few seconds before returning her gaze to Royce. "Thank you."

"Anytime. I mean it."

Jason returned. "They're home and said for us to come over. Make a grocery list, and Uncle Jace will run me to the store while you sleep." He hugged Royce tightly, lingering a long time. "Thank you."

"My pleasure. I love you, kid."

Jason smiled and stepped back. "Love you too."

"Abby, are you okay to drive?"

"Yeah," she said. Royce noticed the promise of food, baby supplies, and a nap seemed to boost her energy.

He waited until they drove off before dialing Sawyer and heading back to his surveillance spot.

"My god, it's taken you long enough to call me," Sawyer said when he answered.

"Miss me?"

"Always. What happened?"

Royce filled him in on all of it, except the part where he had momentarily wanted to give the baby to Sawyer as a gift. He did mention the red hair, fair skin, and soft-looking cheeks.

"I feel so bad for Abby," Sawyer said, "but how lucky is she to have you and Jason in her corner?"

Royce thought of the lengths Jason had gone to help his friend. "Maybe the Locke curse is broken."

"A few bad eggs don't equal a curse."

Sawyer's love and devotion warmed his heart. "Well, I guess that means we can call off the surveillance on Benji."

"I'll tell Bones Kitty you love him when I get home."

"Asshole."

Sawyer laughed. "And now that we're down to one suspect, it's time to turn up the heat."

Chapter
TWENTY-THREE

Royce stared at Holly through the monitor from an empty suite at Magnolia Manor they'd commandeered as their operation's command post.

"If I didn't know better, I'd never have known it was you," Royce said.

Holly had pinned her long, lustrous curls beneath a blonde, pixie wig. Her eyes were now aquamarine blue thanks to colored contacts. Holly's large royal blue eyeglasses and artfully applied makeup and contouring helped change the shape of her face. She'd donned a royal blue pantsuit, an ivory silk blouse, and a multistrand beaded necklace that tied the look together. The royal blue stilettos on Holly's feet gave her an extra four or five inches of height. She looked every bit the part of a cognitive therapist meeting with the family of a resident.

Holly's chuckle came through his earpiece. She looked up at the hidden camera in her temporary office and winked. "Told you. I'm so good my own mother wouldn't recognize me."

"Glad I didn't wager money on it," Royce told her.

With no physical evidence placing Ian inside Rachel's hotel room, Mendoza approved a sting operation and worked with Magnolia Manor's director to put it in motion. The nurses had followed through on their concerns for Marilyn's well-being and had restricted Ian from visiting since the middle of the week. The director had personally called Ian and requested he meet with Holly to discuss potential cognitive therapies they could try for her. Ian had enthusiastically agreed and asked if he could see his aunt yet.

The kid either really cared about Marilyn Moynihan, or he was a sociopath. Royce was eager to see how Ian reacted to the line of bullshit Holly was about to feed him.

"I guess it's a good thing I hadn't donated all my wigs and outfits," Holly said. "I was always going to keep a few things around for Jace. He especially likes to play *Pretty Woman*."

"Attagirl," Tara said.

Topher, Diego, and Sawyer all laughed, but Royce gagged dramatically.

"Come on, Holls," he said.

Sawyer bumped his shoulder against Royce's. "She's yanking your chain."

"Am I?" Holly asked, waggling her brows.

Royce checked the time. Ian was due to arrive in fifteen minutes. After tailing him for days, Royce expected him to arrive five to ten minutes early. "Is everyone in position?"

Topher, Tara, and Diego confirmed they were, and Holly gave him a thumbs-up. Sawyer placed a warm hand on the back of Royce's neck.

"I think our boy has arrived," Diego, who was dressed as an orderly and currently staking out the parking lot from his car, said. When he followed Ian inside, he'd just look like an employee returning from a break.

Sawyer pointed to the monitor showing the parking lot feed. A car like Ian's pulled in and parked. A moment later, Ian eased out and headed straight to the door.

A few rows ahead of him, Diego got out of his car with his phone to his ear. He pretended to have a mundane conversation, moving slowly enough that Ian caught up to him, and they entered through the main doors together. Since Diego had been on his honeymoon when Rachel Morgan had been killed, Ian didn't recognize him. They had to be more careful with the others on the team.

From the lobby camera, they saw Ian approach the front desk presumably to ask where he could find Ms. Everly. The woman smiled and pointed to the corridor where Holly's fake office was located.

They tracked Ian's entire journey, and Royce's pulse leaped when he stopped outside Holly's office. After a pause, Ian knocked on the door, which Royce heard through Holly's hidden microphone. Royce marveled as Holly's body language became entirely different from the person he'd loved for nearly his entire life. The metamorphosis from Holly Stein to Ms. Everly was complete.

Holly opened the door and greeted Ian warmly. She closed the door once he stepped inside. They shook hands, and she invited him to have a seat.

"I appreciate you coming in to meet with me today on such short notice," she told him.

"No problem, but I was surprised someone like you works on a Sunday."

"It's hard to keep office hours in this line of work," Holly said. "And the nursing director is very concerned about your aunt's well-being."

"She seemed fine when I was here the last time," Ian told her.

Holly opened a portfolio and picked up a pen. "When was that?"

"Um, Tuesday," Ian said. "She seemed more tired than usual but otherwise fine. Later in the evening, the nursing director called and said Aunt Marilyn was extremely agitated and had to be sedated. She informed me a restriction on visitations would be best until Aunt Marilyn was calmer. She assured me I could call as often as I wanted."

"I see," Holly said and continued to jot down notes.

Ian sat taller and slightly leaned forward to see what Holly was writing. "I called every day. Sometimes twice. Each time they told me the same thing."

Holly lifted her head and met Ian's gaze. "Which was?"

"She was still extremely agitated like they'd never seen before."

"Uh-huh," Holly said and wrote a few more lines. Her convincing act made Royce smile. He glanced over and saw a matching expression on Sawyer's face. "Has anyone told you the specific things"—Holly's voice trailed off as she checked her portfolio—"Ms. Moynihan has been saying?"

Ian scrunched up his face. "No, but I'm not exactly sure why that's a concern. I mean, she has dementia and seems to be lost in a different decade most of the time. There are moments of clarity, but they're few and far between."

Holly took a deep breath. "What I'm about to say might be very disturbing."

Ian swallowed hard and said, "Okay." His voice sounded like a lost little boy, and for a few seconds, Royce worried they'd been wrong about him. He used the controls to zoom in on the guy's face. Ian's right eye started twitching, a sheen of sweat covered his forehead, and he rubbed the skin behind one ear.

Sawyer picked up a pen and wrote, *NERVOUS,* on a memo pad. Royce nodded and returned his attention to the screen in front of them.

"May I refer to your aunt as Marilyn?" Holly asked.

"Of course."

Holly referred to her notes for a few moments, triggering Ian to bounce his knees and chew his bottom lip. She glanced up suddenly and he stilled.

"Sorry about that," she said. "I just wanted to double-check a few things."

"It's okay."

"I'm not sure how to say this," Holly said.

"With words," Ian said, his frustration showing in his voice. "Rip off the bandage and let me have it."

She tipped her head as if considering it. "Marilyn said you're trying to kill her."

Ian gasped and jerked like he'd been shot. "What? That's crazy."

"She's alternated between 'he's a killer,' 'he killed her,' and 'he's going to kill me' for hours on Tuesday and every day since. It's caused quite a stir in the memory care unit's dining room."

"Christ," Ian said, scrubbing a hand over his face. "Why do you think she's talking about me? As I said, dementia patients are known to relive things from their pasts. Couldn't this be one of those instances?"

Holly set her pen down and studied him. "Are you aware of past abuses such as these in her life?"

"No," Ian admitted. "She never married or had children, and no one in the family mentioned any type of abuse."

"You're Marilyn's only visitor?"

Ian nodded. "I hate to say this, but she wasn't well loved by the family. Forgotten mostly and tolerated whenever the first wasn't an option." Ian narrowed his eyes. "Is it possible she's completely fabricated something?" He straightened in his chair, and his expression brightened. "Maybe it was something she saw on television? A detective show, perhaps. Aunt Marilyn used to love those, especially the British ones."

"I have asked about that, of course, but the only thing the nurses recall seeing on her television were *The Price is Right* and the news at noon."

"Well, there you go," Ian said, throwing up his hands. "The news broadcasts are filled with stories about murders and chaos."

"True," Holly said, making another note. "They've talked nonstop about the murdered Magnolia Queen contestant this past week." She stiffened, then flipped the pages on her portfolio as if searching for something. "Ah, that might explain why she claimed to have killed the queens this week during a particularly heightened state."

Ian's mouth fell open and all the color leached from his face. After a moment, he snapped his jaw closed. "I'll need to speak to the director about limiting the types of television she watches if this continues. All week long, I've felt like I'm the one being punished."

"Oh, no," Holly said. She crossed her hands over her heart. "I assure you, the staff at Magnolia Manor has only the nicest things to say about you."

Royce held his breath while waiting for Ian's reaction. They wanted to push him to reveal something on camera or take steps to expose his crime another way, not make him paranoid. Royce was already concerned Ian would get spooked by the new faces loitering around or recognize one of them from the investigation.

Ian visibly relaxed. "So, what can we do to help her?" he asked.

Holly outlined a therapy strategy the director had given them. She even pulled out a brochure from her portfolio that expanded on her suggestions.

Ian engaged with Holly during the conversation but didn't ask a single question. Royce thought it could mean one of two things: he was on to them and was just playing along, or it didn't matter what Holly had to say because Marilyn Moynihan wasn't long for this world.

"Can I please see her? I don't have to stay long. I just want to pop in and tell her I miss her and love her."

Holly smiled sweetly. "Let me call the nurse's station to see how she's doing."

She picked up the phone and called the memory care unit where Tara answered. Her disguise was simpler. She'd donned a wig with long braids and a headband and a pair of pink scrubs. A padded bodysuit and a chunky cardigan helped to alter Tara's shape. There was no way in hell Ian would recognize her.

Holly inquired about Marilyn and learned she was resting comfortably. After thanking the nurse, Holly hung up and smiled sadly.

"I'm afraid she's sleeping."

"I promise not to wake her," Ian said. "I'll just pop in for a second. Please."

Holly pursed her lips together as she thought it over. "Okay, she said. But just give me a minute. I'll clear it with the staff." Then she phoned Tara again and let her know Ian was coming by for a brief visit.

"Thank you," Ian gushed.

"My pleasure," she said. "Let us know what you think about the therapy suggestions."

Ian smacked his empty palm with the brochure before tucking it away. "Will do."

They watched Ian walk through the corridor. He spoke to or nodded to each of the nurses and staff members he encountered on the way to the memory care unit. Ian started with a leisurely stroll but picked up the pace as he got closer to Marilyn. He passed a trash can on his way and tossed Holly's brochure into it. Royce and Sawyer exchanged a knowing look. Their plan had worked. Ian picked up the phone outside the locked unit and called the nurse's station. Tara answered and buzzed him in once he identified himself.

Ian didn't glance in her direction, and his pace picked up exponentially. His stride was purposeful and intent.

"Where's he going in such a hurry?" Sawyer asked.

"We all know the answer to that."

Royce switched his attention to the monitor displaying Marilyn's darkened room. Ian slipped inside and quietly shut the door behind him. He didn't turn on the light as he crept deeper into the space.

"Aunt Marilyn," he said in a creepy voice. "You've been a naughty girl, spilling our secrets, and I can't have that." He stopped by the small loveseat in her room and picked up a pillow before stalking closer to the bed. "I truly hate to do this. You've taught me so much about life. Without you, I never would've found the courage to kill that whore. A man should never have to kill his hero, but you've betrayed me just like everyone else I've ever trusted."

Royce's heart thundered in his chest as Ian reached the bed with the pillow outstretched in front of him.

"Thanks for everything, Aunt Marilyn. I'm going to miss you."

"Go," Royce whispered into the microphone.

Two things happened simultaneously. Topher, wearing a snowy white wig, sprang up in the bed and leveled his gun at Ian's chest, and Tara burst through the door with her gun trained in front of her.

"Police! Freeze!" they yelled together.

Sawyer, Royce, Holly, and Diego sprang from their spots and ran to assist. By the time they arrived, Ian was kneeling on the floor with his hands cuffed behind him. A tiara was tangled in Topher's wig, and the whole mess rested askance on his head. The nightgown he'd borrowed would probably be ankle-length on an average-sized woman but looked like a minidress on him. It was hard for Royce to take him seriously.

They all high-fived and congratulated each other on a job well done.

Ian was sobbing incoherently and unwilling to talk after they read him his rights. Royce and Sawyer escorted him from the building while the rest of the team wrapped everything up at the scene.

Royce secured Ian in the back of the SUV, then glanced up in time to see Drusilla getting out of her old sedan. He couldn't believe the vehicle was still running nor could he comprehend the joyful smile spreading across her face when their eyes met.

"Hey, give me a minute," Royce said to Sawyer without looking away from his sister. He felt like she might disappear if he so much as blinked.

"Take your time. This shithead isn't going anywhere."

Royce took two steps toward her, then froze. He'd decided to be patient and wait, yet here he was ready to barrel down on her. He opened his arms and hoped like hell she wouldn't leave them empty. The smile slid from her face, and Royce thought he'd pushed too hard. A choked sob escaped Dru, then she launched herself at him. Royce caught his sister and held her slight frame in his arms. He fought off his tears because he had interrogations to conduct, and he didn't want Ian to think he was a pushover.

She buried her face against his chest and cried. "I'm so sorry. I never should've asked you to choose between Sawyer or us. I love you, Ro."

Royce pulled back and cupped her face. "I forgive you, Dru. And I love you too."

Over her head, Royce saw the first news van coming down the road toward Magnolia Manor. "Oh shit," he grumbled. "The vultures are here. Gotta go. We'll work this out, okay?"

Dru nodded. "Still causing trouble, I see."

Royce laughed, dropped his arms, and took two steps back. "Always. Promise me you'll show yourself some grace," he said.

She smiled. "I'll try."

Royce blew her a kiss, then hurriedly climbed into the SUV.

"Everything okay?" Sawyer asked.

Royce figured his dopey smile spoke volumes. They'd solved four homicides, and he'd gotten to hug his sister. She'd said the two things he needed to hear most. Royce started the engine and headed out of the parking lot. "Couldn't be better," he said.

Back at the precinct, they booked Ian and placed him in an interrogation room to stew for a bit.

"The arrest is only the beginning," Sawyer said, sounding as tired as Royce felt.

"Will that be the title of your biography?" Royce asked.

"Maybe."

They still needed to tie this investigation into a neat bow for prosecution, which would involve hours executing search warrants, conducting interviews, and chasing down every piece of evidence that could tie Ian to Rachel's murder.

"The truth is, I may never be able to prove Marilyn killed those three young women," Sawyer said. "Even if I can, Marilyn's health prohibits her from standing trial for her crimes, so this is bittersweet."

"All we can do is turn over whatever evidence we find to Mendoza and Babineaux and let them decide how to proceed. It's why they make the big bucks."

"And get all the gray hair," Mendoza said from behind them.

"Chief," Royce said.

Mendoza smirked. "Nice work, you two."

Sawyer's phone rang, and he looked down at it. "Felix," he said, stepping away. "I promised him an exclusive for his help. He's probably just reminding me. I'm sure word of an arrest has already gotten back to him." Sawyer stepped away and answered his phone, leaving Royce alone with Mendoza.

The chief studied Royce until the silence became awkward.

"Chief?"

"Was I wrong about you?" Mendoza asked.

Royce laughed. "Probably, but can you be more specific?"

"I chose you to spearhead our Explorer program efforts because I saw you displaying early signs of burnout, and you're too damn good to lose. I thought working with the kids would be good for your soul. Looking at you now, smiling after a big arrest… Was I wrong?"

Royce thought back to the recent conversation with Jason and Abby. It had felt really good to help them. It was one of the first times in months where he hadn't felt exhausted, which was a miracle in and of itself since he'd been pulling long surveillance shifts. Royce thought about baby Noah and the family he'd one day have with Sawyer.

"No, Chief. You weren't wrong. I am very much looking forward to the new chapter in my life."

He glanced over at the love of his life and winked. New *chapters*.

Chapter
TWENTY-FOUR

Their first conversation with Ian had been a complete waste of time. He stared ahead and didn't even acknowledge Sawyer's and Royce's presence in the room. They tried several different tactics for forty minutes while the search warrants for his home, vehicle, and work locker were signed and delivered.

Sawyer handed Ian off to the guard, and the teams set out to execute the warrants in hopes of finding physical evidence tying Ian to Rachel's murder and Marilyn to the original three Magnolia Murders. Sawyer felt the latter was a long shot, but his worry had been without merit.

Ian was Marilyn's sole heir, and he had inherited her home and its contents when she'd moved into Magnolia Manor. The proof of Marilyn's crimes had been tucked away in a Victorian trunk at the foot of a massive antique bed in a fussy room. The space was pristine and completely devoid of dust, which meant Ian kept it spotless. It almost felt like a shrine. Sawyer had seen the behavior before with parents who'd lost a child. They'd keep the space immaculate and ready for the child who would never return home again.

What was Ian's deal? Was it a sign of respect? Idolization, maybe?

Sawyer could almost feel the evil emanating from the journals he'd found under a stack of neatly folded quilts. The only sound penetrating his thoughts as he stared into the trunk was the thundering of his heart. The tempo reminded him of the scene in *Jumanji* when the board game was first discovered. The heavy beat warned that opening the leather-bound journals would be both a blessing and a curse for three families.

The search went on around him, but Sawyer blocked out everything as he'd done with Barbara Jean Wright's innocent musings. There was an impressive stack of Marilyn's deepest secrets, but Sawyer immediately figured out the diaries hadn't been stored in order. The years he cared about most were right on top. Had that been Marilyn's doing or Ian's?

Sawyer opened the journal to the night Barbara Jean had died. Tucked between the pages, he found a pale blue satin ribbon. He knew from photos it would've matched Barbara's dress from the night she was crowned. Had she worn it in her hair? Sawyer sucked in a shaky breath and read what Marilyn said about the night. The hate-filled words painted a vivid and ugly scene.

Marilyn had noted Barbara Jean had been too flirty with *her* Neil Henshaw throughout the competition and especially after she won the crown. She'd stumbled upon them kissing in a dark corner. Barbara claimed she hadn't wanted the kiss, but Marilyn had known the whore was lying. She would've taken Neil away from her, and Marilyn couldn't allow it.

The deranged woman described, in vivid detail, gaining access to Barbara's rooms and catching her completely unaware in the bathtub. She detailed her euphoria as she plunged the knife into the young woman's heart. Afterward, she sprinkled the flowers around her and tattooed her shame on her forehead. Marilyn effortlessly blended in with the rest of the crowd at the ball while waiting for the screaming to start once the harlot was found dead. Only then did she slip away.

Marilyn had once hated how people cast her aside and ignored her, making her feel worthless and unwanted. She quickly realized their dismissal was her significant advantage. She waxed on for several more pages about how powerful she felt after killing Barbara Jean. For the first time since winning the crown, she felt like her life had purpose.

Bile burned a path up Sawyer's throat and left an awful taste in his mouth as he continued reading Marilyn's deranged words.

"Hey," Royce said softly. Sawyer looked up from where he sat on the floor beside the trunk. Royce glanced at the leather book in Sawyer's hands and squatted down, putting them at eye level. Royce's gray gaze was filled with concern and more love than one person had the right to possess. It was the perfect refuge Sawyer needed.

"You okay?" Royce asked huskily.

Sawyer swallowed his acidic saliva and nearly choked on it. "No, but I will be." He would not give people like Marilyn Moynihan and Ian Boyd the power to destroy his life. Sawyer snapped the journal shut and shoved it into an evidence bag, then proceeded with the others. He continued digging through the trunk and came up with a knife. It wasn't bloody, and it wasn't likely to contain viable DNA, but he bagged it anyway.

Royce sought him out again a while later. He held two evidence bags in his hand. One contained a pair of lacy black panties that probably came from the set Fake Jake had bought Rachel. Only the bra had been at the crime scene. The second bag held a white gold necklace with a white gold and diamond R pendant. Sawyer had seen Rachel wearing it in several of her social media posts.

It was late when they completed the searches and returned to the precinct. Mendoza had suggested they go home and get a good night's rest and take another crack at Ian the next morning. Neither Sawyer nor Royce were eager to obey their commander. There was no way either of them could sleep.

Royce and Tara took another swing at Ian while Sawyer read through Marilyn's journals. Barbara, Jessica, Amy, and their families were his priority. It broke his heart to read how Marilyn had stalked and killed Jessica and Amy. She'd found Jessica coming out of Neil's room and caught Amy slow dancing with the man on the lawn beneath the moonlight. She'd tucked tokens from each victim between the pages of her journal. After finding Barbara's hair ribbon, he discovered a photograph of Jessica astride a snowy white horse, and finally a leather friendship bracelet Amy had probably made. He wondered if her best friend still had the match. Sawyer planned to return the items to their families as soon as possible.

In the meantime, he kept reading journal pages to find an answer to their most pressing question. How had Marilyn gotten away with it for so long?

He could suspect a connection to Gerald Donovan all day long, but he wanted to find proof. Frustration built when he didn't find what he was looking for in the entries surrounding the three murders. Inspiration struck, and Sawyer checked the file notes for Gerald Donovan's date of death. He picked the journal Marilyn had kept during that time, and sure enough, the proof was right there on the page. She'd written that "Uncle Gerald" had taken her secrets to the grave with him, so she'd do the same for him. Sawyer wondered why she'd used quotations around Gerald's name until he read the last few lines of the paragraph.

I should've killed the sick bastard for what he did to my aunt and mother. And to me for letting that cold fish raise me. All I ever wanted was to be loved by Seymour, but I wasn't his daughter. He took my mother's transgressions out on me but showered my siblings with love and devotion. They can all rot in hell for all I care.

Sawyer wasn't sure when Marilyn had learned Gerald was both her uncle and father, but it was clear she'd used the knowledge to ensure he kept her secret.

He wasn't sure how long he stayed immersed in Marilyn's maniacal musings before Royce arrived in his office to drive them home. Judging by Royce's haggard appearance, another day was on the verge of dawning.

"Did you get a confession?" Sawyer asked him.

Royce nodded, but he didn't look ecstatic about it. He scrubbed a hand over his face and sighed. "There was no remorse, not even a spark of life in him while he recounted how he set this in motion after meeting up with Benji at the party. I suspect he'd been plotting revenge for quite some time, but the reunion was the catalyst. Benji had apologized for hurting him, and the two struck a friendship over their mutual loathing of Rachel Morgan. She and Benji had just broken up because she'd found out about Abby's pregnancy." Royce shook his head. "Ian created the Fake Jake profile and joined all the sites as well as any of the private groups Rachel was in. He first approached her in some television show fan group on Facebook."

"And used what he knew about her to deepen the bond," Sawyer said.

Royce's jaw clenched, and he squeezed his hands into fists like he was fighting his emotions. Sawyer got up and crossed the room. He cupped the back of Royce's neck, and their mouths met in a soft, comforting kiss.

"And he set Benji up so he'd be the focus of our investigation," Royce continued. "He pushed Benji to start sneaking around with Jasmine. Ian lied when he said he didn't know Benji was returning to the hotel with Jasmine, and I now have the messages to prove it. Ian also knew Benji was especially *excitable* and would be finished well before his break. Ian showed up to deliver Rachel's order a few minutes early, and once inside the room, he strangled her." Royce's voice softened, and he rubbed his throat absently. "The sick fucker laughed in her face as she clawed at her skin, trying to get free. He relished telling her how he'd fucked her over and how Benji would soon be bending him over."

"Christ," Sawyer bit out.

"Ian radioed to the front desk to report Rachel hadn't answered the door while standing over her lifeless body. He was writing 'whore' on her forehead with her lipstick while the front desk rang the phone in her room. Then he dragged his feet getting out to his car, hoping the lapse in Benji's alibi would be enough."

"Diabolical," Sawyer said.

Royce quirked his lips up. "Morrison better watch it, or you'll be gunning for his job."

"There can only be one Keith," Sawyer replied.

Royce pulled his keys out of his pocket and extended them to Sawyer. "Take me home."

"Gladly."

"What day is it?" Royce asked when they were in the SUV heading home.

"Monday."

"Already? It was just Saturday a few minutes ago." Royce sighed. "Damn, this job makes me feel old."

Sawyer was about to respond, but he caught a snippet of a news report on the radio. Sheriff Wheeler's voice came through the speakers, and before Sawyer could change the channel, he heard the man boasting about his invincibility. He had no idea what the bastard was referring to, but he suspected it was what Felix had wanted to tell him. His gut churned as his resentment grew closer to the surface, seeking sunlight.

Sawyer changed the channel before he could hear more, feeling Royce's silent scrutiny.

Gripping the steering wheel tighter, Sawyer said, "I can't keep running from this thing with Wheeler. Felix tried to get me to listen to the full, unabridged interview, but I declined."

"You should've listened," Royce said softly.

Sawyer glanced over at him. "Have you heard it?"

"Bits and pieces. Enough to know a major storm is brewing."

Sawyer growled. "Fuck. Tell me."

"I don't want to," Royce replied.

"I'd rather hear it from you."

"Fine. I'll stick to the highlights. Assface has said your promotion is nothing short of nepotism. He's alleged your *filthy rich* parents are the ones who donated the money for the new unit after getting a guarantee you'd be the one running it."

"Bullshit," Sawyer growled. "Is that all?"

"No, baby, I'm just getting started. From there, Wheeler said you're out of your league. You got lucky with the first cold case you solved, and your incompetence is responsible for Rachel Morgan's death. Of course, that part won't age very well, considering we solved all four murders. Felix mentioned your name has been bandied about as a potential opponent for sheriff, and the fat bastard scoffed. Called you a coward who tucked tail and bailed on the sheriff's department when the going got tough."

"Did he now?" Sawyer asked. "I'm not brave enough to take him on, huh?"

"That's where the invincible spiel came from." Royce went quiet for long enough that Sawyer glanced over in concern. Royce was studying him with an indecipherable expression on his face.

"What?"

"Are you going to run?"

Sawyer took a deep breath. "I have to think about it. This isn't something you let someone goad you into doing."

"True." Royce reached over and cupped the back of Sawyer's neck. "For the record, I think you'd be an amazing sheriff."

Sawyer glanced over and smiled. "Thank you."

They arrived home a few minutes later, and Bones gave them hell when they stepped inside the house.

"Grandma has been feeding you while we worked, Bonesington," Sawyer said.

"It is time for breakfast, so you feed the cat, and I'll fire up the shower," Royce said after showing the furious beast as much affection as Bones would allow.

Sawyer apologized profusely for their absence as he spooned the salmon dinner into Bones's dish. When he placed the leftovers in the refrigerator, he spotted the can of squirty cheese. Suddenly, nothing sounded better. Sawyer pulled a pepperoni slice out of the bag, squirted the cheese directly on top of it, and shoved it into his mouth. Who needed crackers?

The sound of Royce clearing his throat grabbed Sawyer's attention. He replaced the can in the refrigerator, shut the door, and smiled innocently at Royce, who stood shirtless a few feet away. He had both hands tucked into his pockets, and the intent look in his eyes stole Sawyer's breath.

Oh my god. This really is it.

"I have something for you," Royce said, his voice husky as he closed the gap between them.

"I hope it's not the cock ring. I don't think I have it in me tonight, er, this morning."

Royce's lips tilted up. "Not a cock ring. Remember how I demanded you love me for the rest of your life?"

Sawyer's breath caught in his throat, but he choked out a yes.

Royce lifted his right hand and held out the gorgeous platinum band Sawyer had coveted every single day since he'd stumbled upon it. "And now I'm asking you. I know this isn't the fancy proposal dinner I intended, but I don't want to go another minute without you wearing my ring." Royce took Sawyer's left hand in his and placed the band on the tip of his finger. "Sawyer, will you marry me?"

Sawyer struggled to see through the sheen of tears gathering in his eyes. He blinked, sending them cascading down his cheeks. "It's about fucking time."

Royce chuckled. "Is that a yes?"

Sawyer kissed him hard. "It's a hell yes."

Royce slid the ring down Sawyer's finger, and they kissed long and passionately until Sawyer forgot how tired he was. He broke their embrace and smiled at Royce when something occurred to him.

"What?" Royce asked.

"Do you know what day it is?"

"You already told me. It's Monday," Royce replied.

Sawyer nodded. "It's February fourteenth. You proposed on Valentine's Day."

Royce pursed his lips, narrowed his eyes, and reached for Sawyer's hand. "I'm going to need that back until tomorrow."

"Too late." Sawyer juked to the right and sprinted out of the kitchen. "No takebacks," he yelled on his way to their bedroom where Royce tackled him to the bed. Soon, they both forgot their names, let alone the date, and the ring remained right where it belonged.

To be continued in *Marriage is Murder…*

Want to be the first to know about my book releases and have access to extra content? You can sign up for my newsletter here: http://eepurl.com/dlhPYj

My favorite place to hang out and chat with my readers is my Facebook group. Would you like to be a member of Aimee's Dye Hards? We'd love to have you! Go here: www.facebook.com/groups/AimeesDyeHards

Other Books by
AIMEE NICOLE WALKER

Curl Up and Dye Mysteries
Dyeing to be Loved
Something to Dye For
Dyed and Gone to Heaven
I Do, or Dye Trying
A Dye Hard Holiday
Ride or Dye

Road to Blissville Series
Unscripted Love
Someone to Call My Own
Nobody's Prince Charming
This Time Around
Smoke in the Mirror
Inside Out
Prescription for Love

Welcome to Blissville Collection (Both M/M Blissville series)
Volume One
Volume Two

The Lady is Mine Series
The Lady is a Thief
The Lady Stole My Heart

Queen City Rogue Series
Broken Halos
Wicked Games
Beautiful Trauma

Zero Hour Series
Ground Zero
Devil's Hour
Zero Divergence

Sinister in Savannah Series
Ride the Lightning
Mr. Perfect
Pretty Poison

Savannah Universe Standalone Books
Invisible Strings
Bad at Love

Standalone Novels
Second Wind

Fated Hearts Series
Chasing Mr. Wright

Coauthored with Nicholas Bella
Undisputed
Circle of Darkness (Genesis Circle, Book 1)
Circle of Trust (Genesis Circle, Book 2)

ACKNOWLEDGMENTS

First, I need to thank my husband and children for their constant support and encouragement. It's not easy living with a writer who often disappears into a fictional world for long periods of time. They do so many things to help me so that I can realize my dream. I love you guys more than words can ever express.

Many, many thanks to Susie Selva for her incredibly thorough edits and to Lori Parks for her keen eye during proofreading. These ladies are consummate professionals and are an absolute joy to work with. And much love to Jay Aheer and Wander Aguiar for this gorgeous cover and to Stacey Ryan Blake for her stunning interior designs. All of you make my books sparkle and shine so beautifully—inside and out. I thank my lucky stars that I get to work with such wonderfully talented people.

Many, many hugs to Melinda James Rueter and Racheal Yunk for bravely reading my rough drafts and providing priceless feedback. Love you, ladies!

xoxo

Aimee

About

AIMEE NICOLE WALKER

Ever since she was a little girl, Aimee Nicole Walker entertained herself with stories that popped into her head. Now she gets paid to tell those stories to other people. She wears many titles—wife, mom, and animal lover are just a few of them. Her absolute favorite title is champion of the happily ever after. Love inspires everything she does, music keeps her sane, and coffee is the magic elixir that fuels her day.

She'd love to hear from you.

Want to connect? All her links are in one nifty location. Click here:
linktr.ee/AimeeNicoleWalker

www.ingramcontent.com/pod-product-compliance
Lightning Source LLC
Chambersburg PA
CBHW021230250626
47155CB00008B/2948